SHAKING THE THRONE

CAROLINE ANGUS

Thank you to the four most important gentlemen in the world for their help – Grayson, Torben, Espen, and Lachlan, to whom I owe everything.

SHAKING THE THRONE

BOOK TWO OF THE QUEENMAKER SERIES

PART I OF THE QUEENMAKER SERIES:
FRAILTY OF HUMAN AFFAIRS

The moderate man shall inherit the kingdom.
That man needs to be the Queenmaker.

London 1529 – Cardinal Wolsey has ruled England in King Henry VIII's name for most of his reign. Now Henry wants to leave his extraordinary Spanish wife of twenty years, Queen Katherine, to marry Anne Boleyn and secure a male heir for the kingdom. Only God can end a marriage, through his appointed voices on Earth, the powerful Cardinal Wolsey, and Cardinal Campeggio sent from Rome in the Pope's place. Wolsey's faithful attendant, commoner Thomas Cromwell, has the mind, the skills and the ambition to secure a royal annulment.

Cromwell's forgotten past in Italy reappears with Campeggio's new attendant, Nicóla Frescobaldi, the peculiar son of Cromwell's former Italian master. While the great Cardinals of Christendom fight the King, the Pope and their God for an annulment, Cromwell and Frescobaldi hold the power over a country at war with its own conscience. Cromwell is called the double-minded man, whose golden eyes make money appear. Now Cromwell wants the power to destroy the Catholic Church in England. Frescobaldi is known as the waif-like creature, the Pope's favourite companion, but Frescobaldi wants freedom from Pope Clement and his Medici family in Italy.

Cromwell and Frescobaldi will place themselves into the heart of religious and political influence as they strive to create an English queen, or lose their heads for their crimes and sinful secrets.

PREFACE

In 1509, King Henry VIII was crowned alongside his new bride, Princess Katherine of Aragon. Katherine had married Henry's brother, Prince Arthur, in 1501, only for him to die months later. After receiving dispensation from the Pope, the couple married and were crowned in a dual coronation, and would go on to have one daughter and lose another five children at birth. After having affairs with several well-known mistresses, King Henry set his sights on Anne Boleyn, lady-in-waiting to Queen Katherine, sometime in 1525. By 1527, Henry set his chief advisor, Cardinal Thomas Wolsey, Lord Chancellor of England, to the task of procuring an annulment of his marriage to Katherine, on the grounds that a man could not marry his brother's widow, without success. The people of England loved Queen Katherine; she had ruled for twenty years, a kind, pious and beautiful Catholic queen all could respect. But Katherine was too old to give Henry what he needed – a son to inherit the English throne. Anne Boleyn was still in her twenties – pretty, sophisticated, intelligent, and young enough to give birth to a male heir. After being in love with Anne Boleyn for years, King Henry had become bitter towards his queen, and also his teenage daughter, Princess Mary, whom he considered too unnatural to inherit the throne, as she was female. Anne Boleyn was a mistress who would not share Henry's bed, and a combination of frustration, longing, and arrogance built in the king. Cardinal Wolsey, at Henry's side for twenty years, and credited with countless successes at home and abroad, and the wealthiest man in England, could not give the King what he wanted, and died in shame in 1530. With the witty Anne Boleyn and her family taking Wolsey's place at Henry's side, and the Protestant reformers beginning to eat into England's Catholic soul, the King could be easily swayed in any direction.

Enter Thomas Cromwell – lawyer and advisor to Thomas Wolsey, a commoner with a smart mind and vivid history throughout Europe, educated in England and Italy, who had ideas on how to create an annulment, and destroy Pope Clement's power in the process. By 1533, Cromwell had ensured King Henry could annul from Queen Katherine, marry Anne Boleyn, disinherit Princess Mary, taken total control over the church in England, and stop Pope Clement from interfering in England's business. Thomas Cromwell was the most powerful man in the kingdom after just a few years, and no one, noble or common, knew what would happen next in their realm, and with the anger of the Holy Roman Emperor due to the King's 'Great Matter' and destruction of the Catholic faith, the threat of war was real. King Henry had a new bride and a baby girl, Elizabeth. Now, Cromwell had to ensure Henry could keep all he had, and finally get a male heir for England.

England's royal inner circle by 1533

King Henry VIII All-powerful, well-educated and athletic ruler of England for twenty years. Aged only 41 years old, a religious, volatile, arrogant man. Father to infant Princess Elizabeth, the now-illegitimate Princess Mary, and a bastard son, Henry Fitzroy, Duke of Richmond and Somerset

Thomas Cromwell King's Chief Minister, Privy Councillor, Chancellor of the Exchequer, Master of the Jewel-House, Steward of Westminster, Surveyor of the King's Woods, Master of the King's Wards, Member of parliament, wealthy merchant and money lender. Former soldier, Italian trader, scholar and banker with the Florentine Frescobaldi family

Queen Katherine Catholic Spanish princess married to Henry since 1509 - pious, respectable, intelligent, and mother to Princess Mary. Decreed no longer queen, Katherine will never give up her title

Anne Boleyn New wife and queen of King Henry. Highly-educated reformer and former royal lady in-waiting

Charles Brandon Duke of Suffolk, and Henry's best friend. Married to Henry's sister Mary, Dowager Queen of France. Member of the Privy Council

Thomas Howard Duke of Norfolk, uncle to Anne Boleyn, close courtier to Henry. Member of the Privy Council

Thomas Boleyn Earl of Wiltshire and Ormond and Lord Privy Seal. Father to Anne Boleyn, along with popular courtier George Boleyn and the beautiful Mary Boleyn, King Henry's former mistress

Advisors and courtiers to King Henry

Sir Thomas More Chancellor of the Duchy of Lancaster, respected humanist, author and Catholic theologian. Loyal advisor to King Henry and champion of Dutch writer Erasmus

Thomas Cranmer Archbishop of Canterbury and leader of the Convocation of Canterbury. Highly-educated theologian, humanist and ordained priest, and supporter of Martin Luther.

Bishop Stephen Gardiner Trained in canon (religious) and civil law, and master secretary to the king.

Eustace Chapuys Imperial Ambassador to England and champion of the cause of Queen Katherine on Charles V's behalf

Powerful Italian figures in 1529

Pope Clement VII Pope of Rome and leader of the Catholic faith since 1523. Member of the powerful Florentine Medici dynasty. Imprisoned during the sacking of Rome by Charles V's soldiers in 1527

Charles V of Spain King of Spain, Holy Roman Emperor, King of Italy, King of the Romans, Lord of the Netherlands and Duke of Burgundy, ruler of the German and Austrian states controlled by the Roman Empire. Nephew of Queen Katherine of England

The Medici dynasty Multi-generational family in control of the Republic of Florence. One of the wealthiest families in Europe, creator of two Popes, including Clement. Ousted from Florence in 1527 during a siege, only to be reinstated with full control and wealth in 1531, especially **Alessandro de' Medici,** Duke of Florence, the last senior member of the original Medici generation, illegitimate son of Pope Clement

Nicóla Frescobaldi Effeminate bastard son to the late Francesco Frescobaldi, a wealthy Florentine merchant and banker. Reclusive favourite courtier of Pope Clement, highly- educated man of business, now master secretary to Thomas Cromwell

Well known figures in Europe in 1529

Erasmus of Rotterdam Dutch Renaissance humanist, Catholic priest, social critic, teacher, and theologian. Creator of the Latin New Testament bible based on Greek texts

William Tyndale Creator of the English language bible, translated from Greek and Hebrew texts. Supporter of Protestant reform. In exile from England and against Henry's annulment

Martin Luther German theologian, excommunicated priest and creator of the Protestant Reformation and the German language bible

Niccoló Machiavelli Recently-deceased Florentine diplomat, politician, historian, philosopher, humanist, and writer. Creator of political science

King Francis I of France Popular young King of France. Well-educated writer and patron to Leonardo da Vinci. Signed the peace treaty at the Field of Cloth of Gold with England

Stephen Vaughan English merchant, royal agent and diplomat, and best friend to Thomas Cromwell

Popular English courtiers in 1529

Ralph Sadler Former ward and now master secretary to Thomas Cromwell and courtier to King Henry

Richard (Williams) Cromwell Nephew to Thomas Cromwell and member of the Pricy Council

Sir Thomas Audley Barrister and Speaker in the House of Commons

Richard Rich Popular lawyer and member of parliament

Thomas Wriothesley Lawyer serving Thomas Cromwell

Sir Henry Norris, Sir Francis Weston, Sir William Brereton, Sir Francis Bryan, Sir Thomas Henneage, Sir Thomas Seymour, Sir Nicholas Carew Members of the privy chamber of King Henry

Mark Smeaton Talented young English composer and musician at the royal court

Sir Thomas Wyatt Diplomat, politician, poet, loved friend of Anne Boleyn and Thomas Cromwell

Hans Holbein the Younger Popular German artist under Thomas Cromwell's patronage, given royal favour for his extraordinary portrait talents

NOTE

While all the world knows Thomas Cromwell, the man himself spelled his name 'Crumwell' and it was pronounced 'Crumell' during his life.

This book, like others in the series, uses the term "Protestant" when talking about the Reformation and the reformers, even though the terms was rarely in use in Germany until 1533, and in England from 1539. The term "evangelical" was in use during this period, however, I have avoided this term as much as possible, as the meaning has changed significantly over the centuries. For clarity, most mainstream Protestants are referred to as reformers, while the fully committed Protestants are named Lutherans. Calvinists in southern Germany and Switzerland are referred to as Calvinists, and the extremist Protestants of this time period are referred to as Anabaptists and/or Sacramentarians. I use all of these terms in the book series, and are kept separate for ease of reading. The term "Protestant" remains throughout the book as a catch-all phrase, to distinguish reformers from Catholics, who are also referred to as papists.

I have used only pounds in England, as the English currency of the period was complex. Approximately, £1 in Cromwell's period is £350 today.

'All who contribute to the overthrow of religion, or to the ruin of kingdoms and commonwealths, all who are foes to letters and to the arts which confer honour and benefit on the human race, are held in infamy and detestation.'

~Niccoló Machiavelli
The Discourses: I, 10, 1517

'…for ye know, by histories of the bible that God may, by his revelation, dispense with his own Law'

~Thomas Cromwell,
Letter to Bishop Fisher , 1535

Chapter 1 – November 1533
Austin Friars, London

Timeth turns our lyes into trouths

'Catholic, Protestant, all makes no matter; for I shall die a sinner for the justice I administer.' Nicòla's rose-gold eyelashes fluttered, such was the strength in which she held her green eyes closed. Tears perched upon her lashes, waiting to ripple down her dark olive cheeks.

'God gives us the power of His spirit, and the sword of His word. True contrition shall deliver souls to heaven.' Thomas Cranmer, Archbishop of Canterbury, knelt opposite to Nicòla, his purple robes flowing around the carpets beneath their knees. His hands closed over Nicòla's clasped in prayer. Behind the altar was Nicòla's bedroom, or more precisely, the bedroom of Thomas Crumwell, her master. Before them; William Tyndale's English Bible, handwritten by the man himself. Also, Martin Luther's German translation, and, for Nicòla's comfort, a Catholic Latin bible. Crumwell may have yearned for Protestant reform, yet Nicòla's soul, away from the ears of her master, struggled with reformation. Cranmer and Nicòla were firm friends, yet in times of prayer, in times of struggle, Cranmer also proved himself a man of true piety, patient with Nicòla's fear for her soul.

'Can contrition and repentance truly come to me?' Nicòla whispered, one tear making its defiant roll down her cheek.

'At the heart of the Christian faith, contrition shows that a soul is ready for repentance. The old religion and the new; it makes no matter, my child. Absolution will come through the regret you now feel.'

'Father, forgive me, for I have sinned. I know you came yesterday for my need to confess and repent, but again I feel burdened with my deeds.'

'Tell me.'

Nicòla felt Cranmer's hands move against hers, a gentle gesture. She opened her eyes a little to see him before her, his eyes closed, his dark hair over his face a touch. While Cranmer preached to king and country about the virtue of reformation in England, in private, Cranmer allowed Nicòla her need to adapt from Catholic idolatry and into the light of God.

'Oh, Thomas,' she whispered as she closed her eyes again, forgetting to address him formally. 'I walked into the Tower of London, my stride strong, my will determined. I walked into the cell of Elizabeth Barton and I struck her across the face. Not a word. I watched as others hurt her, beat her, kicked her. I watched as others tortured her accomplices. I interrogated them; I screamed in their faces. The power I feel, disguised as a man, the favourite man of Thomas Crumwella, the most powerful man in this realm, makes me a monster. I watched as men were put to the rack, I heard their screams and yet I did nothing. How can God want me to do this?'

'Elizabeth Barton is a heretic, a traitor. She is a traitor to her faith. Those men who stand accused beside her represent all the corruption and abuse of the Church itself.' Cranmer's hands shook over Nicòla's, and she opened her eyes again. Cranmer stared back at her. 'God gave Barton and her men the chance to repent, Nicòla. She claims to speak with God, to hear His words. Barton claims Mary Magdalene writes letters to her. She claims God tells her the future. Barton sins so deeply that there can be no salvation for her soul. They have forced you to torture Barton. Someone must do God's will.'

'What if Barton is like me?' Nicòla asked. 'I am a fantastical creature. The mind of a man trapped in a woman's body. That is how I am explained. But I am a woman! You know well the frailty of my affairs. What if Barton is the same? A woman, confused by her calling in life, used by that heretical Friar Bocking and the others in Canterbury?'

'Whatever the cause, Barton speaks. She spoke to the King himself, prophesying his death. That is treason on its own. She taints the minds of influential men. Perchance she is ill in the mind; perchance we shall never know. But what Elizabeth Barton has done is use God's word against the King, against many of us. That is treason. She calls for us to be Catholic and to stop religious reform. She wants to keep England in the darkness.'

'And for that, I must sin, abuse bodies, harm others, alongside Crumwella, alongside Ralph Sadler, Thomas Wriothesley, Richard Rich. We cloak ourselves under Crumwella's name and commit sins.'

'Let us pray. Mighty Lord, you have fashioned the universe, and brought order out of chaos. We thank you for bringing order to our lives. Help us respect the authorities you have established, for the sake of the world and for the Church. Guide us by your Spirit to serve Your will, and give us the courage needed by early reformers, so that in our time we may confess our faith in your Son Jesus Christ, in whose gracious name we pray. Amen.'

'Amen.' Nicòla made to cross herself, but stopped; for that was a

Catholic gesture, not Protestant. But after years by Crumwell's side, it remained a habit. The pair wandered away from the corner of the enormous bedroom, past the bed where she and Crumwell slept in sin many nights, to the fire burning in silence beside two plush chairs and a table for wine. Nicòla leaned on the back of one chair and sighed.

'Thank you, Thomas,' she said, her Italian accent rolling the letters of his name. 'I fear the truth of my sex makes me weak.'

'Even the strongest man can be averse to torture,' Cranmer replied, folding his hands together. 'There is no need to feel ashamed after committing violence. We broke a country away from the Catholic faith. Violence happens all over Europe for this reason.'

'King Henry looks to you as archbishop, to Crumwella as chief minister, to bring these changes.'

'It is Crumwell who broke the Catholic Church in England. All must bow to Henry now. I owe my position in this country solely to Crumwell. I owe my life to Crumwell.'

Poor Thomas Cranmer. The Lutheran faith of the German States stated clergy did not need to be celibate, so he married Margarete in Nuremberg and shipped her to England in a crate. Now they had a son, also named Thomas, and both mother and son still lived in fear for their safety, hidden from the King until Henry decided if English priests could marry. Margarete moved often, so no one knew much of her. She lived in the Austin Friars nursery with her son at present, along with Jane, Nicòla's daughter by Crumwell, already three years old. But Margarete could tarry nowhere long, lest be arrested, the archbishop likewise.

'As long as we have the favour of Master Crumwella, we are safe,' Nicòla replied. 'Have you been at the King's side recently?'

'Yes, just yesterday,' Cranmer said and invited himself to sit down in Crumwell's private room. Few got into Crumwell's huge bedroom; even the maids scurried with fear. 'There is an anger in Henry, I must confess. His new daughter vexes him with anger, but also much confusion. His marriage to Queen Anne is sound, in both God's eyes and the law. We defeated the Pope. Yet God gave Henry and Anne a daughter, not a son for the throne.'

'Henry believes that God has given him the Princess Elizabeth to punish him for his sins against the former Queen Katherine.'

Cranmer nodded as he watched the fire. 'Queen Anne has been out of confinement after the birth for a month now, yet the King barely goes to her. She wishes to make a son as fast as God can deliver another pregnancy.'

'Surely Henry loves his new daughter. One of the ugliest babies I have laid my eyes on, God forgive me, but still Henry's child.'

Cranmer stifled a laugh. 'You have visited with Her Majesty?'

'I have, a few days past. Crumwella suggests I call on the Queen often now she is back in London instead of Greenwich. Anne delights in her daughter; they even keep the child in Anne's rooms, not the royal nursery! What the child lacks in looks she makes up for in her mother's love. Crumwell spends much time in private with Henry, while Henry urges for further legislation, to make the Act of Supremacy legal. Soon we shall all have to swear an oath that the King rules the Church, not the Pope.'

'And we shall be better for it.'

'We need no more of the Pope.' Nicòla remembered Pope Clement in the Apostolic Palace in Rome. Gone was the handsome man of his youth who inspired her lust. He had forsaken her now, thought her a heretic. The Pope's bastard son, Nicòla's husband, had also ceased in demanding her to return home to Florence. At age three and thirty years, Nicòla had more than destroyed her Catholic soul. It was almost twenty years since her love affair with Pope Clement, then only Cardinal Giulio de'Medici, and even nearly four years since she married his depraved Moorish son. Without God giving Nicòla a home, Crumwell allowed her to live safe in England.

'How is Thomas?' Cranmer asked. 'For I have barely seen him.'

'We are much busy at court. Master Crumwella is working on the Act of Succession, so Princess Elizabeth can be heir to the throne, and the Act of Supremacy, recognising Henry's religious authority. Not only is Crumwella the King's Chief Minister, set above all others, he runs the Exchequer, the Jewel House, the Hanaper, he sits in Parliament, and now Henry has made him the Steward at Westminster Abbey, now also Surveyor of the King's Woods! One man can only do so much. We have only so many clerks, messengers, attendants…'

'And spies.' Cranmer smiled. Everyone knew of Crumwell's creatures. Nicòla, "the Waif" was the chief creature of the English court.

'There are rumours of rumblings in Ireland. The Dublin councillors are not happy with the Catholic Church's destruction. Many northern lords are also complaining. Crumwella must see to quelling both factions. He seeks the head of Elizabeth Barton on a spike. Crumwella seeks the heads of Sir Thomas More and Bishop Fisher. He seeks to push Bishop Gardiner from court for good. Crumwella is the King's Chief Minister and Secretary of State. And every nobleman at court hates him for it.'

'I am the Archbishop of Canterbury, leader of the Church in England, under His Majesty, of course. There are bishops, archdeacons, priests, all who wish to defy me. I know what it is to be a common man raised so high all hate him. I lack Crumwell's political knowledge, his deftness in his choices and movements, his ability to take on so many tasks at once. You and he have that art of memory skill. You speak Greek do you not, Nicòla?'

'Yes, Master Crumwella taught me Greek last month while we were away from court.'

'The whole language, in one month?'

'That is Ioci, Archbishop. It is the powerful skill of remembering all. That is how Master Crumwella can recite the New Testament from memory alone.'

Cranmer shook his head. No one in England studied Ioci, the ancient Greek method of remembering everything. 'You know of the Greek expression, "polymath." It means to have the ability in many subjects, having the complex knowledge to solve many complicated issues, using many bodies of work all learned by one man.'

'You believe Master Crumwella is a polymath?'

'With no doubt. Crumwell can think of parliamentary legislation and religious reform, but be…'

'Torturing heretics in the Tower, despite being a man of almost fifty years,' Nicòla finished the sentence.

'I have passed forty years and I could not sustain such a life. There are no exciting soldier-of-fortune stories in my history,' Cranmer smiled inwardly. 'I worry for Crumwell, Nicòla,' he continued. 'He rises so high; he works so often.'

'Master Crumwella believes his reforms to England are a legal matter, using religion as a cover to change a country. He leaves the religious needs of the realm in your good hands. His soul seems at ease, despite all he handles.'

'Yet, he hides you in his life. A woman, dressed as a man, works in the royal court as Crumwell's master secretary. A woman married to another man. You violate this country's social conduct laws, Nicòla. They should remove you to your husband in Florence. You, by right, should be Duchess of Florence, yet are a lowborn man's attendant.'

'You, sir, are Archbishop of Canterbury yet your wife serves in my daughter's nursery, along with your son. King Henry could topple you with one word. I could be toppled also, but while Crumwella does whatever Henry wishes, then I feel safe. I know, every morning when I wake, that they could throw me back in the Tower where I was years ago. This is the world we have created, Archbishop Cranmer; a dangerous world, even for ourselves. As Machiavelli once wrote, "there are two methods of fighting, the one by law, the other by force: the first method is that of men, the second of beasts; but as the first method is often insufficient, one must have recourse to the second." But we must pay a hefty price for owning such power.'

'Now I have annulled Henry's marriage to Katherine and the Boleyns have their queen…'

'Anne is the Crumwella queen, not the Boleyn queen. They may think they have power with Anne on the throne, her father as the Lord Privy Seal, but we know Master Crumwella holds the power.'

'Well indeed. Now that marriage is real in law and before God, what of your marriage? Will there be an inquiry into that, if you so wish?'

'And risk telling the world I am hidden as a man?' Nicòla brushed her newly trimmed rose-gold hair behind her ears. She wore her all-black Crumwell livery, even a black overgown lined with black fur to stay warm in the brisk late autumn. Her brighter clothes, which gave away hints of her feminine nature, had disappeared away again at Crumwell's instance.

'I can, as Archbishop of Canterbury, rule that Thomas Crumwell may take a foreign wife, one in need of an annulment. As the new marriage would be in England, with an English man, I can rule on the wife's annulment. What the Pope of Rome says matters none.'

'I married in the eyes of God, in the Apostolic Palace, before the Pope himself. I said the words before God.'

'Did you not swear before God to marry Crumwell too, before King Henry and his Anne?'

'I did.'

'And you consummated your marriage to Alessandro de'Medici?'

'No. Alessandro is living in Florence happily with his head mistress, and the other girls. To gain an annulment, Alessandro would be the one to ask. A wife cannot petition for an annulment from a marriage.'

'If your husband were to ask for an annulment, then your marriage would fall short and be ended.'

'But Alessandro needs to apply to the Pope. The Pope will not grant his son an annulment.'

'I can try to help you, Nicòla,' Cranmer continued. 'We can canvas the scholars of Europe… as we did for Henry and Anne.'

'Henry is a king. I am a whore.'

'Crumwell wants your marriage annulled, or at least ruled invalid.'

'I had carnal relations with the Pope, my father-in-law, when Alessandro was still in the nursery. Surely that rules the marriage invalid.'

'Yes, but it would also be spoken of, in front of the Convocation of Canterbury, before I could rule the marriage invalid.'

'And we cannot see the King's Chief Minister in the company of the Pope's whore,' Nicòla sighed.

'I do not think I can help you without revealing your nature to the world, Nicòla, no matter how much Crumwell wants it done. We could try a secret ruling of the Convocation…'

'There are no secrets in the English court, parliament or convocation,' Nicòla scoffed. 'There are many spies, so it would never work.'

'If Crumwell's Act of Supremacy laws are in effect, perchance all we shall need is the King's consent. He knows of your fantastical nature and could rule in your favour.'

'Mayhap once we have a legitimate son in the cradle we can ask,' Nicòla suggested. The sound of a distant tolling bell echoed through the private chambers. Master Crumwell had returned to Austin Friars; a rare event at present.

'I shall retire to my private rooms,' Cranmer said and eased himself from the warm chair. 'Please, thank Crumwell again for letting me tarry at Austin Friars to visit my wife. If they found Margarete and baby Thomas, we would all be in grave danger.'

'Margarete is welcome hither until after Christmas, then we shall move her out to Crumwell's new house in Dewhurst for a few months. We shall keep your new family safe.'

Cranmer allowed Nicòla to kiss his ring and he shuffled along the darkened hallway, his purple robes smooth on the bare floor. Nicòla knew Crumwell would go to his library and offices, where Ralph, who ran Austin Friars, would probably still be working. Ralph had been in Crumwell's care since the age of seven and now had a baby with his new wife Ellen. Both Ralph and Cranmer had sons named Thomas. Had Nicòla's last baby not been stillborn, there would have been three babies named Thomas in the nursery with baby Jane. Nicòla sat before the fire and waited; they would flood Crumwell with papers from the lawyers and clerks still working in the offices on the ground floor. But it was not long before someone rushed into the private rooms with wine and cheese on a silver tray. Rather than a maid, it was Ellen, Ralph's wife. She was one of the rare few who knew of Nicòla's truth and thus allowed in the private bedroom.

'Master Frescobaldi.' Ellen bobbed in a curtsy as she placed the tray on the small table before Nicòla. Despite knowing of her sex, and after time to get used to the notion, Ellen still choked a little when calling Nicòla "Master."

'Mrs. Sadler,' Nicòla said with a smile. 'Crumwella and Ralph are in the library, I assume?'

'Yes, Master Crumwell and Mr. Sadler appear to be in much cheer. I thought to bring this tray, as Master Crumwell will retire shortly. I shall tell him you are hither.'

'Tell them to take their time,' Nicòla smiled. 'Archbishop Cranmer has retired for the night.'

Ellen curtsied again and rushed from the room. Nicòla sipped the sweet red wine and closed her eyes. The image of kicking Elizabeth Barton in the face flashed before her and she quickly opened her eyes.

The door to the chambers opened and Crumwell appeared in the bedroom moments later. He tossed his black bag and hat on the Turkish carpets and dashed over to Nicòla, and he pulled her into his embrace the moment she stood up to him. Only when he finally ended their kiss, could she see how tired he appeared.

'Tomassito…' she began.

'I know, they forced you to interrogate Barton and her heretic bastards without me today, and I thank you for your pains. Ralph has already told me Barton gave away no news?'

'No, she maintains she speaks with God,' Nicòla replied, still in his embrace.

'I could not leave the King today. He greatly needs every detail about his son's wedding.'

'Bastard son.'

'Well indeed, but I shall not be the one to remind the King of his son's illegitimacy,' Crumwell said, and guided his love back to her seat. He sat down across from her and grabbed the wine. 'Henry loves that boy, named for him,' Crumwell sighed. 'A young son, just fourteen years and now marrying a noble girl. If only we could make him legitimate.'

'If any person can, you can,' Nicòla replied.

Crumwell raised his eyebrows in agreement as he gulped the wine, most unlike him. The silver streaks in his dark curls caught the light of the fire. 'I have thought to make a law, designed so they need no heir of the English throne to be born legitimate, and then Henry could choose his successor.'

'That could spark civil war!'

'And I know it, Nicò. Still, I must keep all options open. The wedding at Westminster shall be grand indeed. Lady Mary Howard may not wish to marry Henry Fitzroy, but it pleases her father, old Norfolk. It pleases Lady Mary's brother, for he and Fitzroy are close friends. Fitzroy may be a bastard son, but he is the Duke of Richmond and Somerset, and Lord-lieutenant of Ireland. Henry loves his son. Even the King of Scotland speaks highly of Fitzroy. Naturally, our new queen hates the wedding plans. Fitzroy, and Katherine's daughter, the former Princess Mary, are equally hated by Anne.'

'But we draft laws so baby Princess Elizabeth can rule over Henry's other children,' Nicòla argued.

'That does not stop Anne from complaining,' Crumwell said and gulped his wine again. 'She has been queen but six months and already finds fault in the role, and in her own world. I do loathe that woman.'

'Pray to God we get a legitimate son in the royal cradle and all will not matter,' Nicòla replied.

'But what of you, my love. What of Jane?'

'Our daughter is well. It has been a week since I saw you, Tomassito.'

'I hate when we must work apart. A week is too long to be apart from my most wonderful and adored wife.'

'I am glad you are so assured in our marriage.' Nicòla swore to marry Crumwell before God and the King, but that did not overrule her lawful marriage in Italy.

'And I also am assured in the abilities of you, my master secretary. After the Fitzroy-Howard wedding, we shall travel to Greenwich Palace to prepare for the royal Christmas and New Year celebrations.'

'We prepare The Company of Merchant Adventurers of London banquet on your behalf. All have replied they will attend, except the governor.'

'John Hutton is most ill. Stephen Vaughan shall take his place as governor of the Company when Hutton is dead. Tis a shame Vaughan shall not return to England this year.'

'I know he is your closest friend, but Vaughan is safe in Antwerp. He need not get burned as a heretic for his Protestant views.'

'England is my country now. They shall burn no more Protestants. Those days are gone.'

'Now we shall burn Catholics,' Nicòla replied, unable make eye contact with Crumwell.

'No, I shall burn no one. I shall take the heads of heretics and traitors.'

Now Nicòla raised her gaze to meet the double-minded man's golden eyes. Crumwell softened in his position in the chair and took her hand. 'I received word from Gregory today.'

'Is he well?' Nicòla thought often of Crumwell's only son; a boy of female favour and not as intelligent as his father.

'Very well, and happy to move to Dewhurst after Christmas. He shall enjoy being tutored there, and Cranmer's wife and son shall be there for months. Gregory shall be fourteen in a few months. I shall soon need to find him a wife.'

'Must you, Tomassito?'

'A pre-contract only. Do you wish to hear scandalous talk?'

Nicòla noticed a twinkle in Crumwell's beautiful golden gaze. 'What have the creatures heard?'

'An affair at Wulf Hall, one of the Seymour households. Catherine, wife of the eldest son Edward, has been sleeping with her father-in-law, old Sir John Seymour. Such disgrace! Two of the Seymour girls, Lady Jane and Lady Elizabeth, have been called home from Anne's court. Now Edward's two sons may not be his heirs, but perchance his own half-brothers!'

'Idle talk, surely.'

'It harms Edward's chances of rising at court, with Sir John out of royal favour. A decent man, by all accounts. But no longer.'

'As if King Henry cares for faithfulness,' Nicòla scoffed.

'We need Queen Anne pregnant before Henry finds himself a mistress. That is all we need to worry about for now.'

'Such is the glory of ruling England,' Nicòla replied.

Crumwell took Nicòla's hand again, and she looked at his reddened knuckles, a sign of interrogating people in the Tower. 'We shall rule together, you shall see.'

Chapter 2 – November 1533
Westminster Abbey, London

*Lyes can be formd from trouths, but trouths cannot be formd from
lyes*

If it were possible to feel pity for King Henry, now would be the
moment. There he sat, under his golden cloth of estate, his new queen by
his side. There were to one side of the altar in the Abbey while Archbishop
Cranmer praised everyone. The nobility gathered for Henry Fitzroy's
wedding, Henry's beloved illegitimate son to the Duke of Norfolk's only
surviving daughter, Lady Mary. The bride and groom, both aged fourteen
years, looked equally solemn, young Fitzroy nervous, Mary almost fearful.
Rare late November sunshine streamed into the Abbey, illuminating the
beautiful occasion. It reflected off the groom's dukedom coronet and hurt
Crumwell's eyes for a moment.

Crumwell, sitting straight and stiff in the front row of guests, flicked his
golden eyes away from the ceremony to Nicòla beside him. She sat perfectly
still, her face without expression as she listened to Cranmer's words.
Further along, the Duke of Norfolk sat with his hands clasped over his
enormous waistline, fingering the livery collar of the Order of the Garter
which hung from his shoulders. His thick legs moved his widespread feet, a
huge man uncomfortably dressed in his best, sweat running down his neck
onto his white ermine coat.

But it was the groom's father which took Crumwell's attention. Henry
sat there, one elbow on his throne, leaning forward as Cranmer spoke. His
bastard son would be a husband. His precious child born of Elizabeth
Blount, Henry's one-time mistress. The intelligent and likeable son could
never be his father's heir and it hurt the King. The boy was laden with
honours, tutored well, charming, diplomatic, corresponded with the Scots
King and met the French King in person. Perchance it was worth making

26

Fitzroy legitimate through the law if the Church would not recognise him. With Queen Anne failing to produce a son, perchance Crumwell should have hitched his wagon to the Fitzroy cause, not the Boleyn movement. Fitzroy's only problem was his cough, which followed him everywhere. Some said he coughed just like Henry's brother, Prince Arthur.

The King looked so happy as he leaned forward to not miss a word from the Archbishop, nor the words of his son and the bride. The King adored the boy, kept away from his father so often. He had lived in the royal nursery with Lady Margaret Bryan after Princess Mary grew up, and now Princess Elizabeth had taken Fitzroy's place in the nursery. Fitzroy bore his mother's looks; pale, blonde, thin, so unlike Henry himself. The King bore so much pride in seeing his son married while young Fitzroy looked terrified at the prospect.

Queen Anne was the reason Crumwell felt pity for the King. Anne could not have appeared more angered at the idea of a public wedding in Westminster Abbey. She herself married Henry in a tiny secret ceremony, no lavish event for her grand day. Few enjoyed her beautiful coronation. Now, with a daughter in the cradle, Anne had to endure her husband's bastard receiving a royal wedding. Anne's dark eyes frowned at the altar, the bride her maternal cousin, her jealousy there for the court to witness.

Crumwell's attention snapped back as everyone bowed their heads in prayer. An English prayer, for English men. They had completed a wedding in Westminster Abbey without a Catholic Mass. The change was coming to England, and Crumwell knew he had the power to control all.

'I f-f-feel certain you are most p-p-proud of this occasion, Crowmell,' said stuttering Norfolk as he watched his daughter get into a litter with her new husband, to travel to Whitehall Palace for the wedding celebrations.

'Crumwell.' All these years and Norfolk still pronounced his name wrong. 'And yes, as Steward of Westminster Abbey, I am most proud to host a wedding for the King's son.'

'Bastard son,' Norfolk sniffed.

'If the Duke of Richmond was good enough to marry your daughter, surely you have respect for the boy,' Crumwell replied as Nicòla appeared at his side, one step back in deference to her master.

'I meant you m-m-must be proud b-b-because you have made sure the King d-d-does not marry his s-s-son in the Catholic faith. My d-d-daughter has been dis-dis-disrespected today.'

'I serve at the King's pleasure, Your Grace,' Crumwell replied and looked out at those of the court as they left Abbey's main entrance. 'We all serve at the King's pleasure, and he wanted a reformed ceremony for his only son. We are not bound to Rome any longer.'

Norfolk looked around the black-clad Crumwell to Nicòla. 'Your little

Waif is h-h-hither as a guest at my daughter's w-w-wedding,' he scowled.

'We have married your daughter before God today, Your Grace,' Nicòla replied as she bowed in respect for the wide duke. 'A fine match for a duke's daughter. If we named Fitzroy as legitimate, it would make your daughter the future Queen of England. You know this; we all know. Master Crumwella would be the man to make sure such a law change could aid your daughter.'

Norfolk looked to Nicòla and back to Crumwell; they all knew the details. Norfolk had been living at his palace in Kenninghall, with his young mistress Bess Holland, away from her role as Queen Anne's lady-in-waiting. Norfolk despised Crumwell and Crumwell adored it.

'I n-n-need your help,' Norfolk muttered as the crowd dispersed from the Abbey, the King's guards keeping the public well away from the nobles. 'But n-n-now is not the day for such discussions.'

'No indeed, the wedding of your daughter is not the occasion in which to discuss you banishing your wife,' Crumwell muttered with a smile. 'The entire court knows your wife, aunt to the Queen herself, detests you.'

'At least I have a wife, and a m-m-mistress. You seem unable to do your duty b-b-by a woman.'

Crumwell just shook his head and smiled over the surrounding lords.

'B-b-but,' Norfolk continued, 'there is always the Waif's bastard niece in your h-h-house. The child of the Frescobaldi daughter. How is your s-s-sister in Florence, Waif?'

'The Duchess is well, living outside of Florence at a Medici country estate,' Nicòla lied.

Crumwell noticed how much she lowered her tone when talking of her "sister" in Italy. No one else would ever know Nicòla and Nicòletta were the same person.

'If your s-s-sister is such a powerful woman in Florence, married to a Medici d-d-duke, why can she not raise her b-b-bastard in her own household?' Norfolk continued, already knowing all the details.

'The Duchess chose not to keep her daughter with her when she married the Duke of Florence,' Crumwell answered for Nicòla and shuffled slightly to shield her from Norfolk's gaze. 'Master Frescobaldi brought the child to England.'

'Because you are the father, Crowmell?'

'Crumwell! And I do not have time to travel to Florence to even see the Duchess. I am too valuable to the King.'

'Mayhap you are n-n-now, but you were not always so valuable, not v-v-visible at court,' Norfolk mumbled. 'And "Master" Frescobaldi? Master of what?'

'A new estate we are building at Dewhurst.'

'I thought that t-t-to be one of your n-n-new acquisitions,' Norfolk frowned. 'Surely the Waif-creature has n-n-not amassed so much favour, not as a foreigner. Though, you admire f-f-foreigners, do you not? I h-h-hear you have a German nurse in the h-h-household of your bastard.'

Damned Norfolk had a spy in Austin Friars again and watching Jane's nursery no less. Cranmer's wife in the nursery would need to move again, for her protection. 'What sort of villain does it take,' Crumwell said through his gritted teeth, hidden behind a cold smile, 'to place a spy in my household to watch the wards I adopt? We all take in wards, Norfolk. I am Master of the Wards at His Majesty's pleasure. I have a child in living in my house, and you place spies among the staff I use in my nursery? That sounds like a man of lewd appetites.'

Norfolk's face fell in pure horror at the accusations, and he waddled away in a moment. Crumwell felt Nicòla's hand on his shoulder. 'Worry not, Tomassito,' she uttered.

'I shall have to search through the staff at Austin Friars with haste. And remove Margarete from the nursery. She can stay with Richard and Frances at Stepney.'

'Now is not the time to discuss such,' Nicòla replied and frowned her green eyes in the sunlight 'But yes, your nephew could take good care of Margarete.'

'Spies we have in Norfolk's household suggest he locks up his wife and deprives her of her household, jewels, clothes, even food some days,' Crumwell continued.

'Stop letting that man anger your humours,' Nicòla cautioned.

Crumwell sighed, but to his left appeared Charles Brandon, the pompous Duke of Suffolk. Another wide-waisted man with his pristine ermine furs and over-confident demeanour. Beside the man of fifty years stood his wife, who was soon to celebrate her fifteenth year. The sweet young girl gave a gentle smile to Nicòla but did not dare to look at Crumwell.

'Common Crumwell,' Suffolk said in his deep voice, his greying beard, filled with breadcrumbs. Perchance his child bride was too frightened to brush it clean. 'You sat with us at the front of the proceedings.'

'At His Majesty's request,' Crumwell replied. 'You are looking well, Your Grace, so soon after the death of your wife.'

Suffolk's mouth puckered with anger and he patted Catherine's hand on his arm. 'Have you met Lady Catherine Willoughby, daughter to Baron Willoughby de Eresby and Maria de Salinas, lady-in-waiting to the former Queen? Catherine is the new Duchess of Suffolk.'

Duchess Catherine curtsied a little without looking up to Crumwell. 'A pleasure, Mr. Crumwell.'

'Bow not to Crumwell!' Suffolk snorted.

'Un placer conoscerti, Duquesa Catherine,' Nicòla uttered and bowed.

The young girl looked up at hearing Spanish, her mother's language.

'Crumwell's Waif-creature is the brother to the Duchess of Florence,' Suffolk told his wife. 'He is such a futile little thing.'

'I met your mother, several times when Queen Katherine still lived at court,' Nicòla told Catherine.

'Lady Katherine, Dowager Princess of Wales,' Crumwell reminded Nicòla. No one could call the mighty Katherine a queen now, not with Anne Boleyn on the throne.

'The former Queen Katherine is my godmother,' Catherine said in such a meek tone that Crumwell almost had to lean down to hear.

'My son, Henry, is most ill,' Suffolk added. 'It is fortunate we have a competent nursemaid in Catherine's mother, after all her years as a lady to Queen Katherine. Tis sad that Queen Katherine cannot have her closest advisor and friend with her any longer.'

'Lady Katherine, Dowager Princess of Wales,' Crumwell repeated.

'If you say so, common Crumwell.'

'Mr. Crumwell…' Duchess Catherine pleaded.

'No, there is no sense in petitioning Crumwell for a favour, my dear,' Suffolk interrupted his wife. 'For he only serves himself.'

'Do you speak Spanish, Your Grace?' Nicòla asked him, and Suffolk shook his heavy head.

'Escribe,' she said to young Catherine, who nodded as Suffolk pulled her away from the pair.

'What did you say?' Crumwell muttered. 'For her to write to you?'

'We may not have to help her in what she needs, but I feel sorry for a child linked to that fat old man, old enough to be her grandfather. Remember, any idle rumour we can gain is a help to us.'

Crumwell gazed up again, to see people forming around him; any time he stopped moving, people gathered, hoping to have a moment in his ear. Many were clutching notes; they had come prepared to push a request to Crumwell. He nudged Nicòla with his elbow and she promptly moved into the crowd to collect requests on his behalf. But there stood his longtime friend and enemy, Stephen Gardiner, whom he beckoned forward with joy.

'Bishop Gardiner,' Crumwell said, and bowed deeply, knowing Gardiner understood him to be mocking his position. 'Such a shame you were not asked to officiate this lavish occasion.'

'The marriage of a bastard son to a weak Howard girl, cousin to an over-reaching queen?' Gardiner replied. 'Why would I debase myself?'

'You came as a guest, so I can presume you are now as debased as the rest of us.'

Gardiner waved a dismissive hand at the Abbey beside them as if none mattered to him. 'Do you know what tomorrow is, Thomas?'

November 29. 'Of course, I could hardly forget.'

The two men stood eye to eye; once two common men, bound by a third. November 29 marked the third anniversary of Cardinal Thomas Wolsey's death. Once, Crumwell was Wolsey's lawyer, Gardiner his secretary. Now Gardiner was a bishop and the King's Chief Secretary, Crumwell the King's Chief Minister and controller of the country's parliament and finances. One a fervent Catholic, the other a devout reformist; never again would Gardiner and Crumwell sit on the same side of an argument.

'What do you suppose Wolsey would have made of all your changes, Thomas?' Gardiner asked.

'What would have Wolsey made of your lack of ability to stop my changes?' Crumwell countered.

Both men continued to stare at one another. They both abandoned their master, their patron, their friend at his moment of humiliation in different ways. Crumwell felt every man in England knew of his hurt, his embarrassment at doing so. Gardiner seemed to walk away without a scratch on him.

Gardiner glanced around others in the crowd, who had given them a moment to talk in private, Nicòla holding back petitioners with her charm and swift words. 'You are being played as a fool by the King, Thomas,' Gardiner continued. 'The country will not turn away from the Catholic faith. The King will not. He used you and Cranmer for his own ends. Henry still believes in all the meanings and virtues of being a Catholic, just using Protestant lies to abandon his wife in favour of his whore.'

Crumwell steadied his anger; he closed his hands together and set his feet apart a little. He looked to Gardiner in his white robes, his black fur hat slipped forward on his large forehead. 'Stephen, several months from now, I shall introduce a bill into parliament, and by law, they shall arrest you for treason for speaking in such a way about our Queen Anne.'

'Anne is your queen, Thomas, not mine.'

'Indeed, Queen Anne is my queen. And soon, if you do not swear she is your queen, you shall live in the Tower.'

'Will I be tortured, like poor Elizabeth Barton? I hear you interrogate her, Thomas.'

Crumwell narrowed his eyes. 'Perchance you should resign your post as Chief Secretary, Stephen. Perchance it is time we sent you on a diplomatic mission to France.'

'And who would take my place at the King's side?'

'I would; for I have been doing your work for months.'

'If you were to hold the title of Chief Minister, Secretary of State, Chancellor positions in the Exchequer, the Chancery and the Hanaper, the Jewel House, the King's Woods, the Privy Council… am I forgetting any?'

'Many.'

'If you were to hold so many titles, you would rule the country, and place Henry away from wise counsel.'

'I am the wise counsel, Stephen. I get the King whatever he likes.'

'And what favour do you get in return?'

Crumwell looked at Nicòla, conversing with Queen Anne's brother, George. Her safety and his own reputation would get destroyed in a heartbeat if Henry so desired. 'I get to reform the souls of England,' Crumwell replied.

Gardiner scoffed, his waistline jumping with his laughter. 'You change laws, Thomas, not religious views. You may have the illusion of power over religion, but I know, when souls come daily, to hear the true words of God in Latin, as God and the Pope demand, that men like I hold real control over the people. Nothing will defeat the Catholic faith.'

'It shall be defeated, in parliament.'

'Not in the souls of the faithful,' Gardiner grinned. 'I believe men are calling for your head.'

'Peasants perchance.'

'Of course, and you are now high in favour you care not for peasants.'

'Shall we take this conversation to the palace?' Crumwell offered.

'Certainly, for I am sure the wedding celebrations shall be as dull as most court occasions, so at least we can debate. We cannot even put the groom to bed with his bride.'

Crumwell nodded as he watched Nicòla speaking with a woman he did not recognise; a rare event. 'Fitzroy is a delicate son, and Henry does not want him to exert himself in the marriage bed. Henry believes this behaviour weakened his brother, Prince Arthur, and thus he could not survive the sweating sickness.'

'Oh, Prince Arthur, God bless his heavenly soul, was a sickly boy. He had a cough that followed him from cradle to grave, as if he was followed by a demon of coughing. Poor Fitzroy has the same. Are we to believe all royal sons shall die if they enjoy carnal relations when young? Our king survived just fine.'

'Henry does not carry the cough. The King can deny marital bed activities for his son and his wife if he so desires,' Crumwell countered.

'I heard that King Henry is in wonderment with Anne Boleyn in the bedroom. It seems she learned more than French manners in her youth.'

'Sadly, Stephen, I have learned far more about Queen Anne's relations with Henry than I ever wished to know.'

'So, you know she was no virgin when you constructed a false marriage for Henry.'

Crumwell turned back to Gardiner and looked him up and down. They were turning into old men, as much as Crumwell wished to deny it; they had come to prosperity so late in life. 'My queen sits upon the throne. The lies created by Anne's enemies, and my enemies, no longer matter.'

'Perchance just you and I are the winners; we have no dalliances to complicate our endeavours and are the only men in the royal circles who can claim so.' Gardiner was probably the only man at court without women hidden in cupboards. The bishop was probably the only celibate clergyman. Crumwell too was known as a man without a companion; his love for Nicòla would be hidden forever.

Finally, Crumwell's guards had arrived with horses to take him and Nicòla to Whitehall. Gone were the days of being able to move freely around London; everyone knew it was Thomas Crumwell who took away Katherine in favour of Queen Anne.

Crumwell watched Nicòla fold a pile of letters into a bag before she mounted her horse. 'Anything pleasing?' he muttered as they set off for the palace, less than a mile away. Still, being up on a horse and surrounded by Crumwell's men felt necessary now.

'No,' Nicòla sighed. She appeared uncomfortable in her saddle. 'How is Bishop Gardiner?'

'Stephen Gardiner is as boring as the human skull that Bishop Fisher keeps on his dining table at Lambeth Marsh,' Crumwell crowed and several of the guards laughed around him. 'Who was the woman you spoke to just now?'

'She is new to London. Comes from Hever Castle where Lady Mary Boleyn is visiting her children. Lady Mary still does not wish to return to her sister's court but is having financial trouble.'

'Then why not live as a lady-in-waiting to her sister? Lady Mary has been gone from the court for a year; she would be happier here. They provide for her children at Hever Castle.'

'There is a mystery in the Lady Mary, Master.' Nicòla gestured to the guard beside her. He pulled out coins to throw to children as they rode by.

'I am sure, whatever it may be with Lady Mary, that we shall pay for it at some stage,' Crumwell grumbled.

'George Boleyn wants to go with his sister, the Queen, to France next July when Henry meets King Francis again,' Nicòla continued.

'Good, then perchance we can stay home.'

'There he is,' called a loud voice and Crumwell glanced slightly to his left. A man stood in the doorway to a house, filthy hands and messed grey hair. 'Thomas Crumwell thinks himself all high and mighty now he is close to the King himself. Where is the real queen, our Katherine?'

Crumwell did not look at the man but heard him stumble as a guard shoved him without even leaving his horse. Crumwell's queen ruled the people of England now, and none of them liked it.

A few drops of rain appeared; tiny pats landed on Crumwell's black calf-leather gloves. The sky had darkened over all of England.

Chapter 3 – November 1533
St. Paul's Cathedral, London

Nothyng seduces liketh the powyr of lyes

'To call herself The Holy Maid is to slander God's love. She is nothing more than a vain whore, so heinous, so monstrous, so malicious that those loyal to God's grace dare not speak her name!'

Nicòla shivered slightly in the crowd, despite being pressed warmly between Crumwell and Cranmer. Such was the crowd she stood between the tall men, flanked by guards, all squashed among the onlookers. In the square before St. Paul's Cathedral, many Londoners heard the words of John Salcot, a Benedictine monk. The crowd gathered in a circle around St. Paul's Cross, an open-air pulpit. A small lead roof sheltered the monk on the stone steps from rain, but not those on the hastily made scaffold beside him. Every moment Salcot took a breath, the crowd filled his pause with jeers and hisses to denounce the guilty. Elizabeth Barton, The Holy Maid of Kent herself, stood hunched on the scaffold, wearing nothing more than a dirty black shift. Her feet bare, her toes bled onto the wood beneath her, grazed after being dragged before all. They tied her hands behind her back as tight as Crumwell had requested. Beside her stood Edward Bocking, the monk of Christ Church Priory who had encouraged all the nun's predictions. He too wore nothing but black, dark as the bruises to his face and arms, also tied tightly behind his back. Beside him stood Richard Risby, the Guardian of the Observant Friary of Richmond, another man convinced that Barton heard God's voice, could see the future of England. These men and others had made money off Barton for years, by charging people to hear Barton talk of her visions. Now that Barton had "seen" the place in hell where King Henry would go, she needed to be discredited.

'This man, this Bocking character,' Salcot continued in his high tone, desperate to get his voice out over the crowd, 'has continued to lie to us, to speak against our gracious king! Bocking uses his whore, dressed in the robes of a nun, to speak out against our king's lawful and spiritual matrimony with Queen Anne! Bocking shares words of our king's death, the traitor…'

Salcot paused as the crowd hissed and yelled at the threesome on the scaffold. They threw objects Nicòla could not quite see. One, perchance a stone, hit Barton in the face and Nicòla saw tears spring from the woman's blackened eyes.

'The problem remains that neither Barton nor any of her "confessors" have committed a treasonous act,' Cranmer murmured as he clasped his hands over his purple robes. 'We can punish treasonous words, but that may only enhance the maid's followers.'

'Life would be far simpler if we could just behead the lot,' Crumwell muttered. 'I feel Barton is close to confessing that she is a liar, that all this is part of her imagination.'

'We need to denounce them all though, not just the girl. She is a tool used to make money from fake conversations with God. They are stirring up sentiments about Anne, and not good ones!'

'Why not simply change the law?' Nicòla said, her head held high, her lips barely moving. While the crowd again listened to the monk, all three of them knew they were not liked by the audience. Nicòla dared not raise her voice.

'Tis the souls of the faithful I worry for,' Cranmer replied, he too stood straight, an aura of arrogance about him. 'But the laws of England cannot control the thoughts and words of every man.'

Nicòla glanced just slightly up to Crumwell and he shared a crooked half-smile of confidence. 'We could try,' he muttered.

'If it were treason to speak ill, everybody in England would be without a head,' Cranmer continued, his eyes still fixed on the traitors.

'We need to change the rules of what high treason is,' Nicòla replied, her voice barely reaching the men's ears over the cheers of the crowd. 'If you can get attainted for high treason for speaking ill of the King in public, then we can prosecute Barton and her villains without trial.'

'And give Barton the honour of being the first woman to have her head on a spike on London Bridge,' Crumwell smiled.

'Does your spy in the Marquess of Exeter's household have enough news to know that Barton is foretelling the King's death to his cousins?' Cranmer continued.

'More than enough evidence. But we can write false evidence,' Crumwell shrugged.

'Was it you who wrote the words of Salcot hither today?' Cranmer asked.

'I wrote the words today,' Nicòla replied.

'It seems each of you write in an eloquent prose,' Cranmer congratulated her. 'You speak as one mind.'

Salcot gestured for the crowd to be quiet again. 'We must now know The Holy Maid of Kent as The Mad Maid Kent!' he cried, to the laughter of the crowd. 'How else could we describe a woman who fornicates as she does? She has monks and bishops into her rooms, with her on her back, uttering God's words as she lets man after man take her in full sight of each other! These men, desperate to gain carnal relations with a nun, have sold their souls to the devil just to get their hands on the sinful parts of a woman!'

The crowd continued to hiss at the three on the scaffold, their backs facing one another so the crowd could see their beaten faces from every direction. Nicòla glanced along the edge of the front row of onlookers, to see a young girl staring at Barton as they shamed her with false allegations.

'How much longer shall this take?' Nicòla asked Crumwell.

'It looks set to rain much of the day,' Crumwell mused with a quick look at the darkening sky. 'We shall leave them hither to freeze awhile before they take them back to the Tower.'

'Let the people see the heretics,' Cranmer added. 'We will not tolerate this; all must live in a new England with no prophesying.'

Nicòla glanced at the young girl again, silent as her mother hissed at the group elevated before her. A change in fortune, and it could be Nicòla getting ridiculed for whoring, for lying and deception, and worse. Such was the frailty of human affairs.

~~~

Rain it did. But Nicòla, changed into new clothes, always black, always with the best furs to stay warm, walked with speed towards the cell where Elizabeth Barton stayed in the Tower. If Nicòla slowed her pace, she would simply turn and run, so speed aided her nerves. Crumwell and Cranmer were soon to follow, but first, Nicòla was to speak to Barton.

A guard opened the wooden door which creaked on old hinges. The smell of the room hit Nicòla, more so than the dank hallway and long-unwashed guard. No light came from the tiny window, up so high it was almost in the roof; but a candle flickered in the corner, set on the damp stone floor. Elizabeth Barton sat curled in a ball in the dark corner, hay on the floor about her. She pulled her legs up under her shift. Nothing but her eyes moved as she looked at Nicòla while the door closed behind her. Barton, with her freshly shaved head, had a trail of blood past her left ear, her skin bruised and dirty. Unlike Nicòla's time in the Tower, Barton's would never end.

'They send the smallest man to hurt me,' Barton mumbled, not moving from her spot. 'Is this so their dark souls can feel less burdened when God forces them to answer for their choices?'

Nicòla looked at Barton's hands, broken fingers balled together, shivering in the cold. She brought her own gloved hands together. 'It is your soul we worry for, Sister Elizabeth,' Nicòla replied. 'Perchance you are an innocent woman, cruelly used by the men in your priory. If you tell the truth and say God never spoke to you, that Mary Magdalene never wrote to you, that you never saw the King's death in a dream, mayhap you can be spared.'

'I see God,' Barton replied, her high-pitched voice sounding close to tears. 'They all believed when I spoke lovingly of our king, and they tolerated me when I spoke against the annulment of the Queen. Only now, when I see the truth, that the new queen will show our king to hell, do you punish me?'

'I care none for motives, Sister Elizabeth,' Nicòla sighed. 'I wish this to be over.'

'You are foreign,' Barton replied.

'What is this to me?'

'When I speak of the evil foreigner at court, Mr. Crumwell gets most frightened.'

'What?'

'I told Mr. Crumwell that an evil foreigner lived at court and was hiding in plain sight, ready to destroy the will of God. Mr. Crumwell beats me every time he enters my room, but always more when I tell him of the foreigner.'

Nicòla swallowed hard; Crumwell had said nothing. 'You speak of a direct threat to our king, so naturally, Master Crumwella would be most upset.'

'No,' Barton almost whispered, her voice so weak. 'It scares Crumwell that an evil woman shall end him.'

'Perchance you, Sister Elizabeth, are the evil foreigner, a stranger, a commoner, looking to be part of a world in which she does not belong.'

'At first, I believed the evil foreigner to be the false queen, the whore Anne. She speaks with a touch of French in her voice. She is no noble in the court of a king. But no, the foreigner has sunset-coloured hair.'

Nicòla knew her black hat covered her hair, trimmed short and tucked away.

'Are you to beat me again?' Barton mumbled.

Nicòla had no chance to reply; behind her, the door unlocked, and she turned to find Crumwell and Cranmer both there, also dry and changed, warm for interrogation in the Tower. Just the sight of them made Nicòla sigh with relief. In the dank cell, lit by one flickering candle, one could easily feel forgotten.

All stood silently as the guard brought in a solitary chair before locking the door. Crumwell looked from Barton to the seat. She did not even blink. Nicòla strode over and grabbed Barton by the collar of her shift. The fabric soaked Nicòla's glove, with rain or blood, she could not be sure. The beaten and starved Barton fell easily into the chair with Nicòla's shove, hunched forward in the seat before Crumwell and Cranmer.

'All the world shall know of your shame,' Crumwell said, his voice deep and grating, a sound he only made when under threat, like a trapped wolf.

'The world shall know of yours,' Barton muttered.

Crumwell lashed out so suddenly even Nicòla jumped away. He slapped Barton with the back of his hand and her whole body moved with the blow. Fresh blood appeared on her lip as Nicòla grabbed Barton by the shoulders, so she stayed on the chair.

'Sister Elizabeth,' Cranmer said in a tepid and gentle tone. 'Your visions are mischievous and filled with sedition and treason.'

'Sir Thomas More did not think so.'

'We shall charge Sir Thomas More with misprision when he recovers from illness, so too Bishop Fisher. They shall be harmed for deliberately keeping your visions a secret.'

'I speak God's words,' Barton replied.

Crumwell struck her again and she began to cry. With one sharp move of his head, Crumwell gestured for Nicòla to move away. Crumwell leaned over, his face so close to Barton's they almost blended together in the darkness of the cell. The Collar of Esses, Crumwell's chains of office which hung about his shoulders, hung its golden Tudor rose close to Barton's bloodied face. 'You are a whore!' he screamed in her face, she so weak she made no reply. 'You are a harlot!'

'No,' she whispered.

'Liar! Vain, deceitful traitor and heretic!'

The screaming frightened Nicòla, who took a few steps away. She drew close to Cranmer, and he too looked shocked by Crumwell's anger. Crumwell's angry voice sounded straight from hell.

'Repeat after me!' he yelled, each word slow and menacing. 'You are a whore!'

Barton sniffed through her tears. 'I am a whore.'

'What?'

'I am a whore,' she cried.

'You feign visions from your own imagination!'

'My visions are feigned from my imagination.'

'You tell lies to satisfy your accomplices!'

'I lie to satisfy my accomplices.'

Crumwell shifted his feet slightly, his legs apart to steady himself over the frightened nun. 'You lie to obtain worldly praise!'

'I lie to obtain worldly praise.'

'Good. Now you have learned how to confess.' Crumwell lowered his voice now, yet still spat on Barton's face as he spoke.

'If I die,' Barton mumbled, 'I can see your wife in heaven and tell her of your sins.'

Nicòla's eyes flashed wide the moment she heard the words. Barton's confession a moment ago would have saved her from weeks of torture and interrogation, but now she had sealed her own fate. Crumwell balled an angry fist and smashed it straight into Barton's mouth. The chair tipped backward with Barton crumpled atop it, landing with a violent crash. Crumwell stood over the body of the nun and punched her again in the face, two, three, four more times. The intense anger shocked Nicòla as she edged even closer to Cranmer, who appeared frozen in surprise. Crumwell forced his boot into Barton's face, his hand now coated in blood. He kicked her stomach, but her limp body did not respond, merely moved like a dropped sack of flour. Crumwell paused and wiped his mouth with his left hand; blood had landed on his face from the woman's body before him. He glanced up at Nicòla with the angriest glare from his golden eyes; no one could mention his wife or daughters.

'Heavenly Father, in your grace and mercy, offer forgiveness of sins, life, and salvation to all whose faith is in Your Son, Jesus Christ. Lead us from the paths of sin to repentance and humility, trusting in Your Word and promises,' Cranmer muttered, the cell now filled with silence and fear.

Crumwell tried to steady his breathing but jumped in surprise when the body at his feet moved, writhed on the dirty stone floor. Barton's frail body quivered and trembled, her neck arched back as her broken hands shook and contorted like raven's claws.

'Mayhap this is one the seizures they spoke of,' Cranmer uttered as he stepped cautiously towards the shaking body. Crumwell refused to mutter a word in reply. 'What if she claims to have heard God when she awakens?' Cranmer wondered with a furrowed brow.

'I have seen this before,' Nicòla said, at last finding her voice. 'One of my sisters, Francesca, she did this during the sickness which took her life. Her fever rose and rose, and at the height of her pain, she twisted and shook…' Her words trailed away as she watched the bloodied body slow its painful twisting.

'What if God has come to this poor child?' Cranmer asked.

'Blasphemy,' Nicòla replied as the body rested still once more. 'Barton is sick in the mind, or sick in the body. Just another woman shaped to the whims of the corrupt churchmen who have used her for their own gain. This woman is a tool, used by all those who wish to hear God's words, who wish to have control over their lives and God's rules. She is common and that fuels her following; she feels familiar to the commoners. Why would

God seek to come to the vessel of one so plain?'

Crumwell looked at the silent body beneath him; her face so bashed her features were no longer visible. He stepped over Barton and blew out the lone candle in the room and banged on the door. They finished their work for another day, in the name of King Henry.

Chapter 4 – December 1533
Whitehall Palace, London

Those gents did hold togyther with lyes

Thomas Audley's eyes lit up the moment he sipped his wine. The plump Lord Chancellor sat across from Crumwell at his desk in the private office of Crumwell Chambers, his wide shoulders laden in grey furs. 'I love a warmed wine!' Audley exclaimed. 'And the flavour is one I have never tried!'

'You can thank my master secretary,' Crumwell replied and leaned back in his high-backed throne of a chair. Behind him, raindrops hit the windows, the Thames hidden in the darkness. 'Tis an Italian recipe. Lemons and oranges soaked in wine with a mixture of spices and seeds sourced from Venice where the traders have returned from the east.'

Audley sipped his spiced wine again and tried to look not at Crumwell's healing knuckles. Crumwell hid his hand on his lap, beneath the desk's edge. 'But you did not come to discuss wine, Lord Chancellor.'

'Indeed not.' Audley set down the silver goblet and clasped his hands over his wide waist. 'I came to discuss Ireland. They like none of the Reformation changes, Thomas. They talk about refusing the Act of Supremacy.'

'The King rules the Church of England, and Ireland is part of Henry's realm. There is nothing else to discuss,' Crumwell shrugged.

'They could revolt against His Majesty. I know not what to do.'

Crumwell sighed. Why did no one in this government ever think ahead? This issue had been quietly on his mind for some time. They should have sent Fitzroy to rule Ireland, but now it was too late to let Henry's bastard rule; the Irish would no longer accept him. 'The Deputy of Ireland is the Earl of Kildare. He got himself injured with what was called a "gunshot" wound. He is to be recalled to England. I shall install one of his rivals, Sir

William Skeffington to be a deputy. He is for the Reformation and the Act of Supremacy. Also, Kildare's rival, Archbishop Allen in Dublin and the Butler family shall have greater authority at Dublin Castle. Then, one by one, we replace councillors in Dublin with favourites of mine.'

'How does one become a favourite of yours?'

'Bribes, of course.' Crumwell threw Audley a crude smile and the Lord Chancellor nodded. 'I can control Ireland from this very desk.'

'And the northern lords? They too are powerful against the Supremacy.'

'The Dacres and the Cliffords are feuding in the northwest. I shall lay charges of treason upon Baron Dacre and have Henry Clifford, Earl of Cumberland, appointed warden in the northwest. That shall ease the tone. Dacre can be acquitted in time; but by then, he shall have lost all control. He has been talking with Scottish lords and that is treason.'

'Shall you seek to rule the north of England and Ireland?'

'If I must. Ireland shall be easy to rule on the King's behalf. I shall send commissioners to Ireland to make sure the Reformation goes ahead; any person who does not wish to be searched for harbouring Catholic books and idols shall have to pay handsomely for the privilege.'

'How do I gain such bribes?' Audley laughed and sipped his wine again.

'You stay as the pious and attentive Lord Chancellor, Thomas. Leave the rest to me.'

'I fear there shall be little need for me to do anything in my role as Lord Chancellor if you are so busy,' Audley sighed.

Crumwell resisted the urge to smile. He wanted to be Lord Chancellor; he had cleared the path for himself, only to have Audley pulled from parliament to take the role, a move Crumwell still failed to understand. Still, as King's Chief Minister, Crumwell could do as he pleased.

Someone knocked on the door and Crumwell frowned; Nicòla was not in his chambers, unable to take care of his dealings. Why could the other lawyers and clerks not take care of messengers? But the door opened and there stood Sir Henry Norris, one of the King's gentlemen.

'Sir Henry,' Audley said as he turned in his chair. 'Have you come in search of Crumwell's famous Italian wine?'

'Perchance I should try it,' Norris sighed. 'Mr. Crumwell, it is the King. His temper has taken the most alarming turn. He received a message, sender unknown to me, and His Majesty has fallen into a most violent rage. The King is in his privy chamber and seeks to be alone.'

'Then why come hither? Why not send for Queen Anne?'

'Mayhap she is the source of the anger,' Audley muttered. 'This is the moment to retire.'

Crumwell showed Audley and Sir Norris to the main doors of his chambers before rushing along his private hallway to the King's rooms. He knocked gently on the door as he stood in the dark but heard nothing. With great care, he opened the door and peered in, to see no guards or gentleman-ushers there to receive visitors. But one carpet in the centre of the room had a large red bloodstain, smeared through its otherwise pale colours. 'Your Majesty!' Crumwell cried, his heart pumping in his throat.

King Henry appeared around the corner of one of his bookcases with an angry red brow. He looked from Crumwell to where he stood by the matted carpet. ''Tis wine, you fool!' Henry said and tossed a book on the large dining table in the middle of the room. He quickly rounded the wooden edge to Crumwell and smacked his chief minister across the face. Crumwell fell to the ground in shock at the outburst.

'Forgive me, Your Majesty.' Crumwell muttered, one hand against his smacked cheek.

'How dare you come into my rooms without permission? You are nothing but a knave!'

'I worried for your safety, Your Majesty,' Crumwell cautioned, and pondered; was it safe to stand?

'I can care for myself!' Henry burst towards him and hit him. Crumwell stayed on his knees to quell the King. Henry paced back and forth before Crumwell, rubbing his hand across his top lip, messing his short orange beard. Sweat came from his balding head and ran beside his ears to his ever-increasing neck, which pulsed with angry veins.

'Why is there never good news?' Henry asked and stopped right before Crumwell, his codpiece painfully close to Crumwell's sore face.

'There is much cheer at this time of year, Your Majesty. I shall quell Ireland. Elizabeth Barton and her confessors shall be attainted for high treason as soon as the House of Lords approves my new bill.'

'Still not good enough!'

'Bishop Fisher and Thomas More are both charged with misprision and shall have to answer for their crimes against your marriage.'

Henry seemed to relax a little. He raised his eyebrows as he thought. Finally, something which calmed the King. But only for a moment.

'I have had a disarming letter from the Emperor's ambassador.'

'Oh, Eustace Chapuys is the problem,' Crumwell sighed. 'That is most understandable, Your Majesty.'

'He has been writing to my former wife, and my daughter!' the King fumed.

'This is unacceptable.'

'Oh, get up off the floor, Thomas. If someone is to kneel before me, at least be it a woman!'

Crumwell stood up and smoothed his black doublet and hose. He dared not to suggest he find a mistress to entertain Henry; it would only fuel his rage again. 'Perchance I could talk to Chapuys on your behalf, Your Majesty. He and I have not spoken of late, however…'

'Where is the Waif, Thomas? I hear Chapuys likes to spend time with the Waif.'

'Frescobaldi is in the company of Her Majesty this evening.' Nicòla was probably in the Queen's apartments sipping wine and gathering gossip from Anne's ladies while Wyatt and Smeaton both adored the Queen for her entertainment. 'Chapuys likes to stir up trouble with Frescobaldi, Your Majesty. Chapuys questions Frescobaldi about the Duchess of Florence,' Crumwell sighed. 'He vexes me as he vexes you.'

'No one can question the Waif!' the King spat. 'If the world knew I let a woman dressed as a man to be an advisor to my chief minister, I would be mocked throughout my realm. Make sure your creature keeps her secrets hidden! Chapuys has written to me about Katherine. He discusses her placement at Buckden Palace. They say Katherine is most ill this winter and suffers a great deal.'

Crumwell held his tongue. If Katherine were to die, perchance it would not be so bad, for it would calm many people who still held disdain for Queen Anne.

'I did not leave Katherine to hear news about her. She is banished sixty miles north and yet if Anne knew I received news about Katherine…'

'We shall make sure Her Majesty hears nothing,' Crumwell tried to calm Henry again, lest be struck once more.

'My daughter, the Lady Mary. I want her household dissolved; all her servants are to be dismissed at once.'

'Even the Countess of Salisbury, Your Majesty? She has been at Lady Mary's side most of her life.'

'Margaret Pole would be wise to leave now while I give her the chance!' Henry fumed of his distant cousin. The Pole cousins were some of the last remaining people alive with Plantagenet blood in their veins, a last remaining threat to Henry's crown. 'Lady Mary is to be sent to Hatfield. She is to wait upon Princess Elizabeth.'

The former Princess Mary, daughter of the mighty Queen Katherine, was to be a servant to the infant Anne Boleyn bore the King? Surely even Henry would not do such a thing to Lady Mary. 'Your Majesty…'

'Enough! Anne wants Mary to be a servant to Princess Elizabeth at Hatfield and it shall be so!'

'We could send Lady Mary to live with her mother…'

'Her mother?' Henry shrieked, and hit Crumwell across the face again, throwing him to the ground. 'With Katherine and Mary together, they would raise an army and take my throne!'

This time, Crumwell stood again and did not look the King in the eye. 'I shall make sure Lady Mary's household is dissolved before Christmas, and she is to reside at Hatfield in the service of Princess Elizabeth.' Crumwell bowed low to the King and turned to his private hallway.

Damn the King's temper; Crumwell had no desire to quell it tonight. Along the private hallway were the bedrooms set aside for those privileged enough to tarry in Crumwell Chambers. As Crumwell flew past his own door, he heard a noise. On inspection, he found Nicòla there, sitting on the bed with a tired expression.

'I have never been happier to find you,' he muttered as he closed the door and leaned upon it with a sigh of relief.

'I found you not in your office,' Nicòla replied. 'I could take no more of the Queen's ladies tonight. Why is your face so red? Is it the wine?'

Crumwell knelt before Nicòla and rested his head on her warm lap. She stroked his hair and sore cheek. 'The King struck me a few times.'

'What?' Nicòla cried and cradled Crumwell's face in her small hands. 'Why would a king seek to harm his most loyal subject?'

'He is angered by a letter from Ambassador Chapuys and I got too close.'

'I care not for what is to blame, only that you are safe.'

'It is no more than I dispense to others. Perchance it is God, seeking to punish me.'

'I know something that can bring you much cheer, Tomassito. Come with me.'

The room being used was near to Crumwell Chambers, tucked away in a nearby building inside the palace walls. Nicòla subdued the heavy lock to the printing room and held the torch so Crumwell could see his latest creation. Inside the darkened room, all the servants gone for the night, sat his new German printing press. At seven feet long and three feet wide, its tall body sat in silence, paper still upon its bed, ready to be stamped with ink.

Crumwell took the first pamphlet from a stack in the far corner, holding it to Nicòla's torch. *The Denunciation of Pope Clement VII*

'All is finished, and the pamphlets are ready to be sent across the country,' Nicòla said with delight. 'Just as you ordered; these booklets against the Pope and the Catholic faith will go out to all, so they can be educated in their churches, told how Protestant reform and the Act of Supremacy is the best choice for them. We will have them swearing oaths to the King in no time. They will forget Elizabeth Barton and her revelations, and the King will control his people and their religion, as sworn by the people themselves.'

'And if people do not agree with our pamphlet, denouncing the Pope and the Church?'

'We can imprison them.'

'Or take their heads,' Crumwell muttered.

'I thought you did not want to mark your reformation with blood.'

'If we take Elizabeth Barton's head for high treason, then it shall be too late for that worry. Blood will flow like a river.'

''Tis your choice, Tomassito,' Nicòla said and placed the pamphlet back on the pile of printed parchments.

Crumwell put his arms around her and kissed her forehead, keen for a moment's peace. 'You will soon have Ireland under your control and England must follow. Let us retire to Austin Friars tomorrow, to see Jane and Gregory. Let us celebrate the epiphany and then let us take heads.'

'Do you ever feel as if creating a queen was the wrong decision?'

'It was our only choice, as it was the King's command,' Crumwell shrugged.

'Then why is the world darkening?'

'Only God can say.'

Chapter 5 – December 1533
Greenwich Palace, downstream London

Everything they sayd is taynted, every day was a lye

Nicòla tore through the hallways of the palace. People stared as she ran past them, wondering of the panic, but she cared not. News of Crumwell's master secretary running through the palace would soon spread, more since Frescobaldi had been spending time with the Queen. The two guards posted outside the entrance to the Crumwell Chambers saw Nicòla coming, and opened the doors, forcing several petitioners to get pushed aside. Nicòla stopped for no one; she ran through the antechamber filled with clerks putting their careful handwriting to paper and came to a sudden halt in the double doorway of Crumwell's private office. He sat in his throne of a seat, surrounded by six of his attendants, all listening to their master.

'Leave!' Nicòla demanded.

Crumwell looked up in fright, his golden gaze looking her up and down. 'I am arranging papers for the House of Lords,' he argued in a slow tone, half his mind worried for her, the other still deep in legislation.

'La regina è incinta!' Nicòla cried, waving her petite hands in the air. She knocked off her black cap with the motion, rose-gold hair sticking out at strange angles in the fuss.

'No!' Crumwell gasped and stood up in such a manner he knocked back several men standing about him. 'Get out, all of you!'

The second Nicòla closed the doors and locked them, Crumwell was before her, his eyes wide in panic. 'The Queen is with child?'

'I have come directly from her rooms. I know not if the King even knows,' Nicòla said, her smile so wide it hurt her cheeks.

Crumwell cried out with joy and picked Nicòla up at the waist and spun her around, the pair of them laughing with excitement. Queen Anne may have failed with Princess Elizabeth, but the chance had come again so soon.

'The King must have climbed into her bed the moment she was out of confinement,' Nicòla continued as Crumwell set her upon her feet. 'Anne has only just missed her course; I heard talk among the ladies. Lady Wingfield and Lady Shelton gossiped that the Queen had the King into her bed nightly through November in desperation. Lady Stanhope called it unseemly to do such, with a baby fresh from the womb. Lady Seymour looked unhappy.'

'Lady Seymour? Jane or Elizabeth?'

'Jane Seymour. She so loved her last mistress, Queen Katherine, and she wishes dearly for the former Princess Mary to be restored to favour.'

'Another Boleyn baby is just what we need,' Crumwell said and rubbed his hands together with joy. 'We must inform the King.'

'I suspect Anne wishes to wait until she is sure.'

'If the ladies are whispering, soon the news shall spread. I shall order more wine for the Christmas feast tomorrow. Once Henry hears of a son on the way, he shall be toasting everyone in London!'

'Perchance all the worry over the birth of a girl can be put behind us.' Nicòla watched the glowing smile on Crumwell's face. Indeed, not many smiles graced his cheeks since the birth of Princess Elizabeth. Henry had become irate since the birth of his daughter, despite his love for the baby. The world seemed to lean towards angst, darkness and bad humours. Eight months from now the world could either rejoice at a new heir to the throne or be set on fire in horror with another princess in the cradle.

'We shall celebrate,' Crumwell said as he banged his fist against his desk with joy. 'As soon as I have the papers for the House of Lords organised, we shall leave for Austin Friars.'

Nicòla picked up her hat and smoothed her curls. 'Never have I been more grateful to appear as a man,' she sighed. 'For to be surrounded by ladies-in-waiting would be a torment I could not bear.'

'There are other men in the Queen's chambers, surely. For she has 250 servants in her accounts.'

'Yes, Henry Norris visits often, and Wyatt and Smeaton are in constant attention. There is a young man, Thomas Tallis, who is a composer, new to London. He is friends with Wyatt and the Queen has enjoyed his musical knowledge. But the ladies…. Tomassito…'

'Should I be worried?' Crumwell folded his arms.

'I know the ladies are there to wait on Anne, but sometimes I fear they wait for her to fall from grace,' Nicòla sighed again. 'Bess Holland is there as a spy for Anne's uncle, Norfolk. The Seymour girls support Queen Katherine, as does Margery Horsman. The Countess of Worcester is a difficult woman, that Elizabeth Somerset. I know not where her loyalties lie. Margaret Shelton is so dim, Bridget Wingfield is haughty, Jane Boleyn is a bore. Only Nan Bray, Lady Cobham, seems to care for the Queen, and that is only the ladies in attendance today. Tomassito, I cannot bear to spend time in the Queen's chambers.'

'Henry wants Anne entertained by the Italian Waif,' Crumwell shrugged.

'Henry wishes me to spy on the Queen and report to you,' Nicòla spat back and dropped herself in the chair at her desk in the far corner. 'You also use me as a spy, since you cannot stand spending time with your own queen.'

'Let us not lose our joy over the greatest prize of them all – a boy in the cradle,' Crumwell said and Nicòla smiled in return. 'We can still create an England where it is safe for our children to flourish.'

A swift knock echoed on the doors and Crumwell spun around on his heel. 'No!' he yelled, but the knocking persisted. 'I said no!' he yelled.

'King's orders!' echoed back.

Crumwell opened the door and there stood Edward Seymour, elder brother to the Seymour ladies in Anne's rooms. Nothing like his sisters, Edward was a quiet gentleman, who served Henry in his private chamber on occasion. He must have been at court to fetch his sisters' home to Wulf Hall for Christmas. Edward had two young sons, but his wife now lived in a convent; she had embarked on an affair with Sir John Seymour, her father-in-law. Everyone laughed openly behind poor Edward's back. His sons may be his half-brothers. Finding a new wife had not come easily for Seymour.

'Mr. Crumwell,' Seymour said, his voice now lowered and respectful. He stood tall in Tudor green doublet and hose, his large hands clasped before him.

'Edward Seymour, we have not seen you at the court of late.'

'My father has been serving the King in the bedchamber, as I am sure you are aware. My father and I do not serve the King at the same time.'

Nicòla smiled a little, despite her desire not to; Seymour wanted to stay away from his father.

'King Henry requests you in his presence chamber at once,' Seymour continued. 'I am sorry to disturb.'

'Am I to play nursemaid to an angry king once more?' Crumwell's lip had only just healed since Henry's last angry outburst.

'His Majesty is in a fine mood, perchance eager to get all matters completed before we retire to enjoy the epiphany. Henry requested your presence, along with that of "The Waif" at once.'

Nicòla stood up from her chair and smoothed her doublet. As it was, Crumwell had allowed her to wear clothing other than black, wearing a deep red with golden embellishments, which set off the rose colour in her hair, again neatly tied back. She crossed the room and nodded once to Seymour, already feeling the chill of being away from the nearby fire of Crumwell's office.

'Edward Seymour,' Nicòla said, her accent rolling the final letter of his name. 'I believe there are not many at court who have failed to make my acquaintance.'

'It is said you often move at night, Mr. Frescobaldi, and often through private hallways only used by few.'

'There are many rumours made of me. Who knows what they shall say next about the King's favourite creature.'

Seymour smiled, a tiny laugh passing his lips. After a scandal such as his at Wulf Hall, it came as no surprise he too wished to tarry in the shadows.

The King wandered around his presence chamber, hands perched on his hips, his eyes gazing out the window. Nicòla stood one step back from Crumwell as they bowed upon being announced into his presence. 'My daughter is to join me later,' Henry said as he wandered towards Crumwell and Nicòla, not troubled with any greeting. 'Elizabeth is a good child.'

'A fair royal princess,' Crumwell replied.

Henry eyed a few of his attendants in the corner, and waved them out, the guards following them also, and the doors closed in the far corner of the room. No one lurked now, the door through the privy chamber also closed tight. A rare occasion. 'My Anne,' Henry whispered, and scratched his orange beard, as he did when nervous, 'she likes it not when I speak of certain things, certain people.'

'Your Majesty,' Crumwell said with sympathy, 'allow me to take care of any worries and the Queen shall hear no names which trouble her.'

Henry smiled, but he looked worn. Dressed informally, but with a large fur over his shoulders, he seemed a man older than his one and forty years. 'Do you presuppose that God is angry with me, Thomas?'

'No, Your Majesty. I have great reason to believe God is indeed shining His light upon you.'

'Why?' Henry paused and glanced around Crumwell to Nicòla. 'Have you been in the Queen's apartments, as I asked?'

'Yes, Your Majesty. I have been there many days this week.'

'And?'

'And your queen is in fine spirits, in fine health and proud to be with you through this most holy of celebrations, with your daughter at your side.' Nicòla said nothing of the pregnancy looming; for it was not her place to say of the idle rumours of women.

'But Mary is my daughter also.'

'We have moved the Lady Mary to Hatfield, as requested, Your Majesty,' Crumwell explained. 'Lady Mary is set up in a room best suited to attendants of Princess Elizabeth and shall begin her time in the child's presence after the epiphany.'

'The Welsh, they love Katherine, they love Mary,' Henry sighed. 'They support them, and their Catholic cause more than they support me, their king!'

'We are quelling the anger in Ireland and we shall endeavour the same in Wales, Your Majesty.'

Henry appeared worried; not angry, not busy, instead distracted and lonely. 'And what of Sir Thomas More? Anne says I am not to mention his name either.'

'Sir Thomas has begun a steady recovery of his recent illness. He is officially attainted with the charge of misprision, of harbouring news and colluding with the criminal Elizabeth Barton.'

'What shall be the sentence?'

'A fine, Your Majesty, of £300. Bishop John Fisher has also been attainted and faces the same punishment.'

'Is it enough, though, for the people to stop thinking that Fisher and More are both wiser than their king?'

'Only a fool would dare to do such a thing,' Nicòla muttered, and Crumwell half turned to look to her behind him.

'By no manner, may it be lawful for the noblest King of England to divorce from the Queen's grace, his lawful and very wife,' Henry recited. 'That is what Thomas Abel, Katherine's priest, said in his book.'

'All copies of Abel's Invicta veritas have been found and burned, Your Majesty,' Crumwell replied. 'Abel too is attainted for misprision, along with four other inciters of Barton's lies. They are all imprisoned in the Tower and shall not get released. The bill I will force through the House of Lords in February shall see them all executed. Only Fisher and More have the choice to beg for your pardon, Your Majesty.'

'It has been over a year since Anne and I married in Calais, Thomas. As you would know. Yet all this trouble has not ended.'

'All in due time, Your Majesty. Soon all shall swear you are the Supreme Head of the Church and that Princess Elizabeth is the rightful heir to the throne.'

'I do this because Anne does not want Mary to inherit,' Henry admitted.

'Queen Anne shall one day breathe easily around the Lady Mary,' Nicòla said quietly. Once there was a son in the cradle, Anne would reign over all. 'One day, your son shall be born, and the sun shall never set over England.'

'I hope you speak rightly, and not only because you wish to soothe me, Waif. I hear your father-in-law, the Pope, is still much ill in Rome.'

'I suspect so, Your Majesty, but I hear nothing from Rome or Florence.'

'Good.' Henry looked Nicòla up and down, and it made her shiver. 'Thomas, would there be a way of setting Anne aside but not have to go back to Katherine?'

Crumwell doubled over in a coughing fit and Nicòla reached over to help him. Henry already wanted to dethrone Anne? Crumwell's queen?

'Do excuse Master Crumwella, Your Majesty,' Nicòla said as Crumwell got himself together.

'Your Majesty,' Crumwell croaked, 'you could easily set aside Anne and embrace the Catholic faith again, citing the Pope's ruling that Katherine is still your wife. There would be no way to supplant Anne with another. It is Katherine and the Catholics or Anne and the Reformation.'

Crumwell paused and looked at Nicòla. He had to tell Henry the news. Nicòla nodded once in agreement.

'Your Majesty,' Nicòla said loudly, 'I heard talk in the Queen's rooms.'

'What is this to me?'

'Talk that the Queen was due for her courses to begin last week, yet they have not done so. Queen Anne suspects she is with child but is not yet certain.'

Suddenly Henry's face lit up like a bonfire of delight. He threw off his heavy fur coat and embraced Crumwell tightly. 'Could it be true?' Henry asked, breathless with excitement.

'There is every chance Queen Anne is right. But I am sure only she can give you the fine news at the ready moment.'

'I must go to the Queen,' Henry said as he gave Crumwell a hefty slap on the back, enough to make him lose his footing. 'I had almost forgotten why I called you hither on this miserable afternoon.'

'It matters not, I fear,' Crumwell replied.

'Oh, indeed, but it does. I need a new Recorder of Bristol. It comes with great London chambers that I believe you can use for your work.'

'Me, Your Majesty? The Recorder of Bristol?'

'Why not? You seem to cope with so many of the offices I command you to lead. Bristol needs a new judge.'

Henry dashed from the brightly decorated chamber toward his privy chamber, and Nicòla heard his deep voice calling to his attendants to fetch the Queen at once. 'Do you suppose Henry will tell Anne that I shared her secret?' Nicòla asked.

'No, he will make it sound as if the whole conversation is his own idea,' Crumwell replied. 'You know he must appear as the wisest man in England.'

'The Recorder of Bristol?'

'A solicitor who works as a judge in Bristol, or least makes decisions from chambers in London, for cases being heard in Bristol. They shall pay a goodly fee to us.'

'That sounds busy.'

'We have many lawyers to act for us. We can use many of our staff from Austin Friars' offices to oversee Recorder cases. We shall rule this country before you know it.'

Chapter 6 – February 1534
Whitehall Palace, London

Within every lye, a cruymb of trouth

The House of Lords caved to Crumwell's demands. They always did. Who could refuse the King's Chief Minister? It gave stuttering Norfolk something to do, while Suffolk was away at Westhorpe Hall; his son and heir was dying. Thomas Boleyn was wandering around with a grin like the devil, and the King swaggered with pride; Anne was indeed pregnant and had just missed her third monthly course. Not that Crumwell cared about what any person did with their time. He had to create new high treason laws, so they could hang Elizabeth Barton for speaking ill of the King. The House of Lords did not dare complain. The world needed to give Henry what he wanted; everyone had already suffered enough from the King's whims over the last few years.

'It is the end of February; and had I been home in Florence, we would soon look for the ever-lightening sun,' Nicòla mumbled from her desk.

Crumwell glanced at his secretary, but she did not turn to face him. 'Poor Secretary Frescobaldi, doomed to live in England with its long dark winters,' he teased.

Now Nicòla turned in her seat and showed him a sly smile. 'I would not leave this palace for all the world. But this…' she gestured to the chest of mail at her feet, which she sorted… 'brings us nothing but bad tidings.'

At once Crumwell's mind shot to Alessandro de'Medici in Florence. For months he had written to Nicòla, begging his wife to return to Rome, as the Pope was ill and desperate to see his favourite in case he died. Crumwell could not dare tell Nicòla of the letters and let her go home, lest they trapped her there, unable to return. Pope Clement himself had not once written, a worrisome sign; for if His Holiness died and Nicòla discovered she could have gone to him before his death, she would be livid at Crumwell's lies.

'You seem so troubled,' Nicòla frowned and caught Crumwell's golden gaze. 'I shall deal with the correspondence. We have many hundreds of men at your will. Fear not, Tomassito.'

'What do you read?'

'A letter from one of our creatures in Warwickshire. A priest, Ralph Wendon, is predicting that they shall burn a queen at Smithfield. Wendon hopes that queen will be the whore and harlot Anne.'

Crumwell covered his eyes with a weary hand. Life held enough curses without the creation of prophecies as well. 'I shall have him arrested.'

'Another letter speaks of a woman hither in London, one Elizabeth Amadas, who says that King Henry tried to take her as his mistress and she escaped him. Amadas believes that Henry is cursed by God's own mouth and will be banished from England by a Scots army before midsummer this year. Mysterious monks living on an island will come to England and summon the Commons and the Lords to create a Parliament of Peace.'

'Elizabeth Amadas?' Crumwell spat and stood up from his desk. 'She married Robert, the goldsmith who ran the Jewel-House until I took over! She remarried, to Thomas Neville, Speaker of the House of Commons. I spoke to him yesterday!'

'No,' Nicòla said as she watched Crumwell pace around his desk, his dark overgown swishing with the speed of his tight steps, 'the letter alludes to her husband being a sergeant-at-arms.'

'We must find which Elizabeth Amadas the letter speaks of and have her locked up at once!'

'There is plenty more,' Nicòla sighed and picked up a pile of letters. 'James Harrison, parson of Leigh, is calling Anne a whore in church. A Welsh priest, William ap Lli says he wishes to bash the King's head soft. Dan John Frances, a Colchester monk is calling the King and his councillors heretics. He stated that when Henry went to meet King Francis at Boulogne, the Queen's grace followed his arse as the dog follows his master's arse.'

'Enough!' Crumwell cried, which brought a halt to the clerks working in the next room. He clicked his fingers twice, and they all returned to their work. 'Round up every letter, send them to Richard Rich and instruct him that all must be arrested. Letters from our creatures are evidence of crimes.'

'At once.'

Crumwell watched Nicòla set aside what appeared to be over 100 letters. 'Be there any good news among the correspondence?' he asked and finally stopped his pacing.

'There is a letter from the Lady Mary from her new lodgings at Hatfield,' Nicòla held up. 'Perchance you should read this personally. Lady Mary is of too greater importance to have her letters read by me, and are private.'

'Master Crumwell?'

Crumwell turned to the sound of one of the gentlemen-ushers in the doorway. 'A messenger from the Tower for you.'

Crumwell clicked his fingers twice and Nicòla left the room to deal with the issue. Crumwell opened Lady Mary's letter and frowned. Her usually beautiful handwriting seemed laboured, messy, as if she had tried to write against a soft surface. Perchance she needed better rooms at Hatfield. Young Mary spoke of the humiliation of having to serve infant Princess Elizabeth, and that her champion, Ambassador Chapuys could never get time to speak to Crumwell on her behalf. Lady Mary was regularly ill and was banned from seeing her mother. She felt shame for being named a bastard in Crumwell's Act of Succession legislation, which was now but weeks away from becoming law.

'Tomassito?' Nicòla spoke quietly as she came back into the office. 'Be you well?'

'I must write to the Lady Mary. No matter what happens, Henry loves his first daughter over the new Princess Elizabeth. They must see us as kind to her while not disobeying Henry's demands to silence her.'

'I have a more pressing charge,' Nicòla replied and glanced over her shoulder; no one was near. 'Bishop Fisher, from his cell in the Tower, is speaking heavy words and terrible threats against you.'

'Mayhap I shall visit him in the Tower, get him moved to far worse conditions than he now enjoys.'

'Fisher wants a confrontation.'

'Then let us give him one.'

The gentleman-usher returned, this time with a young messenger dressed in black. 'Master Crumwell, the King awaits your presence in his privy chamber.'

'For what?' Crumwell said over his shoulder, irritated by the constant insistence on his time. 'I have a country to run from this room.'

The young messenger appeared confused at the words from the King's Chief Minister. Nicòla rounded Crumwell's desk and tossed the boy a coin and dismissed him.

Crumwell stood with his eyes closed, Lady Mary's letter still in his hands. 'Prepare a barge to the Tower, we leave with great haste. Give me but five minutes with Henry,' he instructed Nicòla as she took Lady Mary's letter from his hands.

A run along the private hallway to Henry's privy chamber left Crumwell feeling breathless. The past years had seen him living in much luxury and his waistline matched the indulgence. To add to his ageing and gaining of weight, if his marriage to Nicòla was not legal, he would constantly fear another man might steal Nicòla away.

Henry sat in a chair by the fireplace, a fur over his shoulders as he read. He closed the book but did not look up as Crumwell came in and bowed low. 'Thomas, I had a thought.'

Oh splendid, interrupted for a thought, Crumwell imagined saying.

'I thought to make Richard Page my official Keeper of the Privy Purse. That way, as Page works hither in the privy chamber, he can oversee all my accounts. You, of course, shall see all paperwork and accounts to make sure all is well.'

'Sir Richard is Recorder of York, and Vice-Chamberlain to Fitzroy.'

'Page is to vacate York.'

'Page was a fine man in Wolsey's household. He would do the job admirably, but, he is not always present at the palace. Could he share the role with Henry Norris?'

'That is why I ask your opinion, Thomas.' Henry reopened his book. 'I have a pressing issue you must remedy at once.'

'Your Majesty?'

'It is Katherine. I want her moved from Buckden Palace, six miles west to Kimbolton Castle. It is well-fortified, a decent moat and gardens. There I can hear nothing from her, no one can visit her, and the damp climate can keep her silent. Suffolk shall visit Katherine, oversee the tally of her household, which we shall reduce, along with her staff. Any jewels from the royal collection shall be taken from her and given to Anne. This includes her personal jewels and plate she brought from Spain when she married my brother.'

To take her belongings, given to her by her parents 35 years past seemed unduly harsh. 'Your Majesty…'

'Anne is my wife and shall wear all the royal jewels. Katherine is to have nothing. I shall not be swayed. Suffolk shall leave within the week.' Henry re-opened his book.

'Well indeed, Your Majesty. I am to the Tower to interrogate Bishop Fisher.'

'Fisher can have a pardon if he begs my forgiveness. He must pay the misprision fine, but he must beg for a pardon from me.'

'We could leave him in the Tower until he dies,' Crumwell scoffed.

'The Pope would fume endlessly.'

'From next month it shall be illegal to call him the Pope. Clement shall be the Bishop of Rome and no more.'

'Everyone shall be for me or be dead,' Henry replied, still reading his book.

Crumwell had executed forty people in the last year for heresy, down from around one hundred a year under Thomas More's watch. He had no desire to increase numbers.

'You may go,' Henry said, and finally looked up to Crumwell, deep purple lines under his blue eyes. Sleep again eluded the King. Crumwell bowed politely but as he turned the King gestured to him. 'One more issue,' Henry said and closed the book. 'Suffolk shall travel from his home at Westhorpe Hall, and I need someone to travel from London to witness Katherine's move.'

'I confess I cannot, Your Majesty, for the work to get the Act of Supremacy, the Act of Succession and the Second Annates bills through Parliament…'

'No, they are the greatest laws passed in England, second to you creating the Church of England. No, I wish to send the Waif.'

'My secretary, Your Majesty? Frescobaldi is much needed for the Parliament reforms.'

'I can trust no other. For the Waif would never do anything which could harm you or herself.'

Another test. Every so often, Henry would devise tests for Crumwell, despite his constant fealty. A gentle threat to Nicòla would make sure Crumwell would heed to Henry's every whim. Katherine would never submit to Henry, she would always be a Catholic. While Crumwell trusted Nicòla completely, he wanted none of the Catholic reminders of her life in Rome with the Pope. That man wanted Nicòla at his side again.

'I can trust the Waif, can I not?' Henry asked. 'Your little creature has not turned back to the faith of her father-in-law and his house of corruption?'

'Frescobaldi receives no correspondence from either Rome or Florence. The Pope is in ill health and has not written.'

'The Pope's bastard? Does he write to his wife?'

Crumwell looked to his flat shoes on the new carpets beneath him. He burned every letter Alessandro de'Medici sent. Henry let out a wicked laugh. 'Jealousy is a sin, Thomas.'

'My priority is this realm. What the Pope and his family want is to rule us. They have the Roman Emperor's power behind them and threaten war. Their words have no place in this country.'

'Do you still trust your Waif? You married her in God's eyes, even though she is married still by the Pope's laws.'

The King was still married to Katherine by the Pope's laws, yet he seemed to care little. 'I trust Frescobaldi with my life, Your Majesty.'

'Good, because I do not want to see you lose your head, or the Waif lose hers.'

Chapter 7 – February 1534
Buckden Palace, Cambridgeshire

The moor you defend a lye, the angryer you are

Nicòla stood in the courtyard of Buckden Palace, having just crossed the bridge and entered the grounds. In the centre stood a new tower, surrounded by an older wall made of solid brown brick. Her riding boots sank in the mud, so Nicòla continued to pace to stay above the sticky mess. Charles Brandon, the pompous Duke of Suffolk, came towards her from the doorway of the main tower. He looked different – thinner, his beard greyer than ever. He had been housed at Westhorpe Hall in Suffolk more often these days, for his son by his late wife Queen Mary, was once again sick. It would not be the first son and heir Suffolk would lose to illness if young Henry did not survive the winter.

Nicòla adjusted the black fur over her shoulders as Suffolk stood before her, the drizzle overhead leaving little beads of water on his dark blue cap.

'The King's henchman sends his creature to watch me?'

Nicòla bowed, regarding Suffolk, but could not be calm in her words. 'I come at His Majesty's request to help Katherine, Dowager Princess of Wales.'

'At Buckden, Katherine is referred to as a queen.'

'Once Master Crumwella's new laws pass, that shall be treason.'

'And you think that is just? That a commoner can change laws to remove Queen Katherine's title? I fail to understand how rules can be changed by men not worthy enough to stand in Queen Katherine's presence.'

'You ask why I was sent? Because the King cannot trust Your Grace. We have a new queen now. You claim to be noble, you claim to be the King's greatest friend. Do you even believe in the King's new religious changes to this realm?'

'I believe in making changes to unseat the Catholic corruption in England.'

'You are the son of a standard-bearer, are you not, Your Grace? The son of a man killed in battle by King Richard while defending a flag?'

'I am a military commander and my father died with great honour. I was raised alongside the King. I married the Dowager Queen of France, King Henry's own favourite sister, and have been the most favoured at court for as long as you have been alive,' Suffolk seethed and clenched his fists. 'What are you? Some effeminate creature, stalking Crumwell's halls like a spider wearing black furs too valuable to cloak your disfigured little body. You climbed out of the Pope's bedchamber and into Crumwell's.'

It was not even a lie, but Suffolk still believed Nicòla a man and accused all those in her life to be evil by her association. 'I am the sole heir to a wealthy house, known for centuries to be trustworthy, intelligent, pious and beloved. I came hither to Buckden Palace to pay a former queen the courtesy such a woman deserves, and to keep my eye on a courtier whom the King no longer values as much as he once did. Remember the words of Machiavelli, my Lord; la disciplina in guerra conta più della furia. Discipline in war counts more than fury.' Nicòla swept around Suffolk and did not dare look back. It might have been five years since Suffolk beat and arrested her in Blackfriars monastery, but she would never stop feeling scared of him. Crumwell had the King's total safety, but Nicòla would never have the same confidence.

The palace was in disarray as Suffolk's men pulled apart the apartments when Nicòla wandered through, unasked about her presence. The men were itemising things as they boxed them, and servants mixed between them, several ladies-in-waiting watching helplessly as the already small household was carved up once more. The walls were bare, as were the floors. The main dining hall had a small table only fit for around twenty people. All the fireplaces were cold, many windows without curtains to shield out the winter. It almost felt colder indoors than out.

Along one cold hallway came a lady-in-waiting, a short blonde woman, her pale golden gown dirty around its hem. Nicòla paused and bowed, to see the woman smile just a little. 'I know you,' she said. 'You visited Her Majesty at Windsor several years ago.'

'Nicòla Frescobaldi, secretary to Thomas Crumwella,' Nicòla obliged.

'I am Lady Elizabeth Darrell. I heard the King was sending someone from London to watch over the Duke of Suffolk and his men. Fear not, Mr. Frescobaldi, for we can trust the Duke completely.'

'Is this so?' Nicòla asked as they walked in time along the hallway, the windows illuminating the space. 'The King is worried over Suffolk's fealty.'

'His Grace married the King's sister. Queens Mary and Queen Katherine were friends for many years. Katherine was heartbroken at the loss of Mary last year and could not even attend the funeral at Bury St. Edmunds Abbey. The Duke carries fealty to Katherine on behalf of his late wife. He even remarried the daughter of Katherine's greatest friend.'

'It worries King Henry that Suffolk cares too much for Queen Katherine and hates Queen Anne.'

'I think Suffolk hates Anne as much as he loves Katherine. Queen Katherine and Suffolk have never been close, for Suffolk often helped Henry gain time with his mistresses, and many other shameful endeavours over the years, but Suffolk respects Katherine. He respected her place in the nobility, her place set above all others.'

'The daughter of two sovereigns anointed by God,' Nicòla replied. 'A crowned queen in this realm, ruling for over twenty years.'

'You sound most sympathetic to our cause, Mr. Frescobaldi. But I thought you worked for Mr. Crumwell; you seek to destroy our queen.'

'Master Crumwella carries no disrespect or ill-will to Katherine. He seeks to promote Queen Anne as it is the King's orders and desires. What the King wants, the King shall have. We all serve someone. Might I be permitted to see Katherine?'

'She rests in her privy chamber at present. None of the Suffolk's men dare go in there to take Katherine's most private possessions.'

'I shall do no such thing.' Nicòla waited at a small door while Lady Elizabeth disappeared inside to attend to her queen. Buckden Palace was the opposite the lavish life of Whitehall Palace, with its happy king and a secret heir in Anne's belly. Warm, decorated, with the best of everything, Whitehall owned all the exquisite enjoyments of England to Anne while Katherine sat in cold poverty, but not as forgotten as Henry would like. Hither, a tiny base of support for the "true" queen reigned.

'You may enter,' Lady Elizabeth said as she peered around the door once more. 'Queen Katherine is much ill at present, so I ask you raise your gentle voice a little when you speak with her.'

Nicòla stepped inside and Lady Elizabeth excused herself. The small room had the only working fireplace Nicòla had eyed in the palace, God be praised. Warm curtains hung over the windows, pulled back to find the dull light of the wet day. A single carpet rested on the floor, beneath a chair where Katherine sat, beside the fireplace. Katherine, her greying hair pulled tightly under a gable hood, sat with a book in her hands, furs covering her thinning body. Her pale face looked over in surprise at Nicòla. To be in the presence of Katherine drew the air from Nicòla's lungs. She possessed a regal essence, a living being that held both noble and godly powers on Earth. Nicòla bowed low, relieved to be in the warmth and light of the former queen.

'Nicòla Frescobaldi,' Katherine said, her accent as strong as ever. 'You came alone all this way?'

'Yes, Your… Majesty.'

Katherine smiled, but a cough passed her lips, as if being happy caused illness itself. She beckoned Nicòla over, but Nicòla did not dare to sit in Katherine's presence. She stood with her hands, fresh out of her riding gloves, clasped before her as Katherine closed her prayer book.

'Mr. Crumwell sent you to come and take away the few things I have left?'

'Master Crumwella only serves at His Majesty's pleasure. He wishes no disrespect to you.'

'Crumwell keeps my daughter Mary from me. Crumwell refuses to meet with Chapuys to discuss my daughter. Crumwell stands at court and in parliament and tells everyone that the whore of Christendom is queen in my place! Crumwell changes laws to suggest that being a faithful Catholic is now heresy!'

Nicòla could expect nothing but distress and anger from the great Spanish queen. Nicòla said nothing, and her green gaze fell to her dirty riding boots on the carpet.

'You, you came to me, on behalf of the Pope himself. You came to me and said Rome was on my side, that I would be queen. Yet the Pope has done nothing, he had not ruled my marriage valid, he has not named me Queen of England still, five years after hearing my appeal.'

'Pope Clement is ill and I fear, not of sound mind.'

'My priest, Thomas Abel, has been removed from my household by Crumwell's orders.'

'Thomas Abel was the man who smuggled your illegal letters to Rome, Your Majesty. It is understandable that the King wanted him punished.'

'How long has Crumwell known Thomas Abel smuggles letters for me?'

'Years, Your Majesty.'

Katherine leaned back in her seat and watched the small fire for a moment. 'Do you swear I am still the Queen?'

'I swear to the allegiance of my masters, Your Majesty. I am a servant.'

'You swear to Anne Boleyn then, do you not? Pray for her in my place?'

'My personal thoughts are not welcomed or encouraged, Your Majesty.'

'Look at me.' Katherine paused as Nicòla rose her eyes from her feet. 'Why are you still hiding as a man? Was that not only for your mission to spy on Cardinal Campeggio? That was five years ago.'

'Pope Clement tolerates me living as a man, has done so for almost twenty years, Your Majesty.'

'Why?'

Looking upon Queen Katherine was like looking upon God. To lie seemed impossible; she appeared to be the ultimate ruler, yet without any malice or desire to control. Only a woman could be so. 'It is often said I am a man trapped in the body of a woman,' Nicòla explained.

'The same has been said of me. Yet I rode at the head of an army, belly full with a baby, to defeat the Scots and kill their king. Why must you hide under doublet and hose?'

'Because I am not a sovereign sent from God to light the Earth like you, Your Majesty. I am but a servant.'

Katherine smiled at the comment. 'I want you to sit.'

Nicòla let herself sit on the chair opposite Katherine, but sat on the very edge, ready to jump to attention in a moment. 'Why does the Pope like you so?'

'The Pope was not always God's chosen man. He used to be just a man. I used to be a young girl.'

Katherine turned her head away, her eyes closed at such a notion. She paused for a long moment before turning back again. 'As women, we must accept the frailties of men and their needs.'

'And I have done so. I hold nothing but peace in my heart for the Pope.'

'But you serve the man casting God from this realm?'

'I serve the man driving corruption and idolatry out of the Church, but God shall never be thrust from England.' Every word hurt Nicòla. When forced to explain her actions with Crumwell and the Protestant Reformation, she felt deep shame. To cast Catholicism from her heart gave her a shame she could not explain; and Crumwell would dare not hear a word.

'You are married, I fear. Your husband is the Duke of Florence.'

'The marriage stands firm. I have not pushed for an annulment.'

'What is the point of the Reformation? To destroy marriages ordained by God?'

'I wish not to be married to the bastard son of the Pope, Your Majesty. I desired none of this. My father desired this marriage.'

'My father desired my marriage to Arthur, Prince of Wales. I was set to sea at fifteen to marry a stranger who could speak not one of my languages. I lived in poverty after the death of the kind prince, the only person in England I trusted. For seven years I waited in hope while God cleared the way for me to take my throne in England. I have lived a long life, and now I am cast into the shadows, hidden away. Why should I, a princess by birth, a queen by marriage, a ruler by blood and by right, be forced to endure men's plans, and yet can defy God's orders? Why should you leave God, your Pope, and your own husband to help change the laws of the land to suit yourself? What then? Will you marry Crumwell? Is he your new master now? Running from one bed to another? You are not free, young Frescobaldi. As a woman, you shall never be free.'

Every tear which ran silently down Nicòla's face stung with the pain of truth, of sin. Queen Katherine was a woman set far above Nicòla, by God's choice, and yet she languished while Nicòla lived in relative freedom. The woman, whose very existence held the alliance between England and Spain together, gave legitimacy to the Tudor dynasty, helped recreate England after the War of the Roses, could not be free, so how could Nicòla be?

'Yet Crumwell sent you to watch over me?'

Nicòla wiped the end of her nose with her hand and took a deep breath. Her vision blended with tears as she looked to the Queen. 'Master Crumwella was under orders to send me hither. It is a test, set by King Henry, to ensure Crumwella's fealty.'

'You are Mr. Crumwell's most precious possession?'

'I am.'

'Why?'

'I am the mother of his only living daughter.'

Katherine crossed herself and pulled her rosary beads from the folds of her skirt. Nicòla ached; no one carried them now, and Crumwell banned them, a part of idolatry he did not wish to see. 'Would you not be safer in Florence, at your husband's side, doing your duty? You could live openly before God as a woman and as a wife. God has decided your fate.'

'Men decided my fate and used God as an excuse.'

'You do have some fight in you,' Katherine scoffed.

'I am a daughter of a merchant, a moneylender. I have travelled through Europe and studied law and finance with some of the greatest minds. God gave me a fine mind, but I alone nurtured and educated that mind. My honour was taken by a man who should not have done so, and I became the creature I am now, the beast you see before you. I did so to avoid the shame of having no virtue while the man who took my honour went on to take the highest role on Earth. I am who I need to be. I am married to the man my father chose, and he took the inheritance my father gave me. Master Crumwella simply lets me be who I am in my disguises. Crumwella may be a man and he may be my master, but he has not forced me in any way. I can respect no other master but him.'

'I must confess I like your defiance, Frescobaldi.'

'The King, in his own wisdom, knows of my truths. King Henry allows me in his court in my guise as a hidden creature. He tolerates my being, he indulges my needs and is entertained in return. He may see me as a conduit to the Pope, but I am as free as any woman can be, given the hand dealt to me by God.'

'And how is my husband? Is he well?'

'King Henry is well and healthy, Your Majesty. He had been much disappointed in the birth of his daughter, but he has other things to make him merry.'

'His false marriage to the whore?'

'The marriage is calm, Your Majesty.'

'Shall Henry ever turn back to the Catholic faith?'

'King Henry has turned his back on little of the Catholic faith, Your Majesty. While he has accepted the beliefs of Protestant marriage and its ability to end marriages, he continues his rituals and prayers in the Catholic faith.' And that was true; Crumwell was trying to banish idolatry and yet it appeared daily in churches where Henry worshipped. Archbishop Cranmer was displeasured over the whole situation as he tried to reform the people in his loyal congregation.

'And my daughter?'

'Princess Mary has been moved to Hatfield.'

'Do you think you could get Mr. Crumwell to petition Henry? So that Mary and I can write to one another?'

'I could but try, Your Majesty.'

'Is Mary well?'

'Princess Mary has been ill but Hatfield has physicians available and Henry has allowed Mary to see the physicians freely.'

'Does the bastard Elizabeth live at Hatfield?'

'Yes, Your Majesty. Princess Mary is with her sister.'

'Half-sister. Bastard sister,' Katherine spat and Nicòla nodded in agreement. 'Tell me, did the King send you to gain news from me?'

'I was sent, Your Majesty, to get the last of your jewels.'

'Never!'

'The royal jewels are possessions of the King.'

'You mean possessions of his false wife. My jewels shall not adorn Christendom's greatest whore!'

'Alas, Suffolk has been ordered by the King to take your jewels, including your Spanish jewels.'

'Those jewels were given to me by my mother, Spain's greatest queen and warrior! Never shall they be given to the whore. They belong to the Queen, and that is me. They will one day adorn my daughter.'

The strong knock at the door startled both Nicòla and Katherine. The Duke of Suffolk entered moment later, bowing low in respect as Nicòla stood. Suffolk looked to the Queen and took a long pause.

'You have come to pull my chamber apart, have you not?' Katherine asked.

'I am afraid that is the nature of it, Your Majesty. You are to move to Kimbolton today. It is but six miles. Any items you are free to keep shall be sent to you in coming days.'

'But I am ill,' Katherine said and grabbed Nicòla's hand. 'I cannot go today! Please, do not take the items that belonged to my dearly departed mother!'

'I am under orders to move you today, Your Majesty,' Suffolk sighed. 'I have orders to remove you by force.'

A group of ladies-in-waiting huddled in the doorway, ready to help their

Queen so no male hands dared touched her. Katherine stumbled to her feet and held Nicòla's hand to steady herself. 'Please, do not let my jewels adorn a whore,' Katherine cried, tears in her pale blue eyes. 'Not everything of the past must be crushed. A woman's life is hard enough!'

'Your Majesty, Kimbolton is made ready for you. It is a pleasant enough manor and you will be comfortable until your personal effects arrive.'

Nicòla stood helpless as men appeared in the room from a small side door, ready to pull the warm haven apart on Henry's orders.

'Please,' Katherine cried as her ladies rushed to her aid. 'For mutual love and respect of the Pope, please do not take my things from me, for they belong to my daughter.'

'I will help your daughter, I swear upon my life,' Nicòla said.

Queen Katherine fell into her ladies' arms as she was pulled from the room in tears. As she left the room, Nicòla glanced to Suffolk and held his brown stare. They both knew the injustice of Katherine's life and could do nothing to save her now. It was the life of a woman; for it could easily be Nicòla dragged away, banished from her own daughter one day, all on the whim of a man.

Chapter 8 – March 1534
Hampton Court Palace, London

Hystory is a set of lyes all agreed on

Music played during dinner, but Crumwell barely heard it. He could not be sure if it was the wine or the prosperity that made him drunk with happiness. He sat in Hampton Court's vast dining hall, golden tapestries lining the long room. Henry and Anne sat at the head table together while around one hundred invited courtiers sat down to the finest meals. They now forgot the Lord Chamberlain's seating arrangements several hours in, people mingling among the tables, allowing Nicòla to sit at Crumwell's side at their table of ten. Everyone could eat whatever they wanted, though Crumwell had the best of everything. A tray of oysters sat before Nicòla, though she did not eat. Neither the swan, nor the venison, nor the veal, nor the pheasant. She would smile at proper moments when others laughed in merriment, cheered at Crumwell's latest wins, but then her sullen face would return. Her petite fingers held her wine, but she seldom brought it to her lips.

Around the table sat Bishop Gardiner and his beaked nose, Sir Thomas More, freshly forgiven for his recent misprision charge, and stuttering Norfolk. Lord Chancellor Audley sat there too, his waistline expanding by the month, much like Crumwell's, the scourge of a good life. Missing was the pompous Duke of Suffolk, as his son Henry, of only ten years, had passed away. The boy was the King's nephew and the second time Suffolk had lost a son bearing the King's name. But that was all hidden away at Westhorpe Hall. It was forbidden to mention the death of the King's nephew, the son of Henry's late favourite sister.

The Act of Supremacy had passed in parliament, but it was Crumwell, not the King, who reigned supreme. The Act stated Henry and his heirs were to be the only Supreme Heads of the Church in England, under the title Ecclesia Anglicana and could enjoy all the honours and dignities, immunities, profits and commodities of said dignity. They could not call the Pope "the Pope," only the Bishop of Rome. Every prayer book in England needed to be altered. The Act of Succession stole freedoms even further. Now, every person over the age of fourteen years would swear an oath, swearing against an allegiance to the Pope, and instead to the King himself. They had to swear Henry and Anne's marriage was lawful, and only Princess Elizabeth and further siblings could be heirs to the throne. Any person who refused was now against the King, and that was treason, and Crumwell would make sure everyone who spoke against the King would be punished with all fierceness. Even to speak against the Oath was misprision, and now that could be punishable by death. Even to speak, wish or think of harming the royal family, its realm, its laws, its titles was high treason, and high treason carried a death sentence. They held every man and woman in England under pain of death against the laws Crumwell created for His Majesty.

Finally, the last part of the Annates law, started two years ago, meant they could send no money to Rome; profits from the Church stayed in England. Now that money went straight to the King's Exchequer, which Crumwell also ruled. The level of power in one man's hands had never been greater, and everyone knew it.

Lord Chancellor Thomas Audley raised his glass from across the table in Crumwell's direction, and Crumwell shifted his gaze away from Nicòla at his side. 'Thomas, I cannot believe all you have done for this most mighty of nations.'

Crumwell bowed his head in respect to Audley. 'You helped word this precise law, so I must not take all the credit. To you also, Norfolk.'

Norfolk acknowledged Crumwell as he stuffed his mouth with oysters.

'Do you feel much pride, Mr. Crumwell?' More asked, where he sat with chunks of pheasant before him, a knife stabbed into the flesh. 'In your heart, does it feel right to take away the power of the Catholic Church?'

'You are pardoned of misprision charges, Sir Thomas,' Crumwell replied. 'I think it prudent for you to quieten your temper and your Catholic sympathies. Misprision is a charge of high treason now.'

'You want my head on a spike, do you?' More challenged him.

'I seek only peace.' Crumwell threw More a smug grin.

'We shall have peace,' spoke the ever-tepid Archbishop Cranmer. He too raised his glass to Crumwell, and they smiled at one another. 'We shall have a safe and pious reformation in this country. I shall see to it personally that every church adopts the Protestant faith.'

'And Crumwell will see everyone opposed will be punished with much cruelty,' Gardiner sniffed. 'But at least you released old Bishop Fisher from the Tower at last.'

'Fisher begged for a pardon, like the King wanted,' Crumwell said and gulped the last of the wine. At once a servant stepped forward to refill the cup. He glanced down the table to see Ambassador Chapuys staring at Nicòla. They had not spoken since Chapuys' threat to expose Nicòla's identity six months ago. Chapuys had held his tongue all that time – he knew to expose the Pope's favourite courtier would cause much anger back in Rome. Crumwell could have Chapuys beheaded if he had to, and Chapuys knew it. Crumwell knew how untouchable he was and revelled in the power.

'So, what is next for the all-powerful Thomas Crumwell?' Gardiner asked across the table. 'For surely as the sun rises in the east, you have done all you can for the King.'

'I seek to do none but the King's will and pleasure. Should we all not do so?' Crumwell asked the table.

'Does your heart not hang heavy with the weight of pain you cause in this realm?' More asked, his beady eyes frowning from the other end of the long table.

'You hold your faith in high esteem, Sir Thomas. For my heart shall not be hurt as I ruin the laws set upon us by Rome. They shall not harm me as I hunt out corruption, abuse, bribery, adultery, idolatry, and superstition from the lives of every Englishman living.'

'And you should not hurt for that, Thomas,' Cranmer said. 'I rule the convocation and shall help the people of the realm with reformation, not harm them.'

'The only ones harmed shall be secret papists, who favour the Bishop of Rome over their own anointed sovereign,' Crumwell added.

More and Crumwell stared at one another and Crumwell knew the time had come. Sir Thomas More would never denounce the Pope in favour of the King, even with Henry being his closest friend for years. Chapuys was the ambassador the Holy Roman Emperor, excused from taking the Oath. But Norfolk was not, Gardiner was not, and as both deeply Catholic, Crumwell would love to see them wince in agony to submit to the Reformation. Nicòla would sign without pause; for she stood at Crumwell's side day by day, hour by hour, as he tore the Church apart. Her pope, a sick old man desperate for her companionship, would never see her again. Just the thought of crushing these men once placed so high above him made Crumwell laugh out loud, to the surprise of all at the table. He grabbed Nicòla's hand and held it, despite being in full view of the guests. She smiled and pulled her hand away, no doubt to bring Crumwell to his senses.

'Surely crafting the laws of the land at the pleasure of the King is dangerous, Thomas,' Gardiner said.

'I think the will and pleasure of the King should be law. That could be my next law.'

'So, you admit wanting to rule this country yourself,' Norfolk said. 'I am certain that is treason.'

'I want to serve my sovereign,' Crumwell laughed. 'For there is a woman at the King's side, Queen Anne, with the heir to the throne in her sweet belly at this moment. Yes, all the rumours are true, Queen Anne is halfway to creating a son.'

'You said that last year and we gained Elizabeth,' Gardiner snorted.

'You are either for these changes or you are against, Stephen,' Crumwell warned. 'No one is safe any longer. Your past allegiances, past positions or past deeds mean nothing in this new age.'

'Crumwell!' the King bellowed, and the dining hall fell into immediate silence. Crumwell stood and nodded, regarding his king. 'You seem entertained this evening.'

'I was just telling your guests I believe your will and pleasure should be law in this country.'

'That would make quite a country indeed,' Anne said and took Henry's hand.

'A strong law to serve your future son, Your Majesty,' Crumwell said, and he heard Gardiner scoff across the table.

'Do recite some of the Oath of Succession you wrote with Audley and Norfolk and our dear absent Suffolk. Your mind can surely remember every word, Crumwell,' the King continued.

'Whatever be your will, Your Majesty.' Crumwell looked out over the noble faces looking back at him. 'You shall swear to bear faith, truth, and obedience alone to the King's majesty and to his heirs of his body of his most dear and entirely beloved lawful wife Queen Anne, begotten and to be begotten.'

'So help you God, and all Saints, and the Holy Evangelists,' Cranmer called out.

The King applauded Crumwell and it forced everyone to abide and join. Henry gestured for Crumwell to sit and he slipped back into his seat, ignited by all the wine, cheer and confidence.

'We shall have no opposition, shall we, Crumwell,' Henry said, more to the party than to him.

'No, Your Majesty. Even from cowards such as Bishop Gardiner.'

Several gasps echoed around the hall as Gardiner stared back at his once friend, now an adversary. But Crumwell felt far from finished. 'Bishop Gardiner has done little, all but nothing, to aid the creation of the Succession, and does not like the strict wording of the Oath. Gardiner stomps around the court with his long nose and greedy eyes, ready to tear down any person who talks ill of his precious Bishop of Rome.'

People laughed quietly in their seats, partly due to the comments at Gardiner, possibly more due to Crumwell's audacity to speak such before the King. But Henry laughed too, and Gardiner rose from his seat, bowed to Henry and left, followed by one hundred pairs of eyes wide in wonder.

Crumwell felt Nicòla's foot move against his own under the table. He glanced at her and she looked right back at him, her green gaze surrounded by an angry brow. Crumwell had gone too far.

But Henry agreed not with Nicòla's worry. 'Gardiner will be most tempered in the morning,' the King laughed, and everyone joined. 'Fear not, Crumwell, for I shall make sure everyone at court swears to the Oath and their position.'

From the far corner of the dining hall, a messenger entered and went quickly to Ambassador Chapuys' side. Nicòla gasped beside Crumwell; the letter bore the official seal of the Pope himself. Just for Nicòla to think of the Pope made Crumwell's heart ache.

The King must have noticed the messenger also. 'Tell us, Ambassador, what is so urgent from Rome that you cannot wait.'

Chapuys raised his wide eyes from the parchment and moved his lips, with no sound forthcoming.

'Speak up!' the King commanded. Chapuys threw a look to Crumwell and at once Crumwell jumped from his seat and snatched the letter from him. The Pope's handwriting once more, not seen by Crumwell's eyes for quite some time. Clement's wide scrawling letters, attached to the large official red seal of this office.

Crumwell's silence affected the King at once. 'Crumwell, with me!' the King commanded, and he jumped from his seat, causing everyone to rise in a panic to pay respect. Crumwell flew past everyone, catching Nicòla's eyes for just a second before he left the hall into a private room.

Henry stood feet wide apart, hands on hips as if bracing for ruin. 'What be the news from Rome?' Henry begged, and wiped sweat from his top lip.

'Pope Clement the Seventh of Rome, after seven years of deliberations, has ruled in the matter of your marriage to Katherine of Aragon. The Pope has ruled the marriage entirely valid under God's law.'

'Under God's law?' the King screamed and shoved Crumwell hard in the chest. Crumwell tripped, landing hard on his back. 'God's law is my law!' Henry screamed, spittle flying onto Crumwell's clothes.

'Tis too late,' Crumwell implored the King. 'England has broken from Rome and the laws of this man no longer matter in the affairs of England or your marriage.'

'Get up.' Henry stepped back from Crumwell.

'Your Majesty,' Crumwell said as he struggled to his feet, his head spinning with wine and confusion. 'The Pope can rule in the judgement of Katherine if he so desires. But the law of England states he has no jurisdiction over affairs. The queen in England is Queen Anne, who is at dinner, right now, carrying your legitimate heir.'

'Oh, Katherine will adore this news. She shall receive the judgement at Kimbolton, and she shall hold the paper to her chest and thank God and the Pope for the ruling. All she wants is to be queen.'

Queen Katherine had done no wrong. Crumwell, even at the height of his prosperity, which came during Katherine's downfall, could not speak ill of her or her daughter, Lady Mary. Crumwell suspected Nicòla's constant unhappiness of late stemmed from meeting Katherine again. 'I shall continue to do my duty, Your Majesty,' Crumwell said, breathing heavily after the sudden fall. 'The Pope is now the Bishop of Rome. A bishop with no rights over your soul or your country. Any person speaking of this news, or even daring to call Clement "the Pope" may be arrested.'

'Even your Waif?'

'Even Frescobaldi must not utter the word "Pope" to any person.'

'Everyone must sign the Oath of Supremacy, and the Succession immediately.'

'Within weeks, Your Majesty, I swear before God. A God not corrupted by the Catholics any longer.'

Henry nodded and took a few deep breaths. 'We make changes, starting tomorrow, Crumwell. Be in my chamber right after Mass.'

Henry swept from the room as Crumwell bowed, and he folded the letter into his hand, the parchment tight. It was time to take down his many enemies.

Chapter 9 – April 1534
Whitehall Palace, London

Sumtymes you must lye to fynd the trouth

'Be it true?' Queen Anne stood at the window at the end of the long
room and placed one hand on her growing belly. Her lavish golden gown
gently floated over the baby inside her, her dry hands catching on the fabric
slightly as she rubbed her stomach.

'Is what true, Your Majesty?' Nicòla asked and clasped her own hands
together before her.

'Is it true that Mr. Cremwell feeds the poor from his kitchen at Austin
Friars every day? I heard he provides hot food and drinks to the poor of
London every morning.'

'I heard rather than lining up for food outside the friary on Broad Street,
the poor now line up at the back door of Mr. Crumwell's home,' Lady
Margaret Douglas said. She stood close to the Queen, her rich red hair
flowing freely about her slender shoulders.

'Austin Friars provides food for 200 people every morning and then
again in the evening,' Nicòla told the room. 'The same people can return
and new people are welcome. Master Crumwella tries to feed as many
children as he can with supplies in the house.'

'Quite the noble cause,' Lady Jane Boleyn said on the other side of the
room, where she sat with embroidery in her hands. 'With Mr. Crumwell
rising so high at court, I feel surprised he has not taken a wife.'

'It is not my place to question my master's private dealings,' Nicòla
replied and moved her feet a little wider apart. She was the only "man" in
the Queen's chambers today. Crumwell had sent her to pay favour to the
Queen, as the King liked spies watching his wife.

'Lady Margery,' Anne turned and looked for the maid she spoke of, who sat by Lady Jane. 'I quite believe you like Mr. Cremwell in a way which would be becoming. Or you, Lady Jane?'

Jane Seymour, who sat on cushions on the floor as she patted Anne's little dog, looked up in shock. 'I shall only marry as my father bids.'

Nicòla regarded the Queen's rooms as a nest of vipers. Each one of these women reported the idle talk of people at court; Anne was not safe, not treated with enough respect. No one trusted any other. As she gazed around, Nicòla noticed Margaret Shelton, Queen Anne's cousin, was missing from the ladies, though perchance it was not of worry, as ladies left the household constantly, always ready to be replaced by someone eager to be at court. However, Lady Margaret's absence was not new, though she was regularly wandering at court. Henry Norris seemed to speak with her at length, but the suggestions of a relationship between the pair seemed unlikely.

Across the long room of Queen Anne's private chamber, the chamberlain opened the door and revealed one of Crumwell's gentleman-ushers. He bowed low and scurried like a timid mouse in Nicòla's direction.

'Tell us not that work shall spirit you away from us,' Queen Anne called to Nicòla. 'We have barely even sported with you today.'

Nicòla smiled at Anne but already felt relief at the chance to leave the Queen's rooms. The young black-clad usher gave Nicòla a smile of familiarity and whispered in her ear. 'Master Crumwell urges you to come at once. A boat is made ready for you. You are to leave for Lambeth Palace with Master Crumwell at once to meet with Archbishop Cranmer.'

Nicòla frowned at the young boy. 'That is the whole message?'

'Yes, Master Frescobaldi. Master Crumwell said you are to bring nothing with you but your wits. I am to lead you to the boat and leave with haste, as we are against the tide.'

Crumwell hid nothing from Nicòla; if they were leaving now without warning, it surely was in aid of an enormous upheaval.

'Rush off to your Cremwell, Waif,' Anne said before Nicòla could excuse herself. 'For we know you are but Cremwell's shadow and he can barely act without your company.' The Queen smirked, the only woman in the room who knew of Nicòla's great secret.

The moment Nicòla stepped upon the boat, guards pushed them from the dock outside Whitehall and she sat beside Crumwell, pleased by the gentle warmth in the afternoon air. Crumwell sat with his hands balled up on his lap, his eyes firmly on his secretary.

'What is this?' Nicòla asked the moment she was seated comfortably in the centre of the boat. The boatmen had them at great speed in no time, a feat against the tide of the Thames. Indeed, Nicòla had never moved along the river at such speed. 'Is there something wrong with Cranmer?'

'No, all is well,' Crumwell replied and then leaned forward in his seat closer to Nicòla. 'I have a grand plan, but all must come together with such haste. Indeed, only today I came up with this plan, after speaking with His Majesty.'

'I do so love a plan. Shall this be entertaining?'

'I fear there shall be little enjoyment today,' Crumwell said, his face not moving from the stern brow he presented to Nicòla. 'We are to receive two guests, who shall arrive at the same time as us. We shall be presented to Archbishop Cranmer in his main hall. Sir Thomas More has been summoned from Chelsea and Bishop Fisher has also been summoned.'

'Will they swear the Oath today?' Nicòla whispered.

Crumwell nodded just once. Today, both More and Fisher would be faced with the Oath of Supremacy, and no doubt Crumwell already had plans in place if the two men would not sign. For weeks, people had been lining up, waiting to take their turn swearing the Oath. Both Crumwell and Nicòla had sworn it on the first day it was ready, sworn before both the King and Queen and Archbishop Cranmer. Everyone at Austin Friars had already done so. Crumwell's men across England were rounding up people, forcing them to swear. Today, Crumwell would catch two of his biggest adversaries.

~~~

Archbishop Cranmer stood with a slim face, his eyes dark in contrast to his vibrant purple robes. They stood in the lavish main hall of his palace, a long narrow table laid out in the centre, where light flooded from an immense stained-glass window high in the ceiling. Among the colours rested the Act of Supremacy and Act of Succession. There rested the words Crumwell crafted, the words every English person had to recite, swear their alliance to, sign their name to, all ready for the occasion. Crumwell stood with Cranmer, his own expression dark as his black coat, while Bishop Gardiner stood in white, on the opposite side of Cranmer, as if to keep his person as far from Crumwell as possible. Nicòla felt cold in the room, alone in the corner while the three powerful men awaited their company.

As the main doors opened on the opposite side of the hall, the doors echoed an eerie creak through the wide space. Only two people came forward, followed by four royal guards who blocked the doorway. Bishop Fisher ambled to meet the Archbishop and his attendants, his old feet carrying him with caution. He wore robes of white, a black cap perched on his bald head. After being arrested and fined for misprision, Fisher looked worn, gaunter than usual, a man of already four and sixty years. Alongside him walked Sir Thomas More, the burner of Protestants. The men had been pardoned for supporting Elizabeth Barton, but Crumwell would pardon neither today if they did not swear the Oath. More, like Crumwell, also wore black, though the mighty Collar of Esses, shining in its gold finery, now swayed over Crumwell's shoulders, instead of More's. Younger than Fisher by almost ten years, More walked with far more confidence, yet the result for each man today remained equally desperate.

Crumwell and Gardiner both stood with their hands clasped behind their backs, equal height, equal posture. They both moved their feet every so often to control their powerful stance. They probably never noticed they appeared so similar. Cranmer did all the talking; all the minor greetings and plain respects needed in the presence of the two men who were ready to take their lives into their hands.

'You know what is to be done,' Cranmer explained to the two men opposite him at the table. 'You are to take the Oath, and you need, by law, to sign the document which contains the preambles of the Acts of Supremacy and Succession. You both must swear that King Henry is the leader of the Church and that Queen Anne and her children are lawful and legitimate.'

'I will not swear anything to Crumwell's queen,' Fisher said and threw an evil look in Crumwell's direction, one angry enough to make Nicòla shiver in the corner.

'I shall be happy to take the Oath of Succession,' More said, much to Cranmer's surprise.

'Please. Do read the Oath aloud at once, Sir Thomas, so that our ears may hear your words in praise of our king.'

'I can easily swear to our king and swear Queen Anne is His Majesty's only lawful wife, and that Princess Elizabeth is the rightful heir to the throne. I cannot swear that the King is the Supreme Ruler in all matters spiritual and ecclesiastical. I can never claim the King is above papal authority.'

'I cannot even swear that much,' Fisher added. 'I shall never swear that Anne Boleyn is queen over Queen Katherine.'

Crumwell turned slightly to Cranmer. 'If Fisher and More swear to the Succession but not the preamble containing the Supremacy, that will suggest both men believe in papal authority and not the King. If they believe in the Bishop of Rome, and not the King's authority, then they believe the true Queen is Katherine, not Anne. If these men can pick which lines to swear to, then every man in the country will think he can pick.'

'Quite true,' Cranmer mused and looked to More and Fisher again. 'You must swear the entire Oath and cannot pick which parts to believe.'

'I am hither today, as the King's representative, to hear you swear the entire Oath,' Gardiner told the pair.

'Have you sworn the Oath, Bishop Gardiner?' More asked and eyed him across the table.

'I have not,' Gardiner replied.

'I have arrested four Carthusian monks from Middlesex,' Crumwell said. 'They are on their way to London in chains, to be placed in the Tower. If you like, Bishop Fisher, Sir Thomas, you can today join them in the Tower. I have the King's authority to arrest you today for high treason for failure to take the Oath.'

'Arrest me,' Fisher spat in Crumwell's direction. 'I shall swear none of the Oath.'

'I wish to swear to part of the Oath,' More struggled and ran his hands along the parchment on the table, to find the words he believed. 'I, Sir Thomas More, do utterly dedicate in my conscience....'

'No more,' Crumwell replied, and swiped the Oath from the table, its glorious handwritten words thrown onto the stone floor. 'Guards, arrest these two men.'

The four guards, which Cranmer had so readily arranged for this occasion, stepped forward, two men each on the side of the far older and superior men. Neither fought being grabbed by the shoulders. 'Sir Thomas More, I arrested thee in the name of King Henry, for failure to take the Oath of Succession and for high treason,' Crumwell said, his voice now cold and steady. 'Bishop Fisher, I arrest thee in the name of King Henry, for failure to take the Oath of Succession and for high treason.'

But then Crumwell turned to Cranmer and Gardiner. 'Stephen, you too have not taken the Oath and you shall be arrested also.'

'I am the King's Chief Secretary,' Gardiner scoffed. 'And you have no permission from the King to do so. You may bully me, humiliate me before the court, but cannot arrest me.'

'Yet.' Crumwell stared at his foe as More and Fisher were pulled from the main hall without another word. 'Yet.'

Chapter 10 – April 1534
Whitehall Palace, London

The cruelst lyes are sayd in sylence

Crumwell walked through the crowds as if he no longer saw them. With each confident stride, the guards either side of him did the same, parting the crowds in the palace hallways. All knew better than to hand him a letter or petition today. Nicòla walked a step behind him, as he expected, though a few times she nipped the fur edge of his long coat with her shoes. People still tried to hand items to Nicòla, and several times the guards fell back to push people from her. Crumwell made it clear; in case of a crisis, the guards were to fall back to Nicòla before him. Death threats came in waves now; for Crumwell arrested Sir Thomas More and Bishop John Fisher. Any person in the land who defied the Reformation, or the new queen, now had a strong cause to hate Crumwell and his dealings. Enemies had reason to attack; allies had reason to shy away, and everyone's alliances seemed hard to trust. Crumwell was no longer a commoner who created a queen, he was also a man who would gladly destroy men far above him in rank. Had it honestly taken this long for the fools of the court to understand how strong Crumwell had become? He stood daily at the King's side, he had webs which stretched across England into Wales, Scotland and beyond. He almost ran Ireland thanks to his plan to replace the Dublin Council members with friends, and ran the King's finances, and had eyes on every single petition that crossed the King's desk. Queen Anne was a queen because Crumwell said she could be a queen, and the people of England could no longer be Catholic because Crumwell told them that Protestant reform was better for their souls. Rising so high while being quiet proved a most valuable decision.

Guards parted all those standing in the King's antechamber, and Crumwell entered the presence chamber without any need for an announcement. His guards stood at the door with Nicòla, and Crumwell found the room devoid of any person but the King himself, Bishop Gardiner, Thomas Boleyn and Thomas Audley. 'Your Majesty, Lord Privy Seal, Lord Chancellor, Bishop Gardiner,' Crumwell said with a bow, almost choking on the final title. Never had things been so bitter between the pair. To think once they were friends under the watchful eye of Cardinal Wolsey.

At once the King began to turn pink in the face and Crumwell held his breath. Was Henry to rage once more? Was he to turn violent again, which had crept into their daily meetings? But no, rather tears began to prick at Henry's blue eyes, one feeling Henry constantly refused to reveal to the world. 'Crumwell, now you have arrived, there can at last be justice,' Henry said and turned away from everyone, wandering in the direction of the window. He pulled his soft red sleeve to his face, and everyone pretended not to see the King wipe his tears.

'I am ready to assist Your Majesty, but I must say Lord Chancellor Audley can administer justice on your behalf at any time.' Crumwell glanced at Audley, who made a gesture which suggested total confusion over the King's dilemma.

'More and Fisher are in the Tower,' Henry said, still not turning back to the group.

'Of course, Your Majesty,' Crumwell said and stood tall, his hands clasped before him. 'More in the Bell Tower, next to the rooms of the Lieutenant. Fisher has been put one floor below him. Each is still able to send and receive mail and have books and personal items in their rooms. They are comfortable, but not too comfortable, I promise you. I have been to their rooms personally.'

'And the others who have refused to take the Oath?'

'I have monks in the Tower, but there has been little resistance to the swearing to the Oath. People are lining up to swear without question, Your Majesty.' In truth, the Oath had only been made official three weeks ago and not many people had the chance to sign at all.

Now Henry turned back to the group. Crumwell stood to the left of Henry, with Nicòla behind him against the wall, and the other three stood to the right of the King, all slightly hunched in stature, all lost over the point Henry wanted to make. 'What do I do if a man in my court refuses to take the Oath?' Henry asked.

'With thanks to the new treason Acts passed last month, Your Majesty, any person can be arrested for failure to take the Oath,' Audley explained.

'It is at your discretion to decide if someone's behaviour is treasonous, Your Majesty,' Boleyn added.

'By not signing the Oath, Your Majesty, any man shall be arrested without delay,' Crumwell told the King.

Henry leaned a little to look around Crumwell. 'Waif-creature, step forward.' Crumwell's heart began to pound at once, so fast it felt ready to rise from his throat and appear on his tongue. The King spoke of treason and wanted his Nicòla?

'You are a creature of Rome, the creature of the Pope,' Henry began and wandered forward to Nicòla, who had stepped forward and bowed to the King. 'The hands of the Pope himself must have been on you since you were born.'

'Tis true the Pope and I have been known to one another for some time, Your Majesty,' Nicòla replied, her eyes down, her voice plain but even.

'And the Oath, which Crumwell has taken so much time to create?'

'I have sworn the Oath, Your Majesty. I signed before you, with many other courtiers when the papers were first ready.'

'You are a favourite of the Pope, you are an Italian by birth. You are a strong Catholic from one of the most piously controlled countries in Christendom. Yet you swore the Oath.'

'Of course, Your Majesty. I believe in your marriage to Queen Anne and I believe in changes to stop corruption in the Catholic faith.'

Henry gestured for Nicòla to step back, and she took several wide steps, passing Crumwell on the way. Crumwell's heart began to ease as she stepped back, the scent of her washed hair lingering a moment. Crumwell turned his face a little and looked to Gardiner whose face had gone as white as his robes. All seemed to move into place in Crumwell's mind. Gardiner had not sworn the Oath. This was the moment to strike.

'Your Majesty, is there a person who has failed to take the Oath and troubles you with their behaviour?' Crumwell asked as innocently as he could.

'Crumwell,' Henry sighed, 'I need a new Chief Secretary. This person is supposed to be the person I trust most in the world. Now, as King's Chief Minister, you oversee so much of the court, of the parliament, the country. Yet, you are the only man who can act as Chief Secretary.'

'I would be honoured to take the place at your side and deal in all matters on your behalf, Your Majesty.' This role meant total control, head of the table at the Privy Council, power within the Lords in parliament, and even walk ahead of some noblemen at court.

'How?' Henry despaired and threw his hands in the air in the direction of Gardiner. 'How could you, the Chief Secretary of my court, refuse to take the Oath, Stephen?'

'I…' Gardiner stumbled, and Crumwell swallowed hard, 'Your Majesty, I have been much busy…'

'Will you take the Oath or not?' Henry bellowed, throwing everyone off their guard.

Gardiner managed to stand tall. 'I oppose the Act of Supremacy and the Act of Succession.'

This was the moment Crumwell needed to throw Gardiner in the Tower.

'Am I not anointed by God?' Henry cried as he walked straight up to Gardiner, who stepped back in submission.

'Yes, Your Majesty.'

'Am I to be obeyed in my realm?'

'Yes, Your Majesty. But I cannot swear the Oath.'

'You swore to the submission of the clergy not two years past. Any reason you have to deny my right would be treason.'

Crumwell's lips wanted to grin, as his enemy was about to fall. Only moments ago, he feared it might be Nicòla in trouble. He felt sweat on his forehead from the sheer terror that came from Henry's daily moods.

'You are banished from court,' Henry said, strangely calm at once. His voice, deep and strong, conveyed little anger, more disappointment. 'You must leave the court at once and have no freedom to return until such time you are ready to obey your sovereign. Only I can decide when you are ready to serve me once more. You are to be considered in disgrace and are not to speak or act for the court in any case. There are guards waiting to escort you from the court and you are to leave London at once.'

Crumwell stood still as stone as Gardiner passed him, but their eyes followed one another, and the world slowed for a moment, as if to let Crumwell revel as his only real opponent at court was suddenly banished, and all without a single dealing from Crumwell himself. God found ways to thank his subjects in the strangest of ways. Henry paused until Gardiner was gone from the room. 'You shall be formally appointed the Chief Secretary at the next council meeting, Thomas. You shall be the one to draw up the paperwork.' Henry laughed and slapped Crumwell on the shoulder with a rough hand. 'I shall also give you lands and grants for all your hard work on the Oath. How about I make you the Constable of Hertford Castle in Hertfordshire? That shall be a kind reward. Perchance you could take the role jointly with your nephew, Richard, for he is much beloved by me also.'

'I thank His Majesty for such generosity.'

'Take your little Waif and go about your work, Thomas, for I am to visit my wife and her goodly belly.'

Both Crumwell and Nicòla bowed as they left the room, with the doors opened by Crumwell's guards, the sound of waiting courtiers flooding the space. 'Oh, and Crumwell,' the King called over to him, loud enough to hush voices in the next room, 'ensure that from today, those at court address you as Chief Secretary Crumwell.'

Whispers followed Crumwell and Nicòla back to their chambers. By the time they were safely back in their offices, Nicòla's hands were laden with letters pushed to her when the guards looked away. They stood in the antechamber, where clerks and lawyers sat, adding and working.

'Take heed,' Nicòla called out, and at once all stopped to listen. Several men appeared from an adjoining room to hear Nicòla's gentle voice. 'From this day forth, Master Thomas Crumwella is to be addressed as Chief Secretary Crumwella, Chief Minister to King Henry.'

A hearty round of applause encircled Crumwell as his loyal staff came to offer their kind words. By the time he had relayed the news of Gardiner's banishment, Nicòla had already retreated to her desk and had opened some correspondence. Crumwell closed the double doors and locked them. He turned to Nicòla in the corner and leaned back on the wooden doors for a moment, his smile so wide it hurt his round cheeks. 'Let us celebrate,' he said and clapped his hands together. 'An informal party tonight, hither in the chambers, and then we shall travel to Austin Friars towards the week's end and celebrate officially. I must send news to Ralph at once, and to Richard, for he is now joint Constable to Hertford Castle!'

Nicòla turned in her seat and looked at Crumwell with a face so darkened that Crumwell shivered. She stood slowly from her chair, paper in hand. She took but two steps in his direction and stopped, half offering the letter to him. 'Che cosa nel sangue di Cristo?' she said, her voice deep.

'What be this?' Crumwell asked. Nicòla only swore on the blood of Christ when most distressed.

'Why have I received a letter from my husband who is in Rome with his father? Alessandro says he has written to me many times over these past months and worries I reply not! He writes this letter in code, as he worries the correspondence is being stolen. Every man in Europe knows letters in England are read by the spies of Thomas Crumwella.'

Alessandro de'Medici had written monthly for some time, ever since the birth of Princess Elizabeth. Crumwell had read all the letters, even if only in the code which he could not break. He detested every call for help from the depraved Medici. He could never have his wife back in Florence.

'Have you been hiding correspondence from Italy?' Nicòla accused her master. Her eyes almost caught fire in anger under her stern rose-gold brow as she held out the coded letter.

Crumwell could not lie to his Nicòla. 'I hid the letters out of love, out of safety,' Crumwell implored. He threw himself to his knees, not wise for a man of almost fifty and gaining weight by the day. 'The letters started arriving when the princess was born, and we were urgent to create the Oath of Succession. Life has been so joyous for us, so peaceful. We have been happy with our children.'

'If all is well and safe, then why hide letters from me?' Nicòla asked, and tossed the letter, which floated onto Crumwell's desk. 'Where are the letters? Alessandro writes that the Pope is stricken ill, has been for some time. Pope Clement cried for my care, my presence, and you have denied the leader of the Catholic Church that comfort in his time of need.'

'I was scared you would leave for Rome!' Crumwell cried and clawed his hands together as if in prayer. 'I am an ageing man with a widening waist, and in Italy, you are praised with a life of luxury and can reign as the Duchess of Florence.'

'Abandoned Duchess of Florence, in a false marriage which could easily be undone.'

'The Bishop of Rome loves you!'

'He is the Pope, Tomassito! I care not for your laws of calling Giulio the Bishop of Rome. He is Pope Clement the Seventh, as decided by God. Just because the King cannot stand his precious wife Katherine, we are to not call the Pope by his title? Every day, I deny all I have ever known, ever learned, by praising the new Church of England and I do this because I love you. Yet you trust me not, and your vanity leads you to lie and hide. I shall not go to Rome; that is impossible. I would be kidnapped and put in a Medici villa under guard as the Duchess until I produce an heir. I turned my back on Rome five years past and yet you trust me not, believe me not. You listen not. After all the wise counsel I have given you, after all the ideas and conspiracies I have created, of which you gain all the rewards. I stand hidden in men's clothes just to have the right to be a person, to walk a step behind you so you feel powerful. I must deny I am the mother to my own daughter each time I visit her. I am called her uncle. Her uncle! No one questioned my sex because I am considered ugly with my dark skin and the pink-stained hair of my father. I am called the Waif, too weak to be considered a real man. I am a freak, a creature, scurrying about the court like a rat after its master. All I endure I do so for you and yet you trust me not with my own correspondence from my husband.'

'You said I was your husband,' Crumwell pleaded and pulled at the edge of her doublet. 'You swore before God I was the only man you wanted as a husband. Please, Nicò, for all the love I bear for you, please cease your anger. I trust you; I do not trust the Italians.'

'Without Italians, neither of us would be as successful or educated as we are,' Nicòla replied, and swatted away Crumwell's hands. 'Only I decide what to write to Alessandro, for he is my cross to bear. Already I have felt angry for months after being forced to see Queen Kathrine hidden away even more, pushed into poverty, knowing her daughter is alone and unwell. I thought all men hated their women, but you were different. Instead, I find you are the same.'

'No, Nicò, please,' Crumwell begged, unable to find any more words. Nicòla had never unleashed her rage on Crumwell, and suddenly the lack of her favour caused pain in his chest.

'I am to Austin Friars to visit my daughter,' Nicòla replied. 'Or shall you deny me rights to leave the court to visit Jane?'

'I shall come also.'

'You are the Chief Secretary of the King's court. Just moments ago, you were celebrating your victory, revelling in your win.'

'I would have no such prosperity without you. Let me fix this.'

Nicòla wavered over Crumwell, rather than moving away. Tears welled in her green eyes; she was angered not; rather hurt, betrayed.

'Let me right my wrongs, Nicò. I shall start with sending money to Katherine at Kimbolton, and Lady Mary at Hatfield.'

'I have already done so from my own pocket. Let me deal with Rome and Florence. And stop your gloating over the banished Gardiner. Your pride shall see you punished by God. You are but a servant of the King, like everyone. Your head could be on the block as easily as any person. One day it could be you banished.'

Still on his knees, Crumwell wrapped his arms around Nicòla's body, feeling her tremble with disappointment. 'I beseech Thee, O Most Blessed Trinity, to shed the fire of Thy merciful love upon this most frigid heart, to let shine upon this most darkened mind, the light of the Son, in whom alone is every grace and truth. Have pity on me, most merciful God, and regard not my sins and offences, but in Thy mercy, forgive me yet again, and grant me the graces to serve Thee now in fidelity and truth,' he recited, his eyes closed as he leaned his face against her warm body.

'A Catholic prayer,' Nicòla lamented.

'In honour of you and your father, who saved me in the Catholic faith and made me the man I am today,' Crumwell said.

Nicòla pulled Crumwell's arms and he rose to his feet, eager to wrap his arms around her. Never had Nicòla's confidence wavered in him. Never had Nicòla been angry or upset, no matter the urgent and crippling acts they sometimes needed to endure. God sent a warning; Crumwell could easily lose all he wanted in the pursuit of the King's happiness.

Chapter 11 – April 1534
Whitehall Palace, London

A lyar knows she is a lyar

'Et ne nos inducas in tentationem, sed libera nos a malo. Amen.' Nicòla whispered the end of the Lord's Prayer and crossed herself as she looked out the window of her bedroom. The sun had not quite surfaced upon this fateful day, April 20. Grey whispered across the sky, the world ready to rise from its bed and say its daily prayers. But no more Latin, for Nicòla had to pray in English now, because of the man who rested behind her, his arms wrapped tightly around her naked body. Thomas Crumwell, the most powerful man in the country, had the nation's throat in a noose. A week had passed since Crumwell took the closest position to the King, that of Chief Secretary. A week since he fell to his knees and begged for forgiveness from Nicòla. His repentance appeared honest; it was the detail that Crumwell would knowingly deceive her, the person he claimed to trust most, which lingered between them. Nicòla slept in his bed at night knowing he was truly sorry, but also that she truly had no choice but to forgive him.

The warmth of Crumwell's body moved against her back as he stirred from his sleep. His hands moved against her body, wandering as he ended his slumber. Today the charges they had concocted against Elizabeth Barton would see her hanged at Tyburn. No one had "heard" her confession but Crumwell. Barton had merely repeated but a few words he forced into her. She had been put to the rack, her arms and legs torn from their sockets. She had been beaten, screamed at, starved and humiliated. Now, the careful papers Crumwell wrote in his own hand, stating her fake confession, sat with the bill of attainder, meaning she would receive no trial. Today Barton would die, along with her closest allies, by Crumwell's demand, to satisfy Henry's vanity.

Again, Nicòla stood between Crumwell and Cranmer on a day of violence and ridicule. They stood with Ralph Sadler, who had travelled the three miles from Austin Friars to join the proceedings. The group stood together, flanked by several of the guards from the Crumwell Chambers, all on the scaffold where Barton would be hanged and beheaded, and her co-conspirators all beheaded. The scaffold was wide enough to take care of these acts, yet Nicòla could not wish to be far enough away. She had watched Richard Roose be boiled to death at Smithfield for her own crime several years ago, and it still haunted her. This time, though, Nicòla may not have been guilty of the crime, but she did not wish to see a woman hanged because of the lies she told to satisfy the whims of the men who ruled her.

'What are you holding?' Ralph asked Nicòla as he pushed his blonde hair from his eyes; the spring wind twirled around everyone on a grey day. Nicòla looked to her gloved hands; a letter one of Crumwell's spies shoved into her hand as she dismounted her horse on arrival. He had come and gone from the crowd so fast, Nicòla could not be sure who delivered it, perchance a guard.

'Idle rumour from one of our little creatures,' Nicòla opened the folded paper. The letter went unsigned, but the crude lettering suggested a boy working on behalf of Henry Norris, one man closest to the King in the privy chamber. 'It says Henry Norris visits the Queen's chambers not to pay favour to Lady Margaret Shelton, as he claims. Norris is not keen to court Lady Margaret. Lady Margaret is to be King Henry's new mistress, and Norris fetches her to the King's bed when needed.'

'It was only a matter of time,' Crumwell mumbled as he closed his hands together and looked out at the large crowd there to watch the spectacle. 'Queen Anne must take great care with her child and Lady Margaret can hold Anne's place in Henry's bed.'

'Can no man simply wait for his wife?' Nicòla scorned as she closed her angry fingers over the letter.

'Not a king,' Cranmer said as he smoothed his purple robes, the golden cross about his neck perfectly centred. 'We must accept the fault of men, especially a king. Only God can judge.'

'Yet any woman who does work in a man's bed shall be tainted for her whole life,' Nicòla spat.

'The Reformation shall increase the rights of women,' Cranmer said. 'You are well read, Nicòla, and I know you understand this. It is unnatural for men to abstain; a woman has no sexual needs.'

'Do you forsake your wife when she is with child, Archbishop?' Nicòla asked, not looking up to any of the surrounding men.

'I do not.'

'And you, Ralph? Ellen has already borne you one child and is preparing for another after only two years of marriage. Do you forsake her?'

'No,' Ralph admitted.

'Our existence at court is based on Anne being the Queen,' Crumwell uttered. 'Without Anne, we would be lost. The Reformation is safe if we have Anne's cousin in the King's bed while Anne creates an heir, and we should thank God for such a happening.' Crumwell paused and Cranmer and Ralph both nodded. 'Or it could be all of us lined up on a scaffold when an act of attainder is readied.'

An attainder created by you to give people no rights or safety, Nicòla thought but brushed it aside. Anger against her precious Crumwell would do no good. But attending executions had to stop for Nicòla personally; it rattled her too much. The crowd rose in cheers and Nicòla saw the six get led to the scaffold, the executioner already in place. The crowd appeared a strange mix - some cheered for the killing to begin, some booed and jeered, others called out in praise for their Holy Maid of Kent.

They dragged Elizabeth Barton forward to face the crowd before the noose was tied to her neck. She was barefoot, covered in just a dirty and misshapen white shift, her long dark hair matted to itself, many parts of her scalp bald and bloody. She hung in the arms of her jailers, her limbs broken from torture. How any person could endure such agony surpassed any strength God could offer. Barton took one look to Crumwell, her eyes surrounded by bruises. Nicòla knew Crumwell had convinced Barton that confession was the only way to make a good death. What went on in the Tower's underground rooms defied Nicòla's knowledge.

The crowd silenced to hear the Maid's final words. 'I am the cause not only of my death, which I richly deserve… but also the cause of the death of the people who will suffer with me… I said anything that came into my head. I, full of the praises of priests, fell into pride and foolish fantasy… but now I cry to God and beg the King's pardon,' Barton called out over the crowd, her words littered with tears.

'God bless you!' a woman called from the crowd and others joined.

Cranmer gestured for the guards to complete the proceedings. They dragged Barton back to the noose where the hangman awaited her. They held the poor girl in place as they tied the noose around her neck, and the crowd cried out as the noose snaked about her skin. Cranmer gestured to the men in charge to hurry; for the crowd could easily turn in favour of the Maid instead of the execution order all too easily. Barton turned her feeble head one more time and looked at Nicòla. 'Next, it shall be you,' she called, barely heard, even up close. 'One day it shall be you on the scaffold for your sins.'

'Hurry along,' Crumwell barked, and they easily lifted Barton off her feet. With her hands tied behind her back, her body twisted and lurched on the end of the rope for what felt like an eternity to Nicòla, as if she were to await her own death on the gallows. The crowd continued to call out as the woman, probably ill in the mind, used by men of the Church, slowly choked to death for the sins claimed by others. The rope had been useful, for Barton's body had a little fight left.

'Tell me why I must watch such scenes,' Nicòla said.

'Because this furthers our cause, and because our anointed king requested us as the witnesses to this occasion. Because those who further their causes are a direct threat to the realm we have created,' Crumwell replied. His words appeared steady, but Nicòla felt the back of his hand against hers, the tiniest of comforts, all a man could offer to his "male" attendant.

'God our deliverer,' Cranmer cried out as executioners put Barton's body down to be beheaded, 'defender of the poor and in need of salvation; when the foundations of this Earth move, give strength to those who uphold justice and fight all wrongs in the name of your son, Jesus Christ our Lord.'

'Amen,' Nicòla, Crumwell and Ralph all recited, along with the crowd.

Nicòla shut her eyes as the axe fell on Barton's neck, even though her soul had already departed. They dragged her dripping body away, her head carried in a basket, to be the first woman to have her head mounted on a spike on London Bridge. They would dump her body at Newgate, forgotten in an instant. Five men stood awaiting in Barton's blood, their heads to be brutally hacked before the crowd. Edward Bocking, the Benedictine monk who encouraged Barton came first, not allowed to speak before his death. The executioner struck him plain, one chop and the brown-clad man was gone. After him came John Dering, another Benedictine monk kneeling in Bocking's blood as his life ended. Henry Gold, a priest, cried as his head got pushed onto the blood-soaked block, same for Hugh Rich, a Franciscan friar, and then finally Richard Rigsby, a fellow Franciscan friar. In what felt like only moments to Nicòla, the entire nest of traitors was dead, the basket filled with blood-soaked heads with their gaping wide eyes. No one would dare prophecise about the King again. The Marquess of Exeter's wife would not dare hire another woman to foretell the future again, not with this much blood spilt. The King would be best pleased. Cranmer felt certain God would be pleased.

'We took control of this country because Protestants were being burned by Sir Thomas More,' Nicòla commented as they pulled away the bodies, the heads collected to get spiked at the London gates. 'Now we kill Catholics.'

'We kill traitors,' Crumwell said. 'It is them or us. It is the life we all chose. Think of Queen Anne, an innocent woman chosen by the King. It is her destiny to have the King's son, whether she wanted the role or not. We must serve our masters. We must choose sides, and we are on the side of reform, on the side of the Boleyns. It is not our place to decide what is right and what is not.'

'If not us, then who?' Ralph asked, appearing paler than ever after the beheadings.

'We do God's work, and He shall guide us,' Cranmer replied.

'Might I be given leave to accompany Ralph back to Austin Friars to visit my daughter?' Nicòla asked.

'If that is what you wish,' Crumwell sighed as the group left the scaffold, the crowd already dispersing. 'I shall send guards with you.'

'No, you need the security,' Nicòla commented, noting the bitter expressions on the faces of commoners.

Crumwell took Nicòla aside as they headed to their horses. 'The Maid was wrong, Nicò,' he mumbled. 'It will never be our turn on the scaffold, I swear it.'

'If it is our turn, please tell me you would save your own head and live for Jane's sake.'

'If I was to have my head struck off, I would do so to save you. For that is the only reason in the world worth dying for.'

Nicòla looked up to Crumwell and his golden gaze. They seemed to age faster than ever. At four and thirty years, Nicòla felt as if her bones were long past their best. 'If it were you on the scaffold, I would be there, holding your hands, screaming for them to show mercy.'

'Believe none of Barton's words, for she could not see the future. She could not hear God. God does not speak through whores found writhing in the mud. The people of England are on a perilous journey towards reformation and we need to help them.'

'Unless they kill us first.'

'Ride back to Austin Friars and hold our daughter tight, stroke her rose-gold hair and marvel at her beauty. Seek all that is good, and you shall find it in Jane. Find my Gregory and kiss him for me. I shall send a barge to you before nightfall to bring you back to Whitehall. From tomorrow, all those in London will swear the Oath and the dark times shall be over. I shall not kill those who refuse, I shall have them imprisoned. The worst is over. I have no will to kill people, Nicò. That is not the Church I want to install in this country, one imposed with fear and death. Never again shall you have to witness an execution.'

'As admirable as your ideas are, Tomassito, whether they can come true is another matter entirely.'

Chapter 12 – July 1534
Windsor Palace, Berkshire

Lyes require commytment

Even the double-minded man needed time outdoors occasionally. Crumwell pushed fifty acts through parliament in a year, and another fifty statutes, each at least 100 pages in length. With the summer progress of 1534 limited to palaces close to London due to Queen Anne's pregnancy, Crumwell could keep up with work and still be at the King's side every day. Crumwell spent time in the gardens with Henry, indulging in a spot of archery, neither of the men beaten by any of their attendants. But today Crumwell got away, to go for a walk in the wide quiet spaces surrounding the palace, in search of Nicòla.

There she sat hidden behind a tall hedge. Nicòla had tossed her black doublet on the grass and sat in just her hose and a white linen shirt, her feet dipped into a pond. Her rose-gold hair sat on her shoulders, moving just a little in the soft breeze. A letter sat in her hands, yet her gaze drifted off into the distance, over the nearby hedges and off to the tall trees which surrounded the gardens. Crumwell took short silent steps in the dry grass as he approached, his heart a little nervous to disturb Nicòla. The last months had been difficult, ever since Nicòla came back from her visit with the former queen. Crumwell too had moments when he wondered if he could stomach the sacrifices of the Reformation, and now, the strain wore on Nicòla and the love she bore for Crumwell.

Nicòla jumped as he appeared beside her but said nothing. Crumwell sat down beside her, his back to the pond so he could look upon Nicòla's face instead. His tired bones ached as he settled on the grass, but to sit down in the silent garden also soothed so much.

'Do you remember the light?' Nicòla asked without looking at him.

'La bellezza della luce,' Crumwell replied. At once the beauty of the light of Florence came to mind; how the city glowed in a bright sunshine that never crept as far north as England.

They sat so closely their arms almost touched. Crumwell put his hand down on the grass, his fingers touching Nicòla's hand, the most he could do in public. Stretching his legs out on the grass felt like a luxury afforded to his younger self.

'I cannot recall a time when you looked more beautiful,' Crumwell commented as he watched her gaze off into the distance.

Nicòla let out a gentle laugh. 'I feel sorry for you, Master. For you could not have picked a mistress any less attractive.'

'I would call you wife sooner than call you mistress. And you have moments of true beauty which shine through any costume you may wear.'

'When?'

'Such as the moment you came back to Austin Friars those years ago, with infant Jane in your arms.'

Nicòla turned now to Crumwell, their faces close. 'I was so frightened that day, frightened that you would turn me away.'

'You appeared not frightened, but innocent.'

Again Nicòla laughed, and Crumwell wondered how long it had been since he had heard the sound. 'I am many things, but never innocent.'

'In moments of silence, I am remembered of how much I adore you.'

'I fear you may have been in the company of those practising courtly love, Tomassito, for it has made you soft.'

Crumwell laughed but his eyes gazed at her lips. 'I wish I could kiss you, before the world, before God.'

'I believe God knows our sins already,' Nicòla whispered.

Crumwell laughed again and looked out over the garden. 'The world could burn today, and we would have no knowledge of it.'

'Do you know what is happening with your Subsidy Act for taxing during peacetime?' Nicòla asked.

'No.'

'Neither do I. What of the poor relief bill or the new trade and agriculture laws?'

'I know nothing.'

'Neither do I. What of George Boleyn in France on the King's behalf, being an embarrassment. Or of Reverend Lee in the Welsh Marches being trouble, or the Irish lords sending bribes to prevent their castles being searched by government men?'

'I know nothing.'

'Neither do I. Do you know who is running the King's mistress into his bed? Who is collecting all the letters from our spies all over England?'

'I know nothing. As I say, England could burn, and we would never know.' Crumwell turned back to Nicòla as she still gazed upon him.

For the briefest of moments, the weight of the kingdom did not sit upon their shoulders. 'If it is so soothing to be free of the world, why do you hold such a weighty letter in your hands?' Crumwell asked, and tried to see the writing on the paper. Italian.

'I was reading while you were with the King, and I needed time to think on many things. As you did not need me, I walked, but ended up hither some time ago.'

'Who dares to write my love?'

'My husband does. He bears news I needed to understand for myself before I shared.'

'And?'

Nicòla sighed and folded the letter, many pages written by the depraved Alessandro. 'He writes with much news. His mistress, Taddea, she is with child again. Their son Giulio is thriving in Florence. He shall be two years old soon. Alessandro mentions that many families the Medici and the Frescobaldi know in Florence have been stocking weapons. Alessandro has raised taxes on the people of Florence to pay for the building of his grand fortress, and they have drafted men from the ducal territories to continue the build. Many are unhappy, it seems. The city is not at peace. Some noble enemies have been gathering gunpowder. I know not why Alessandro wishes to share so much with me, but he also hints at happy tidings.'

'The health of the Bishop of Rome?'

'No, the "Pope", for it is still legal to call him Pope in Italy, is still unwell, still wishes me to return to Rome to visit him. But rather he writes of the Holy Roman Emperor. Alessandro has met with Emperor Charles several times and his daughter, Margarete of Austria, who is still in need of a husband. If we could annul our marriage, Alessandro would be free to remarry. He has already taken my father's vast fortune and spent it, so it is time to abandon me and remarry for the family. The Pope could marry his bastard son to the Holy Roman Emperor's bastard daughter at last.'

'Shall Clement give you an annulment? If he loves you as much as he claims, he would end your marriage to his wicked son.'

'The people of Florence will care none for an annulment between Alessandro and myself. I am only the Duchess by marriage. No one has seen me in Florence for almost five years. But their Duke marrying the Emperor's daughter; it may frighten them into submission thanks to Charles' armies, or they may rebel and tear the city to shreds. Pope Clement shall be aware. The current tensions shall need to be quelled because any annulment must be blessed. Clement is ill; there is the talk of a successor if he dies. The favourite is Alessandro Farnese, Dean of the College of Cardinals. He has five bastard children, all powerful and connected, and many grandchildren rising in favour. Farnese bears love for the Medici name but would care nothing for annulments. But perchance Farnese would grant an annulment with ease as he has no issue to consider. If Emperor Charles wants his daughter married to Alessandro, I am likely to gain the annulment of our dreams.'

'You could be Mistress Crumwell by law as well in as in the eyes of God and His Majesty.'

'Shall I then need to live as a woman, Master Crumwella?'

'No, for I like to disguise you close to me.' Crumwell took off his hat and tossed it, public place be damned. He kissed Nicòla full on the lips, a long lingering kiss which turned to another and another. But a shrieking cry echoed through the garden and Crumwell and Nicòla jumped up in a moment. To get caught kissing his secretary would destroy Crumwell and he knew it. But as they stood on the edge of the pond, they could see no one.

As Nicòla pulled on her shoes, another cry echoed; a woman's voice. Nicòla grabbed her black doublet off the grass and the pair set off towards the sound of agony. Through the hedges stood the Queen, with several of her ladies and a solitary guard. Queen Anne stood hunched over her goodly belly, holding her baby tight as two of her ladies held her to standing.

'Get her inside,' Crumwell cried as the pair rushed to the group, still dishevelled from their peace in the garden. Crumwell eased the ladies aside and took Anne's arm over his shoulders to hold her weight, and Nicòla took up the other arm to get Anne back in the palace.

'Oh, Cremwell, please, you must send for the doctors and the midwives and the King,' Anne cried as she got carried along, her face showing fear, her hair already covered in sweat.

'Worry not, Your Majesty,' Crumwell strained through his voice as he carried his queen, 'for many can bear fine kings early and survive such an ordeal.'

Long before they reached the palace the guards came running to carry their queen. For all the fun by the pond, the moment Crumwell and Nicòla left the palace, the country started to burn. The son England needed was suddenly in danger.

'You must go to the King at once,' Nicòla said, panting from the rush with Anne. 'Henry must hear this from you, otherwise, they shall give him the news with no care and in a rush of blind panic.'

'You stand guard in the Queen's rooms, so we can hear what is happening. I shall keep the King at bay for now. Could a baby live if born this soon?'

'The Queen is seven, eight weeks from delivering.' They paused for a moment; their son Thomas was born at that age and had no hope of survival. 'God help us all,' Nicòla said, and Crumwell just turned in a panic to find Henry still out with his longbow.

~~~

Crumwell tried to calm Henry, who stumbled upon hearing the news of his beloved Anne. Rather than wait in his apartments, Henry insisted on being close to the Queen's rooms, close enough to hear the cries of a woman struggling with the truth of creating new life. Crumwell stood in the hallway gallery with Henry, all his gentlemen banished, so as not to see Henry's worry and grief at the thought of losing yet another son. When the door opened at last, after hours of hearing Anne's cries, Nicòla appeared. Crumwell knew they had confined Nicòla to the antechamber, not the bedroom, being in her guise as a man, yet the face on Nicòla told them all. The precious second child of Henry and Anne was dead.

Without a word spoken, Henry stumbled to the floor in despair, crying out in pure torment. Crumwell fell to his knees beside his king, and Henry turned and pounded a fist into Crumwell's mouth in anguish. Crumwell fell onto his back, grateful to land on the carpets rather than the stone floor. The moment he sat upright, Crumwell watched Nicòla get punched by the King, who had jumped to his feet in a moment. Nicòla too fell to the floor when hit by the ageing monarch, who stepped over her body to enter the Queen's chambers. Crumwell struggled to pull Nicòla up, her face stuck in surprise. They sat on the floor, stunned by the moment, the air shadowed by Henry's cry choking from the bedchamber beyond.

'A boy,' Nicòla said as Crumwell placed a hand on her reddened cheek. 'A blessed son, perfectly formed yet too small for life. The poor child never took a breath. Poor Queen Anne was so desperate to hold the child inside her. I could hear her ladies telling her to push, but she did not wish to do so; for she wanted to preserve the son within her. Alas, God wanted to take this royal boy to heaven.'

'Why would God forsake us like this?' Crumwell sighed.

'God was not in that room,' Nicòla shook her head. 'God would not take a blessed boy away.'

The King entered the hallway just as the pair got themselves to their feet. Henry stumbled from the chambers alone and looked to Crumwell with total surprise, as if he had forgotten he and Nicòla were ever there. 'You are to tell no one,' Henry muttered. 'No one is to know what happened. This baby shall never be mentioned. God has not forsaken me or my reign. He has not forbidden me male children. This baby never happened, this pregnancy never happened. Write nothing. Do you understand me, Crumwell?'

'Yes, Your Majesty.'

'I am not forsaken by God,' Henry repeated.

'No, Your Majesty.'

'I shall have a son from Anne's belly.'

'Yes, Your Majesty.'

'We shall travel to Greenwich once Anne is ready. No baby happened, Crumwell. No pregnancy. No confinement, no birth, nothing. History shall not know of this moment. We are not cursed.'

'Never, Your Majesty. This is a private worry between yourself and the Queen,' Crumwell soothed the man who had just punched his sore mouth and hit his precious Nicòla.

Henry disappeared back into the Queen's chambers again and Crumwell turned to Nicòla. One afternoon in the garden and England burned.

Chapter 13 – August 1534
Austin Friars, London

We live insyde the lyes we beleeve

Crumwell had not moved about with such care in some time. With the King and Queen still on progress at Windsor, much of the court away while Henry pretended Anne's stillbirth never occurred, the chance to be at Austin Friars gave a rare feeling of pure freedom to celebrate Jane's fourth birthday with both her parents and her brother Gregory. It was a glorious chance to see the magnificent changes at Austin Friars as Crumwell's star continued to rise and money flooded his accounts. Ever the man to be in control of every detail, Crumwell planned a lavish dinner party to be held while also overseeing details of how many people had signed the Oath. One moment he mentioned how many had taken the Oath in the Welsh Marshes, next he would talk about how much venison was to be served at dinner, all while Nicòla scurried behind him, trying to write his words. Every single remembrance which came from Crumwell's mouth needed to be written. It would take clerks all day to file the notes.

Crumwell stood, hands on hips, and looked out over his dining room, now doubled in size. A table for twenty was being laid by Ralph's wife Ellen and her maids, the finest silver and fabrics being used, candles being carefully put in place. Now huge doors opened the dining room up into the garden, just as Francesco Frescobaldi's dining room had once done back in Florence. Out in the garden, young Jane was running on the grass between the flowers, chasing one of Nicòla's precious peacocks. Her little rose-gold ringlets bounced as she squealed more than the fleeing peacock, or the nursery maids chasing her.

'Master?' Nicòla asked, and he turned his head a little to her, his eyes still on his daughter in the garden. 'I have a letter from Lady Alice, Sir Thomas

More's wife. She wishes to speak with you, to appeal for her husband in the Tower.'

'And what shall I say?' Crumwell shrugged, and his nephew Richard nodded as he entered the room.

Crumwell clicked his fingers at Ellen, and she hurried all the maids from the room. 'For seven thousand, three hundred and forty-two people have sworn the Oath so far, but More is too special to sign?'

'You could say... worry not, Lady Alice, for I have no wish to chop your husband at the neck,' Nicòla ventured.

'Sir Thomas once threatened to expose you,' Crumwell reminded her.

'That is no reason to cut a man at the neck. Ambassador Chapuys threatened the same but quickly quietened his threats.'

'Ambassador Chapuys only quietened because the Emperor told him not to expose you, and only because the "Pope" wanted your identity to stay quiet,' Richard added.

'I wish Gregory would come out,' Crumwell said. 'He seems determined to sit at Ralph's desk in the offices all day.'

'Gregory is a quiet boy, let him be,' Nicòla replied.

'Gregory will soon be fifteen years old, and today his greatest issue was to make sure the barber gave he and you the same short haircut. At fifteen, I had left home, sailed to France, and joined a mercenary army ready to face Italy.'

'Yes, you were one of the few not slaughtered at Garigliano,' Nicòla added. 'Be pleased Gregory gets to grow in such peaceful times and become a good man as Richard and Ralph have done.'

'Who is the master of his household?' Crumwell grinned, and Richard laughed.

'So... Lady Alice?'

'Yes, allow her to come to Austin Friars and plead More's case,' Crumwell sighed. 'But More is a threat who must take the Oath, as seven thousand, three hundred and forty-two people already done.'

'How many times are you to repeat that number, Master?' Richard asked.

'I hope it shall rise and I shall revel in the number every time.'

All the plans for the magnificent feast seemed worth it, just to see the light in Crumwell's eyes when his long-time friend, Stephen Vaughan made his return to London. He had spent so long living in Antwerp as Crumwell's man there but his correspondence with William Tyndale left a target upon Vaughan. Now he was the governor of the Company of the Merchant Adventurers of London from Antwerp, and now also president of the Factory of English Merchants in Antwerp, dignified roles Crumwell would once have sought had he not risen in royal service.

Nicòla stood two steps back from her master as they all lined up to wait for Vaughan and his new wife Margery. As long as Crumwell ruled, More could not threaten Vaughan. No one could threaten Vaughan and his Protestant beliefs and friendship with the Lutheran writer William Tyndale anymore. In the entranceway, filled with the lavish tapestry given to Crumwell after Wolsey's fall, all waited in patience, but Crumwell dashed out into the fading evening light to meet his friend in Austin Friars' courtyard. Nicòla watched as a short man, about her age, embraced Crumwell with a huge grin. Vaughan was a small person, his wife similar, with dark red hair and a shy demeanour. Nicòla stood up straight and perfected her royal blue doublet to meet Crumwell's old friend.

'This…' Crumwell said and pointed to Nicòla after he had introduced Gregory, Richard and Ralph, 'is Master Nicòla Frescobaldi.'

'I feel as if I already know you, sir,' Vaughan said with a merry greeting. 'The son of Francesco Frescobaldi of Florence! I am pleased you have become part of Crumwell's household, for he and your father were much similar. I met your father but once when I was young when he worked with my father. I must thank you.'

'For what, Master Vaughan?' Nicòla asked, pronouncing his name a little rough in her accent.

'For working as Thomas' secretary and not as a merchant, for you and Thomas together would destroy my business throughout Europe. I could not compete against you!'

The whole group laughed at the easy conversation, but Vaughan's words caught in Nicòla's mind. As a man, she could do as she pleased, worked as she pleased. Yet she constantly served only one man and neglected all her own skills in recent times, her skills as a lawyer, a merchant, a moneylender and investor. The thoughts of feeling trapped beneath the dirty business of making and supporting a queen never seemed to fade these days.

Silver adorned the dining table, the wide doors opened to the summer air, and thankfully the plague in London ran quietly this summer. Nicòla sat in peace between Gregory and Ralph. Vaughan's wife sat across from Nicòla, an English woman whose accent now seemed laced with her Flemish life. Along with Ralph's wife sat Richard and Frances, Thomas Avery, Thomas Audley, and Thomas Cranmer and his wife Margarete, all men self-made. The comfort and ease of conversation and lack of etiquette made the evening gentle, peppered with the talk of children out in the garden, not hidden away like royal offspring. Jane and Gregory played Stephen's namesake son, and daughters Katherine and Mary. For one night, it could be easy to think the weight of the kingdom did not lie upon the Crumwell household. They were just a group of wealthy merchants all with children keen to touch Crumwell's pet leopard in the garden.

'Ralph, here,' Crumwell said as he waved a chicken leg toward his adopted son, 'shall now be Master of Sutton House in Hackney, as the place is almost complete. Master Richard Crumwell, Privy Councillor, shall have a new home at Stepney Green, named Great Place, which is fitting, close to my place in Stepney. Nicòla shall be master of a manor in Dewhurst in Surrey once it is complete, and my adopted daughter Jane shall own a home in Mortlake. Gregory shall be gifted lands in Essex, Kent and Sussex.'

'Is there any part of England you have not bought?' Vaughan laughed to his friend, a friendly hand on Crumwell's shoulder.

'For myself, I have leased Allfarthing Manor in Wandsworth,' Crumwell added, 'and even a little land up in Lincolnshire, to collect the yearly rents.'

'For a total of £417 a year,' Nicòla boasted.

'So, you have indeed brought all of England,' Vaughan repeated.

'For you, Stephen, I have bought a manor here in London for you and your family while you live in England. I know you shall only be hither some time with your new role in the chancery and an official spectral role at court…'

Nicòla watched Vaughan and Crumwell embrace again over the great gift. Never had Crumwell lavished so much on one man.

After a huge thank you for much good fortune, Vaughan said, 'so, Thomas, tell me, how many have sworn the Oath?'

'Seven thousand, three hundred and forty-two,' Nicòla, Ralph and Richard all said in time, to the laughter of the group. 'And growing by the day,' Nicòla added.

'As we are in good company, I shall show you my gift, Thomas,' Vaughan added. He had a servant bring him a small box, put on the table between Crumwell and young Gregory. Vaughan had brought a new printed copy of William Tyndale's New Testament. 'I know you can recite the New Testament,' Vaughan explained, 'but Tyndale has updated his version, with more view to both Luther and the Greek texts. There are words and phrases never uttered by English lips until now,' Vaughan gushed. 'This copy has a personal inscription from Tyndale for you, Thomas. Tyndale is in hiding in the Low Countries, I know not where, but I received this gift. Tyndale has used a new word – atonement – which he has ascribed, a reconsolidation between God and any man who seeks His peace.'

'I believe atonement means to be "at one" with God,' Cranmer said for the group, possibly the only other expert beside Crumwell on the new bibles.

'One day England shall be at one with God,' Crumwell said to the group, everyone filled with wine and summer merriment. 'No purgatory, no penance, just peace.'

Yet all around the table knew pain would be needed if the Reformation was to encompass England, but Nicòla smiled and hid the thought.

'They have made Master Crumwell the Constable of Berkeley Castle,' Richard told Vaughan.

'As we are in the company of common men and women and no one at court shall hear,' Vaughan said, and raised his glass, 'long live King Crumwell.'

While it was treason to utter such words, no one repeated the toast but still raised their glasses. Crumwell's star soared, and God help the men who tried to stop him now.

Chapter 14 – September 1534
Greenwich Palace, downstream London

it is haarder to lye to someone's fayce

Crumwell yawned as he sat back in his throne of a chair behind his desk. Being at Greenwich to be close to the King was easy during the summer; picnics, hunting, sports, and while Crumwell only took part in some, it left him tired while trying to hold on to his dozens of other roles in the royal court. He opened his eyes again and watched Nicòla across the room, reading letters from the chest of mail which arrived for the morning. Crumwell absently clicked his fingers twice to instruct her.

'Tis a letter from the new Duchess of Suffolk,' Nicòla replied without looking up from the page. 'She writes in the hope of privacy. Her mother, Baroness Maria, is living with her daughter at Westhorpe Hall, but desperately wishes to travel to visit the former Queen Katherine. The Duchess begs you, Tomassito, to ask the King to allow her mother to visit Katherine.'

'We deprive Lady Katherine of all comforts and that includes her closest friends,' Crumwell replied and folded his arms over his chest.

Nicòla dropped the letter upon her desk. 'Lady Maria has been Queen Katherine's lady-in-waiting ever since Katherine came over from Spain to marry Prince Arthur! That is my whole lifetime ago! Lady Maria loved Katherine as a sister. She named her daughter after her; Queen Katherine is her daughter's godmother.'

'Lady Katherine,' Crumwell amended Nicòla's words. ''Tis the King's orders. I cannot change this.'

'You are the only man who can change these laws. Let Katherine see her daughter, her friends. What harm could it do?'

'Katherine could give her friends letters, who could send them to Emperor Charles, asking him to invade England for her, and kill us all.'

'If the Emperor were to take England, he would have done so by now. Charles is also the Spanish king. He has too many issues to worry about rather than his aunt's divorce. Invasion from the Turks will always be Charles' biggest worry.'

'I am not preparing to take the risk; we destroyed a queen and made another, and now we can have the Reformation and can have total control of England. Katherine is a casualty of that.'

'You minded when Cardinal Wolsey was the casualty of these changes. You loved Wolsey, and he died; Katherine has people who care for her. One day we could be casualties. Will no one show us mercy?'

'Mercy is in short supply, Nicò.'

'Shall we not be the ones to supply mercy?'

Crumwell sighed; Nicòla was right to offer mercy, but such mercy could incur the wrath of the King.

The main door opened out in the offices and in came one of the gentleman-ushers, with Sir Francis Bryan. Crumwell clicked his fingers to dismiss the usher, but Bryan waited until they shut the doors behind him.

'You need to go to the King's rooms,' Bryan offered at once.

'È impossibile rimuovere un inconveniente senza che emerga un altro,' Nicòla mumbled. It is impossible to remove one inconvenience without another emerging. Machiavelli had a quote for any occasion.

'This be of honest consequence, and I seek to stop rage before it occurs,' Bryan offered and adjusted the strap which held his eye patch steady. 'Much ruin is occurring at this moment in the Queen's apartments. Her sister, the Lady Mary Carey, has arrived unannounced and is with a child.'

Crumwell bolted upright in his chair. 'Mary Boleyn is with child?' he croaked, almost unable to hear his own voice.

'And with the Queen still grieving the loss of her own son, Anne is most vexed at the sight. Her sister, a widow, with child!'

'Who is the father?' Crumwell's mind searched for possible suitors, but Mary seldom came to court.

'They say Mary married in secret to a man named William Stafford,' Bryan explained. 'Some man of no fortune.'

'Stafford?' Crumwell groaned. 'The King shall force us all to wither in fear. Does Henry know of this?'

'I think not but shall in no time.'

Crumwell charged to the King's rooms, Bryan and Nicòla trailing behind. Henry paced back and forth, his hand on his forehead as Anne sat by, yelling the most tearful words to him. Indeed, Henry and Anne had spent little time in each other's company since losing the baby; Anne kept quiet in her rooms with her ladies, and Henry was still with his mistress,

Margaret Shelton. Crumwell barely saw Anne these past weeks since their arrival at Greenwich; much of the palace was empty as they hushed the Queen's pregnancy from the world. Any time and peace away from Anne Boleyn was gratefully received by Crumwell.

Anne sat in a soft chair, tears on her face. But rather than upset, Anne appeared most angry. Crumwell waved Bryan away, who slunk off to hide in the corner with the other men of the privy chamber, all in the far corner of the light, spacious room, eager for gossip.

'In God's name, Anne, calm yourself,' came the voice of her father as he entered from a door on the other side of the room. Boleyn too appeared flushed red in the cheeks. Boleyn paused when he saw Crumwell, his hands folded before him. A glance of relief appeared on Boleyn's face as he took a deep breath.

'You shall address me with the title I deserve,' Anne shot back to her father. 'Be not angry at me, for it is your older daughter who is the whore and liar!'

'Your Majesties,' Crumwell interrupted and bowed. 'Lord Wiltshire,' he added politely to Boleyn.

'This is a family problem, Cremwell,' Anne snapped at him. 'Run along and play your conspiracies elsewhere!'

'Speak not harshly to Thomas!' Henry chided his wife. 'For he is the Queenmaker. You should bow at his feet!'

Crumwell pursed his lips; the hostility between the King and his wife had not yet mended, despite the baby they equally grieved.

'Crumwell may be the only man who knows how to fix such an issue,' Boleyn told Anne as he folded his arms over a grey doublet. Sweat trickled along his face beside his ears, even more in his pale grey hair. The hunch of Boleyn's old back appeared more pronounced than usual.

With one angry wave, Henry dismissed his men in the corner, the room closed to all but his wife, father-in-law and Crumwell. 'I like this not, Thomas,' Henry said, his voice warning of impending wrath.

'Your Majesty, please, tell me what you need.'

'I need my whore of a daughter not to be pregnant!' Boleyn spat back.

'I want my sister's secret marriage undone!' Anne added.

'I want Mary away from court!' Henry added. Henry never dealt with intimate issues well. War, no problem. Anger, it was a specialty. Anything to do with matters of the heart and Henry panicked and hid away. To have Mary Boleyn back, a woman he took to bed ten years ago now, caused Henry much embarrassment. Henry had got Mary pregnant before, both children hushed away from both their mother and father.

'I can do two of those things, Your Majesty,' Crumwell said. 'With no knowledge of Lady Mary's state, I could find only a remedy to the baby upon its birth. As for Mary away from court, that is easily arranged. I can send lawyers to check the marriage to whomever Lady Mary has taken to her bed.'

'She is Mrs. William Stafford now,' Anne snorted. 'Married to a common man! A man of no standing or fortune.'

'My daughter is sister to the Queen of England!' Boleyn cried. 'She is a jewel for us to remarry at our pleasure. We could form many an alliance with her hand, and she turns back to whoring, as if this is still the days of the French court!'

'Who is this man?' Crumwell asked.

'The second son of Sir Humphrey Stafford, former Sheriff of Northhamptonshire.' Boleyn spoke every word as if they were cursed.

'Sir Humphrey is the son of Sir Edward Stafford, executed for treason,' Crumwell added, the name coming from his memory. 'He has lands in Buckinghamshire, Warwickshire and Staffordshire. The attainder against the family has long been dropped, by your word, Your Majesty.'

'He is a Stafford!' Henry replied as he stormed towards Crumwell. 'Stafford!'

Crumwell wiped Henry's spittle from his face. 'A very distant relation to the Stafford dynasty, I believe,' Crumwell commented.

'Stafford is the strongest bloodline of all remaining Plantagenets!' Henry screamed and shoved Crumwell with two hands. Crumwell thumped against the wall and steadied himself. Henry moved no closer, praise God.

'Stafford was once one of His Majesty's gentleman-ushers,' Anne said across the room. 'My sister married to an usher? Surely she committed some misconduct for which they can charge her.'

'We are certain they married before God? Married according to the law?' Crumwell asked, his voice plain.

'Mary has signed paperwork from a priest who married them in London six months ago when Stafford was on leave from Calais, where he now again resides. Mary has been living in Warwickshire with her father-in-law, and not at Hever Castle as expected,' Boleyn explained.

'If Mary is with child…' Crumwell began.

'She is very pregnant!' Anne cried and threw her dainty hands in the air. 'She has a goodly belly and shall bear the child before Christmas!'

'I believe Sir Humphrey Stafford married Margaret Fogge, did he not? Sir John Fogge was the treasurer for your grandfather, King Edward, Your Majesty, and many other posts besides. Fogge was the daughter of a Woodville princess, making her a cousin to your mother, Your Majesty. William Stafford would be your third cousin.'

'And thus, a distant Stafford cousin to the Duke of Buckingham, whose head I had struck from his neck for treason!' Henry replied. It was unlike the King to mention such an act; he liked to remove himself from any treasonous dealings. 'And those Staffords have always supported Katherine.'

'I am the Queen now,' Anne said.

'Shut your mouth, you stupid girl,' Boleyn swore to his daughter.

'I will not!' Anne said as she swept from her seat. 'My sister has married a soldier based out of Calais, who only comes to England while delivering packages for Lady Lisle, who is married to another Plantagenet!'

'A love match,' Crumwell mentioned and looked to the King. 'Have we all not made missteps in the name of love?'

'I wish I had such luxury,' Boleyn spat back.

'Lord Wiltshire, please escort your daughter back to her rooms, for I believe she needs to rest,' Henry said through gritted teeth, though his eyes fixed upon Crumwell. He moved not an inch as Boleyn took Anne from the room, both equally hostile. Crumwell continued to hold himself against the wall, Henry before him, hands on hips.

'I care for none for this,' Henry sighed. 'None. I care not if my former mistress is with child.'

'But she is the Queen's sister. If Stafford married Mary after they discovered the baby…'

'Indeed, he did, came back from Calais and wed her at once,' Henry interrupted.

'Then Mary is guilty of misconduct. But to punish her for this, this whimsical act of love, shall do nothing but draw attention. Banish Mary from the court. Cut off the allowances her father pays. Mary's older children…'

'I refuse to acknowledge either of them,' Henry snapped.

'They are officially fathered by Mary's first husband,' Crumwell said calmly, hoping Henry would again quell his temper. 'Both children are taken from Mary's care and are wards of Queen Anne. Let Mary settle in the country with her poor husband. Forget her.'

'Can it be so simple?'

'Indeed. For there could be no great match for Mary Boleyn. She is known as the great whore of Europe. Had Mary been virtuous, then we would have gained her a fine marriage long ago. No, Your Majesty, they have lost nothing in this affair.'

'I have but one mistress,' Henry said and wiped sweat from his upper lip. 'All others are to disappear once I have used them.'

'Naturally, Your Majesty.' Henry was strangely secretive about his mistresses. The first ones years ago were never mentioned. They only remembered Elizabeth Blount because she bore the handsome young Henry Fitzroy. Mary Boleyn needed to disappear from memory.

The King moved away from Crumwell, and slunk into a soft chair, his temper gone. He gazed out the window for a long moment before speaking again. 'Have you had many mistresses, Thomas?'

'Enough, Your Majesty.'

Henry laughed and gestured for Crumwell to sit across from him, and Crumwell accepted with delight that Henry bore no anger. 'Be there such a thing as taking enough women to bed?'

'I prefer being married, Your Majesty, to a generous woman.'

'But your travels, France, the Low Countries... Italy! There are countries filled with mistresses-in-waiting.'

Crumwell smiled in remembrance. 'A long time ago.'

'How long has the Waif been your mistress?'

'Five years.'

'There is a good mistress,' Henry said and leaned forward in his seat. 'The first girl I bedded, a French girl, my sister Mary's French tutor. Jane was wonderful. I made her one of Katherine's ladies when I wed, as a favour. She became useful many times, especially when Katherine was with child. Jane became the Duke of Orleans' mistress for a while too. Another woman was a Stafford, like this soldier cousin of mine. Anne Stafford, she was the stepdaughter of my great uncle Jasper. She was wonderful and discreet. Elizabeth Carew, you know, Sir Nicholas' wife? She has been discreet and useful on lonely nights for twenty years now! But these Boleyn women, to bed two sisters, is not the excitement many men would believe. And some gossiped that I also slept with their mother, but no, I would never invite that trouble.'

'I can imagine,' Crumwell said and leaned his elbow on the arm of the chair, his chin in his palm. The days of needing to be formal with Henry were long past.

'Would my affinity with Mary be cause to annul from Anne?' Henry asked.

'Why would you do such a thing, Your Majesty? Anne is twice as beautiful as Mary, thrice as intelligent, and bore you a legitimate daughter.'

'And a dead son. God is angry.'

'I fear God is too often blamed for such things.'

'Do you mean to suggest the stillbirth is my fault?' Henry demanded.

'No, not at all...'

'You do! You mean to suggest the death of my son is because of me, not God's will? You say I should be content with Anne, so you must believe I am to blame!'

Henry leapt from his seat and before Crumwell could even rise, and swiped him across the face with a tight fist. Crumwell fell to the ground in an instant. 'Get rid of this Boleyn whore, or I shall set you the task of ridding me of Anne, whom all call Crumwell's queen, rather than mine! You are only hither because you made me a new wife, Thomas. You may have made Anne, but I made you, and I could kill you. I could reveal the secret of your perversion of that Waif creature. Imagine the punishment I could inflict on her! Every man at court could take their turn with your whore! If today does not end well, if that whore and her commoner baby do not disappear, you shall!'

Crumwell stumbled to his feet and left the King's rooms without a word. Outside the door stood Sir Francis Bryan, waiting for his master's call. 'You are well, Tom?' Bryan sympathised.

'Yes, Sir Francis,' Crumwell muttered, feeling blood on his lips, 'your brother-in-law, Nicholas Carew. Where is he?'

'In London, seeing to his work.'

'Your sister, the Lady Elizabeth Carew?'

Bryan smiled, a crooked smile thanks to the pressure placed upon his wrinkled cheek around his eye patch. 'The King needs a whore tonight?'

'A sturdy one for that temper. I know he is bedding Margaret Shelton, but tonight may take a more experienced woman.'

'Say no more, I shall send for my sister.'

'Henry will not want his wife,' Crumwell sighed.

'Your queen not as enticing?'

'Only Henry can marry for love, bed for love. Everyone else makes him furious.'

'Mary Boleyn is banished from court and sent back to her father-in-law?'

'Yes,' Crumwell replied as he wiped blood on his sleeve. 'Keeping one Boleyn girl in Henry's good graces shall be hard enough.'

Chapter 15 – September 1534
Whitehall Palace, London

One hundryd shaydes bytween a trouth and a lye

Nicòla gasped as she woke. She rested on her stomach in Crumwell's bed, the curtains drawn around them, the room dark. Crumwell too stirred from slumber. Nicòla paused for a moment; no one was to come to the private rooms. Crumwell's chambers had three large bedrooms; one was for visitors, such as Ralph or Richard, one for Nicòla, where she pretended to sleep, and Crumwell's room, which adjoined her own. But the knocking came not from Crumwell's door; it echoed through from Nicòla's room, the adjoining door open. No one ever came to knock on Nicòla's door. The night guards were under strict instructions never to enter the private hallway to the bedrooms, as it continued through a small hallway to the King's privy chamber.

'What shall I do?' Nicòla asked into the darkness.

Crumwell fumbled to light a candle in the darkness. The tender flame illuminated his weary face. 'Go into your room and call to who is there. Unlock nothing until you know of the man on the other side.'

Nicòla fought on her gown over her nightclothes and lit a candle off Crumwell's. She closed the adjoining door and tiptoed to her main door with an enormous bolt attached at Crumwell's instance. 'Who calls? Nicòla asked, instant fear in her tone. Was tonight the moment she got exposed as a woman and sent to the Tower? She struggled to smooth her curls with only one hand, to appear as masculine as possible, her nightgown having to do the work of her chest binding cloths, tossed on the floor.

'Master Frescobaldi?' came a gentle voice. ''Tis me, John. I bear a letter for you. The messenger said I had to wake you; the letter warns of grave urgency.' John was a guard posted on the doors to the Crumwell Chambers, a young orphan boy Crumwell had taken in not two months past.

'Who is the messenger?' Nicòla asked, afraid to answer the door.

'He says he is one of Crumwell's men at the port.'

Nicòla unbolted her door and held her candle before her to see young John in his new grey livery. 'Sorry, Master Frescobaldi,' he pleaded. 'I know I am not to enter the hallway. But the letter bears a ducal seal and comes with instructions that suggested all haste and no manners.'

'Tell the messenger to come at sunrise and I shall reward him for his haste. See he has a bed and meal.'

As soon as Nicòla put the heavy bolt back in its place, Crumwell came through the adjoining door from his room, wrapped warmly in his fur coat. 'Who shall I have whipped?'

'Twas only young John delivering an urgent message, Tomassito. A letter bearing Alessandro's seal. You cannot hide letters from Florence. I get them first.'

'I said sorry for that, Nicò. Forgive me for not wanting your husband to write to you.'

Nicòla sat down on a chair by the fire, which glowed red in the fireplace, small and almost dead. Sunrise could not be far away now. She fingered the red seal, hesitant to read the words. An urgent letter from the Medici Duke of Florence could not bring good news.

'Shall I read it?' Crumwell offered.

Nicòla shook her head as she broke the seal and unfolded the paper, Crumwell's candle held close for her tired eyes. 'He has named me as Nicòla, not Nicòletta, so he means to shield my identity against spies. We can feel grateful for so much.'

With humble reverence and due commendations to my brother-in-law Nicòla Frescobaldi

This letter comes to you in haste, a swift note to be sent on the first ship leaving port. More detail shall be sent presently. You will be saddened by the secret news that our most revered and humble ruler, Pope Clement, has died this day. No words can express the pain and turmoil of such ruin. My dear father, a man as precious to me as to you, has gone. Father wrote to the Emperor to say goodbye, and to me. His Holiness marked many treasures for you, but you need to come home to receive them in Florence.

Our alliance with the French is now broken. The Sacred College of Cardinals has already been summoned, but eleven cardinals shall be excused from voting, nine of them cardinals made by Medici popes. You know what this means for us. We have no allies in the conclave, and they shall follow the choices of King Francis and Cardinal Medici, who has no love for me.

My dear sister is in Paris, trapped to her French prince, alone and without her dowry paid. We must work together at this fragile time as your England turns heretic around you. Be not sour in our true faith, for one day you shall return to us in the Holy See. With the great loss in our hearts, the amount in which this death shall pain Nicòletta will be immense. Nicòletta shall need great guidance. Just two days ago, His Holiness asked his painter, a man named Michelangelo, to create a painting of The Last Judgement in the Sistine Chapel. He requested all the angels and virgins have rose-gold hair, like his Nicòletta.

Wait but a little, for more news will follow

Alessandro de' Medici, Duke of Florence
This day of our Lord Settembre 25

Without a word or glance, Nicòla handed the letter to Crumwell and shivered as he gently took it from her fingers. The Pope was dead. Cardinal Giulio de'Medici was dead. Twenty years had passed since he took Nicòla as a mistress, stole her virtue. Twenty years since her father discovered the secret and felt forever shamed. Twenty years since her father decided to dress her as a man and made her into his secretary, because as an educated and soiled woman, Nicòletta Frescobaldi had no value. Nicòla had played her part as a good son, a merchant, moneylender, banker, lawyer, so well she did not know who she was any longer. Once the lover of a cardinal, then secretary to her father, then the wife of her lover's son. The creature. Crumwell's Waif. All because a man in cardinal's robes fell in love with fourteen-year-old Nicòletta Frescobaldi of Florence.

Nicòla felt herself slipping from her seat but did not try to steady herself. She fell in a heap on the floor as the tears flowed. Her father was now long dead. The Pope was now dead. Freedom had at last come, and yet far too late for salvation. The first sob gave way to a wail of heartache. Crumwell fell to her side on the floor and held her tight against him to muffle the sound of her cries in the silence of the palace. Nicòla could not even be sure why she cried; for the man she loved in the past, the Pope he became, or for the old, weak man, surrounded by his favourites who took excessive favours and emptied the papal treasury. But while a Medici sat on the papal throne, Nicòla's secret was safe. All that was gone – but so was the guilt of leaving Italy for good.

'Father of love, hear my prayer. Help me know Your will and to do it with courage and faith,' Crumwell whispered in her ear as the wails turned back to sobbing. 'Accept my offering of myself, all my thoughts, words, deeds, and sufferings. May my life give You glory. Give me the strength to follow Your call, so that Your truth may live in my heart and bring peace to those I meet, for I believe in Your love.'

'Amen,' Nicòla sniffed. She rested her cheek against Crumwell's shoulder and closed her tear-soaked eyes, nestled against Crumwell. 'I know not what saddened me, for I never wished to return to the Holy See.'

'All things end, good or bad. Relief comes in many forms. Be in remembrance of one thing; that the Pope used you as a trifle, but I love you.'

'You must take this news to the King at once. The news of His Holiness' death has not been swift. They shall have summoned the College of Cardinals to the papal conclave before releasing the news. The Pope had been ill a long time, so plans for a new pope shall have begun before his death.'

'Who becomes Pope means nothing. Henry is Head of the Church in England. We rule this country; No Pope shall rule England again.'

'A new pope could be aligned with enemies of England, or the French king. They are powerful allies against England.'

'We can only see who shall be chosen as the new Pope.'

'If Alessandro has aligned with the French king, the decision seems clear to me.' Nicòla sat up and wiped the remaining tears from her cheeks. 'Cardinal Alessandro Farnese is Dean of the Sacred College and is considered a neutral cardinal. Farnese was made a cardinal because his sister was the Borgia Pope's mistress. There are twenty cardinals made by Clement who can vote, another thirteen made by his uncle, Pope Leo. The Medici connection is still in play. They educated Farnese in humanism at the instruction of Lorenzo de'Medici at the University in Spa, a similar education to mine. Medici sympathy on the papal throne is best for Florence. The Italian, French and Imperial factions should agree to Farnese taking power.'

'But the most important question is, will Farnese give you and Alessandro an annulment?'

Nicòla managed a gentle smile. 'That is your worry? You have turned a whole country from the Catholic Church, making powerful enemies, yet you wonder of my annulment?'

'Please do not leave for Florence. Alessandro would never let you leave again.'

'I care nothing for what treasures the Pope's death has bestowed upon me,' Nicòla sniffed. 'I shall never leave you.'

~~~

Nicòla stood in silence in the King's presence chamber as Crumwell went ahead into the privy chamber to tell the King of the Pope's death. She heard the King's cry of joy through the thick palace wall. Nicòla prayed for home, for the Pope's soul, as much as she could, but the feeling of loss had already turned to relief. After only a few minutes, the door to the privy chamber opened and Crumwell beckoned Nicòla inside to the King. The privy chamber appeared oddly dim in the early morning light, the sun not yet shining through Henry's windows. Only a candle set upon his writing desk stirred, the opulent room of golds and greens dull and subdued. Henry stood still in his bedclothes, feet wide apart, his hands clasped together, almost as if ready to pray. Both men looked in eagerness to Nicòla as she bowed.

'Well, Waif, the man whom you have been reporting on has died,' Henry said. 'As a mark of respect, I shall not try to be so happy about Clement's death in your presence. I am but a humble gentleman.'

Nicòla worked hard not to move her expression, lest show her contempt for the King's words. She said nothing, though her eyes shifted towards Crumwell for a moment.

'I suppose all shall struggle in panic to appoint themselves the new Bishop of Rome,' Henry continued.

'The College of Cardinals is ready to meet in the papal conclave.'

'Corrupt bastards all bribing their way to the top,' Henry commented.

'Things are done fervently in Italy, Your Majesty.' Nicòla could barely raise her voice to even speak, so disheartened and broken by the news. After all those years of being the favourite of the Pope, to think he was not in the Apostolic Palace in Rome, at his desk, having a servant pour wax to set his seal on all his letters, seemed too much to imagine. London truly was home now, for there was nowhere left to turn.

'We need none of Rome, Your Majesty,' Crumwell said with all confidence. 'You shall be the Head of the Church in England, far from Rome's corruption. You shall be the Supreme Ruler of England in all matters. Your marriage to Anne is the only legitimate match you have ever made.'

'Still, our enemies would be much soothed if this new Bishop of Rome would rule my marriage to Katherine invalid.'

Nicòla sighed out loud and understood her misstep too late. Perchance the lack of sleep had affected her courtesy. Henry looked at her in surprise, his red eyebrows raised in suspicion. 'Yes, Waif, do you have any thoughts to share?'

'I cannot speak on behalf of the Catholic Church, Your Majesty.'

'Yet that is the reason I allow you in my court beside my Chief Minister, in the form which you are permitted to live.'

'Pope Clement prayed long and hard over your marriage, Your Majesty. He truly cared for making the right decision. He ruled in favour of Katherine and the validity of your marriage without a doubt. A new pope would care not for an annulment. That is why Master Crumwella broke your country away from the Catholic faith. The opinion of Rome does not matter. Master Crumwella has saved you from the opinions of Rome. A new pope will no doubt seek to excommunicate you from the Catholic faith as a show of strength against Protestants. You must be ready to fight with your conviction that your new Church of England is the right decision.'

'And is it the right decision?' Henry asked.

'Of course, Your Majesty, and a new pope may wish to form an alliance with you and leave all the hate in the past. The break allowed you to marry freely and gain a legitimate heir by your wife,' Crumwell commented.

'Only Anne has given me no son,' Henry sighed. 'Yet I am most pleased to hear of Clement's death. How did he die? It is usually poison with you Italians, is it not?'

'Rumours mix, Your Majesty, yet the full news on the death shall arrive from Italy presently,' Crumwell explained.

'Thank you for bringing me this news,' Henry said to Crumwell and placed a gentle hand on his shoulder. Not weeks ago, Henry had punched Crumwell so hard his bottom lip split open. 'To reward you, Thomas, I shall name you Master of the Rolls. This comes with the Rolls House hither in London. You shall be the first secular Master of the Rolls, the highest judicial position in the land. The Rolls House on Chancery Lane is a grand and ancient manor. All the records of the Court of Chancery shall be in your hands, worked by your household on all matters of equity, and shall have greater power than common law courts. The private cases of the country shall come to you at the Rolls House. You may leave us, as I am to tell my wife of the good news about the Pope's demise.'

Crumwell and Nicòla exited the privy chamber, Crumwell's golden eyes in a frown as he made calculations. Nicòla took out her notebook as he would surely soon give orders.

'How lucrative is the post of Master of the Rolls?' she asked as they left the presence chamber, their long coats skimming the stone floor.

'The post outshines most, just in bribes alone,' Crumwell said, his voice low despite the palace still quiet early in the morning. 'The Chancery manor is big enough for us to set up our own court.'

'Have we not done that at Austin Friars?'

'We can move much of our work to the Rolls House; all government work can be done from there, Ralph can run it, and let Thomas Avery run Austin Friars. Richard can work from Austin Friars on royal court matters and be on the Privy Council. The number of courtiers, of patrons and envoys sent to us will be like a swarming of bees searching for a hive. This manor shall prove most useful, and is only one mile from Whitehall, and the same again to Austin Friars.'

'Not that it is safe for us to walk that far in public any longer,' Nicòla mumbled.

'It shall ease the pressure upon our other offices.'

The pair turned into a hallway to find Imperial Ambassador Chapuys there, dressed in his usual drab grey furs, Crumwell and Nicòla both stunning in their black velvet and fur sewn in silver thread. Chapuys gave the smallest nod of his head in acknowledgement, and Nicòla almost heard him whine in pain at having to be civil.

Chapuys looked right at Nicòla, ignoring Crumwell entirely. 'Is it true?' he asked, his French accent soaked in a weak tone.

'His Holiness passed away two days after writing a goodbye letter to Emperor Charles. Has your master not written to you? The Pope has been with God for weeks now.'

'Rumours told me of a letter sent to you, Mr. Frescobaldi, sealed by the ducal arms of Florence. I know His Holiness has been sick for some time… do we know the cause? Was he murdered? Poisoned?'

'I know not,' Nicòla sighed. 'Pope Clement had three tasters for this food and wine. But he travelled constantly and has been complaining of ill pains for years. I have known His Holiness, God rest his soul, to be gravely ill for a year now, Ambassador Chapuys. This comes as no surprise, I am certain.'

'I shall write to my master at once,' Chapuys replied. 'They shall already have summoned the cardinals to the papal conclave.'

'Indeed, Ambassador,' Nicòla said, and stood tall. It felt so nice to have the upper hand over an adversary. Crumwell probably felt this way daily.

'After eleven years of the Medici Pope, and his uncle a pope for years before him, the Medici family shall still have much control over the papacy. The Medici popes created almost all the cardinals.'

'Most true, Ambassador Chapuys,' Nicòla said. 'While there may be no more Medici men on the throne of God, the influence shall reign for some time.'

'Any idea of who shall be the next pope, as you are… the… brother-in-law of a powerful Medici duke?' Chapuys asked and looked Nicòla up and down.

'My opinion would be Cardinal Alessandro Farnese, Dean of the Cardinals' College and the Duke of Parma. Cardinal Farnese is a Medici man, educated in Pisa, has five children and healthy grandsons. He would do well to preserve the Catholic faith. Your master, Emperor Charles, has had too much influence over papal matters. I sense that shall now end.'

'A new pope could mean war.'

'If a pope wants war, he can have war,' Crumwell interrupted. 'As can your Emperor. For you threaten us, you sneak about our palaces and cause nothing but dissension. We rule, Chapuys. Remember well.'

Nicòla and Crumwell swept past Chapuys back towards their chambers. Nicòla knew it would serve well to turn her grief into a wish to turn England from Rome forever, just as Crumwell wished.

Chapter 16 – January 1535
Greenwich Palace, downstream London

One spoils everythyng with their lyes

King Henry may have been at the head table of the dining hall, but Crumwell felt like a king. After lavish meals, processions and parties for the epiphany only weeks ago, yet another opulent evening could have felt wasteful. Though not when it came to Crumwell, who was sitting like a king on this throne, seated not far from the King and Queen themselves. By Christmas, the final parts of the Act of Supremacy and Act of Succession had completed their journey through parliament, Crumwell's new treason laws were in place, restricting a man's right to speak ill of the King. Sir Thomas More and Bishop John Fisher were still locked in the Tower. Everyone bowed to Crumwell.

Especially now. For today, on the twenty-first day of January, the King had bestowed a new honour on his Chief Minister and Chief Secretary. Henry awarded Crumwell the title of Vicegerent, or Vicar-general. Crumwell now had enough power over the churches in England to keep them or shut them down. Every new law Crumwell crafted seemed just to oppose any person who defied the King's new marriage. Crumwell had no political superior.

Across the table where Crumwell leaned back in his seat, his arms crossed over his chest, appeared Queen Anne's father and brother. While the elder Boleyn, Earl of Wiltshire served as Lord Privy Seal, Anne's brother George, Lord Rochford, did little, which was why Crumwell intended to send him abroad on dull diplomat missions, if only to get the slippery Boleyn out of the way.

'My Earl of Wiltshire,' Crumwell said as the elder Boleyn sat down, and flicked his eyes to his son. 'And my Lord Rochford.'

'Chief Secretary Crumwell,' Wiltshire said with a crooked smile. 'You have won so many titles at court I fear I no longer know how to address you.'

'Vicar-general Crumwell shall suit me,' Crumwell laughed in a gentle tone. The wine of the evening had gone to his weary head. The dining hall wore a dewy glow, so warm during the dead of an English winter.

'I am certain we can make you a lord before long,' Rochford said as he considered his wine.

'You believe none the rumours of your wife being in love with me, do you, George?' Crumwell asked with a snort of laughter.

'That woman?' Rochford laughed. 'No, for the court is filled with beauties and there is much fun to be had.'

Crumwell glanced up to where Nicòla positioned herself, her back to the wall as she waited like a patient servant to her master. It was Rochford's own wife, the Lady Jane, who whispered into Nicòla's ear, the conversation locked away from the party. The shine from Nicòla's new necklace, a huge jewel-laden cross on a gold chain, shined in the candlelight and gave Crumwell an angry shiver. A gift sent from Florence, a trinket owned by the dead Pope now hung around Nicòla's neck. Yes, the cross was beautiful, gold and covered in diamonds, yet it hung around Nicòla's neck, leaned against her deep red doublet, and reminded Crumwell of all Nicòla had done in Italy.

Rochford followed Crumwell's gaze to see his wife speaking with Nicòla. 'My wife is no doubt filling your Waif with gossip,' he said and sipped his wine. 'Gossip about my sister.'

'What news is there of Her Majesty?'

'My daughter is with child,' Wiltshire said with his crooked grin at full stretch.

'God's blood!' Crumwell sat forward and raised his glass. 'To the health of the Boleyn queen!'

The three men raised their glasses together, and Crumwell glanced up again for a moment; many people hovered close by, eager to have a word in his ear. None could speak with him; they had to be called, for they could not touch Crumwell now. He was above all others.

But Crumwell's old friend Thomas Audley could join. He slowly came to the table and Crumwell eagerly gestured for him to sit down. 'Lord Chancellor,' Crumwell said with a smile and rested his hand upon Audley's fat shoulder. 'Come and join in my revelry.'

'Many congratulations on your appointment, Thomas,' Audley said as the Boleyns nodded a welcome hello. 'I am certain you have already considered your first task in becoming the Vicegerent.'

'I shall create the Valor Ecclesiasticus, England's largest survey of the land and its value. The King has privately awarded me the task of crossing all of England and Wales to assess both the value and spiritual morality of every monastic house. The eight hundred or so monasteries shall be very closely checked. I shall have the profit of their lands, the very buildings, and all their relics and false idols. Every man and woman in England shall be assessed, and either left to their work under my watchful eye or destroyed.'

'Destroyed how?' Audley asked.

'I shall choose.'

'No one shall call my daughter a whore again,' Wiltshire said, and raised his glass to Crumwell. 'To the Church created to make Anne a queen shall hold this country.'

'And shall change the country throughout history, my Lord,' Crumwell replied. 'Gone are the days of monasteries and churches sending bribes to maintain their debauched lives. I shall send my most loyal men across the land. I may even attend a few myself.'

'And where shall all these riches go?' Audley asked.

'To any person I wish to receive the bounty. I follow the King's orders, and as the ruler of this country, the money is his, at his discretion.'

'There are things you can do to rise even higher in the Queen's reverence,' Wiltshire mumbled and looked over to his daughter at her husband's side. 'Many speak ill of Anne and it hurts her. Privately, her anger against the Dowager Princess Katherine and the bastard Mary vex Anne greatly. It would do well for those women to no longer be upon this Earth.'

'That may soothe Queen Anne, but we cannot find any reason to harm either Katherine or Mary,' Crumwell sighed. In truth, he would never harm either of them, although they would never swear the Oath. They were innocents in Henry's quest to rule both his earthly and spiritual realms.

'Where be Archbishop Cranmer on this evening?' Audley asked and took another drink.

'Called away to an important meeting. Cranmer is a good friend and ally and shall control the Protestant Reformation with faith, vigour, calmness and honesty.'

Across the room over the heads of the Boleyns, Crumwell noticed Nicòla staring back at him. Her stern look told him to move at once. 'You must excuse me, gentlemen, for even at my celebration I must attend to the kingdom.'

Nicòla pulled Crumwell into a dark corner, against a heavy red curtain which shielded them from the cold glass. 'I have just received word from Stepney, where Cranmer is with his wife and son.'

'Has Margarete delivered of their new child?' Crumwell asked. They continued to move Margarete around manors at intervals, so no one knew Cranmer had a wife, but surely the secret of the German accent of Margarete would one day be noticed in Crumwell's properties.

'Messengers brought a note directly from Cranmer. Margarete struggled a whole day and night with the birth. She delivered of a daughter without life.'

'Oh, Thomas,' Crumwell sighed for his great friend, who should have been at court tonight to celebrate their new power. Instead, he would baptise his deceased daughter in her mother's weary and heartbroken arms.

'The child was to be named after the Queen herself, had she not been stillborn. And less than six months since Anne's own stillbirth.'

'Yet our Queen is with child again,' Crumwell said. 'At least some good news comes tonight.'

'I do not wish to ruin the night with this sad news from Cranmer. I only request we bring Margarete and baby Thomas back to Austin Friars to be close to Cranmer. He shall be back at Lambeth Palace to resume duties within days and that would be cruel to them both.'

'I shall have Margarete Cranmer brought directly to Lambeth Palace. The Archbishop's palace is so large that having a woman, niece to a foreign friend of Cranmer's at Lambeth shall not seem strange. People can think Cranmer is caring for a friend while she is in London. That can give Thomas and Margarete some time to heal.'

'You are a good man, even if you are rising in enough favour to destroy the fabric which holds together the towns of England,' Nicòla smiled.

'Those filthy monasteries are going to get pulled apart. The Catholic Church rules us no longer. I do God's work. I do the King's work.'

'The King's work is to plant a seed in Anne,' Nicòla replied with a sly smile. 'Sorry to sour your party but I felt you ought to know of Cranmer's misfortune at once. I shall send a barge to collect the Cranmer family back as soon as Margarete can travel. These people are our family.'

'You are permitted to enjoy yourself tonight.'

'Tomassito, you sat down to a twenty-course meal. It has taken five hours to complete. We servants have stood in the corner for all that time and I am tired! My day began eighteen hours ago and my back hurts!'

'One day, you shall sit beside me at all events, Nicò, I swear it. I wish I could kiss you at this moment.'

'Hush, for you have indulged in much cheer and must quieten your tone!'

'No, I must leave this party and take you back to my rooms. For I have been offered several women, some noble, some whores, to stretch the enjoyment of my new appointment. Fools; they know not I have the most precious jewel of all in my bed.'

Nicòla rolled her green eyes but her smile continued to twinkle. 'With permission, Master Crumwella, I shall retire to your apartments and ready the rooms for your arrival after the evening is done.'

'Thank you, kind secretary,' Crumwell said and gave a smug grin. He could wait not to leave the event and have her. Crumwell waited until Nicòla disappeared before he presented himself before the table of Henry and Anne. Henry leaned over to Anne, his cheek almost pressed against her shoulder, wine and warmth wearing down Henry's usual public face. Only when he saw Crumwell bow before him did Henry sit up straight.

'The man of the hour,' Henry said and raised his glass. 'I trust all is well in my kingdom, Thomas.'

'Indeed, Your Majesty. Lord Wiltshire tells me that Her Majesty is in a delicate condition of great cheer.'

'England deserves a great cheer,' Anne said with a smile. Pretty smiles seldom graced Anne's face since the death of her son last summer. But that had passed, for another baby would grace the royal nursery.

Crumwell bowed again. 'I shall retire, Your Majesties, as tomorrow I shall begin my work under my new title and continue my work on all my other posts.'

'We shall have to ennoble you soon enough, Cremwell,' Anne said as she took Henry's hand. 'Sometimes I fear you have more power than Henry, yet you are unliked in England, so perchance you understand many of my fears.'

'I am only hither to serve, Your Majesty.'

'From tomorrow, you shall start serving me by pulling down monasteries and punishing those who upset my queen,' Henry said, his cheery smile gone.

'Worry not, all will change, Your Majesty, as we banish fake relics and immoral sin.'

'I hope so, Thomas, I hope so. I have raised you high, and it is time I had total control. There be nowhere for traitors to hide in Crumwell's England, I hope.'

'Nowhere, Your Majesty, I will stake my life upon it.'

Chapter 17 – February 1535
Whitehall Palace, London

Better to be coomforted with a lye than hyrt wyth the trouth

'Be it true?' Thomas Wyatt asked under his breath.

'Be what true?' Henry Norris replied. The pair sat together with Nicòla, in the weak winter sunlight which trickled through a large window into the Queen's apartments. When Nicòla came into Anne's rooms, it instantly reminded her that they were once the main rooms of York Place, Cardinal Wolsey's palace, these rooms Wolsey's private offices. Now the rooms were opened and light, Anne sitting on a throne of a chair, on a pedestal, higher than the other seats so she looked down on everyone. A queen above everyone in every respect.

'The lady.' Wyatt gestured with his head at Lady Margaret Shelton. The pretty cousin of the Queen, Margaret had dark hair always pulled back, her round face sweet with an affectionate smile for Norris.

'If, and I say, if, I wish to marry again, I shall take my time in asking for Lady Margaret's hand,' Norris said with a sniff. Wyatt was only teasing; he knew Norris had no intention of marrying Lady Margaret. Norris was the head gentleman of the privy chamber to the King, keeper of the privy purse; Norris was the one who snuck Henry's mistress into his rooms, out of sight of Anne's spies. Lady Margaret had been the bed-mate of King Henry for a year now, luckily still not pregnant. The notion that Norris wished to remarry was a lie for when he was spotted with Lady Margaret. Norris could sit in the Queen's room daily, playing spy for the King, and know when to take the mistress to the monarch.

'If you were to marry,' Nicòla said to Norris, 'I am certain the King would reward you handsomely.'

119

Wyatt laughed under his breath. The King always married his mistresses off when he got bored, with a cash payment to the husband who wedded the soiled goods. And Lady Margaret's time was almost complete.

'I have larger issues, for my brother, John, who is usually an usher in Henry's outer chamber, is much worse in his illness,' Norris replied.

'I am sorry to hear it,' Wyatt said and threw a look to Nicòla; no more teasing for the day.

Nicòla sighed. 'I do wish I could return to my work,' she muttered, as she watched Lady Margery Horsman and Lady Margaret Douglas playing with a dog which Anne kept in her rooms. 'I know not how courtiers bear sitting about for so many hours a day just to pay favour to the Queen.'

'I would not wish to be attendant to Secretary Crumwell,' Norris replied. 'For that task appears utterly thankless.'

'It has its advantages,' Nicòla replied and looked out the window to the Thames behind her. Just the thought of being on the water created nausea.

A sharp cry brought Nicòla's attention back to the room. Anne, who had gone to sit by a window in the dark corner where she could rest her swollen feet, cried like a wounded child as she held her stomach. At once, everyone in the room was on their feet; the pregnant Queen in pain brought abject fear in all hearts. Lady Jane Seymour was at Anne's side in a heartbeat.

'Tell me what you need,' Jane said as she tried to help Anne to her feet.

'I want my baby,' was all Anne could wail in reply.

'Fetch Dr. Butts,' Nicòla said to Wyatt, and he left without a second look. 'Norris, tell the King at once that Anne is ill.'

'No,' Anne pleaded. 'Henry will divorce me if I lose another baby.' Tears rolled down Anne's ever-paler face. She clutched her stomach, her ladies all desperate to hold their Queen. But even from a distance, Nicòla could see the blood appearing on Anne's silver gown. The moment Anne saw it too, she cried even louder. This was no place for a man, but Nicòla forgot all about being safe in her guise, and only thought of the moment she bled out her own precious son.

Nicòla helped Anne through the doorway to her bedroom, while Nicòla and the women laid Anne on the soft sheets. She rolled onto her side, her hands cupping between her legs, her palms instantly covered in blood.

'If my son dies, so shall I,' Anne wept, her black eyes shut tight. The other ladies all stepped back in fear of what was happening. Nicòla glanced over at them, all inching closer to the doorway, but refused to do the same.

Nicòla knelt beside the bed, her face close to the Queen's. 'Your Majesty, I shall do anything you command.'

'Tell no truths to Henry,' Anne whimpered. 'Henry cannot know the cause.'

Nicòla glanced to the women in the doorway, all huddled together in a mass of worry and damask gowns. Only a few were married; none had children. They had experienced none of the fate of their Queen.

'Tell me, what do you feel in your hands?' Nicòla asked quietly. She could not dare look under Anne's clothes, for Nicòla was a "man," and could never presume to act in such a way.

'I want Georgie,' Anne wailed as another pain seared through her stomach.

'Lady Jane, fetch your husband and your father-in-law at once. Lord Rochford and Lord Wiltshire are entertaining in the King's rooms today.'

'Please, help my baby,' Anne cried out loud. She writhed on the bed as she rolled onto her back, which showed the full horror of the blood on her dress. Her ladies all gasped in fright, which made Anne opened her eyes in panic. She brought her hands to her face, speechless by the blood before her.

'Everyone out!' Nicòla cried as she jumped to her feet. She could rely on none of these women. 'Go and wait for the Boleyns and the doctor. No one leaves the Queen's rooms, lest you suffer the anger of my master!'

The moment the door shut, Nicòla climbed onto the bed and Anne sat up, sweat running from her dark hair, now untying itself from delicate pins. 'The pain has paused but a moment,' Anne whimpered.

'I am a man in clothing only,' Nicòla said. 'Do you trust me?'

Anne nodded, clutching a handful of her silver silk, blood smearing its shiny fabric. Nicòla carefully pulled Anne's dress higher and higher. Her knees upwards were stained with blood, pooling and smudging on her delicate skin. Nicòla did not have to take all of Anne's dignity, for she did not need to pull at the dress right up to see what was happening. A lump covered in blood sat among the fabric. A baby? Nicòla could not be certain. Anne would only be two months gone; most women knew nothing of their child now. Nicòla knew little of other women's monthly courses. Were all women the same? Living as a man, the conversation would never arise.

'Your Majesty, do you often get pain with your courses?' Nicòla asked and looked to Anne's face rather than the smears of blood. Anne nodded a weak gesture. Nicòla pulled Anne's dress down a little and laid the Queen onto her back.

'My courses are a constant blight upon me,' Anne sniffed, tears still rolling freely.

'How many courses have you missed?'

'I missed this month, and last month.'

'Could it be that you are not with child, but simply missed a course by accident, only to suffer double now?'

Anne's weeping eyes shot straight to Nicòla. 'Could it be true?'

Nicòla shrugged, for the only baby she ever lost was almost fully grown. Monthly courses were not dinner conversation in the Crumwell Chambers. 'Perchance only God knows of such things.'

'I was not with child, I was wrong and got a terrible course,' Anne said. She seemed much better at once. With the lump out and all the accompanying blood, the pain appeared to have lessened. Anne still held her stomach, sweat on her pale brow, but at least the screaming stopped.

The bedroom door banged open and there stood Thomas and George Boleyn. George ran to the bedside at once, not even seeing Nicòla sitting at the feet of the Queen. Thomas Boleyn strode in with a heavy slam of the door. 'We have sent for the doctor,' he announced. 'What have you done to the child, girl?'

'Father,' Anne wept as George helped his sister to sit. 'Frescobaldi says perchance I was not with child at all, it is but women's courses. God has decided to not give me a baby.' Anne stopped as another pain came on, her frown burrowed, but she panted rather than cried out this time.

Boleyn's eyes shot to Nicòla. 'What would you know of this? Why would you, a creature to Crumwell, even dare to be hither?'

'Nicòla helped me, Father,' Anne said as she used a bloody hand to wipe a tear from her lips. 'You know Nicòla's truth.'

Boleyn paused; he long knew the truth about Nicòla, and cared not, as he cared for no one about him other than his own family. ''Tis a fine plan to tell the King of a simple problem with women's courses,' Boleyn muttered. 'But you must leave us,' he commanded Nicòla. 'Tell everyone who shall listen – Anne did not lose another child. There was no baby. If Henry hears this, he is less likely to abandon his wife. Get Crumwell to spread this news.'

Anne broke into fresh tears and George held her close, rocking his sister with great care. Nicòla had no choice but to leave Anne with her family, who cared more for her womb than of her welfare. Nicòla charged past the ladies-in-waiting, not even troubling with eye contact, just as Dr. William Butts entered the Queen's rooms. Nicòla only gestured to show the doctor the way and left the rooms without a whisper. With luck, Dr. Butts would reach the same conclusion that Anne had never been pregnant, or at least the Boleyns could persuade him. Henry would replace Anne if she lost another child, Anne thought so herself. But they would not consider a misunderstanding of her condition such an issue, Henry could simply slip back into Anne's bed again rather than having a mistress shoved into his.

Nicòla spoke to no one until she entered the Crumwell Chambers. With nothing more than nods of acknowledgement to the guards and clerks, Nicòla charged into Crumwell's private office where he sat, surrounded by half a dozen clerks, all receiving instructions, the mail chest open on Nicòla's desk.

'Uscire!' Nicòla ordered everyone out, her voice as deep and loud as she could muster. The sound of her voice snapped Crumwell's head up from his papers in a moment. With a double click of his fingers, he dismissed all the young men, who filed out without a word or look. Nicòla slammed the doors on everyone the moment the final footstep left the office.

'Poor tidings, Tomassito.'

Crumwell held his hands upwards towards her in search of news. 'Tell me and we shall fix all.'

'Not this,' Nicòla sat down across the desk from her master. 'Anne has lost the baby.'

'God in heaven,' Crumwell groaned and placed his face in his hands. Nicòla watched his greying dark curls bounce a little as he shook his head in despair. 'How could this happen once more?' he mumbled through his fingers.

'All is not lost.'

Crumwell looked up again with a stern brow. 'How?'

'Anne permitted me to look up her skirts.' Nicòla paused Crumwell's eyebrows raised so high they almost disappeared into his hair. ''Tis but a long tale. But the Queen was in pain, bleeding, and no one dared to touch her anointed body. Anne allowed me to check the problem. There was blood, there was pain and some… how you say… coaguli?'

'Clots,' Crumwell replied. 'A clot of blood. Did you see this ill-fortuned mess?'

'I did see and it did not look like the presence of a child, with my limited knowledge of the whole process.'

Crumwell nodded slowly and took a deep breath. A difficult matter for any man, no matter his knowledge. 'So, Anne was pregnant, but is no longer?'

'Anne admitted to having difficulty in this womanly trouble, so God may not have given her a child, not a whole healthy one.'

'I am glad Anne had you there, and not me. Has Henry been sent for?'

'Yes, Norris was present, and he sent for the King. Wyatt got Dr. Butts to the Queen's rooms and Lady Jane got the Boleyns. They shall manage the truth before they tell the King of the loss.'

'Supposed loss.'

'Anne seemed amiable to the notion that we tell the King it was a poor calculation of dates, not a miscarriage.'

'I too am amiable to that cause. Henry shall be much placated by this news.'

'Henry would not forsake Anne, would he? For their love is true, is deep. Henry changed a nation for Anne's love.'

'I am marked by wrinkles over the change,' Crumwell shrugged. 'But you know Henry's temper. But no, I truly believe he shall tarry with Anne, despite matters such as this. But he has not yet fully recovered from the loss of last year's son, so this shall not come as good tidings. We must set to distract Henry as much as we can, so our Queen remains safe in her position. And pregnant once more in great haste.'

'Anne shall need time, a few weeks at least before we push her into the marital bed,' Nicòla warned.

'Henry shall know of this by now.'

'I shall set out to find our King at once and try to limit this damage. The Boleyns are present and that is of great relief.'

'What if Katherine was right?' Nicòla pondered. 'What if God truly does not believe in the marriage of Henry and Anne?'

'Tis the people who must agree on the marriage. Or they shall set all alight, starting with us. Henry's anger is the only consideration for us now.'

Nicòla sighed and rested her elbow on the desk, her eyes resting in her palm. 'Henry is not the only consideration, Tomassito.'

'What else? Do you mean Anne?'

'No, me. I have considerations.'

'What?' Crumwell's tone changed in an instant.

Nicòla looked up to see a worried expression. 'Queen Anne has been wondering of a child of late. She is a mother, she knows the signs. But perchance she was wrong. Perchance there was simply something within her causing illness and it played upon her desperation.'

'Tis possible.'

'And have I got the same illness? I have not suffered from my courses for three months. I must conceal my courses, so I never forget them, due to…' Nicòla made a waving gesture at her body, not wishing to discuss this with Crumwell.

'You have missed three courses and said nothing?' Crumwell squeaked.

'Queen Anne was too hasty in speaking up, and now she is paying for it with humiliation and despair.'

'Are you with child?' Crumwell whispered.

'I fear it is possible.'

'There shall be no despair for you!' Crumwell said as he leapt from his chair. He rounded his desk and knelt before Nicòla still in her seat. 'There shall be no humiliation for you.'

'But I am afraid, Tomassito.'

Crumwell took Nicòla's hands in his; he was almost fifty and the signs of a hard life showed against Nicòla's much darker but younger skin. 'We know not why God does such things.'

'God was angry at us when we handed religious power to Henry instead of the Pope. We placed God's power in Henry's hands, and we paid for it, our tiny son ripped from my body, gone to God before even being baptised. We now seek to take more power away from the Catholic Church. What shall God do this time?'

'Perchance God has taken enough, for he has denied Henry a son yet again.'

'I am too old to bear a child, already I am five and thirty years! It shall not be a royal baby this summer, but another Crumwell baby. How shall we hide such?'

'The court shall go on progress without me,' Crumwell said. 'We shall create an excuse. All shall be gone from London, and Austin Friars can be home to the child, with Jane and Gregory in attendance.'

'What if I am wrong, like the Queen?'

'What if you are right?' Crumwell grinned. 'You are my wife, if by God if not by law, Nicò. I rule this country, so I can make certain you have this child safely.'

'After what I just witnessed, I am so frightened,' Nicòla burst into silent tears. 'My last birth was so horrific. Jane's birth saw me almost alone in Rome. I have seen Anne on the bed today, perchance expelling a tiny life which had no chance to live because we constantly anger God…'

'God will not stop us,' Crumwell said. 'You shall bear another child by me. You shall keep your secret, maintain your life in this chamber. I swear it, Nicò. We are unbeatable now.'

Chapter 18 – March 1535
Whitehall Palace, London

Lyes told with confydance are better than weake trouths

Crumwell gently brought his hand to his chin, touching it enough to confirm the immense pain in the writhing lump of agony. The wide gash in his lip had abated some, enough he could now talk without sounding full of wine. His whole jaw ached with anger, with sadness and resentment. He had already been on the ground, flat on his back when the blow came. King Henry had already thrown him against a wall, punched his nose, pushed him to the carpets and kicked him. Henry had reached for the silver candlestick upon his desk as Crumwell rolled himself over in pain and confusion. The thump with the candlestick to Crumwell's jaw was the final blow. All because he was the one to speak with the King after he learned Queen Anne was not pregnant. Henry's devastation was obvious, not just in his beating of Crumwell in the privy chamber, but to all, and had abated none in recent weeks. There had never been a better time to leave the court for a week.

Crumwell put his hand back on the table and looked up. The eight people around the table all looked back at him, Nicòla at the end, ready to write everything said and organised. Her face spoke of worry, no doubt because he was touching his injured face once more. No one knew what had happened, but gossip spread all the same.

'The Valor Ecclesiasticus will be one of the greatest works done under the reign of our king,' Crumwell began. He felt as if he said that about every paper he drafted for Henry over the last five years. But this rang true, not just for the King's love life, but for every English subject. 'This church valuation shall visit every single monastery, abbey, cathedral and the local church. It shall inspect every clergyman, every parish priest, monk, friar, nun, every head of any monasteries, colleges, hospitals and other institutions under church auspices. These men shall be commanded to give sworn testimony to you, the local commissioners, about their income, their lands and buildings owned, and all revenues they receive from any other source. Every donation, every single animal grazing on their land, every so-called "relic" they claim to have will get inspected, catalogued and assessed for its truth and merit. Every document and account book must be read and understood. This work is to be completed before the end of May, and you are to choose your own men who shall help you in this task. The speed at which this must be done is unlike any study which has been conducted in this country. You are to summon all local gentry, mayors, magistrates, bishops, sheriffs, any person of good standing in any county to get this done. There are no excuses, there shall be no delays.'

While the men around the table knew the task ahead, Crumwell could see each of them nervous about the task, not just for the sheer volume of work, but for the hatred and suspicions which would fall upon them. Thomas Crumwell was not a popular man, for he had changed the laws in parliament, and now all religious houses had to pay ten percent tax on everything they owned and earned, after centuries of living tax-free and getting fat off profits. But no more. Henry needed to be abated; Crumwell needed to reform his country and make a fortune.

'We are to begin this task without any guidance from our Archbishop of Canterbury, Thomas Cranmer. I shall be the sole head of this endeavour.'

Heads nodded about the table. While news spread of Cranmer's recent illness, the truth was that Cranmer's secret young son, named for his father, had recently died, plunging the Cranmer couple into fresh grief, right after Margarete's stillbirth.

'How exact must we be?' asked Ralph, who sat next to Crumwell at the table.

'Thank you, Ralph,' Crumwell replied, 'for asking the difficult question. I want you to be broadly precise. They will expect you to estimate low values, you shall be bribed to keep secrets of priests and their dealings. I care not for this; for what bribes they offer you, you are free to keep. But we shall keep these volumes in Henry's private records, and in my own, so accuracy is important. Consider each holding wisely, for this is your only chance to estimate the King's wealth. Henry is the leader of the Church now, and we must do our best. The monasteries not doing well shall be closed immediately. The larger monasteries will be destroyed based on your calculations. If something needs closing, then estimate a low value, for this shall make work much faster.'

Heads nodded all around the table. These men knew their tasks; they knew the risks, and they all swore their alliance to Crumwell. He paused as Nicòla rose from her seat and rounded the table to present more papers needed. As she approached, Crumwell glanced to her stomach, bound tightly under her black doublet; their third baby was not due until the summer, but he still worried for signs of her condition. Crumwell needed Nicòla healthy and available for work, but he would not risk their child again, as he had before while making a queen out of Anne Boleyn.

Crumwell took the list of names from Nicòla's dark hand. 'I am trusting you can fulfil your roles,' he said as Nicòla returned to her seat. 'John ap Rice and Thomas Legh, you are both fine diplomats and you shall oversee the inspections from York northwards. I trust your allies know trustworthy men for this task.'

Thomas Legh was a lawyer of similar years to Crumwell and a cousin to Rowland Lee, a friend of Cardinal Wolsey, and a man who loved to hate Welshmen. Legh had been ambassador to Denmark and Ambassador Chapuys hated him, making him instantly pleasing in Crumwell's eyes. Both he and fellow diplomat John ap Rice, a fine lawyer and member of parliament, would do anything Crumwell asked. Both sought to find fortunes in destroying monasteries.

'And Richard Layton, I have assigned you the south and west of the country, Bedfordshire, Northamptonshire, Leicester, all just the start for you. I trust you can handle such tasks. After all, you inspected Syon Abbey for me and did a wonderful job in uncovering their immorality.'

'I am honoured to do this task,' replied Layton. Layton was a man of Nicòla's years, an archdeacon and loyal to Wolsey, and Crumwell by association. He was a fine man, an honest man, ready to destroy corruption and lewdness in the Church. Nicòla had suggested Layton may be too lenient, being a man of the Church, but Crumwell remained confident in his ally. All the men who remained loyal to Wolsey after his fall would be rewarded now.

'I am worried with the workload, Secretary Crumwell,' Layton admitted.

'Yes, even I see this as a formidable task,' Crumwell sighed. 'That is why I am personally seeing to monasteries in Cambridgeshire, so I have personal knowledge and practice of what we must do. I shall send Legh south to aid you once he is complete in the north, for I believe Legh shall have the task in the north in hand in no time.'

'Thank you, Secretary Crumwell, or should I say, Vicar-general Crumwell,' Legh commented, to gentle laughter around the table.

'I never thought I would see the day the name "vicar" used for my uncle,' said Richard next to Ralph, and everyone laughed again.

Crumwell looked to Richard and Ralph, two men now, once boys he considered his own sons. He smiled; only they could tease Thomas Crumwell.

'Richard Rich,' Crumwell continued, and Rich sat up in his seat and Nicòla cringed. She disliked Rich and Crumwell knew not why; she feared Rich, a lawyer of doubtable morals, would be unfair in his assessment of the

Church, but Crumwell cared not for this. 'Rich, you are to be sent east, starting in Kent. I want those monasteries closed this year, for the rumours say the region has some of the worst. I fear they will not weaken you, though nuns, monks, priests and local men of the area will bribe you to keep their monasteries open.'

'Monasteries are home to the clergy, but also house the sick, feed the poor, educate the local children,' Nicòla warned. 'We must prepare, or resistance shall be strong.'

'That is why I am sending Rich to close these first houses,' Crumwell continued, taken aback by Nicòla's arguing tone.

'The tears of women and bribes of men in Kent shall not sway me. Worry not, Secretary Crumwell,' Rich said, his chest puffed with pride.

Crumwell threw a stern brow to Nicòla, who looked at Rich with anger. Feelings mattered none in this issue. 'Thomas Wriothesley.' He paused as the young lawyer smiled with delight, his stupid white feather in his soft cap bobbing as always. The confidence in Wriothesley never ceased. He now sported the unruliest blonde beard and Nicòla would often ridicule Wriothesley behind his back. 'Wriothesley, I will send you and my nephew Richard to Wales. I understand you may take longer in your matters, due to distance.'

'No, Secretary Crumwell, we shall be brisk in our reports,' Wriothesley said. 'I look forward to being bribed already.'

Everyone laughed but Nicòla scowled. 'I look forward to going through your reports, written in expert Latin, detailing all Church abuses,' she bit, her bad mood becoming more obvious by the second.

Nicòla's words brought Crumwell back to seriousness in a moment, which in turn silenced everyone. 'Richard Page, you and Ralph shall tarry close to London, and as you are a fine lawyer and jurist page, you shall be a fine aid to Ralph.'

''Tis an honour,' Page replied, a young man which had come to prosperity by working for Wolsey and Crumwell. Courtiers swarmed like bees around Crumwell now, as Nicòla as often said, and this would work in his favour. It would take hundreds, if not thousands of men to visit every monastery and church, interview every priest, monk and nun. Everyone had to agree on the decision to close monasteries and abbeys or the plan would fail. Crumwell would have to give out extraordinary payments, bribes and endowments over coming years. He could see the paperwork already, all to appease King Henry.

A loud knock came from the main door in the Crumwell Chambers dining room, and Crumwell growled. 'We are trying to save England, so you better be of great importance!' he yelled. The door opened, and a gentleman-usher stood with Thomas Heneage, one of King Henry's privy chamber men. 'Oh, Heneage, come.'

Heneage entered the room with cautious footsteps, looking around the men at the table. Rich turned in his chair and looked up and down at Henry's attendant, dressed all in green. 'Heneage, should you not be fetching a mistress somewhere for our king?' he commented.

'I am soon to be Gentleman of the Stool,' Heneage replied. 'That is the most prized role in Henry's chamber.'

'Be careful, Heneage,' Crumwell said and leaned back in his chair. 'That role belongs to Sir Henry Norris, the King's greatest friend. Be careful whose job you covet.'

'I come hither for Master Frescobaldi, Secretary Crumwell. His Majesty requested Frescobaldi come at once to the presence chamber.'

'Why?' Crumwell replied.

'I know not, only that it is to be now.'

Crumwell sighed as Nicòla stood up at once and straightened her doublet and hose, her hair pulled under a soft velvet cap. 'I shall go.'

'We need you, Frescobaldi,' Crumwell said. 'Heneage, please understand that we have paperwork for the first six hundred monasteries we must examine. Can this not wait?'

'His Majesty never waits for anything, Secretary Crumwell.'

Crumwell would not let Nicòla into Henry's presence alone, not in her delicate condition, which Henry did not know of; there would never be a good time to mention Crumwell would be a father again after all of Henry's sad losses.

'Gentlemen, please see to your paperwork and take wine while we are gone.' A double click of his fingers and servants appeared with wine for all, and an usher to brush Crumwell's long black fur coat before seeing the King.

He and Nicòla followed Heneage back to the presence chamber, Crumwell's face already hurting in worry for any meeting, as he had for weeks now. Crumwell was right to go with Nicòla. Henry could be heard before they reached the antechamber. Henry Norris and his brother returned to stand in the antechamber and silently showed Crumwell in with Nicòla. They entered just in time to see Thomas Boleyn disappear through another door, leaving only Henry and a few ushers, all crumpled in the far corner, eager to get forgotten.

'Crumwell,' Henry said, his hand on his hips, his red doublet appearing much too tight for his wide shoulders, 'I asked not for you.'

'No, Your Majesty,' he said as he and Nicòla bowed in time. 'I took the opportunity to assist.'

Henry took no notice as he walked over to the pair and looked up and down at Nicòla. Rather than staring down, Nicòla looked Henry right in the eye which often threw Henry's tempers. Surely even he would not strike a woman again. 'Frescobaldi, tell me of the new Bishop of Rome, Pope Paul.'

'I have met him but a few times, Your Majesty,' Nicòla said, surprised by the change in subject. 'He is a friend of the Medici family and educated in Pisa, Florence and Rome. He was a cardinal in Padua, and his son is Duke of Parma now. Pope Paul, as he calls himself, has recently made his eight-year-old grandson a cardinal.'

'What folly,' Henry scoffed, and Crumwell nodded in agreement. 'Frescobaldi, this country hates my wife. Anne is their queen, but the people like her not. I wish to renew ties with the Pope.'

'Why?' Crumwell cried out and Nicòla watched him with a look of anger and worry. 'Wise, Your Majesty,' Crumwell coughed.

'If the people saw my friendship with the new pope, then they would more readily accept by changes to the Church and my new queen.'

'Most wise, Your Majesty.' Nicòla said. 'You still intend to reform the Church in England, though, as ruler in your own realm.'

'Of course, Rome shall never rule England again.' Henry was still Catholic in almost all dealings, until it came to divorce. If Crumwell wanted to break the Catholic Church, he would need to start with Henry's behaviour in church. 'You are a Medici, of sorts, Frescobaldi. I want you to write to Rome, to this new pope, and tell him that I wish to renew ties with the papal offices. I shall send an ambassador, instead of having Chapuys gossiping in every letter to the Roman Emperor. He writes as if we do not have spies reading every letter!'

'We also have our spies reading his return mail, Your Majesty. Chapuys cannot be trusted.'

'But you must be his friend, Crumwell,' Henry instructed, and Crumwell felt a pain in his chest. Be friends again with Eustace Chapuys? After he threatened to reveal Nicòla's womanly identity?

'I can write to the new Pope, Your Majesty,' Nicòla said, bold as a knight in a joust. 'Secretary Crumwell and I are to Cambridgeshire tomorrow. Perchance we could stop at Kimbolton Castle and visit the former Queen Katherine.' Nicòla paused for only a moment as Henry's face turned the red of his doublet. 'If the Pope can read that the former queen is well, then he shall be kinder to you, without question. Knowing you care for Katherine, even though she was never your true wife, shall soften Pope Paul's opinions on England. I have nothing but love and admiration for Queen Anne.'

'I know you do,' Henry mumbled and looked at the calf leather shoes on his feet. Nicòla had been there for Anne that day of the possible miscarriage and Henry knew it; the pain of the loss lined his ever-ageing face. 'So be it; visit Katherine if you choose, but your role is to ensure Paul likes England and understands my role as the King and Supreme Leader of the Church of England.'

'As you wish, Your Majesty. It shall be a delicate matter, but we shall endeavour.'

Henry dismissed the pair, and the moment they left the rooms, Nicòla muttered, 'the only thing the new pope shall do is excommunicate Henry from the Catholic Church. Pope Paul is the new leader of the counter-Reformation. First, Paul shall send an army through the German States towards England to kill reformers like us.'

'Then we should find good cause to close monasteries and make Henry rich and beloved, and fast, in case we have war,' Crumwell replied.

'I fear we shall all have our heads upon spikes for this monastery dissolutions.'

'I will gladly lose my head to save yours, Nicò.'

'Oh no, Master Secretary, we are all keeping our heads. Promise me.'

Chapter 19 – March 1535
Kimbolton Castle, Huntingdonshire

Humility is trouth, and pryde is lying

Once the horses stopped at the edge of the moat around Kimbolton Castle, Nicòla understood how much she had been sliding in her saddle. By her best guess, the baby was only halfway to its time, just enough to be a pain while riding. Luckily, most of the other symptoms of being with child had passed, a slight relief while being out on the road. The week spent travelling around Cambridgeshire had been a cold one, but not just the weather.

The moment Thomas Crumwell, Vicegerent to the King, poked his nose into the workings and finances of a monastery, the clergymen within would step back in fear. Crumwell would march the halls of monasteries, his heavy black furs sweeping behind him, ready to destroy the lives of the priests, nuns and monks who called monasteries and abbeys home. Every time Nicòla picked up an account book, clergymen would stare at her in hatred, mutter things about her foreign accent, curse her dark skin. Monks would desperately try to stop laymen's hands touching their fake relics, to avoid being discovered. Nuns would cower in fear, which upset Nicòla the most. Being a woman in any life was hard, and she sought not to hurt the women of the convents being searched.

Anglesey Priory, Blackfriars Cambridge, Huntingdon Austin Friars and many more in a week. Crumwell took a liking to the last one, named alike their own Austin Friars at home in London. Nicòla could see Crumwell pulling apart monasteries in his head – some destroyed, others given away as bribes, some kept for himself. The mission would enrich Henry and his men along with controlling the power of religion. At each place, Crumwell left local men behind to complete searches as the London group rode on to Kimbolton Castle.

The bridge slowly came down over the moat and Nicòla sighed a little and rubbed the base of her back. At once, Crumwell was at her side, his black horse right against hers. 'Are you well?' he asked.

Nicòla nodded and brushed a strand of rose-gold hair from her face, her black gloves damp from the earlier rain. 'How long do we have to visit with the Lady Katherine?'

'This visit must be as short as possible, for we have another thirteen miles to cover before we reach Bedford for the night, and then the fifty miles home to London starting tomorrow.'

Nicòla smiled a little and Crumwell gave the tiniest of smiles back. They argued the night before; Nicòla admitted to Crumwell that she had sent money to Mary Boleyn, enough to help her move to Calais where her commoner husband worked as a soldier. Mary Boleyn had not been discussed by any person and wrote to Crumwell many times asking for help, as banishment from her family meant poverty. Nicòla had sent Mary Boleyn money after the stillbirth of a daughter, so she could move and be closer to her husband stationed far from home. At least in Calais, Mary Boleyn was out of sight of the court and her angry sister. Still, Crumwell like none of Nicòla's decision to send her own money to the ill-liked Boleyn girl. It went against a direct command from Queen Anne, against the wishes of the King.

They moved through the halls of Kimbolton Castle in silence, a huge yet freezing space. The cold castle had been redesigned and rebuilt not ten years past, but being so large, and lived in by so few, the castle appeared mostly closed; rooms bare, and windows uncovered.

Lady Katherine, or Queen Katherine as her servants still called her, allowed Crumwell and Nicòla into her presence in a large and warm parlour. She sat at a fireplace, a book on her lap. Her black dress appeared worn and dusty, her shoulders limp and covered with a dirty-looking fur. Katherine had appeared distraught at her last meeting with Nicòla, as she was taken away from Buckden Palace. Now, in this chilled prison, Katherine appeared most ill; both Nicòla and Crumwell paused at the sight.

'I hear you are Secretary Crumwell now,' Katherine spoke as Crumwell and Nicòla bowed before the old queen. Her blue eyes searched the pair for clues of their visit.

'Dowager Princess,' Crumwell greeted her with her new title. 'I see news travels far from the court.'

'News travels everywhere, Secretary Crumwell. Please do not call me a dowager princess, for I was only that after the death of Prince Arthur. I am called Queen Katherine in my household as my marriage to Henry is still lawful.' Katherine would never give in. This argument had gone around so many times, surely even Katherine was sick of hearing such words.

'Queen Katherine,' Nicòla acknowledged her, knowing it would irritate Crumwell, but wished to calm the ill woman.

'Nicòla Frescobaldi,' Katherine replied and let out a gentle cough. The weather in Huntingdonshire, a damp place, did nothing for Katherine's health. Her sharp Spanish accent spoke Nicòla's name to perfection. 'It has been some time since you visited me at Buckden. What brings you, and my husband's most important adviser, all the way north?'

'We are hither to speak to you about the new Pope,' Crumwell replied.

'Pope Paul the Third,' Katherine said, her voice low and crackling. 'I have had no correspondence with the new Pope, for I have the most important letter I ever need from Pope Clement.'

'The ruling that your marriage is legal,' Nicòla added.

Katherine turned and gestured to a servant in the far corner of the room, who came over. Katherine whispered in her lady's ear, and the woman scurried over to the box in the far room. She came back with the ruling on the royal marriage; at once Nicòla could see the signature of Pope Clement on the page and thought of him dying alone in Rome without her. The six months since his death had passed quickly, but the pain and confusion had not yet left. Clement's holy cross of gold still hung around Nicòla's neck.

Katherine's pale fingers ran over the careful Latin words of her marriage ruling. She gazed at Nicòla and lost her easy smile. 'I am sorry, Mr. Frescobaldi, for you have suffered a personal loss in the death of our Pope, God rest his soul.' Katherine paused and crossed herself. 'How is the son of Pope Clement?'

Nicòla shot a quick look at the lady-in-waiting, hopefully out of hearing. She looked like the woman Thomas Wyatt sometimes wrote poetry to Lady Elizabeth Darrell, who would know little of Nicòla's situation, if any at all. 'I must confess I have not had many letters from Alessandro de'Medici in recent months, Your Majesty. But to lose one's father, and one who protects his son from his great enemies is surely a great loss.'

Katherine looked up and down at Crumwell, his hands clasped before him. 'You wear the turquoise Wolsey ring, the ring magically capable of controlling the King.'

'I believe not in superstitions, my Lady,' Crumwell replied.

Katherine sighed and leaned back in her heavy chair. 'What brings you to Kimbolton, Crumwell?'

'I know you are in correspondence with your nephew, the Holy Roman Emperor, and with his ambassador, Eustace Chapuys.'

'I am not allowed to send correspondence; Henry banned such.'

'And yet letters still flow. I have eyes everywhere, Lady Katherine. Let us not pretend. I will not tell Henry of such details. We come hither before you to say King Henry wishes to renew his bonds with Rome, with the Emperor and the new Pope.'

Katherine crossed herself again, at once her true-blue eyes alive with joy. 'Henry has changed his path?' she gasped. 'I presupposed you came to force me to sign your new Oath of Succession! But no? Henry intends to turn back to his faith, his family?'

'His Majesty wishes to renew alliances with the Emperor, alliances strained since your annulment, Lady Katherine. He wishes to find favour with the Emperor and his ambassador. There is no reason for there to be anger between His Majesty and the new Bishop of Rome.'

'Pope, not just a bishop,' Katherine snapped. 'If Henry wants alliances and favour from Rome and my nephew, he must leave his whore and their bastard daughter. Henry must return to his true wife, me, who is to be at his side. To turn his soul to the Catholic faith and away from reformers such as yourself, Secretary Crumwell, is the only way Henry shall find favour in Rome.'

Nicòla glanced at Crumwell, his golden eyes weary. They knew all of this; Katherine would never help Henry in securing the friendship of the Pope or the Roman Emperor. 'Your Majesty,' Nicòla said again, to appease Katherine's refusal to accept her annulment, 'we come hither to know if there is anything you need to make your stay at Kimbolton a comfortable one.'

'You mean you wish to bribe me with furs and servants, wines and silver plate, so I tell my nephew and his new pope that I am well cared for? It shall never work.'

'We did not think so, either, Your Majesty,' Nicòla said. 'But we are not your enemy.'

'You are!' Katherine scoffed. 'Crumwell, you are known as the Queenmaker. To make your precious whore queen, you had to destroy me. You even tried destroying the Catholic Church in England! For what? So the King can get a son on his mistress? Henry and I have a perfect, healthy, intelligent daughter to rule England, and yet Henry wanted to get a son on that Boleyn woman!'

'I cannot hold the throne of England for Lady Mary,' Crumwell replied. 'Do I think your daughter could reign? Yes, of course, I do. With parents such as yourself and His Majesty, Mary could be nothing but suitable. But His Majesty wishes to give his throne to a son to make the role of monarch safe. A woman on an English throne never worked; there would be civil war. England has seen enough death. King Henry's father ended the War of the Roses and a male heir is the only way to stop war returning to these shores. I am sorry, Lady Katherine, I truly am. No one is more capable of being an English queen than you. But King Henry remarried after your marriage was found unlawful by the English Church. His Majesty rules the

Church, reform has come to England and your papers from Rome shall not change a thing. His Majesty wants to make peace now, while he waits for a male child from Queen Anne.'

'I shall die before I care for anything you say. I am a Spanish princess and an English queen. You cannot force me to acknowledge any religious change in this country. You cannot banish me any further; for at Kimbolton I am already forgotten. I am ill and starved. They keep my precious daughter Mary at Hatfield House, as a maid to the whore's bastard girl. You have destroyed me, and my daughter, in the making of your new queen. I want you from this castle at once.'

Crumwell bowed in silence and stepped away but Nicòla paused. Her eyes met with Katherine's. 'Your Majesty,' Nicòla said politely.

'Be careful,' Katherine said and reached for Nicòla's hand. She grabbed it tight the moment Nicòla outstretched her fingers. 'You and I have come from another world to this land, one where they hate people like us. I have borne six children and lost almost as many. I have seen many other women with child, some elated, some with the news hidden. I see you and what you carry. They will one day turn on you like they did me.'

Nicòla gazed down at her belly, which she swore was not showing her condition; all thought her male, so surely no one suspected. But Queen Katherine certainly did.

'Sometimes the road to our rightful place is a long one,' Nicòla uttered.

'God be with you,' Katherine said and released Nicòla's hand. 'Some of us have been sorely tested by God, and I will die one day, knowing Henry is my true husband, our daughter the rightful heir of England. Crumwell shakes the throne, but he does not sit upon it. Reckoning shall come and you must decide where you wish to make your stand.'

Chapter 20 – March 1535
Austin Friars, London

A man can tryp over his own lyes

One of Crumwell's beloved hawks sat upon his left arm, the new leather glove Nicòla bought him for Christmas keeping the bird's claws at bay. Despite the beautiful bird being right before him, Crumwell had trouble seeing his pet. His left eye saw little, its socket swollen and heavy. Nicòla had gently touched his face earlier in the day, and the pain seared through his cheek for hours. Despite placing a cold cloth on the skin, Crumwell's eye continued to swell, as if someone had punched him in a fight. Now, when Crumwell swallowed, he felt his throat too had swollen. Still, best to say nothing, for he had felt ill for the trip around Cambridgeshire but had kept it secret.

'Are you quite well, Thomas?' asked Chapuys.

Crumwell turned his head to the ambassador who too had a bird on his arm, another Crumwell hawk, one of fifty kept at Austin Friars. It had been some time since Chapuys had visited Crumwell's main home, and it would take more time again for Crumwell to feel comfortable in his presence. Yet, Henry wanted a renewed relationship with Rome, so the Holy Roman Emperor's ambassador needed to be entertained. Already Chapuys had petted Crumwell's leopard, only brought out for the best parties, the finest of guests.

'I am well,' Crumwell replied and raised his arm a little, readying the hawk to fly away, Chapuys' bird following. Above them, the hawks circled around the large garden of Austin Friars, no doubt entertaining the nearby residents as early evening set over London.

'Thomas, you do not look at your best.'

'These past weeks have been out of my usual habits, and perchance I have eaten too many of the fine offerings,' Crumwell jested. Ginger, nutmeg, figs, oranges, marzipan, many of Nicòla's favourites. She had accompanied Crumwell on multiple monastery visits, ridden hundreds of miles in recent weeks, all while being with child. Now she could rest back in London, all her treats laid out for a jovial evening at Austin Friars.

Over Chapuys' grey fur-coated shoulders, Crumwell noticed Ralph and Richard setting up the longbows for more pre-dinner activities in the wide square garden. The canaries chirped while the hawks flew overhead in the fading light; Nicòla stood with Gregory nearby, as she fitted his new hawking glove made especially for his thin arm. Jane stood at Nicòla's feet, watching her elder brother look upon his new glove with delight. Gregory was fifteen years old now; and yet Crumwell had little idea of what would be become of his young son. Jane would soon be five years old and spoke English, Italian and Latin. Already Nicòla insisted on Jane's schooling being perfect; they had already employed many tutors.

'So, your Mr. Frescobaldi,' Chapuys continued, catching Crumwell's attention once more.

'What of him?'

Chapuys narrowed his eyes for a moment. 'Has Mr. Frescobaldi been receiving letters from the Duke of Florence?'

'No, indeed not. The Medicis are quiet, have been since the death of their pope, which had much effect I suspect.'

'Indeed, though Farnese, Pope Paul – is a popular Medici friend. But I thought perchance Frescobaldi had received word from his sister, the Duchess.'

This time Crumwell narrowed his eyes, one being so swollen it lost itself. 'Duchess Nicòletta? Why do you enquire after mail from my secretary's sister?'

'There are rumours in Rome. It is said that Emperor Charles wishes to marry his bastard daughter, Margarete of Austria, to Duke Alessandro. Of course, they could not marry if Alessandro de'Medici did not first annul his marriage to the only Frescobaldi daughter.'

This was it; if Charles wanted Alessandro de'Medici as his son-in-law, then it could be a way of having Nicòla's marriage annulled. Finally, Crumwell could marry Nicòla legally, not just in God's eyes. Friendship with Chapuys suddenly appeared to have a personal benefit. But his vision blended once more, and Crumwell swayed upon his feet.

'Are you well?' came the voice from Archbishop Cranmer. 'Your face does not look fine.'

Crumwell turned to see his other dinner guest behind him, dressed in his usual purple robes.

'Thomas,' he said with a smile. 'They had not informed me of your arrival. I am glad you have decided to join us tonight.'

'I arrived just this moment.' Cranmer stopped and threw the pair a stern brow. 'Thomas, your face is much swollen. I am sure you understand this.'

'Indeed,' Crumwell smiled again. Now his lips felt fat. ''Tis nothing, I am certain.' Cranmer's arrival brought Ralph and Richard over, whose faces frowned as they too drew closer across the grass. Was his face that ill-looking? 'You all worry so, but it is no matter.'

'You are not the first person to utter such today,' Chapuys commented as the men stood together in a circle. A hawk swooped down and landed on Crumwell's arm, eager to receive a piece of orange.

'I received a letter today,' Chapuys continued. 'It says the new Pope likes to gamble.'

'That may the only thing I like about him,' Crumwell replied, to the laughter of the group.

'That may be so, but the Pope is a terrible gambler. He loses almost every hand of cards, every game of dice. Already he owes money.'

'No Pope should be in debt to any man,' Cranmer frowned. 'This is why we are a country of reform. The Catholic Church is now headed by a man who likes to gamble; hardly a Christian advisor to the masses.'

'The last Pope had a bastard son who married Crumwell's secretary's sister. That is much worse than gambling in idle time.'

'Perchance we should go indoors, and I can beat you all at gambling. Except you, Thomas,' Crumwell teased Cranmer.

'You paint me as a man of no fun!' Cranmer jested. Hardly; for Cranmer had a wife hidden out of the city, now hiding at Dewhurst in Surrey, a home in Nicòla's name. They could afford to mourn their lost son no more, but some good news did prevail, for already Margarete was with child again, soon after the stillbirth of their daughter just months ago.

'Is it true you invited Stephen Gardiner to dine with us tonight?' Cranmer continued.

'Indeed, for I want to tell our friendly bishop that he is to go to France as a diplomat for the King. I think we shall all do well to have Gardiner out of London for a while! We have pressing issues to plan in coming months, and I wish not to have Gardiner's sympathetic Catholic heart casting its opinion. But Gardiner shall not visit tonight.'

'Do you speak of those monks who have been arrested?' Cranmer asked. 'They are all in the Tower as we speak.'

'And they have committed what crime?' Chapuys asked. 'Be it those monks who refused to sign the Oath of Succession?'

'Indeed,' Crumwell said and swallowed hard. His throat felt laced with stone. 'Robert Lawrence, the new Prior of the Beauvale Charterhouse in Nottinghamshire, refuses to swear the Oath, and uses his influence to dissuades others from signing.'

'And what is the punishment for this crime?' Chapuys added, a stern brow added to his words.

'As we have new high treason laws, ones stricter on such crimes. Refusal to sign the Oath is punishable by death by hanging, drawing and quartering.'

'If you do this, it shall make these Carthusian monks into Carthusian martyrs,' Chapuys replied. 'Thomas, this shall go against the Catholic Church, against every man of Rome you wish to align with your king.'

Crumwell's swollen eye twitched as his hawk took off from his arm again. This strange pain was such a blight at such a busy time. 'Let us go inside to talk, but let the dinner talk be of things other than quartering.'

The small party of six sat around a table, filled with the most lavish meal served at Austin Friars in some time. Crumwell wished to treat his precious Nicòla, who sat at the opposite end of the end of the table to him. Ralph and Richard talked with each other, Crumwell and Chapuys listening in, but Nicòla and Cranmer were in their own conversation, one nobody else could hear. Cranmer had brought his wife Margarete to Austin Friars, as always, in a crate to protect her privacy, and she was elsewhere in the house, most likely with Frances and Ellen. Only once Chapuys left could they have Margarete in their company. Nicòla hated the treatment of Margarete, who had not long lost two children. Crumwell longed to create an England where Nicòla could be his wife freely and Margarete did not have to be treated as Cranmer's dirty sin.

Chapuys noticed Crumwell staring at Nicòla and Cranmer's discussion. 'What creates such a serious face upon you?' he asked Cranmer across the table.

Nicòla looked up to Chapuys. 'We were discussing the role of women in the Church and within society,' she answered for the Archbishop.

Chapuys laughed off any notion. 'Women have their place. Silent and grateful.'

'You are a man who took holy orders. Do you believe men such as yourself can also take a wife?' Nicòla probed him.

'Why would I need to do such thing, for I live as ambassador to the Holy Roman Emperor, in the court of King Henry. I have seen the harm marriage does. No, a man who has taken holy orders cannot marry; you sit next to the Archbishop who would most certainly agree with you.'

The whole table sat in a stiff silence for a moment. But Chapuys was not finished. 'And what of you, Mr. Frescobaldi? For you have been in court for five years and have not taken a wife. Or is there is a marriage for you back in Italy?'

'I fear your desire for gossip has given you lies, Ambassador,' Nicòla spat back. 'L'astuzia e l'inganno serviranno un uomo meglio della forza ogni volta.'

Chapuys crossed his arms as he scoffed at her words. Nicòla looked to the confused faces around the table. 'Tis a line from "Discourses on Livy" from Machiavelli; "cunning and deceit will serve a man better than strength every time." Ambassador Chapuys prefers lies and gossip as he holds no real power.'

'I use cunning and deceit, you claim?' Chapuys cried. 'Secretary Crumwell adopted your sister's bastard daughter, did he not? Smuggled into England by you to be raised as a Crumwell in Austin Friars? Surely such behaviour tells you that marriage is essential for a woman, and the only role she needs to play. Your sister committed a grave sin in having a bastard child. The cunning and deceit comes from your sister, not I.'

Crumwell, even with his swollen eye, could see Nicòla lick her lips and pause in anger. At best, Chapuys named Nicòla's "sister" a whore. At worst, suggesting Nicòla herself was a whore, a whore with the audacity to play the role of a man at a royal court.

'How is Duchess Nicòletta?' Chapuys continued to bite. 'I hear that my master wishes to marry his daughter to the Medici Duke and annul the marriage the Duke has with Nicòletta Frescobaldi. That will make your sister, the mysterious rose-gold beauty no one ever sees, to be a woman who is soiled goods.'

With an angry flick of her wrist, Nicòla tossed her sharp knife in Chapuys' direction, and it stuck deep in the wood of the table just before the Ambassador's empty plate. A gasp came from every man at the table at the quick response.

'Eustace, speaking in such tones is not permitted in this home,' Crumwell barked. 'Duchess Nicòletta is the precious daughter of my patron. I must ask you desist at once.'

'You shall find the next knife in your tongue!' Nicòla cried from the other end of the table. Nicòla seemed far angrier than Crumwell expected; perchance her heavy workload and the baby made for a difficult mood.

'I expect such empty threats from you, Mr. Frescobaldi, as you seem too weak and fragile to hurt a man. Still, you must have a redeeming quality. Thomas keeps you so close, and you are a man as delicate as a girl, who kept close company with a filthy and corrupt pope, even in his bedchamber I heard. 'Tis no wonder your sister has become something of a gift, handed about the Medici men, much like yourself.'

In just one nimble movement, Nicòla had a foot up on the table. She jumped forward from her seat and forced an angry fist right into Chapuys' mouth. None of the men reached to stop her, all stunned by the violent outburst from the English court's gentlest attendant.

Crumwell opened his mouth to command Nicòla to stop, but he could not even gain air to create a sound. He gasped a few times, catching everyone's attention, and Nicòla slunk back to her seat. Crumwell glanced at the blood on Chapuys' lips.

'To hurt the Ambassador,' he croaked, 'is to hurt the attentions our king wishes to pay to Rome.' He paused and swallowed; his wine sat beside his meal yet appeared so far away, much too far away to reach. Through narrow vision Nicòla leaned forward at him; at least Crumwell thought she did.

'Never hurt the needs of our king,' Crumwell coughed. He felt himself sliding sideways in his chair but could not hold on to anything. He caught sight of Nicòla rushing towards him as he closed his eyes, ready to hit the floor, and he longed for its coolness to soothe his brow. But the feeling never came; Crumwell landed on nothing but a relieving sensation of emptiness.

Chapter 21 – April 1535
Whitehall Palace, London

It is not a lye if everyone undyrstands

Nicòla looked to her fingertips perched on the edge of Crumwell's desk. She stood in front of his throne of a chair, his desk piled high with papers. Across from her stood Richard, his hands clapped together in patience. She glanced up and remembered Richard had spoken. 'I confess I find it hard to listen,' Nicòla admitted.

'I too,' Richard replied and straightened his posture. 'But I am hither to serve you, Nicòla.'

'I need you to be my man in the Privy Council, and in parliament. For I never wish to visit either of those places. I have enough difficulty with the King and his private council.'

'The Boleyn Council.'

'How are they taking the changes?'

Nicòla just shrugged. Nicòla cared none for gossip now. Crumwell had been delirious in bed for a week. Young Gregory was there to hold Crumwell's hand if he awoke lucid; Cranmer stayed close to pray, to deliver the last rites if needed. Nicòla wanted to be there, but the court and the country would not run itself in Crumwell's absence. He begged her to tarry at court for the King. Whatever illness threatened to take his life, he wanted no disease near Nicòla or the baby. He pushed Nicòla away from Austin Friars, where he slept frail in his bed, sweating through the sheets, suffering fits in his sleep, mixing his words, unable to even take water. His powerful golden eyes no longer gleamed with cheer, now dull and slow, trapped in their discoloured sockets. When Crumwell drew breath his lower lip shook, every breath a gasp of shock. His shaking hands clung to the edge of a blanket, his body so tired the blanket seemed as heavy as rocks against his aching bones. The swelling of his face had suddenly gone, replaced with a whole body of torment and the doctors did not understand what was wrong. Which led to Nicòla's newest worry.

'Richard, two guests are sailing from Calais, and their ship should arrive tomorrow, and I need you to be there to escort them to Austin Friars.'

'Would you dare bring in people at such a time?' Richard threw a stern brow back to Nicòla.

'Two new doctors shall attend upon our master. They are Jewish doctors, who fled Spain very young and have been living in Brussels for some time.'

'You would bring Jews to England to treat Uncle Tom?' Richard cried. 'You cannot bring Jews to England!'

'This is no matter of religion, it is a matter of knowledge and healing. Your English kings may have expelled Jews from England, but my home has always had a Jewish presence. Many Jews expelled from Naples came north to Florence with wealthy patrons. Now I seek help for England's most powerful man. Those doctors are Jewish men, trained by their fathers who got expelled from Spain many years ago. Do not let your fear guide you towards hatred, Richard. I seek to save Crumwella's life.'

'I shall speak with Ralph.'

'Ralph is to run the Master of the Rolls offices in Secretary Crumwella's absence. Did our master not put me in charge of his works?'

'Yes, but…'

'But you see me as a weak woman, when I have lived these twenty years as a man, can work as a man, think as a man, be a man.' Nicòla paused; beyond the slightly open door behind Richard, she could hear movement. There would be a line of people waiting for instruction, but the voices seemed to have quietened, something the office seldom did.

'I am sorry, Nicòla, but I worry if you bring such… doctors to the bedside at Austin Friars.'

'The last Pope, God rest his immortal soul, had a Jewish physician. He believed the Jewish can understand how blood travels through the body, and could help us know how illness travels, which could find cures. These men are well-versed in the new faith, for they had to hide their own beliefs many times. Fear not, Richard. All they need is their safe passage from the port to Austin Friars.'

A knock upon the doors swung one door open, a gentleman-usher there with a look of trepidation. 'Excuse me, Master Crumwell, Master Frescobaldi, but the Bishop of Winchester is upon us.'

'I shall be to parliament,' Richard said to Nicòla. 'For we shall begin the trial of the monks who refuse to swear the Oath.'

Nicòla nodded, and Richard left, off to listen to the latest gossip around London on their master's behalf in case he was lucid enough to listen. Nicòla fell back into Crumwell's chair and ached to be back at home at his bedside. The two-mile barge ride to Austin Friars seemed so far, too far. Nicòla got but a moment of silence before the Bishop himself strode into the office.

'Bishop Gardiner,' Nicòla sighed and sat up straight, not troubling to rise for Crumwell's most beloved enemy.

'Mr. Frescobaldi,' Gardiner replied as he sat himself down across the desk. 'Your appearance leads me to believe the rumours of Thomas' health are not exaggerated.'

'I wished for Secretary Crumwella's health to be private, but you know the court…'

'Well indeed. I come in friendship, Mr. Frescobaldi. Truly, I do. For all the anger between Thomas and I, never would I wish for him to die so soon.'

For another to speak of Crumwell dying made Nicòla gasp; no one had spoken aloud of such a ruin.

'Has the doctor understood the illness? Be it plague?'

'They believe no plague, for his skin shows no sign of the illness, God be praised.' Nicòla sighed and sat forward, her elbows on the desk. 'He would have succumbed by now with sweating sickness, for he stumbled one week ago. For now, only God knows of Crumwella's ailment.'

'I have known Thomas for many more years than I care to admit, and I have never known him to be ill. Not once.'

'You are far from the first to make such a claim, Bishop. We had been riding in Cambridgeshire this past month, and Crumwella, he seemed not himself.'

'How so?'

'He complained of a sore neck often, sometimes he would speak and slur a word. Crumwella complained of tiredness or shortened breath, pain in his back, his knees. He jested he was just old.'

'But perchance an illness was already upon him.'

'He stumbled at a dinner with Chapuys.'

'Oh yes, that dinner. You had your fist in Eustace's mouth.'

'And I regret it most ardently, Bishop Gardiner. Perchance my anger pushed Crumwella too far, causing his stumble.'

'And his health has gotten worse since he took to his bed? There are rumours of a swollen face, of gasping for breath, of sweating.'

'All those things. He cannot sleep for long, for he jumps himself awake. He cannot remember a thing, which is a serious worry for a man like Crumwella. One moment he is in pain, then his body is numb…'

'And Archbishop Cranmer is by his side?'

Nicòla nodded and took a deep breath. 'I know you suspect Crumwella's death.'

'And no one could replace him. No one can be Thomas Crumwell, except Thomas Crumwell. He holds offices and titles no man has ever had before now. May I visit Austin Friars?'

'Do you wish him well, or rejoice in his illness?' Nicòla shot back.

'I came in peace only, Mr. Frescobaldi, I promise on God's word. For I am to sail for France on a diplomatic mission.'

'You fear Crumwella shall die before your return.'

'I fear what his death would do for the country, but at least the monasteries would be saved from dissolution. As I say, I came in peace only.'

'All the court swarms upon Crumwella. They all want to speak to him, to be in his favour, to beg for his time. I got a letter to Crumwella just this morning, from Elizabeth Seymour, the wife of the late Sir Anthony Ughtred. She just gave birth to a daughter and now needs a new husband. She is but seventeen years and thinks she could marry Crumwella! Such is the wish to be close to Crumwella's prosperity that even young women such as a Seymour daughter wish to be at his side.'

'Surely the Seymour girl would better suit Gregory,' Gardiner scoffed.

'I think Gregory would better suit the Church, but as an only son he must marry and breed.' Nicòla threw her hands in the air in frustration. 'A man such as Crumwella may not die, he must live forever to serve his king and queen.'

'Thomas' queen is no longer thriving,' Gardiner said. 'Anne angers Henry with her presence. I cannot attend court any longer due to Henry's dislike for me and that is not an ill-fortune. But I heard you, Mr. Frescobaldi, now run the court in Thomas' absence.'

'I conduct paperwork, Bishop Gardiner, and that is all. I see that the careful plans and workings of my master continue so he may return to full health with God's help and lead this country into the light of the reformed faith. It may be best you not visit Austin Friars, but instead, take your Catholic beliefs and enjoy your time in Paris. You are most liked in France.'

Gardiner could take the gentle hint in Nicòla's tone. He slowly rose from his chair and Nicòla did the same. 'Then this is farewell for now, Mr. Frescobaldi. While Thomas and I have not been close in some time, I wish him no ill will. I seek not to take his place at court, indeed I pity any man who dares to come after the great Thomas Crumwell.'

'Smooth sailing and safe travels, Bishop Gardiner.'

Nicòla waited until the double doors of the office closed before she eased herself back into the seat and placed one hand on her belly. The baby would be over halfway to its birth by now, her waist stretching under her wide doublet. Just the thought of Crumwell in his bed, thrashing about as he sweated, next trembling with cold, his teeth chattering, his dull eyes rolling backwards made her clap a hand over her lips to stop a frightful sob.

Her instincts held her back from constantly running to his bedside, but the wife in her, the mother in her, wanted to be close to Crumwell as his child stirred in her belly.

'Almighty and Eternal God, you are the everlasting health of those who believe in You. Hear us for Your sick servant Thomas, for whom we implore the aid of Your tender mercy, that being restored to bodily health, he may give thanks to You in Your Church. Through Christ our Lord.' Nicòla crossed herself, something banned in Crumwell's presence and unnecessary in the reformed faith. But only God could save them now.

~~~

Nicòla stood between Ralph and Richard, each of them stretched as tall as they could, their hands clasped before them. They stood outside the front door at Austin Friars, the courtyard bathing in bright sunshine, the fountain twinkling in the centre.

'Mark the date on the calendar,' Ralph muttered under his breath as the gate to the property bolted shut. King Henry appeared with some thirty men accompanying him to Austin Friars. This was not his first visit, but before had been informal dinners. Now, the King came to the bedside of his master secretary, his vicar-general, his chief minister. For Henry to leave Whitehall for Austin Friars told the entire court just how ill Crumwell was now. The King would never visit someone when he was ill; once he even left Anne Boleyn ill with sweating sickness and rode away to safety. Yet here was a king terrified of illness, riding to visit a sick member of his court. It would conflict enemies of Crumwell; their enemy was close to death, yet the visit showed just how high Crumwell sat in the King's eyes.

Henry's face told of an unforeseen happy expression as he dismounted his horse. His gloves tossed to an attendant beside him, Henry strode with heavy wide steps over the stones to the three who bowed in time.

'Tell me honestly,' Henry said to the group as he frowned in the sunlight, 'how bad is it?'

They all paused; Crumwell would order them to say he was recovering or at least out of danger, yet none of them could utter such a lie to the King.

'We know not the illness, Your Majesty,' Nicòla admitted to Henry. 'We have both your physician whom you kindly gave to us, along with doctors who were friends of my father when he lived in Brussels.'

'Yes, I know they brought ashore several Jews in London on Thomas Crumwell's orders,' Henry sniffed. 'Had it been anyone else, I would question such a secretive visit by foreigners without permission to come and go. Are you the one who used Thomas' name to gain these Jews entry into the country?'

Nicòla nodded quietly and averted her gaze to her feet. The Jewish men brought to London had soothed Crumwell's pain and fever but could not understand the illness.

'Thomas is the only man at court whom I trust,' Henry said, 'so I will not question the arrangement. If Thomas needs other doctors, he shall have them. Please, let us not tarry. Take me to Thomas.'

Henry passed both Ralph and Richard who melted away into the hallways of Austin Friars, much like all the servants of the manor house. Henry encountered no one as Nicòla showed him to the third floor where Crumwell's private room awaited. All the attendants and nurses were tucked away for Henry's visit, and Nicòla noticed the King look pale as he stood at Crumwell's bedroom door.

'Fear not, Your Majesty,' Nicòla tried to calm him, 'for after three weeks of illness, none in the house fell ill, neither any of the attendants who spent ample time in Crumwell's room.'

'Not yourself?' Henry eyed her.

'Nothing, Your Majesty.'

'For some say of late that you do not look in total health.'

Nicòla resisted the urge to touch her slowly expanding belly. She prayed Crumwell would recover before her baby showed through her doublet and bindings, so she could enter early confinement outside London. 'I can promise you that I have no illness which could spread to you, Your Majesty.'

Nicòla opened the door for the King, who walked in ahead of her. His long steps became dainty and gentle as he entered the room, slowly crossing the carpets towards Crumwell's bed. Someone had pulled the green curtains back to view Crumwell in bed, covered right up to his chin. The fire across the room flickered gently, just enough to keep the room warm for the attendants, as Crumwell, when awake, complained of the intense heat.

Crumwell did not stir as Nicòla sat on the edge of the bed and took his hand. A chair placed close to the bed waited for Henry, who eased himself down, his blue eyes never leaving the man before him. Nicòla shook Crumwell gently to wake him, but he did not respond.

'This… this is not what I thought to expect,' Henry mumbled, and slowly brought a hand to his mouth, shocked by his own words. 'Not the sweating sickness?'

'Dr. Butts has said he has never seen a case like this. The season was too cool for a sweating sickness outbreak; London is free of the disease at present. Those who survive sweating sickness show some recovery within a week of their first stumble. It may take weeks before they return to their health, but alas, Secretary Crumwella has shown none of the same traits who suffer the illness.'

'And what of the other doctors? Who are they?'

'Doctor Toledo and Doctor Salomon have thoughts but no conclusion.'

Henry sat up straight. 'And they are Jews?'

'They were men who had to leave Spain many years ago, while still children. Both travelled to the safety of Italy. Now they are educated as doctors like their fathers before them and live in the Low Countries. They have Jewish names, Your Majesty, and raised by Jewish parents. Yet everyone accepts them in Brussels as men of science and learning.'

'They are Jewish doctors.'

'They are the sons of the men good to my father and my family. I know you banned Jewish people and their faith, Your Majesty. I called upon these men to help, for perchance they had learned of the new ideas coming from the German States, learnings about health.'

'They are still Jews.'

'I understand, Your Majesty. These men are trying to navigate a new world, not so unlike yourself, as you change the religion of this country. The doctors are well-educated as humanists and reformers, and the learnings of their fathers' faith. We live in difficult times and I have trusted their learnings, all while listening to the care of Dr. Butts.'

'And what have these Jews learned?'

'They have studied, at great length, how blood moves about the body. They believe if they can find a spot where blood is not moving as it should, it may to tell us the area of the illness inside the body.'

'Does it work? Has he been bled?'

'Even Dr. Butts felt bleeding him would do no good. Perchance the plan to follow the blood shall help. Secretary Crumwella's heart is beating rightly, so the doctors say. He is sweating out an illness, and his face is not as swollen as once seen.'

'I hit Thomas in the face and I thought I caused his sickness.'

'No, Your Majesty, no one is to blame for such a problem.' Nicòla paused; she felt livid every time Henry hit Crumwell, and it had become common since Anne's last miscarriage. 'Secretary Crumwella has not slept a good night in more than a year, Your Majesty. His workload does not let him rest, as he has the wish to be the best minister England has ever seen.'

'That is admirable, Frescobaldi; but if Thomas dies, who shall replace him? There is no man to take his place.'

'No, Your Majesty, you are right. Secretary Crumwella takes on the role of twenty good men; he holds so many offices he cannot keep count.'

'And what is to become of these offices as he lies upon his deathbed?'

'I have assigned each task to a courtier; then I assigned a group of clerks and attendants to help the courtiers see out tasks.'

'It is taking an army of men to hold on to Thomas' power.'

'Master Sadler and Master Richard Crumwella are helping in a great capacity, but they are also tasked with working on the inspections of the monasteries. The Crumwell Chambers at court is run by myself, the Master of the Rolls office watched by Master Sadler, and the Privy Council matters and the parliament is cared for by Master Richard.'

'You shall all receive a title for helping in this time of great calamity.'

'Every man who serves Secretary Crumwella does so because they wish to, Your Majesty. They wish to be of service.'

'I do not have that level of diligence from my own subjects.'

'All we do is to serve Your Majesty. Toiling for you is our life's work.'

'Should I feel worried, Frescobaldi, of you as a woman? You should be at your husband's bedside day and night praying for his recovery. You should not be running the highest office in my kingdom.'

'I am no wife, Your Majesty, for I must play the part of the humble attendant. I lack certain body parts, but I am a man, as fantastical as I am.'

'You are a wife in the eyes of God and your king.'

'And I am grateful for such an honour. There is news I shall annul my first husband if the new Pope permits.'

'I wanted you to bring us closer to Rome, and yet you are punching the Imperial ambassador like a drunkard in a brothel and wanting an annulment of your Italian marriage!'

The raised voice startled poor Crumwell in his bed. His golden eyes slowly opened, and he shifted his weight a little to focus on who sat there. His dry and cracked lips formed a tiny smile when he saw Nicòla and tried to tighten his fingers around her hand. But when he turned to see the King, he fumbled and made to rise.

'Move not, Thomas,' the King commanded. 'Do not rise for your king and speak not. I came to see you in your time of great need.'

'Your Majesty,' Crumwell whispered and swallowed hard. Nicòla ran to fetch him water, which he could only take in tiny drops.

'I came to see the recovery you are due to make!' the King said, though his expression spoke of fear as he looked at his ever-thinning chief minister. 'Soon we shall gain power and wealth from the monasteries, soon we shall execute our enemies, soon we shall reign supreme. England needs you to rise from this bed completely recovered, Thomas.'

Crumwell tried to speak again but flopped his head back on his pillow. Nicòla reached forward to wipe his sweaty brow as his dull eyes closed again. 'I am sorry,' he whispered.

'Worry not,' Nicòla tried to calm him.

Henry slowly rose to his feet as he watched Crumwell move in a series of contorted twists as he tried to become comfortable again, his body aching with tiny movements. Nicòla got only a few more drops of water into his mouth before sickness took Crumwell's mind again. By the time he settled, Henry had edged himself all the way across the room by the fire, as if he were cold rather than frightened. Nicòla knew better.

'I do regret, Your Majesty, that I could not help Secretary Crumwella to a better state for your visit.'

'No,' the King dismissed her with a wave of his hand. 'I wanted to see the truth. Rumour flies at court and I wanted to see Thomas for myself. 'Tis worse than I thought after these three weeks. The spots on his skin, his falling hair, his fever. I was told to ready for Thomas' death, but I wished not to believe.'

'Who told of such things, Your Majesty?' Nicòla demanded, forgetting herself completely. 'Who would lie so brazenly to you?'

'Lie?' Henry scoffed. 'I see for myself. I came to wish Thomas an easy recovery from his bed rest, and yet I find him so sickly he cannot speak. The doubleminded man has no mind at all! George was right.'

'George Boleyn, Lord Rochford?' Nicòla enquired. 'Lord Rochford believes Secretary Crumwella shall pass due to this illness? Lord Rochford has not been hither, not sent a message of worry nor a gentleman-usher to enquire after proceedings. Your Majesty, once this fever breaks, you shall have your ally back by your side.'

'I shall speak with Dr. Butts, for I believe he is staying at Austin Friars?'

'Quite, Your Majesty. Allow me to show you to the doctor's rooms.'

With the King, eased comfortably in private rooms with his doctor, Nicòla raced back to Crumwell's bedside and took his hand which had come out from under the blankets once more, searching for someone.

'Worry not, Tomassito,' Nicòla muttered as she wiped his brow again. 'King Henry came to see you, to make sure you are recovering with the best care. That is how much he cares for you.'

'Please, do not banish me, Your Majesty,' Crumwell uttered, his eyes still closed. 'I am sorry I rest in bed.' Crumwell interrupted himself with a cough. 'I cannot swim, Your Majesty, I cannot swim.'

Once more Crumwell had lapsed into a madness, so hot and confused he knew not what he said. Nicòla sent for Mercy at once, so they could bathe him. Every time they peeled back his covers, Crumwell's seemed thinner than the day before.

'I shall not lose your place at court,' Nicòla promised him as he opened his eyes again, no doubt relieved by his bed covers being peeled away. 'You shall not lose your life to this fever. I promise.'

In time God may listen. Or else he would take Thomas Crumwell from the Earth as a sign of anger for all he had done to the Catholic faith in England.

Chapter 22 – April 1535
Austin Friars, London

Lyes can be mayde with words and with sylence

It took a lot before Nicòla would agree to rest. The headaches would not stop her. The back pain made her slow but still, she had to work, so Crumwell would not lose his place beside the ear of the King. But once the pains crept around to her front, under the gentle curve of her baby, then Nicòla agreed to rest. She retired for the evening to Austin Friars, to see her precious Crumwell and sit long enough to ease her pains. It seemed so foolish now.

As Nicòla rolled onto her back in her bed, tears which had been falling across her face instead pooled in her green eyes. Perchance the church teachings were true; women cannot rule, cannot lead. Women submit to the will of their husbands, their families. Not working at a royal court, not hiding in a doublet and hose, with men's hats and shirts. Nicòla had thought not of God's laws; God's laws were altered to suit, and someone had to take the anger of God.

Crumwell rested in bed; now staying awake for more than a minute at a time, the deathly illness stalking his soul but still not ready to claim him. Nicòla slept in her bed only one room away, swaddled and padded to ease her belly pain. The pain should have been worse. There should have been more blood. Nicòla had lost a son before, one almost due, yet this new baby was but halfway through its journey to life. So small, born all too easily on the bedsheets where Nicòla desperately tried to stop the birth of her boy. Another boy lost to God. Had God taken this child as a punishment for changing the religion of England again?

Perchance God no longer sought to punish Crumwell for his changes; perchance this time, God sought to punish Nicòla for daring to live a man's life while trying to carry a child. A woman could not carry a child and help run a nation. God made sure of that. Mercy and Ellen again delivered the child, again hid the bloodstained sheets, the body of the child baptised by Cranmer and spirited away.

As Nicòla's body continued to drip blood, tears continued to form in her eyes. The private door which separated Crumwell's room from Nicòla's swung open with great power. No one was ever to use that door, for they would see Nicòla dressed in a shift, her hair down, suffering from a pain only a woman's body could know. But only Mercy's face appeared.

'Oh, Nicòla, I am sorry, but you must get up at once. Tis Thomas!'

Nicòla rolled herself off the bed and onto her feet. With her skin against the cold stone floor, Nicòla tiptoed through the door, silently praying that there would be no blood on the back of her shift. The doctors were all in attendance, and as the curtain about the bed got pulled back, Nicòla felt herself weaken. Not only had she lost another son, now she would lose his father too. Four weeks had passed with Crumwell lying still, his skin grey, his nights filled with fits and cries of pain from his fever. Mercy would never come through the private adjoining door unless something horrific happened.

Crumwell sat in the bed, up for the first time in weeks. A weak smile crossed his pale face when he saw Nicòla limp towards the bed, only a day of recovery given to her body. Dr. Butts knew Nicòla was a woman, and the two Jewish doctors never enquired into Nicòla's life. But he was alive!

Nicòla sat gingerly on the edge of the bed and Crumwell took her hand; for the first time, he had the slightest colour in his cheeks, as thin as they now appeared. The man painted by Holbein not a year ago bore no resemblance to this man, who had lost so much weight in the last month. Gone was the swelling to his face, though the bruises of the cupping experiments remained on his skin.

'I fear I have no remembrance of anything,' he said, finally his voice heard again, quiet but more than a whisper at last.

Tears ran down Nicòla's face, unable to keep her cover as a man at this moment, and she clutched Crumwell's hand to her chest. As she silently cried, Mercy stood by her side, one hand on her shoulder, she too in tears of joy at the recovery.

'I do believe we have witnessed something of a miracle,' Dr. Butts said. 'For I checked on Secretary Crumwell, not an hour gone, and he remained the same. God has performed a miracle.'

'I woke hither,' Crumwell croaked, 'to find myself in bed. I feel I have been hither for some time… I remember Gregory in the room, figures standing around the bed, you, Mercy and Nicòla…'

'The King came to the house to visit,' Mercy replied with a sniff.

'No, Henry hates illness,' Crumwell croaked.

'Another miracle,' Dr. Butts said. 'Shall I inform the King and court of your current state, sir?'

Crumwell looked feebly to Nicòla, who instructed Butts to leave for Whitehall at once. As the doctor sped away, she turned to Mercy. 'Tell Gregory at once that his father has broken his fever. Get messages to Ralph and Richard… and to everyone they need to tell. We are well due for some good news. Awake Archbishop Cranmer from his bed, for we must truly thank God for this miracle.'

Mercy turned away with a happy smile while Crumwell turned his attention to the doctors. 'Who are you, fine gentlemen? Forgive me, but you appear…'

'Jewish,' Nicòla finished for him. 'Dr. Toledo and Dr. Salomon have come from Brussels at my request, with the King's permission. They have discovered remedies to help you recover.'

'You shall feel discomfort in your bruises,' Dr. Salomon said as he touched Crumwell's arm. Crumwell's eyes followed his arm, shoulder and onto his chest as the doctor pulled back his nightshirt to reveal bruising from the hot glass cups stuck to his body. 'We have sucked fluids loose in your body to help you recover from your illness. All shall heal in good time.'

'Now you are awake, we can discover more remedies for you,' Dr. Toledo added. 'We shall start simple. You must drink a broth made of chicken and garlic at least three times a day. You have been suffering a pain of the stomach and garlic shall cure all. But first, more onion water with garlic and mustard.'

'To drink?' Crumwell screwed up his nose.

'And we must get you bathed, Mr. Crumwell, for "hygiène", as the French say, is important in your recovery. You are fortunate to be one of the cleanest English men I ever met, but still, the faster we get you from the bed, the better. Dr. Butts will demand you rest, but we believe in gentle movements to restore your health. Even if you simply sit in a chair and we move your arms for you. It moves the blood and will too help your mind. We must rub every muscle every day as you learn to walk again.'

'Have I been much ill?' Crumwell asked.

'You have been in bed for a month. We thought you so close to death that the King came to the bedside, only to witness you in the fits of fever,' Nicòla explained, to Crumwell's shock.

'Worry not, Mr. Crumwell,' Doctor Toledo added. 'For now, you are awake; not only can we look after your bodily health, we can restore your mind's health. We have heard of your devotion to your faith, and we have said prayer of many forms for you. You should also take a wife, Mr. Crumwell.'

'Would that help me recover?' Crumwell smiled, still holding Nicòla's hand.

'We must balance all parts of your life. We believe this lack of balance has caused your break from health. You are a man much loved by those in your household, Mr. Crumwell, and that shall help your health.'

'Dr. Toledo and Dr. Salomon knew my father when their families passed through Florence many years ago,' Nicòla said. 'Their fathers were doctors forced from Spain and treated Father and the Pope many years past.'

'I shall reward you dearly, and ensure you have safe passage and contacts back in Brussels,' Crumwell whispered to them both.

'We come where our souls guide us, Mr. Crumwell. Worry not.'

'Could I have a moment with my companion?' Crumwell asked. 'For soon my children, born and adopted, of all ages shall be upon me.'

'While their love is needed to help cure your body and mind, we shall ensure they are limited in their time with you,' Dr. Salomon replied, and both men bowed to their patient and shuffled from the room.

'Jewish doctors in London,' Crumwell said, his voice already fading again.

'I have worried you.' Nicòla shuffled up the bed, so she could sit alongside Crumwell and gently kissed his cheek. 'You may come to remember all in time, Tomassito, but know this – the illness you have suffered, something no one can understand, is one of the greatest afflictions many have witnessed. None have suffered worse than this; this was worse than the sweating sickness and the plague together. You have been to the fires of hell.'

'I have been dreaming, I think. I have been drowning in hot water. I close my eyes and see myself sinking in hot water. Thomas More is above the water, yet he will not help me to the surface. He meant to see me dead.'

'More is still locked in the Tower. You must fear not, for we have done our best during your illness. The court continues to function. We will soon find the Carthusian monks guilty of heresy and see them executed. The monasteries continue to be inspected.'

'And you? Pray, have I infected you?'

'You infected no one, my love, for you suffer from an internal destruction, one where you could not breathe, nor eat or drink. You could not cool down, or talk, move, or sleep soundly. Your stomach pained you. Your head pounded. You choked on every mouthful of fluid I tried to give you, fought every wet cloth we sought to clean you with and vomited every day and night.'

'God has been purging,' Crumwell uttered. 'I thought I had paid my debts to God.'

'We have.' Nicòla paused as a sharp pain started between her legs and shot up her back. 'Tomassito, I did my best, I swear. Yet I have fallen short in one regard in your absence.'

'How could it be so? There be nothing in this realm we cannot cure.'

'I am afraid…' Nicòla paused and took a heavy swallow, 'I am afraid God does not see it fit for a woman to both work at court and carry a child. I had to hold your place in the King's favour, and it came at great cost. My crying at your bedside added burdens to a son who could not bear any more. God did what needed to be done.'

Crumwell's weak hand drifted to Nicòla's stomach, and she flinched when he touched the soft mass which should have been solid with a baby boy. 'God took another Crumwell son?' he whispered. 'Why seek to torture me if the price to pay for our sins was the child's soul?'

'The boy's soul is safe, for Cranmer made sure. But I fear I shall forever be in debt to the Lord.'

'I know we must follow God's will, and yet what God would take the soul of a child as payment? And more than once?'

'All I can say to our Lord and Saviour is a great thank you for bringing you back. If I had to trade the life of the baby for yours, I can only submit to God's will, no matter how awful it was to suffer.'

'Are you in much pain?' Crumwell asked.

'It happened but yesterday, but for all the horror, it was not too difficult. I can only beg God to never again send me a child if he has no means to let me keep him.'

'If God has done this to us,' Crumwell said as he rested his tired head on Nicòla's shoulder, 'perchance now we can continue our love knowing God has taken all he can from us.'

'God not yet has our heads.'

'Then we shall have to take heads, for I believe you are no longer in debt to God. Perchance God is in debt to us.'

'God cannot be in debt.'

'Forget the torture we have endured these past weeks, past years, for it is time they treated us like the kings and queens we could be in this country. Perchance your Jewish men are right; for our bodily health to improve we must improve the health of our minds. We must learn to eat well, drink well, sleep well. Love well.'

'I can mourn our baby, but I could not live a day without you.'

'Or I you.'

'Let this illness never be seen on Earth again.'

Chapter 23 – April 1535
Whitehall Palace, London

If soomeone you love deepends on your lye, then it is easy

As much as Crumwell detested to admit it, his new rivet spectacles were rather useful. The silver frame, held by a single rivet which balanced upon his nose, held the Murano glass before his eyes, allowing him to see clearer than he had for years. He knew his old patron Francesco, Nicòla's father, had worn them thirty years prior, yet never imagined himself to be old enough to wear them. Yet now, at court for the first time in six weeks, Crumwell wore new spectacles on his face, a walking staff at his side. At least the staff was beautiful; glorious polished dark wood, a silver knob atop with his initials engraved. Nicòla had it made to appease his indifference to relying on a stick to help him walk. But if wearing the spectacles and carrying a staff got him back to court, Crumwell was ready to do so. Such was the amount of his weight loss meant getting around the court was far simpler than he expected, though all his clothes had to be resewn, now half the man he used to be.

Crumwell stood in King Henry's presence chamber, leaning heavily on the staff when Ambassador Chapuys entered the room. Without the King present, Chapuys wandered over and Crumwell gritted his teeth. News of Crumwell's return to court spread, so a quiet return to work became impossible.

Chapuys looked Crumwell up and down as if judging his existence. 'The rumours are true,' Chapuys squeezed through his French accent. 'You have returned to court at last. Many thought the double-minded man dead, Crumwell.'

'Many have wished so.'

'Many have added it to their nightly prayers.'

'Perchance, Eustace, perchance. Have you come to pick over my bones? I am sorry, but I have not yet finished with them.'

Chapuys laughed just a touch. 'I hear idle gossip you smuggled Jews into England, to cure you with witchcraft.'

'Some would call your Catholic faith witchcraft also, so be careful who you throw such accusations towards, for I am still the Vicegerent of this country.'

'And four monks are on trial now for their lives, all due to not signing your Oath. The judges hearing their cases are men in your pocket!'

'Everyone is in my pocket,' Crumwell said calmly. After the pain of the last six weeks, nothing Chapuys said would bait him into anger. He had not the strength for anger. 'We issued these monks warnings for their treason and hateful speeches against Queen Anne. I gave them a chance to repent a year past, and they refused. Now, if they are found guilty of treason, be it on their heads only.'

Behind Chapuys, Crumwell saw Nicòla come in, her hands full with papers, probably petitions given to her in the antechamber outside. She had fulfilled Crumwell's role at court to her own detriment, and stood hither today, only two weeks after losing a child, and still weak from pain and worry. Before Crumwell could catch Nicòla's eye, the door to Henry's privy chamber opened and the man himself appeared looking worn and weary. Without a word, he climbed the two carpeted stairs to his throne and sat down while everyone remained bowed and hushed.

'Thomas Crumwell!' Henry said when he noticed him standing against the wall. Chapuys swiftly edged himself away from Henry, his flapping lips finally silenced. 'You have come forth once more! How glad I am to see you in our court as we have much to contend with today.'

'Thank you, Your Majesty.'

'You look old,' Henry replied.

'As do you.'

Henry roared with laughter. 'Only you could speak in such words, Thomas. Only you.' He paused and turned to Nicòla, standing firm in the centre of the large room. 'Our dear Mr. Frescobaldi. I see you have come with all we need today?'

'Indeed, Your Majesty,' Nicòla said, her voice low and controlled. She did not even look to Crumwell, which hurt his feelings. Nicòla stood before the King in total confidence; she had watched court for years, stood in silence in the background, yet seemed to have no trouble in stepping forward now.

'How is the trial against the monks from the London Charterhouse? Any confessions? We must secure the public obedience of Carthusian monks, and they must support my marriage to Anne.'

159

'All have confessed to speaking ill of the Queen, Your Majesty, and witnesses testified as such. The first four monks are due to be pronounced guilty and they shall face execution. That sentence will be handed out this week.'

'Is Sebastian Newdigate among them?'

'No, Your Majesty. Newdigate has not yet been arrested.'

'Newdigate was a friend of mine, he worked within my privy chamber before taking up a monastic life. I would not wish to see him quartered. He is not arrested, yet he has not signed the Oaths of Supremacy and Succession?'

'No, Your Majesty, he has not. These first four monks shall be executed promptly, but we shall arrest more. I am sad too that your friend shall be among those arrested unless you expressly forbid it.'

'No, I cannot,' Henry sighed. 'We must punish all.'

Crumwell watched Nicòla, who stood tall to Henry as she calmly spoke about having monks hanged, drawn and quartered. He had spent six weeks fighting in bed, yet Nicòla had lost a child and risen in Crumwell's eyes. She locked her eyes on Henry while she spoke, something many men could not do.

'Let us talk of finer things,' Henry said. 'I am to knight Thomas Wyatt.'

'I think Sir Thomas Wyatt sounds most fitting,' Nicòla replied with a smile. 'He shall be hither tomorrow to thank His Majesty.'

'Splendid. What else?'

'We need to discuss which roles Secretary Crumwella shall cease to hold.'

That startled Crumwell. He leaned away from the wall and leaned on his staff. He had heard none of this. Was he losing places at court? Was he losing positions? And yet Nicòla stood there and mentioned it as if it was acceptable? Now Nicòla glanced at Crumwell. Her green eyes were still and calm.

'Shall we run through the list, Your Majesty?' she asked, her eyes on Crumwell.

'Your Majesty…' Crumwell began.

Henry raised a hand to stop Crumwell. 'I am awarding you the position of Steward of the Manor of Savoy and Bailiff of Enfield in Middlesex, Thomas. Both roles I hope you can handle.'

'Naturally, Your Majesty, and I thank you…'

'Also, the Lordships of Edmonton and Sainsbury, Middlesex.'

'Lordship?' Crumwell asked, his throat already burned for the day, even though he had only broken his fast not two hours ago.

'Can you cope with such a role, Thomas, with your illness?'

'I have made a full recovery… to say I shall make a full recovery with all haste.'

'I shall also appoint you Steward of the Duchies of Lancaster, Essex, Hertfordshire and Middlesex. I cannot make you a duke, Thomas, but I can award the duchies to you.'

'The roles are handled through series of deputies,' Nicòla said as she fiddled with the papers in her hands. 'Secretary Crumwella shall be able to hold such a prestigious role with his other ministerial roles.'

The Duchy of Lancaster was the greatest role, one Sir Thomas More had held, Sir Thomas Audley too, both before being Lord Chancellor. Even with the roles of Chief Minister and Vicar-general, Crumwell still longed for the title. He still did not have the King's Great Seal in his possession.

'Sir William Paulet shall take over much of the work as Surveyor of the King's Woods with Secretary Crumwella,' Nicòla said as if they had decided it without Crumwell's opinion. 'Privy Councillor Richard Crumwella shall take a joint role in the running of Hertford Castle and Berkeley Castle. Ralph Sadler shall take the role of Clerk of the Hanaper, held jointly with Secretary Crumwella. Robert Wroth, who has been working as the Steward of Westminster Abbey in Secretary Crumwella's absence shall continue jointly for now.'

'See, we seek not to supplant you, Thomas,' Henry said. 'Only ease your burden.'

'Running this kingdom is no burden!' Crumwell cried. 'Your Majesty,' he added in hurry.

'We are yet to appoint a new Chancellor and High Steward for Cambridge University, and Commissioners for the Peace for Bristol, Kent, Middlesex and Surrey,' Nicòla added.

'I can manage those roles,' Crumwell spat out, hurt to not have Nicòla on his side. 'I have aides and deputies all who work to keep my offices functioning, Your Majesty. I seek not to rule, only to serve.'

'You may have those titles if you choose, Thomas,' Henry warned. 'But there is worry you are holding all the power in England and that almost killed you. Your pride took over your body, and you failed.'

'I fail at nothing!' Crumwell cried, already feeling sweat upon his brow.

'It has not been a good time to have my Vicegerent of the monasteries in bed, Thomas. For the inspections around England are underway, and the inspection papers are filling offices.'

'I have that well in hand, Your Majesty,' Nicòla said, and again Crumwell felt supplanted. 'At our next monasteries meeting in the privy chamber, we can discuss abuses seen in monasteries and abbeys around your country. Plus, we have new totals on the profits you shall gain from dissolving these corrupt institutions.'

'I can be ready to take over the role as head of monastery inspections again, Your Majesty,' Crumwell cut in over Nicòla. 'I can be ready to discuss them today.' Lies straight from his lips. He felt weak and needed to rest soon. But he did not work all his life to be cut out of important matters of state due to a mystery illness.

'Mr. Frescobaldi has made for a good deputy in your absence,' Henry replied, 'and you should be most proud of the work done by your creature. The work is penance for his behaviour in assaulting the Imperial Ambassador. Frescobaldi has translated many great quotes from "The Prince" by Niccolò Machiavelli for me. Frescobaldi, which quote did you use to explain your outburst towards the Ambassador?'

'Whenever men are not obliged to fight from necessity, they fight from ambition, Your Majesty,' Nicòla recited.

'Yes,' Henry agreed. 'I like to see those who work in my court have such ambition to impress me.'

Nicòla did not flinch, not blink, nothing. Crumwell could see her face lined with pain. She did not seek to supplant him, only save him from his own ambition. She appeared dull, hidden under rose-gold curls. Crumwell's vanity and need for power had pushed them both to their limits.

'Have you heard the Waif's plan for royal progress, Thomas?' Henry asked. 'We are to be away for months, promoting the Reformation outside of London.'

'I confess I know none of this, Your Majesty.'

'Tell us the details,' Henry asked Nicòla.

'The court shall be on progress for almost four months,' Nicòla said, to the people in the room, and listening from the doorway. 'We shall make thirty stops along the way, travelling through Oxfordshire, Wiltshire, Hampshire and Berkshire, starting and finishing at Windsor Castle. Has my foreign tongue pronounced these curious regions, Your Majesty?'

'Well enough. Oh, Thomas, it shall be marvellous, a chance to show off my beautiful Anne and talk of the Reformation we shall push through this country, Thomas. You shall come?'

'I could but try.'

'Try getting more deputies such as the Waif, and perchance you could enjoy this glorious reign of ours. I cannot award titles to Frescobaldi, being the foreign creature of the Crumwell Chambers,' Henry continued. 'I know you reward your master secretary well enough. Frescobaldi, could you suggest a reward for your work?'

'I live to serve my master, Your Majesty. If I could ask for anything, I would ask you to promote Archbishop Cranmer to be the deputy of the Vicar-general position, so you have Secretary Crumwella in charge of the legal matters, while Archbishop Cranmer deals with any religious matters.' Again, Nicòla sought to take roles from him. Crumwell could not believe his own ears. Perchance he was still in bed, raging with fever.

'Another sound decision. We must take care of our Thomas, should we not?' Henry laughed.

'Your Majesty, I am well…'

'You know what we need, Frescobaldi?' Henry said to the room. 'Secretary Crumwell needs a new wife.'

Both Crumwell and Nicòla startled at this suggestion, said where hundreds of ears were in the close distance. 'Your sister,' Henry said and winked to Nicòla. 'Your sister's name?'

'Nicòletta Frescobaldi de'Medici, Duchess of Florence,' Nicòla choked.

'But the Duke wants an annulment, does he not? To marry the bastard child of the Emperor?'

'That is the rumour, yes, Your Majesty,' she replied.

'Your sister will lose her vast dowry if they annul the marriage?'

'Yes, Your Majesty.'

'Does the annulment have good cause?'

'I believe it does. The new Pope is eager to make peace with the Emperor and will undo the marriage sanctioned by the old Pope. Florence is not a safe city, and it needs to be in the embrace of Rome and the Emperor.'

'Your sister, one hidden away in country estates outside Florence, shall need refuge. Her bastard daughter lives in Crumwell's home still, does she not?'

'She does, Your Majesty.'

'Perchance the Duchess shall make a fine bride for our Thomas?' Henry continued to tease.

Crumwell gasped as the floor came towards him. He knew he was fainting but was powerless to stand up to the King's jests and his illness.

Chapter 24 – May 1535
Tyburn, London

People lye when they are afrayd of the trouth

'John Houghton, of the London Carthusian Charterhouse, you are found guilty of high treason. You are to be laid on a hurdle and so drawn to the place of execution, and there to be hanged, cut down alive, your member to be cut off and cast in the fire, your bowels burnt before you, your head smitten off, and your body quartered and divided at the King's will, and God have mercy on your soul.' The words came forth from the panel with ease. Houghton's verdict, along with the others, went just as planned.

In Crumwell's absence, Nicòla had spent much time in the court, listening to the charges laid against the four Carthusian monks who refused to take the Oath. Houghton had been warned a year before his arrest; all the men had been warned. Now, Houghton, Prior of the London Charterhouse, and Robert Lawrence, Prior of Beauvale and Augustine Webster, Prior of Epworth would die at Tyburn. So too would Richard Reynolds, a Bridgettine monk from Syon Abbey. A secular priest from Middlesex, who called himself John Haile, would be executed for speaking against King Henry's new marriage.

The truth of the matter was far removed from the trials. The execution took place on a wet day, the fourth day of May. No sounds of familiar voices placing calm judgement now; the air filled with cries, screams, gasps and shrieks. The smell of Londoners packed at Tyburn to watch the spectacle made Nicòla hold a glove to her face; the wide hat upon her head too thin to muffle the noise of the crowd. Crumwell did not attend; none of the lords attended. Twas not deemed safe. Nicòla went along, left the court when Crumwell had not a moment to notice her missing. She had sat in the court and listened as these men pledged to die for their beliefs, for their

Catholic faith. These men would not betray what they believed and wanted to die the most horrific death. Nicòla had been the one to ensure that Crumwell's trial, which he could not organise from his sickbed, got the result desired by the King. She needed to be the one to witness the deaths.

Hanging each man took longer than expected. Each struggled against the rope, Nicòla close enough to hear them choking. Their bodies, cut down and moving more by chance than effort, wiggled in the light rain as they were castrated and disembowelled. The axe used to cut off their heads and end their pain needed several chops to get through the bone; but the bodies broke apart easily enough. They would all have body parts scattered around London, including in front of monastic houses. Nicòla reported all back to the King.

Nicòla ordered a change of clothes before she went back into the Crumwell Chambers. When she found Crumwell, behind his new spectacles, he sat in his throne of a chair where she had sat these past eight weeks. No more; back to the stool in the corner at the desk dedicated to accounting.

Crumwell tossed his glasses on the table before him with a stern brow. 'Where were you all this time?' he asked as he leaned back in his chair.

Nicòla clasped her hands behind her back, to at least appear formal in the eyes of so many who could overhear the conversation out in the other offices. 'I am sorry, Secretary Crumwella. For I have been at Tyburn this morning.'

With a double click of his fingers, Crumwell gestured at the doors. Nicòla closed them and turned back to see an exasperated expression. 'Why, Nicò? Why would you wish to see something so vile? These men have committed high treason. We were all cautioned not to attend, for reasons of safety.'

'Because people could do to us what was done to those men of God.'

'If those men were good people like us, they would have obeyed their master, the King. For that is the holy law of this country, we wrote those laws in this office.'

'I made certain of those men's guilty verdicts while you were ill. I was the one who made sure all the work you had done continued in your absence. I had to see the end of the whole awful mess.'

'You lost a child – we both lost a child but weeks ago, Nicò. You need not be hither.'

'If I am condemned to this life, it is nothing to see four men cut into strips.'

Crumwell rose from his seat, feeling steady again. 'A many number of things would have ended in ruin if I had died, Nicò. One of my main worries was what would become of you! Now I am returned to health and you seem angry at me for my recovery. I know you are not a vicious person.

I know you are weak from your loss. I held my words when you told the King I needed deputies for many of my appointments. I hold my tongue as you spend every night in your own bed. Yet now you have defied me once again in witnessing executions without guards at your side. How are you condemned in this life? Do you mean our child's loss?'

Nicòla shrugged her shoulders, even she could not understand her recent anger.

'Every night since I recovered from my fever, Nicò, I should have prayed in thanks for my survival. Yet I have begged God to help me relieve the pain I feel when I think of you losing a child while I laid silent in bed, but one room away, and provided you with no comfort. The country could have come apart with my death and I think of you, of our children, our family, our friends.'

'I am angered none by your survival, Tom.' Nicòla could not use the pet name she used for him. 'I could not worry or mourn as a wife at a sick husband's bedside. I could not be in confinement as a mother who lost a child. I had to be hither, as a servant working for his master. All I shall ever be is a servant to a master. If you had died, then I would be in hiding, as Margarete is for being the secret wife of an archbishop. It has been a time of worry. I sought to ease your burden by placing deputies in your place while you fought illness, and now too, so you do not fall back into illness. I am but a servant.'

'You are my wife, Nicòletta.'

'Not in law, and not by words said before a man of God.'

'The King heard our words in marriage.'

'A king who can change the whole Church to relieve himself of marriage when the time is right.'

A heavy bang appeared from the other side of the closed doors. 'Away with you!' Crumwell boomed. 'Nicò, if that is what you wish, we shall say vows once more before Cranmer in the chapel within the palace walls.'

'Even Cranmer would not oblige, despite all his knowledge, for my annulment in Italy is not yet approved.'

'Then we shall increase the speed and get the job done. We can send a secret envoy to the Emperor in Rome, telling him he can get his daughter married to the Duke of Florence because we can secure the agreement of Nicòletta Frescobaldi.'

'And then what? I wear a dress and your reputation is tarnished by my association?'

'I know not how to please you, Nicò!'

The heavy bang appeared again. This time accompanied by the voice of his Crumwell's nephew Richard. 'Secretary Crumwell, urgent news!'

Crumwell sunk back in his chair and Nicòla opened the doors. Richard came in with a rush, a message in his hand. 'News, uncle,' Richard said in a puff from running. 'News from Rome that Bishop Fisher is to be made a cardinal.'

'A cardinal!' Crumwell cried as he stood up again in a second. 'We shall sooner send Fisher's head to Rome than receive a red cardinal's hat in England! To think the Pope would make the traitor Fisher a cardinal, a privilege that once belonged to Cardinal Wolsey! He speaks and writes nothing but treason from his cell in the Tower.'

'Indeed.' Richard handed a pamphlet to Crumwell across the desk. 'This is a new work by Fisher. Tis called "The Ways to Perfect Religion" and is to be distributed.'

'Men have had their bodies carved up today for speaking against the King and Queen. And for speaking against the Reformation we seek to create,' Nicòla said to the pair before her. 'The time has come that Bishop Fisher and Sir Thomas More, who continue to sit in their cells after a year, who speak with one another through secret messengers, have their cases heard.'

'And what do you suggest?' Richard asked, looking between Nicòla and Crumwell.

'The time has come; they were warned of their fates,' Crumwell gruffed. 'Let us to the Tower at once.'

~~~

Nicòla walked with Crumwell, though a step behind, as expected. Both clad in black, they walked the pathways inside the Tower grounds, aware of the silence. Since guards had dragged the monks from their cells at dawn, everything was again locked up tight. At least by travelling on a private barge, it could distance Crumwell from the people of London, all angered at him for the morning's executions.

'What are you to say to Bishop Fisher?' Nicòla asked as they walked, a guard far ahead of them.

'I shall say he has been made a cardinal, and suggest he take back his writings and statements and submit to the King's will, or he shall not live long enough to receive his red hat.'

'Can we stop a bishop becoming cardinal?' Nicòla asked. 'As of now, hat or not, he is to be Cardinal Fisher, by order of the Pope.'

'To spite the King only. Rome does not rule religious law any longer. King Henry rules, he names cardinals.'

'Yet Henry has not done so.'

'Wolsey has been dead not yet five years. Fisher is no man to be a cardinal in Wolsey's place.'

'Perchance no man can be in Henry's eyes.'

Crumwell sighed, not looking at Nicòla as he spoke. 'I wish to let Fisher live quietly, and I shall tell him so. But Fisher is for the Pope at present, against executions, arrests, monastery inspections. Fisher could become a symbol for a larger revolt against the King. If he does not submit to the Oath now, then he faces trial and execution.'

'And Sir Thomas More?'

'More is but a fool, but also a symbol for rebellion. He is a known Catholic, strong in his faith, and against Henry and Anne. Imprisoned, he could be the symbol the people need to refuse the Oath. He too has run out of time.'

'Do you wish for us to execute More?'

Crumwell paused as they came to a door at the base of the White Tower, the most secure building in the centre of the grounds. 'I wish to stop people dying for faith, not promote death.'

'No one can sway Henry,' Nicòla replied as they continued along a dark hallway and up the first set of stairs.

'We can try one more time. Once I tell His Majesty about Fisher's cardinal elevation, Henry will want him dead. The least I can do is give Fisher this one last chance.'

'I wish not to see Fisher,' Nicòla replied as they walked along another hallway behind the guard. 'I believe in the Reformation and yet, when seeing men like Fisher, of another time and of the old faith…'

Crumwell stopped and turned around in the narrow hallway. She need not say any more. 'I permit you to wait outside, Nicò. I need no witness to this meeting.'

'Might I speak to Sir Thomas on your behalf?'

'He threatens to speak your truth,' Crumwell muttered under his breath.

'I am not afraid of Sir Thomas More.'

'Take his books, take his paper and quills. But he may turn vicious.'

The door closed behind Nicòla and she waited in the silent cell. Sir Thomas More sat in a chair across the room by an arched window, the light falling upon a tiny desk. Gone was the man of majesty; after a year in confinement, More had aged at speed; his hair all grey and dry like hay, his skin ashen, his clothes filthy, and the smell made Nicòla hold her breath.

'They send me the Waif?' More said with a dry cough. He troubled himself none to move from his plain chair. Nicòla moved to stand closer to him, not willing to get comfortable in the cell. 'Have I fallen so low I only get the creature which Crumwell keeps in his office?' More continued.

'Harsh words from such a pious man,' Nicòla said as she brought her hands together.

'Time has made me a different man. I cannot stand in this cell, with my wife and daughter crying, begging me, and not become a hardened man.'

'I come bearing news. Bishop Fisher is to be Cardinal Fisher.'

'What glorious news!' A smile spread across More's dirty face. 'The Pope has seen Fisher's determination to hold steady to the true faith!'

'It will see Fisher killed. Which means you are in danger, for you have been imprisoned for a while, and we can lay new charges, Sir Thomas.'

'Such as?'

'Such as you have been conspiring with Fisher within these walls. There are letters in Fisher's room, written by you.'

'No, he burns letters.' More bit his lower lip but it was too late.

'So, the letters are real. You fell into a simple trap, Sir Thomas,' Nicòla teased. 'Men were executed this morning for refusing to sign the Oath. Bishop Fisher, Cardinal Fisher, is likely to die also for this. Yet you also do not swear the Oath and still say the Pope is the Head of the Church. You argue about petty legal details regarding my master's laws.'

'Your master, Mr. Frescobaldi, wrote laws stating a king could be the Head of the Church. You cannot create laws and use them to replace divine teachings!'

'We write such laws. Thousands across England are signing the Oath right now. You need to recant your words, sign the Oath, and you can go home, Sir Thomas. Fisher is being offered that same deal as we speak.'

'And if I do not sign?'

'Today I take your books, your papers and your quills, deprive you of all correspondence. They will give you a trial and then, if guilty, shall be executed at the King's pleasure.'

'Because the King's will and pleasure is law, all thanks to Crumwell.'

'Indeed. Do you deny the King is the Head of the Church? That his marriage to Anne is lawful and his rightful heir is Princess Elizabeth?'

'I stand not against Anne and Elizabeth. I am a true supporter of Katherine, and yet I seek not to argue against the marriage or succession.'

'And Henry as Head of the Church?'

'I have relied upon the legal precedent, the maxim "qui tacet consentire videtur" during my time in the Tower.'

'He who is silent is taken to agree,' Nicòla translated More's Latin.

'I have not expressed a word against the Oath of Supremacy.'

'Yet you have not sworn and signed that the Oath is right. You may not have denied the Oath, but you have not spoken for it either. This argument shall not last forever, Sir Thomas.'

'No man may be the Head of Spirituality!' More said in anger. Nicòla narrowed her eyes. Those were the words she needed to have More convicted of treason.

'You accept the Pope was Head of Spirituality.'

'He is the Pope, chosen by God.'

'God chose Henry to be king,' Nicòla argued. 'What if the law changed, and Henry was no longer the King? Would you accept it?'

'I would have to, as an English subject, though it could never occur.'

'What if a law passed saying Secretary Crumwella was king, would you accept it?' Nicòla asked.

'Again, I would have to face it, if the law was clear. I see not how this could be, but...'

'I imagine this only, Sir Thomas,' Nicòla interrupted. 'What if we wrote a law, stating Secretary Crumwella was the Pope?'

'No such law could be written. No one can make laws to decide a pope. That is a divine choosing.'

'What if the law said Secretary Crumwella was now God?'

'No, because man cannot make laws that decide on the spirituality. Only God can decide such things.'

Nicòla desperately tried to keep her smile to herself; she had what she needed. More had just denied Henry as the Head of the Church, albeit in different words. She knocked on the cell's door once more, and it opened at once. 'See that all books, papers and inks are taken,' she commanded. 'Everything is to be cleared from this cell, as Sir Thomas More shall no longer be permitted to write, read or send and receive anything from his cell. Take the desk and chair too.'

More rose from his chair as guards took away the pile of books nestled into the corner of the room, bathed in sunlight. 'Tu loquerisne Latine?'

'I speak Latin,' Nicòla replied and turned back.

More watched the guard for a moment. 'Is it true?'

'Is what true, Sir Thomas?'

More fixed his eyes upon Nicòla again. 'Vos autem femina.'

More still wondered whether Nicòla was a woman. 'Yes,' she taunted him. 'One of great power, in Rome, in Florence, in London.'

'Fornicariae,' More spat back, calling her a whore.

'And yet no one would believe you, were you to speak out against me. Your King trusts in me, your Archbishop of Canterbury, so many people believe in me, Sir Thomas. You may slander me, as so many have done before. I came today in good faith and you have shown me what path you wish to take. God have mercy upon your soul.'

Chapter 25 – June 1535
The Tower, London

Anger at lyes lasts forever

Crumwell pleaded in private.
King Henry raged in public.
Cardinal Fisher mourned in private.
Richard Rich lied in public.
All of Catholic England prayed.
Of all the sins and wants, all the questioning and avoiding, it was Rich's words which did the most damage. A council of twelve, Crumwell among them, Lord Chancellor Audley at the head, presided over the trial of John Fisher, freshly stripped of his title as Bishop of Rochester. Now a commoner, accused of high treason by failing to swear the King's Oath, would have to argue for his life. Yet there were no words to save the old man from death, for the decision was made the moment Henry decided he wanted Fisher gone forever. And so, Crumwell got Richard Rich to act as a witness to Fisher saying he would refuse to bow to the will of the King. Crumwell wrote the lies Rich was to say, and in return, the role of England's Solicitor General would be in Rich's keeping.

'Fisher falsely, maliciously, and traitorously wished, willed, desired, and imagined, invented, practised, and attempted to deprive the King of the dignity, title, and name of his royal estate, the title of Supreme Head of the Church of England. He stated this in the Tower, on seventh day of May, when, contrary to his allegiance, he said, in the presence of different true subjects, falsely, maliciously, and traitorously, these words: "The King our sovereign Lord is not Supreme Head on Earth of the Church of England."'

The chorus of watchers and jurors of men sat in the court at Westminster Hall and listened to the lies as they poured from Rich's smirking mouth, yet all Crumwell saw was Nicòla's heavy shoulders. For reasons Crumwell never understood, Nicòla despised Rich. She claimed him to be untrustworthy, despite Rich's constant service to Crumwell. But Crumwell and the other jurors needed a witness to Fisher's treason, and Rich was more than willing to keep company with such lies.

Crumwell wanted not to see Bishop Fisher killed, hanged in public, his innards cut from him, his head struck off, limbs chopped away, no. He wanted the people of England to stop rallying to Fisher's defence, to stop believing in the Catholic faith, the faith Henry needed to take from his realm. Everyone needed to believe in Henry's marriage to Anne, now two years old, and they had to believe Henry ruled the Church in England, not the Pope. Fisher was steadfast in his faith; Crumwell had no choice but to admire the man's courage and conviction in his beliefs. But Fisher was ready to be a martyr to his religion, and Crumwell needed to make him one, to spare the wrath of Henry's current rages.

On that warm seventeenth day of June, the court ruled that Fisher had to die for his crimes. The people of London were ready to explode in anger and disbelief at the decision made, not that a single person could swear it startled them. June 24 was the feast day of Saint John the Baptist, executed by King Herod for questioning his marriage to Herod's brother's widow. Even the most foolish man in London could see the lesson in the tale. As the people talked, Henry continued to feel angered, and promised to commute Fisher's sentence to beheading if he was dead before the feast day. So, he left it to Crumwell to see that on June 22, Fisher's head, due to be crowned with a cardinal's hat, would instead be struck off at Tower Hill.

Grey clouds hovered over London on the morning of Fisher's execution. Crumwell stood, Nicòla beside him as Fisher appeared in the main doorway from Bell Tower at nine in the morning, ready to go to the site of his death. Their eyes met for a moment, Fisher a man of five and sixty years, a man kept in the Tower for a year. He was no longer the man Crumwell remembered from all those years before, now he had been worn down by the agony of suffering for his faith. Yet Fisher would die for his God, and he stood, his dark eyes sturdy against Crumwell's golden gaze, a man dressed in his best of black, ready to meet the God he stood for, who stood above his king. Just for a moment, Crumwell had no words to utter; he held the country and their souls in his hands, and yet he could find no words to mark such an occasion.

It was Nicòla, quite out of turn, who found the words as Fisher stood in the meek sunlight. 'And this is life eternal, that they might know thee the only true God, and Jesus Christ, whom thou hast sent. I have glorified thee on the Earth: I have finished the work which thou gravest me to do,' Nicòla repeated calmly.

172

'John 17:3-4,' Fisher replied as he wrung his hands. 'Even in this last hour, I can learn more from our Lord.'

Crumwell turned slightly to Nicòla to see her holding rosary beads between her fingers, forbidden in Crumwell's presence now, hidden from all at court and the King's spies. Yet they sat between her slender fingers. Where Nicòla could have gained them, Crumwell knew not.

Nicòla sank to her knees on the damp path before Fisher, and neither the sheriff nor the guards moved as she did so, none prepared to stop the moment. For none believed in the execution of a bishop.

'O Lord, Jesus Christ, Redeemer and Saviour, forgive my sins against the great Cardinal Fisher,' Nicòla begged her hands clasped before her, her green eyes shut tight.

Fisher reached out and took her hands in his, his skin reddened and scratched from neglect. Nicòla opened her eyes and looked up at the weary face of the man, and it occurred to Crumwell. Nicòla had poisoned Fisher several years ago, and they had boiled his cook to death after taking the blame. Time had passed, but the sin had not yet been cleansed from Nicòla as far she believed.

'Count not my transgressions, but, rather, my tears of repentance. Remember not my iniquities, but, more especially, my sorrow for the offences I have committed. I long to be true to Your Word and pray that You will love me and come to make Your dwelling place within me. I promise to give You praise and glory in love and in service all the days of my life, for what I have done to Cardinal Fisher surpassed the glory I can be bestowed by Jesus Christ,' Nicòla continued, her eyes fixed upon Fisher's.

'There is no offence, however serious, that the Church cannot forgive. There is no one who may not confidently hope for forgiveness, provided his repentance is honest,' Fisher said, to Nicòla's tender and hopeful smile. He placed one hand on Nicòla's head as a tear bubbled in her eye. 'May almighty God bless you, the Father, and the Son, and the Holy Spirit.'

'Amen,' all uttered as Nicòla rose to her feet.

Crumwell swallowed hard as Nicòla stepped back to come beside him once more. All the faces of those around him appeared as his own; all could not quite believe such a day had come. Fisher stumbled, his health so bad from his time in prison he could no longer stand, indeed even the trip down the stairs had been brutal.

Two guards rushed to hold Fisher, who fell into their arms with great anguish. 'Fear not, Bishop Fisher,' Crumwell found his voice, addressing him with the title he lost months ago, by Crumwell's own directive. 'We shall have you carried to Tower Hill, none shall punish you with such a demanding walk.'

Crumwell expected chaos along the short walk Fisher would take to the block, but no. Instead, the crowds who lined the way parted with much peace and reverence for the occasion. Crumwell stood with Nicòla tucked behind him, and they watched Fisher carried in a cart from the gates of the Tower and through the crowd. The people of London may have been willing to submit to what would happen today and would respect Fisher, but they could turn on Crumwell, the man who had begun the evil process of taking their Catholic nation apart. Never would Crumwell dare walk into that crowd with comfort and he would never risk Nicòla's safety. Rather, once Fisher departed, Crumwell and Nicòla left through another doorway, out of the way of the commoners at Tower Hill.

Nicòla stood close, right near the front of the execution. Crumwell questioned nothing, as Nicòla's behaviour had been difficult since his recovery, and losing the baby had seemed to scatter her mind somewhat. If Nicòla thought watching the horror of Fisher's execution was a punishment, or would make up for things they had done, then Crumwell had no choice but to accept Nicòla's choice. Fisher reached out to one guard, to gesture them to halt when he reached the bottom of the scaffold.

'No,' he uttered, 'for I shall walk these final steps alone.'

Crumwell watched along with the silent crowd as Fisher managed to walk up the few wooden stairs unaided, an effort for a man who could barely stand. Fisher stood at the top of the stairs for a moment, and the sun appeared from beyond the clouds, beaming upon his face. His eyes closed, Fisher raised his hands towards the sky.

'Accédite ad mum, et illuminamini, et facies vestrae ne confundaris,' he uttered to himself.

'They looked unto Him and were lightened: and their faces were not ashamed,' Nicòla repeated to herself as she delicately touched the beads still between her fingers.

Forgiveness given to the hesitant executioner, his black gown and tippet hat stripped away, Fisher turned his attention to the hundreds within the small space waiting to see him die. 'Christian people, I come hither to die for Christ's Holy Catholic Church. I thank God that I have not feared death. I desire you to help me with your prayers, so now of death's stroke, I may stand steadfast for the Catholic faith, free from fear. I beseech Almighty God of his infinite goodness to save the King and this realm, and that it may please Him to send the King good counsel.'

Fisher spoke with such confidence, such courage that the crowd dared not utter a word. Send the King good counsel; it stung Crumwell. He was the King's counsel, the man to rule in the shadows. He knew he did right by England to pull them from darkness and into the light of the Reformation. Yet, on this day, with the only sunlight over London shining upon Bishop Fisher, Crumwell had never felt more alone.

'God bless you, Cardinal Fisher,' cried a voice; Nicòla's voice. She was not the only one; it started off a chain of cries of love and faith to Fisher on the scaffold before them all. Voices died away again as Fisher fell to his knees before the block. His tired voice rang out once more, back to Latin for the Te Deum. With each line, the crowd joined in, blindly following the Latin words they did know, which was why Crumwell wished all to pray and give hymns in English. While stumbling Latin poured from many mouths, Nicòla spoke perfectly.

'We believe that thou shalt come; to be our Judge. We, therefore, pray thee, help thy servants: whom thou hast redeemed with thy precious blood. Make them be numbered with thy Saints: in glory everlasting...'

Fisher's voice trailed off with the final lines. The sun continued to shine in just the one spot where Fisher sat, his eyes closed to the light; the executioner placed the clean white handkerchief over Fisher's dark eyes. His skin, worn by time, aged by prison, hardened by injustice, appeared grey next to the innocent fabric bound over his sight.

Crumwell swallowed hard; again, truth sat in the air; either Fisher died, and the Catholic faith got chased away, or Crumwell would be on the block and the Reformation would sink back into Europe. No honesty, no justice, no fairness entered London today. How to worship God was the only subject under discussion and Crumwell had to keep his own head.

Despite the expectation, the readiness and the preparation, when the sharpened axe fell upon Fisher's slender neck, the crowd gasped in fright; it had occurred on such a meek summer's day. How so much blood could squirt from such a thin and weakened body worried even Crumwell, a man hardened by war. The silence wore away as women wept, and men shuffled their feet on the damp ground, their silent faces stuck in hatred.

Crumwell turned slightly to Nicòla, only to see a fresh horror, for in the front row of the crowd, fresh blood from Fisher's tiny neck had splattered upon her dark olive cheeks. Her green eyes flicked to Crumwell, yet she said nothing; God had done this, another punishment, marking her face with the blood of a man she once tried to kill, and for the man boiled in her place years ago.

Without a word, Crumwell took a handkerchief from his pocket and wiped the blood from her face. Crumwell's personal guards had moved ever closer to him and Nicòla as the crowd moved and began their shuffle now the spectacle was over.

'If it is ever me on the scaffold, I wish you to be the last thing I see,' Nicòla uttered as Crumwell wiped her face.

'And I you,' he replied, his voice gentle, almost lost among the people about them. 'Pray us never be upon the scaffold.'

'I work every day to avoid such.'

'Morirei per te,' she uttered as Crumwell wiped the final droplets from her cheeks.

'I would die for you, too. Ti amo moltissimo.'

Nicòla smiled and repeated his words back to him, not understood by the crowd. She loved him deeply too. It took the death of a pious man before them for their rift to cease. Something good had to come from this awful St Alban's Day, the day of the first Martyr of Britain. Hopefully, this head, to be stuck on a pole on London Bridge, Fisher's body dumped in an unmarked grave, would appease Henry's anger and hunger for power. Or any person could be next.

Chapter 26 – July 1535
The Tower, London

Lyes can kill, but so can trouths

Sir Thomas Audley, Lord Chancellor. Sir Richard Leicester. Thomas Howard, Duke of Norfolk. Sir John Port. Sir John Fitz-James. Sir John Spelman. Sir John Baldwin, Lord Chief Justice. Sir Walter Luke. Sir Anthony Fitz-Herbert. Nicòla's eyes ran over each man seated side by side at the bench of the court. Some were friends, some enemies, some strangers. All looked upon Nicòla, standing with her hands clasped together, her expression uncomfortable.

'Mr. Frescobaldi?' Audley prompted her.

Nicòla glanced to her left, and there sat Sir Thomas More, leaning back in his chair, his body of seven and fifty years weak from a year in the Tower cell. The great man himself, talked of throughout Europe as a genius, a humanist, a scholar and religious man, once the greatest friend to the King of England, sat in a chair and waited with patience for Nicòla's words. Close behind More sat Crumwell, the man who had pushed her to this place. Someone had to give evidence against More in court; Nicòla swore it should be Richard Rich again, as he revelled in lying about Bishop Fisher. But no, Crumwell's insistence put Nicòla forward, but Nicòla swore she would only tell the truth. Luckily, the men of the court knew how to frame questions, so the truth sounded guilty.

'Lord Chancellor,' Nicòla said, finding her voice. She turned slightly to face the judges again, there to decide More's fate.

'Please tell the court what Sir Thomas More said to you in his cell in the Tower when you sought to take his books and papers,' Audley said.

Nicòla knew what to say, for the moment More had spoken with her, she knew his words sounded damning. 'Sir Thomas said he believed the Pope was the Head of Spirituality.'

'Indirect c-c-contradiction to the Act of Supremacy, st-st-stating that King Henry is Head of the ch-ch-Church in England,' the Duke of Norfolk replied, his angry voice far louder than Nicòla's.

'Yes, Your Grace,' Nicòla answered and turned to the jury again, away from More's eyes. 'Sir Thomas spoke of God appointing the Pope, as only God could decide who leads the Church on Earth.'

'And what did you ask Sir Thomas afterwards?' Audley asked.

'I asked Sir Thomas if parliament could change a law, stating that King Henry was no longer king, and would he, Sir Thomas, accept the law change.'

'And?' Norfolk pushed.

'And Sir Thomas claimed he would accept that change, as parliament can decide on such matters, even though Henry is king in God's eyes and man's.'

'Go on,' Audley gestured to Nicòla to speak freely.

'I asked if Sir Thomas would accept Secretary Crumwella asking parliament to change the law, and he replied yes, as an English subject, he had to accept such law changes. So, I asked if Sir Thomas would accept Crumwella as Pope if the law was passed in parliament. But Sir Thomas claimed he would not accept the law as neither man nor parliament has any power over God or the Church.'

'And all these w-w-words directly contradict the laws in England that sit within the Act of s-s-Supremacy,' Norfolk boomed once more.

'Mr. Frescobaldi, do you believe Sir Thomas More is truthful in his words? Do you believe Sir Thomas was holding firm to his belief about the King's position in our realm and Church?' Audley asked.

Nicòla turned slightly again, looking over More's head to Crumwell, who nodded only once. Could Nicòla know whether More was telling his opinion, his true thoughts, his idea of the day? No, she could only guess. But she had to do her part in destroying Sir Thomas More.

'Yes, Lord Chancellor,' she sighed, 'I believe Sir Thomas More spoke his true feelings on that day, for he had no reason to lie. His words were the same as other interrogations in recent months. Sir Thomas believes no law change could make any man Head of the Church of England. Sir Thomas thinks himself above the law.' That last sentence was something Nicòla believed. Sir Thomas cared nothing for honesty or truth when he tortured men personally in his home for being members of the Reformation.

From the corner of her eye, Nicòla saw More shaking his head at her words. She caught the expression on Crumwell's face; his stern brow showed how desperately he needed Nicòla to be the witness at the trial. She took another deep breath as a tiny bead of sweat formed at her hairline.

'I believe Sir Thomas More thinks his conscience to be the wisest, most sincere, of all men in England. From bishops to laymen, all take the Oath yet More refuses to do so. He does not stand for his faith, as the late Cardinal Fisher did, nor any monks who have died for this cause. Sir Thomas comes before the court with the belief he need not be held to the laws of England.'

With sudden agitation, More rose from his seat, his long grey beard shaking with anger. More had said little throughout the day of his trial, little to any person in the past year. Nicòla's words had shaken free his patience and restraint.

'You are of no standing,' More seethed at Nicòla, standing only feet away from him. 'You are not credible, and you are but a foreigner from a background no one can understand. You stand hither today as a mere puppet of Thomas Crumwell. You, nothing but the creature from Italy. I am sorry you feel such need to commit perjury, but again, you are not even a real man.'

'That is enough!' Crumwell cried over murmurings of the crowd.

Nicòla turned to More and looked him dead in the eye. 'If the court needs, I am happy to grant you the details of both my birth and my education. Indeed, all be far from these lands, and I may not have the legal experience of Sir Thomas More, of Secretary Crumwella, or of Lord Chancellor Audley, but I have a legal mind. Speak not of perjury, Sir Thomas, for the crimes committed by you speak of worse things!'

'If I did say these words to you in my cell, little puppet, they were said with no malice, and therefore can give no offence to the King! You come hither today, with four charges against my name and yet your only witness in the court is that of the Waif that Crumwell keeps as a pet? This is the guardian of your trial?' More scoffed and threw any angry wave at Nicòla as if to present her like a dead rat.

'You may s-s-seek to discredit the witness if you wish,' Norfolk said plainly, 'but you m-m-must do so in a way that is respectful to the c-c-court.'

More dropped into his seat once more. 'I seek to do no such thing. I seek to discredit the laws that see me hither today, these laws, written by Thomas Crumwell, at the whims and wills of King Henry, which are not just. The laws have no power and I seek nothing from false witnesses.'

Audley rose calmly from his seat to address More. 'This is the kingdom of England, Sir Thomas. In England, the laws of the land are for men to obey. You are an Englishman on English soil and you shall obey the laws.'

The two men looked at one another for a long moment, friends now pitted against one another. Once, not so many years ago, all these men would sit at dinner at Austin Friars and talk as friends and colleagues. Now, Henry's marriage to Anne had separated them to spill blood. Nicòla looked to Crumwell, who nodded to her. What they did today would last for the ages.

'The bishops, the nobles and the commoners of this realm have sworn the Oath, Sir Thomas. Do you presume to put yourself above them all?' Audley asked.

'The numbers are material, Lord Chancellor. I fear for you, though, as you have this farce forever connected to your name!' More screamed, spittle on his chin. 'My conscience is one of the highest learning and I know, in my heart and soul that only the Pope can rule the Church in England. England is but one part of Christendom, and no man can claim to control any part of God's lands! Rome has ruled the laws of God for one thousand years and no man, no Crumwell, can think to change those laws now!'

Nicòla felt shaky, perchance from the air of the court, of the yelling, or from the burden placed upon her shoulders. She put out one hand to steady herself, only to find nothing close by to hold.

'Faint, are you, Frescobaldi?' More questioned. 'Weak, yet it is I kept in a cell for over twelve months past. You are dining with the King in lavish comfort while I sit with rats, and yet you dare to be faint in the court? You have nothing but the heart and stomach of a woman. The mind of a woman. How can the court place any trust in one so feminine and unnatural?'

Nicòla felt someone come up behind her; a gentle turn showed it to be Ralph close at hand, who could sweep Nicòla away in one motion, his firm hand so steady Nicòla's feet barely touched the ground as he moved her away. The onlookers of the court found Nicòla to be entertainment. Nicòla sat on a stone bench outside the court, the summer air going some way to easing her panic of the filled courtroom. The yelling and screaming continued among the men of the court as she sat in a far corner alone, hidden politely from view. In the panic and confusion of such an ambitious case, no one would remember More almost telling Nicòla's great secret to the world. Oh, how she had failed Crumwell today when he depended upon her the most! Had the judges, lawyers and courtiers not been told what decision they had to reach in advance, Nicòla could not be certain they would win this case. More was right; how could a king change the laws and rule a religion? Because he had a Crumwell, that was how. A man smart enough to change every part of every law, thus changing what every man and woman in England had to think and feel and obey.

Crumwell appeared weary when he appeared from the court in search of Nicòla. He rushed to her side on the quiet stone bench, his hand close to hers on the stone, as close as they could be in public. 'What be this?' he asked, his golden eyes searching her face with worry. 'Are you ill?'

'I must confess, after seeing the killing of Fisher, seeing his fear in the moment of death, to stand but a week later to condemn another man is more than I can manage,' Nicòla said with a weak smile. 'If we are to have

Sir Thomas More killed, all of Europe will cry in outrage, and it will be my words that caused it all.'

'We can keep your name from the paperwork as much as possible, but I fear you are, to some degree, right,' Crumwell sighed. 'The trial is over, and the jury has retired to make their decision. I am the man who changed the laws of a country to give a king such powers over the Church, but I never thought I would take part in seeing men killed to uphold these laws. I thought we could be better. I never wanted men to die when we enacted this Oath upon the people.'

'I know this, Tomassito.' Nicòla brushed the edge of her hand against his upon the bench. 'None shall take enjoyment from this trial, not even Henry himself. He shall have to condemn his own lifelong friend because of his love for Queen Anne.'

'Such is the folly of men.'

'Promise me that you shall never change laws or make ill decisions based upon notions for me,' Nicòla said, her voice now as serious as she felt. 'For I am faint today in the heat, but I am not weak as More wishes. And I never wish to be what makes a great man like you weak.'

The rush of panicked footsteps tore their eyes from one another, to see Ralph rushing in their direction. 'Secretary Crumwell,' he panted, 'the jury has announced they are to come back and deliver the verdict to Audley now.'

'But they have been in private just fifteen minutes!' Crumwell cried. 'Are they to resolve all so soon?'

'You told them what the verdict had to be before the trial,' Ralph replied. 'Come, for this is a moment we cannot miss for all the world.'

Nicòla stood in the crowd of men urgent to see the result. Crumwell stood near the front of the court, close to the bench of judges. Nicòla noticed that the Earl of Wiltshire, Thomas Boleyn, and George Boleyn, Lord Rochford, had come close, after being hidden away for the trial. More pulled himself from his seat to hear the verdict brought down upon him by his friend, Audley. The Lord Chancellor rose from his chair and Nicòla could almost feel the breath being held by every man in the room. There were no secrets in what the verdict would be, but fears of More's execution were about to become true, like a nightmare come to life.

'Sir Thomas More, you are charged with high treason, for refusing to accept the King's marriage to Queen Anne, for conspiring with Bishop Fisher while in the Tower of London, for malicious talk against His Majesty King Henry, and for your failure to swear the Oath over the Act of Supremacy. The jury of your peers finds you guilty.'

The court fell into a state of disbelief, but Nicòla could only look at Crumwell, who stood stiff, his eyes upon More. The two men, together through times of good and bad for so many years in the English court, looked to another as all around, men talked and shook their heads. There was no way out of this situation, for Crumwell had made the choice to make Henry happy, and More would never stop his hatred over Henry's supremacy.

Audley waited until the men of the room composed themselves. 'Sir Thomas More shall be carried back to the Tower of London, by Sheriff William Kingston, then taken on a hurdle to Tyburn, there to be hanged till he should be half dead; then he should be cut down alive, his privy parts cut off, his belly ripped, his bowels burnt, his four quarters set up over four gates of the city, and his head upon London Bridge.'

More stood defiant against the words imposed upon him, and Crumwell's eyes drifted from More to Nicòla. He had the same look of resignation when Fisher got beheaded; either More lost his head, or Crumwell did. Nicòla knew those words to be the truth. In the laws Crumwell had made, either you agreed with King Henry, or you died. There were no more choices to be made.

~~~

Five long days passed before Henry commuted More's sentence, and only on July 6 did Henry have More beheaded at Tower Hill. Nicòla could not attend such an occasion, not when her own words helped to condemn the man, a man who stood for the Catholic faith as Nicòla did before she met Crumwell. More hugged his precious daughter Margaret one last time before his execution, so weak he could barely climb the stairs to face the axe. Crumwell told Nicòla later that More recited the Miser Psalm with great devotion as he kneeled before the block.

Have mercy on me, God, in your kindness. In your compassion blot out my offence. O wash me more from my guilt and cleanse me from my sin. My offences truly I know them; my sin is always before me. Against you, you alone, have I sinned; what evil in your sight I have done?

Nicòla chose those same words for her nightly prayer, for those who sinned against More on the day of July 6, who were as condemned as More. A single swing of the axe took More's life, a man devoted to his faith and his king.

Chapter 27 – July 1535
Austin Friars, London

Sumetymes the trouth is uglier than lyes

Windsor sat thirty miles from London where Crumwell watched More's head leave his body, yet Windsor yielded an air of another world, so needed by Henry. For the King could not talk of More's ending, and nothing could be discussed in Henry's presence, as he was to set off on progress, three months of visiting estates around the west and south of London, a chance to relax, let his people see their great King and Queen, and, as Crumwell prayed, for Anne to become pregnant again. A child had not stirred in Anne's belly for some four months now, and the King needed a son, to distract him from the desire to see men's heads on spikes.

Back at Austin Friars, they redesigned Crumwell's private office and the library; now he had double doors which opened out into his gardens. This meant the wide opening doors could stay open, the summer air breezing to his desk, much like the palaces of Florence. The only sound in the house came from the servants, only around 200 people, with many clerks now working from Crumwell's Master of the Rolls offices a few streets away. But the building at Austin Friars continued, men expected to work even in the heat, especially with plague not running rampant in the city this season. King Henry and the court had left from Windsor Castle a week prior, away on progress for three glorious months of peace.

'Do you worry for Ralph?'

Crumwell turned his heavy chair to Nicòla who sat across the room at a desk of her own, dressed in only hose and a linen shirt due to the heat. She appeared as a woman, but only Crumwell's eyes were in the room. 'No, why do you ask?'

'Because you have sent Ralph in your place on the King's progress, and now you are staring out of the window, which you do in times of worry.'

183

'I trust Ralph, everyone trusts Ralph. The King wants to think nothing of the agonies of past months, only of relaxing, of seeing his people and being with his wife.'

'I hear Henry Norris got rid of Henry's mistress, Lady Margaret.'

'Margaret Shelton has been sent back to her parents. Elizabeth Somerset, Lady Worcester, has offered to take Lady Margaret's place, but for now, the King needs to centre his lust on Anne.'

'What a horrid notion,' Nicòla shivered.

'That is treason, Nicò.'

Nicòla looked up from her desk with a light laugh and Crumwell wondered how long it had been since he heard such a sound. Even a smile seemed months ago.

'Before Ralph left on progress, he made sure there was ample marzipan sent to Dewhurst,' Crumwell told her.

'Good, for my daughter deserves her favourite treat for her birthday,' Nicòla replied and went back to reading at her desk. Crumwell sat back in his seat and watched her eyes skimming over a letter. The chest of mail had been dry of late. After the events of the past months, everything seemed dull. At least their daughter's fifth birthday, which they would celebrate at their estate in Dewhurst, was a happy occasion and excuse to celebrate.

'I have a bill hither,' Nicòla said, breaking Crumwell's dreaming. 'Gregory has spent £67 on clothing this month.'

'God's blood!' Crumwell exclaimed and sat up straight once more. 'I must put that boy to work. Or find him a wife and estate to manage.'

'He is but fifteen years. And not for women.'

'Sir Richard Southwell has a place in his household, at Woodrising Manor in Norfolk. Gregory could do well there, much time for hawking and work on his longbow. He could learn statecraft from a Privy Councillor.'

'Southwell lives 100 miles from London! Could we bear having him so far away for months at a time?'

Crumwell smiled; it was not only him who would miss Gregory; Nicòla took him into her heart too. 'When we return from Dewhurst, I shall see about that appointment for Gregory. London is no place to be at present.'

'If only we could go on progress.'

Crumwell raised his eyebrows in agreement but paused when a knock echoed from the door to the library. A gentleman-usher appeared just as Nicòla stepped behind one of the bookshelves, not dressed well enough for any person's eyes. Men brought a mail sack and placed it on the carpets and Crumwell sighed. There was so much work in there that two men carried it.

'What is all this?' he asked.

'It comes direct from Richard Layton, Secretary Crumwell,' one of the men said. 'All from the monasteries where he has completed his inspections.'

With a double click of his fingers, the men left again as Nicòla walked over to join him on the carpets. She sat down at Crumwell's feet and untied the rope on the bag.

'Perchance in here lies gossip for us,' she teased.

'Nothing good could come from that bag,' Crumwell said as she handed him a pile of papers. 'Inspection of Syon Abbey,' he read.

'I saw one of their monks cut into pieces on the scaffold two months past; I dare say you shall not find much to delight you in those words,' Nicòla mused as she looked through the piles in her hands. 'Many of the prioresses are daughters from noble families. We must tread lightly at Syon Abbey, all must be perfect, for it is one of the wealthiest abbeys in England.'

Crumwell fell into reading the papers, Nicòla still on the floor with the bag. 'Do you know of the Cluniac Priory of St. Pancras?' Nicòla asked as she read.

'In Lewes?'

'The inspection has turned up the most debauched things I have heard, and I have lived in amongst the Medici.'

'What do the inspectors claim?'

'The inspection found that homosexuality is rampant among the monks. The Abbot stood and preached that he is "the authority of God the Almighty, the authority of the King and the… the authority of Master Thomas Crumwella"…' Nicòla stopped and looked up to him across his desk.

'This is why I have these inspections, to find these men and turn them out of the Church.' Crumwell knew everyone beyond Austin Friars' walls hated him, but to hear his name used directly still hurt.

'Abbot Thomas Corton of the Benedictine order in Cerne Abbey in Dorset is keeping mistresses in the cellar,' Nicòla said, picking up more papers from the floor. 'He is using monastery funds to marry off his natural children. He has a healthy son to a woman named Alice Roberts who may have been married when she became his whore. At the inspection, they found the Abbot at dinner, with his mistresses at the table ready to be fed.'

'I have a letter from the inspection of the Augustinian St. Mary and St. Lazarus house at Maiden Bradley in Wiltshire,' Crumwell almost cried in reply. 'The Abbot has six children, but says he has a licence from the Pope to keep a whore, due to his "natures" and believes he is forgiven as he only seduces maidens, never married women!'

'They found the Abbot from the Premonstratensian Abbey of London in bed at eleven in the morning, naked with a whore!' Nicòla exclaimed as she read.

'You should not be reading such things,' Crumwell told her. 'As if I need you corrupted by such notions.'

'This is in pursuit of God's Church,' Nicòla said. 'And none of this startles me. The Gilbertine House of nuns and canons in Chicksands have two pregnant nuns, both meddled with by a canon himself.'

'There is a nun living with the Augustinian canonesses in Harrold who has given to birth to "two fair children of her own making", so this paper says.'

'Prior Edmund Streatham of the Crossed Friars hither in London has whores everywhere; he meddles with them in the daytime and procures women for the others in the priory. They found him naked with a woman and bribed one of your men to be quiet.'

'Did the inspector take the money?'

'He did, and reported the Prior,' Nicòla replied.

Crumwell laughed. 'If men are to profit from these inspections, who am I to judge?'

'You are the judge, Tomassito,' Nicòla replied with a stern brow. 'There are not just these lewd acts you must punish. It is also large reports on the dilapidation of the monasteries, of huge running costs, of places not making profits, yet having inventories such as gold and silver chalices, yet no room for the poor.'

'King Henry has never set aside alms for the monasteries, ever since he took the throne. He put the money towards houses of learning and almshouses. Twas a wise decision.'

'Yet now these monasteries are huge costs on enormous swathes of untended land, a big area of this realm, all sitting idle while men meddle with women when they are not gambling.'

'Gambling is a sin none of us can avoid.'

'Whoring can also be difficult to avoid, from all I have seen of men,' Nicòla replied. 'That does not mean we should permit it in monasteries.'

'I need to set up the ecclesiastical court and deal with all of this.' Crumwell put his hands over his face, his elbows on his desk for a moment. 'As Vicar-general, I must oversee all of this. I am the authority over the Archbishop of Canterbury and the Archbishop of York, so it all falls on my shoulders.'

'Both Cranmer and Rowland Lee are your men.'

'I sometimes wonder if Lee dislikes the Oath of Supremacy.'

'Lee submitted and now will have to change the churches in the north on your behalf, or he shall be the next Cardinal Fisher. You must oversee every crime; Cranmer will aid you. You could close those smaller monasteries, and their wealth could go to the King.'

'And take their profitable lands.'

'And put them in the King's hands, or whoever you wish to behest the lands to on the King's behalf. Henry has no mind or stomach for the work involved, but monastery lands could make wonderful bribes.'

'I will be the one to control the Church in England.'

Nicòla slowly got up off the floor as she nodded. In the sunlight, Crumwell could see her skin through her linen shirt, which moved from the breeze blowing in the doors. 'You could attack their wealth by punishing all these abuses. Why else would you inspect all these monasteries? We want to stop the abuses, but you shall have to stop taking bribes from clergy who run monasteries and abbeys. The profits from the dissolution of monasteries are bottomless.'

'I would be a king in all but name,' Crumwell whispered. Even in his own office, Crumwell could not dare to utter such words. Nicòla nodded without a word, and Crumwell rose from his seat. The worry of having to oversee dissolution of the monasteries flooded away, the dream of much power overcoming any fear. 'My court could oversee all – what preachers are permitted to say, where monies can be given or bestowed, who can petition for divorce, instead of relying on the Church to decide such matters.'

'You could change the world with the Reformation. You must create a Bill of the Dissolution of the Lesser Monasteries. Leave the larger ones, such as Syon Abbey and the London Charterhouse for now. That will help abate the anger of the people.'

'I have to be the one to inspect Austin Friars,' Crumwell said and glanced out his window, the roof to the friary in the distance.

'You already lease so much land from the friary, but it could be yours if you closed the place. Already you knock down houses around this manor to make this home greater.'

'Shall we profit from these dissolutions? Is that right?' Crumwell pondered, still looking out the window.

'Tis too late to save our souls, Tomassito; all we can do is our best with what we have left. Tis too late to sit back. You are the Queenmaker, Tomassito. You brought down the great Katherine of Aragon.'

'And I shall forever feel guilty, but I needed Anne.'

'Yet now, Anne needs you. Take your place at the top.'

'Will you come to my bed tonight?'

The comment made Nicòla startle. 'You ask this of me now?' she frowned, her eyes narrow with suspicion.

'You have not come for months.'

'You have been ill.'

'I have been without my walking staff for weeks.'

'Why do you ask this of me now?'

'You stand hither now, prepared to stand beside me in all I do, but no longer in my bedchamber.'

'I lost another child. A woman needs time.'

'And that is all I need to know, if that is the problem. I feared it was more. I shall be fifty years old soon. But I am thin now, half the man I was before the illness…'

'I would destroy the world for you, Tomassito.'

'That is what I am asking of you, with these dissolutions. And remember you do not grieve for our sons alone, Nicò.'

For the first time in months, Nicòla came into his arms. He knew this would be their only moment of peace before their next grasp at power began.

Chapter 28 – November 1535
Greenwich Palace, downstream London

Time turns sume lyes into trouths

'Forasmuch as manifest sin, vicious, carnal and abominable living is daily used and committed among the little and small abbeys, priories, and other religious houses of monks, canons, and nuns, where the congregation of such religious persons is under the number of twelve persons, whereby the governors of such religious houses, and their convent, spoil, destroy, consume, and utterly waste, as well their churches, monasteries, priories, principal houses, farms, granges, lands, tenements, and hereditaments, as the ornaments of their churches, and their goods and chattels, to the high displeasure of Almighty God, slander of good religion, and to the great infamy of the King's highness and the realm.'

Crumwell recited the preamble of the Dissolution of Lesser Monasteries to Sir Nicholas Carew in the Crumwell Chambers dining room as Nicòla closed the door on the discussion. Carew was a conservative, so to see him with Crumwell seemed strange, but everyone wanted Crumwell's favour.

Nicòla returned to her desk to read a letter which lay waiting.

Per il nostro carissimo amico, il signor Frescobaldi

After our very hearty recommendations we, with good consideration, need you to signify unto us by private letter a matter of much urgency. As in earlier correspondence, the discussions for the possible annulment of my marriage to one Nicòletta Frescobaldi, Duchess of Florence, needs due consideration. After much discussion with His Majesty the Holy Roman Emperor Charles V, now is the time to commission His Holiness

Pope Paul on the issue. His Holiness holds the highest office in the Catholic faith, and the right man to talk of such marital dissolution.

As it is known, the Duchess of Florence lives in solemn contemplation at a country estate and needs a man to speak for her. The only living relative known to the Duchess is her brother, Nicòla Frescobaldi, servant to one Master Secretary Thomas Crumwell, Vicegerent of England. Tis now we humbly call upon the Frescobaldi household to commit to a hearing on the issue of annulment, submitted on the grounds of non-consummation and lack of free consent. Let us speak plain of such issues.

We know His Majesty King Henry the Eighth of England is much removed from the Pope and the Catholic Church. This is due to the workings of Master Secretary Thomas Crumwell. Both His Holiness Pope Paul and His Majesty Emperor Charles are much humbly sympathetic to England and wish to see the realm return to the bosom of Rome. An alliance between Rome and England would be necessary if such threats of war were to appear from France or the Ottoman Empire. His Majesty Emperor Charles also wishes to seek redress and comfortable living for his aunt Queen Katherine. We presuppose that Master Secretary Crumwell would have much influence over any such alliance.

As the only living relative of the Duchess of Florence is in the service of one Thomas Crumwell, the Pope asks if an alliance between himself, the Emperor and King Henry may be part of a deal to smooth the way for a marriage annulment, so I, Duke of Florence, can be married to the Emperor's charmless daughter, Margarete of Austria. Tis a marriage to secure Italian alliances and strengthen our relations in times of threats of war.

At the earliest time, I humbly ask that Signor Frescobaldi understands this letter and its meaning, write to discuss such possible alliances, and help create the annulment. Much progress on this matter would well strengthen relations between good Catholic nations, and indeed, in the bosom of God. Thus, indebted to you for your pains taken for me, I bid you farewell.

Florence, this fifteenth day of Settembre

Your friend, Alessandro de'Medici, Duke of Florence and Pisa

Nicòla took in the patient and polite words from her husband, who had not written in some time now. The Pope would give an annulment! Alessandro was far better suited to the bastard daughter of the Emperor, and her dowry would be as large as the one he garnered from Nicòla's father. Alessandro wanted an annulment as Nicòla did, as he went to great pains to be mannerly, and did not address her as a woman, the letter written to, il signor Frescobaldi, not a woman. He alluded to there being a living male and a quiet duchess. He wanted this marriage over, and to keep the shame of being abandoned by a wife who lived as a man hidden for all times. Marrying Margarete of Austria would give Alessandro greater wealth and power over Florence.

But to accept, as part of the annulment, to help broker a deal between London and Rome? Alessandro, and the Pope, far overvalued Nicòla's position in court. Could she speak to the King? Yes. Could she influence Crumwell into making an alliance? Yes. But was that right after so much work to break England away from the Catholic faith and into the light of the Reformation? After all Crumwell had fought for? After all those people who had died? Sir Thomas More's head had only been taken off London Bridge four months ago. Why would Henry even want an alliance?

Nicòla still sat stiffly in her chair, the letter woven between her fingers, her gaze out the window at the threatening winter. Indeed, she did not even hear Crumwell come into the room, his long black overgown sweeping the Turkish carpets.

'I have been with Sir Nicholas, and I learned plenty,' Crumwell said as he closed the doors to the office.

His voice snapped Nicòla from her dreams. 'Be it of any great advantage?' Nicòla said, and blinked a few times, to bring herself back to the present, rather than thoughts of a home far away.

'Well indeed,' Crumwell replied.

Rather than sitting at his desk, he sat down on a chair by the fire, the Greenwich offices large enough to accommodate such comfort. With a double click of his fingers, Nicòla obliged the instruction and came to sit in the other chair opposite Crumwell, the letter still her hands. 'Carew wishes to be a Knight of the Order of the Garter,' Crumwell said as he leaned back in his chair. 'Henry promised King Francis that Carew would receive this honour, and now, Carew wishes to take full advantage.'

'But Carew hates Queen Anne; he knows his hatred makes him unpopular at court. Indeed, Carew is unpopular with you, and close friends with the pompous Duke of Suffolk.'

'Still, as much as I hate Suffolk, to have him as an enemy does me no good. To be friends with Carew would gain me access to stable terms with Suffolk. It shall do us good to have fewer enemies, for we have few friends,' Crumwell mused as he rubbed his chin in thought.

'It never stops.'

'What never stops?'

'The plotting, the scheming, the alliances, the public words which are all lies, while truth and bribes change hands in secret.'

191

'Do you wish to flee to the country?' Crumwell asked with a smile.

'What good is power if you cannot have peace?' Nicòla shrugged. 'You rule this country, you are changing the lives of everyone in England with closing these smaller monasteries. All it does is make enemies.'

'We can hardly stop now, Nicò!' Crumwell scoffed. 'Henry is impatient for a son; we are all impatient for Anne to bear a son. Henry spent his whole summer progress at his wife's side, instead of in a mistress' bed, pounding away at Anne in search of a son. The man is spent now. Carew reports that Henry is tired of Anne after summer progress. His eye is ready to wonder and we need to choose a mistress for him.'

'What fun,' Nicòla mumbled. 'Take Lady Worcester's offer to lie with Henry. Or Carew's wife, who has serviced the King for decades.'

'I know, it soothes no hearts to say such things, but we must keep the King on our side.'

'Tomassito, Carew hates the Queen. You are the Queenmaker. Why trust such a man? He is one of the few who has not lost their love for Katherine.'

'Carew is married to the sister of Sir Francis Bryan, one of Henry's closest friends. He has much gossip, which is always helpful to us. Carew hates Anne's complaints and power over the King.'

'We flourish under the rule of Anne Boleyn, let us not forget that,' Nicòla warned.

'I know, but I must make alliances where I can.'

Nicòla glanced at her letter. 'What of an alliance with Henry and Rome?'

Crumwell laughed. 'What could Rome offer us? For we are free of Rome.'

'Peaceful terms,' Nicòla replied. 'A peace treaty with the Emperor and a pope who will not excommunicate Henry from the Church.'

'You want me at the treaty table with Eustace Chapuys?' Crumwell laughed as he looked at the fire. 'Why would such a thing happen?'

'That is what the Emperor wants. That is what the Pope wants.'

'What is that to me? We need none of their guidance, we are a reformed nation.'

'We are not; we aspire to be a reformed nation. Henry's only care around Reformation is around the subject of divorce. Mass for Henry is as Catholic as ever, in every palace and cathedral in England!'

'Not forever,' Crumwell said as he looked back to Nicòla. 'How do you know the desires of Rome?'

'Alessandro wrote me,' Nicòla offered him the letter. 'Rome will give us a divorce. But in return, they want the influence in the English court to help set up an alliance…'

'A heavy price for an annulment,' Crumwell frowned as he read Alessandro's careful words. The moment he finished the fine Italian writing, he looked up again. 'If I need Henry to look kindly upon the Church and Rome again, then I shall. But not at the expense of the Reformation.'

'I am not asking for such favours.'

'But our own marriage could be law, could be official. Secret as it may be, it would be real for us, for our daughter.'

Crumwell folded the note carefully, and Nicòla could see he was already thinking of such an arrangement. 'To broker a marriage with you, I must ask the King to look kindly on Rome again, at least for a while. Anne is the only obstacle, and Anne is not in Henry's favour at present. Now would be a good time to strike such a bargain.'

'No, Tomassito!' Nicòla rose to her feet. 'We do not alter foreign relations to suit our whims! What foolery! That would make us no better than Henry and Anne. Their love, their lust, has almost destroyed this country.'

'An alliance with the Pope and the Emperor will not anger the people. We could continue the Reformation and closing of the monasteries once we are in Rome's favour again. Once the annulment is ready and Alessandro marries the Emperor's bastard, we can do as we please.'

'They are powerful yet petty men. They will expose my secrets, a woman pretending to be a man, holding a high office at a royal court, and once the whore of a pope. I will be in the Tower and your reputation will be in tatters. I like this not.'

'They could destroy us with that news if we do not accept their terms!' Crumwell jumped to his feet. 'It is time we enjoyed all our works on the King's behalf.'

'The money, the power, the bribes are not enough?' Nicòla sighed.

'Just think; be free of your marriage, annulled by the Pope. That is God's blessing to be free. Could we ask for more?'

'Would I be free in the eyes of God, or has money and power been traded for God's favour?'

'You know how the Church operates. They can buy all freedoms, dispensations and reversals. We have a country to barter with, Nicò. Let us take it slow, and perchance next year, 1536, will be one of true greatness for us both.'

Chapter 29 – December 1535
Greenwich Palace, downstream London

Lyes can seduce better than trouth

Crumwell had been reading a letter sent from Stephen Gardiner in France. Gardiner lamented on the many rumours he had heard, eager to discuss with his sometimes-enemy Crumwell, as he and Crumwell wrote to one another almost daily, despite being angry whenever facing each other.

But a letter which had come by messenger to Nicòla changed the simple evening in the palace. From the hand of the young Catherine Willoughby, Duchess of Suffolk, the child wife of the pompous old Suffolk himself, spoke of dreadful news, with a message begging and pleading for mercy. Mercy was the one thing Crumwell was in constant short supply.

Walking the halls of the palace alone, one of Henry's privy chamber gentlemen let Crumwell through into Henry's private rooms, the only man allowed to break Henry's quiet evening. Not looking like the man Henry wished to display to the world, he instead looked weak and tired, sunk into a chair by the fire, his feet up on a stool close to the warmth. In his hand swirled a glass of wine, a book dropped on the floor. Henry was ageing, and Crumwell admitted to feeling the same. While Henry had laughed about Crumwell's new age of fifty years at the lavish party held only a few weeks ago, Henry himself had reached four and forty years. Quiet evenings by the fire with books did often tempt Crumwell now, not that his work allowed it.

Henry shook himself awake at the sound of someone close by and turned in his seat to see Crumwell there. 'Oh, Thomas, by the grace of God, it is only you.' He gestured to the other chair close to the fire.

Crumwell groaned as he sat down, the chair taking the pain of the day from his feet, sore in tight new calf-leather shoes. 'Did you fear another might enter your chamber?'

'I feared Anne.'

Crumwell could not stop a gentle laugh escaping his lips. Henry smiled in return and turned in his seat. With a dismissive wave, he ordered out the gentleman-ushers and guards, who stood idly in various corners about the room. With the close of the final door, Henry sighed.

'Do you ever fight with your creature, Thomas? Does your Waif not cause you grief?'

'We have fought many times, Your Majesty. She is intelligent, and her temper can use that knowledge. But Frescobaldi is my master secretary while I am her master. The power imbalance means I shall always come out on top.'

'You lucky man.'

'More than anything, I feel guilty when I use that power to my benefit. I wish never to hurt Frescobaldi.'

'Such a strange creature, though. Is it not odd to undress a man instead of a woman?'

Crumwell cleared his throat, for Henry had often been open in many matters, but never about Crumwell's life. 'Think not of a courteous answer, Thomas. I envy you, that is why I ask.'

'Envy me, Your Majesty? How so?'

'I find myself in the most difficult position on this evening. We are ready for the epiphany and yet I feel no such cheer.'

Crumwell closed his hands over the letter between his fingers. 'May I bear your burden, Your Majesty?'

'If only someone could, Thomas.' Henry sipped his mulled wine. 'I have received word tonight that Anne is with child once more.'

Crumwell almost slipped from his seat as he sat up quickly. 'Your Majesty, this is the most profound news! Your son, your precious heir at last!' Suddenly, all of Crumwell's worries faded as he imagined how invincible he would be with Henry out of the way, distracted by the son he longed for.

Henry did nothing but glance to Crumwell from the corner of his eye. 'Forgive me if I do not leap with excitement, for this is the tenth time a wife has told me of a child, and there have been several women I have not married who have said the same.'

'Tis a sign, Your Majesty, that God believes in your marriage. Yes, there has been difficulty, but people will understand once there is a son in the cradle.' Oh, how many times had Crumwell suffered this conversation with the King? Nicòla had lost Crumwell's own son, not a year past, all kept secret. His time to have another son had surely passed, for Nicòla deserved not to endure the heartache a third time.

'I shall keep all excitement for public display, Thomas,' Henry continued. 'I shared my pleasure with Anne and all those who have overheard such words, for we are never truly alone. The Boleyns shall be somewhere in the palace, no doubt huddled together, planning to take over the world with their royal heir. Some days I think old Thomas Boleyn thinks himself the King, not the Lord Privy Seal. He is that, and Earl of Wiltshire, at my command only, and yet he walks around with his stubborn face and haughty tone…'

Crumwell paused but Henry did not finish his sentence. 'I think everyone wishes for a stable country, Your Majesty.'

'I more than any other,' Henry said and tossed his hands in the air in frustration. 'I shall be cautious this time, and as the baby progresses, then I shall gain more hope, I am certain. Anne would not leave my side all summer long while in progress. The people dislike Anne, but she would refuse to hide away. Every night she begged me to come to her bed.'

Crumwell had to destroy the last queen, so Henry could be in that bed, and now Henry complained of the opportunity. Crumwell had redefined religion in England and rewrote the laws of the country, so Henry could be able to slide into Anne's bed every night. There could be no more fickle master than love.

'We stopped at Wulf Hall for a week on progress, as you know,' Henry continued. 'It was marvellous to see the Seymour family again. Old Sir John and Edward have healed their rift over John bedding Edward's wife, and she is now dead, and they remarried young Edward.'

'Indeed, Edward has married Lady Anne Stanhope,' Crumwell replied.

'What was it everyone says of her?'

'That she is more presumptuous than Lucifer.'

Henry laughed in reply. 'I wonder what Edward sees in young Anne.'

'Perchance she does not like Edward's father as much as his first wife did?' Crumwell offered, and Henry roared with laughter again. 'The Seymours be a fine family, though one other son, Thomas, can be a difficult man.'

Henry nodded, deep in thought. 'Ten children, lucky man, old Sir John, though I know he has lost many young, including his first-born son.'

'But three sons and three daughters all still living,' Crumwell said. 'One of the younger daughters, Lady Elizabeth, was widowed a year or so past. She wrote to me, to gain another marriage.'

'What, to you?' Henry scoffed.

'I think she would be a fine match for my Gregory, as she has produced two children already. Lady Elizabeth has been away from Queen Anne's court for some time after the birth of her second child, so soon after her husband's death.'

'Lady Elizabeth is much younger than the other sister among Anne's ladies,' Henry replied. 'The Lady Jane.'

'Oh, yes, Lady Jane Seymour must be ten years older than her sisters. I must confess I pay little attention to the ladies in Queen Anne's company unless I am given particular reason to judge them.'

'Is she not a true beauty, though, Thomas?'

Crumwell stopped for a moment to remember which of the three Seymour girls Henry spoke of; all he could remember was a plain girl, most pale and never with more than a few words to utter.

'Lady Jane served both Katherine and now Anne. The Seymours a loyal family to the throne, ready to serve, with fine minds and ready courage.'

Crumwell remained silent. Yes, Edward Seymour was a fine enough man, though Crumwell thought him a little boring; Crumwell threw the best parties in the court, so when a man like Seymour stood quietly during festivities, Crumwell took little notice.

'Lady Jane is not tall, but she is one of the finest ladies I have ever laid eyes upon,' Henry continued to touch upon this woman. 'Jane is a woman of charm, not in just appearance, but also of character. Jane is simple and chaste, so gentle, almost meek. And she comes from fine stock, one of ten children.'

At once Crumwell saw the situation; while dining at Wulf Hall with an old friend, Henry noticed Jane Seymour, who had been at court for at least five years, mayhap even ten years. Jane was well enough to be a suitable as a mistress, for she was quiet and discreet. But no man had married her in all the time at court, so she was no doubt dull like her brother.

'As you say, Your Majesty, a fine, chaste woman.'

Henry sat up straight in his chair and looked Crumwell in the eye. 'I like Lady Jane very well, Thomas. How could I be so blind to such a lady for so long?'

'You wish to take a new mistress now that the Queen is with child, Your Majesty?' Crumwell asked. 'It would be understandable...'

'No, Thomas, I have Lady Worcester as a mistress. I mean not to take Jane as a mistress. What can be made can be unmade, do you not think?'

'How do you mean?'

'Thomas, you are the Queenmaker, I know they call you the Queenmaker behind your back...'

'Amongst other names, Your Majesty.'

Henry laughed once more, and Crumwell noticed the change in the King's character. Now Henry sat upright, his eyes bright again. Oh no, could it be love? Crumwell had a country to run, never mind Henry's constant need for romance.

'If I were to leave Anne, I would need to go back to Katherine, would I not?'

Crumwell broke out into a coughing fit; he could not discern why, probably the shock of the question. Henry looked so worried he poured

Crumwell wine and handed it to him. 'Your Majesty, I suppose that would be true,' Crumwell croaked after taking a sip. 'You could leave Anne and return to Katherine, claiming you were deferring back to Rome.'

'I will not defer to any person, for I am a king!'

'Precisely, Your Majesty.'

'Could I take a new wife, someone like the fertile Lady Jane, if I were to leave Anne?'

'Leave Queen Anne?' Crumwell cried. 'You have a woman, whom you love, carrying your child and she is your legal wife. The precious son you crave is in Anne right now.'

'Yet she has produced a girl and dead sons, Thomas!'

'As has Frescobaldi, but I would not set her aside.'

'You are not the King of England!' Henry boomed. He paused and regained his posture again, leaving Crumwell ever more worried for his own safety. 'Of course, if Anne were to give me a healthy son, I would honour her as my wife for all of my days. But she has not yet done that.'

'Then perchance all you can do for now is wait, Your Majesty. Care for Anne, nurture her health as the child blooms.'

'And the Lady Jane? She is too virtuous to be a mistress.'

'Lady Jane can continue to serve Queen Anne, as a mark of her good character,' Crumwell bluffed. Now he unfurled the letter in his fingers. 'Your Majesty, I come bearing a letter from the Duchess of Suffolk.'

'Young Catherine?' Henry asked. 'What has Charles done to her now? With child again? He married a girl so young she would have been in the nursery with his sons he got on my sister, had they lived.'

'Duchess Catherine writes on behalf of her mother, Lady Maria. She is still the closest friend to the Dowager Princess Katherine.' Crumwell paused and waited to see Henry's response to hearing of his last wife and her best friend. Henry's face clouded, but he held his tongue. 'Lady Maria requests permission to visit Lady Katherine at Kimbolton Castle.'

'I have denied Katherine her closest ally for years, why should I change now?'

'Because Lady Maria believes that Katherine is desperately ill, Your Majesty. They believe Katherine's health to be failing.'

'Katherine's health has been failing for years,' Henry scoffed. 'I suppose my daughter Mary will seek to see her mother also?'

'Perchance, Your Majesty, if Katherine were to die…'

Henry's eyes met Crumwell. Henry could be free from the shadow of the great Katherine of Aragon. He had known her since she married Prince Arthur five and thirty years past and been an enemy for the last ten years. 'You think I should allow Katherine to see the Baroness in her final months of life?'

'It could do no harm. Besides, if Katherine were to fail now, then the threat of war with Emperor Charles would be removed forever, and you could form an alliance with Rome as needed.' The sooner that Crumwell made an alliance, the sooner Nicòla would get her annulment.

'It could be a trap, Thomas. No, Lady Maria may not see Katherine, nor any person else if they ask. My daughter, Mary, may not see her mother, even if she is to die. I cannot trust any person. Katherine and Mary could plot against me. If they do not accept Anne was my queen, they cannot speak nor write to one another.'

Crumwell knew both women had secret letters sent between them but thought not of it. 'As you wish, Your Majesty.'

'If Katherine meets her end and Anne delivers of a boy, I am saved, and God shall smile upon our Reformation,' Henry said. 'It will be nothing but good news for us in the coming new year, Thomas. Send someone to Kimbolton Castle; send your Waif. Then we shall know the truth about Katherine's condition. If you are to be trusted, Thomas, then we can send only the Waif.'

Crumwell nodded and raised his glass to Henry who replied with a grin. As long as Henry kept away from Jane Seymour, peace may come to the court. Crumwell had sent Nicòla to watch over Wolsey's final hours all those years ago, and she would agree to such a trip, even if he loathed to part with her. Anything to keep the Crumwell queen on the throne.

Chapter 30 – January 1536
Kimbolton Castle, Huntingdonshire

Even if a lye is beautiful, you still face the trouth in the end

'Tis a long trip for one so delicate.'

'Tis a long trip for one so old.' Nicòla eyed Eustace Chapuys standing in the main hall of Kimbolton Castle, some 65 miles from London. Indeed, it was a long way to ride in the grip of winter, and Nicòla was forced to miss the epiphany celebrations with her daughter. But to come face to face with Chapuys, whom she had not spoken with since punching him some nine months prior, was an added punishment.

Chapuys sniffed at the suggestion of his advancing age. 'I come as soon as I read Queen Katherine's health passed beyond the point of salvation. Yet, as I have seen these past days, the Queen is in better health.'

'I am glad to hear such,' Nicòla replied, her hands still in the grip of her riding gloves. The four days ride had been hard, in poor weather, though as the secretary of Thomas Crumwell, she now travelled with a large party of guards and stayed in the best manors along the way. A far cry from the days of riding north to see the final days of Cardinal Wolsey many years ago while poor, outcast and alone.

'I am to take my leave and return to London at once,' Chapuys replied, and tugged on his fur overgown. 'What would bring the Waif so far north? Does Crumwell want to have someone to watch the Queen's death?'

'I come at the behest of King Henry, not my master,' Nicòla replied. 'Secretary Crumwella would find no joy in the death of the great Katherine.'

'The Queenmaker would find no joy in her death? What a preposterous notion,' Chapuys laughed, his voice suddenly raised. 'At last the concubine could be the true wife of Henry if Katherine were to pass.'

'Queen Anne has been queen for three years. I was there in parliament when it was decided. I was there at the Convocation of Canterbury when the law was ruled valid. I was there when Henry married Anne.'

'Are you to chide me for calling Katherine a queen, still?' Chapuys mocked her. 'Are you to run to your master and tell of how I call Katherine a queen, and not the whore? Everyone in this household calls Katherine the queen. She is the true queen.'

'I care nothing for the titles you give, Ambassador,' Nicòla replied. She pursed her lips, thin and cold from the long ride. 'Indeed, no one cares for your thoughts.'

Chapuys looked to argue, but paused as a woman came into the room. It was none other than Lady Maria de Salinas herself, Katherine's great friend, the same one Crumwell denied permission to visit Kimbolton Castle not weeks ago. Nicòla bowed at once to Lady Maria, who recognised her.

With Chapuys quickly dispatched, Lady Maria took Nicòla by the arm and began to lead her through the hallways of the cold and neglected castle. The walls and floors were bare, only a few candles dotted in rooms and halls, no fires lit. Katherine continued to live in her constant position of poverty. Nicòla could only send a little personal funds to Katherine without being caught, and clearly no amount was enough to run a household like Kimbolton.

'Baroness Willoughby, I confess I did not expect to see you hither,' Nicòla said as the women walked alone towards Katherine's chamber.

'Indeed, I am not to be hither at all. I rode as hard as I could in this weather and lied that I was thrown from my horse on the journey. I begged for shelter and a place to rest after my accident, and they let me in through the servant's entrance. Once inside I was able to come to Katherine's side and revealed my appearance.'

'And Queen Katherine? Ambassador Chapuys tells me that she is much recovered.'

'Katherine has been dreadfully unwell, but yes, God has smiled upon her these last days. Indeed, Katherine has eaten food and kept it down, something not done for some time. She has sat up a few times, and even let out a little laugh. The Bishop of Llandaff is within, in case Katherine needs to take confession, and her will has been readied, and Katherine wrote a beautiful letter to the Princess Mary. I swear Katherine shall go to her death claiming she is England's true queen. I know your Crumwell thinks not.'

'That matter is not what I come to discuss, but to report on Katherine's health directly to Henry. His Majesty wanted no official party sent hither, indeed no one knows of my trip, other than my master. King Henry shall not believe any words from Chapuys.'

'The Ambassador loves Katherine, and has even more love for Mary, and yet he does not stop with the gossip!' Lady Maria groaned. 'But alas, his presence did help Katherine's spirits these last days. Chapuys left only after making Bishop Jorge swear he would get a deathbed confession about whether Katherine ever consummated her marriage to Arthur.'

'Ever to the last, Katherine's life must be pulled apart to satisfy the frail affairs of men,' Nicòla mused.

'Quite right, Mr. Frescobaldi.' Lady Maria stopped at a door and pushed it open to reveal a bedroom for Nicòla's use. 'I must confess, I did hear the Duke of Florence seeks an annulment to remarry.'

'Yes, it be true, and much to my sister's relief,' Nicòla smiled to Lady Maria, who smiled in return. Some women had a lifetime of experience and did not question Nicòla or her appearance.

'Please, Mr. Frescobaldi, do take your rest. Katherine sleeps at peace for now, and I dread to wake her, for peaceful slumber evades Her Majesty many days and nights.'

Darkness fell over Kimbolton before Nicòla woke in the bed; all afternoon had passed. She jumped awake, lost in unfamiliar surrounds, her eyes scanning the dim room, only lit by a dying fire in the grate. Sounds shuffled beyond the door; someone must have knocked, startling Nicòla from her treasured rest. A young lady-in-waiting stood with her hands clasped when Nicòla opened the bedroom door, her clean clothes all ruffled by her sleep.

'Forgive me, Mr. Frescobaldi,' she said, and Nicòla recognised her as Elizabeth Darrell, the same lady-in-waiting she met on the last trip to Queen Katherine. Thomas Wyatt spoke of Lady Elizabeth often, the latest object of his affections.

'Pray speak, what be the time?' Nicòla mumbled as she shook herself awake.

'Shortly after midnight,' Lady Elizabeth replied. 'The household is much quietened at present, but alas, Queen Katherine has taken a turn. Sorry, I presuppose I am not to call her a queen in your presence.'

'Forget the titles imposed by kings, Lady Elizabeth. Please, show me to the Queen at once.'

The pair hurried along a freezing hallway and the bedroom door opened to quite a sight. There slept the magnificent Queen Katherine, her long grey hair waving upon soft pillows as her face sat at rest. But her complexion — far from the pale beauty of years gone by, now Katherine appeared gaunt, her skin a mere blanket over bone. Her lips were almost blue in colour, and her hands poked out through white sleeves, appearing like the curled claws of a dead bird.

The room was by no means empty; around the room stood Katherine's last few faithful attendants, all in a state of distress. Lady Maria sat upon the bed next to her friend of forty years, a weak smile acknowledging Nicòla's arrival.

'I must say sorry for my absence,' Nicòla said as she crept closer to the enormous bed.

'Queen Katherine has been most comfortable and at peace for the day and into the evening,' Lady Maria said from the side of the bed. 'She has only recently woken and complained of pain.'

The Bishop approached Nicòla with a worn expression. 'I am Jorge de Athequa, Bishop of Llandaff, and Queen Katherine's confessor. Her Majesty requested you be present while she receives communion.'

'Now?' Nicòla whispered as she saw Katherine's eyelashes flutters against her cheeks. 'You mean to hold communion outside of daylight hours?'

'I know it is forbidden; however, I fear Her Majesty will not survive until the break of day.'

'What changed?' Nicòla asked as Katherine opened her pale blue eyes. 'I was informed of recovery.'

Katherine's tired eyes took in the people around the room as she turned her head on her pillows. She attempted a weak smile to Lady Maria on the bed, and then she looked upon Nicòla. Katherine moved her dry lips and Nicòla knelt at the bedside. 'Frescobaldi, I am relieved it is you who was sent by His Majesty, my husband,' Katherine whispered as she looked Nicòla right in the eye. 'I knew he would not let me die without his watchful eye upon me.'

'I come to see you on behalf of His Majesty,' Nicòla said. 'I was given much instruction on how to you are to be treated and cared for in this time of ill health, Your Majesty.'

Crumwell had told Nicòla never to refer to Katherine as a queen, but who could deny the dying woman the honour? Her throne had been usurped by Henry's lust; Katherine bore the burden but not the guilt.

'I am the true Queen of England,' Katherine said before falling into a coughing fit. Nicòla held Katherine's hand as Lady Maria wiped spittle from Katherine's chin. In the handkerchief; blood. 'I have written to my precious daughter, the rightful princess,' Katherine mumbled as her ladies all drew near to the timid voice. 'Now, I must write a letter to my true husband. I want England to know that I have always wanted to be a true queen to them, even if England has not always been kind to me. I wish not to be blamed for the heresies currently plaguing this country.'

'The people have nothing but love and sympathy for you,' Lady Maria assured her dear friend through heavy tears, and Nicòla stepped back for the bishop to administer confession and communion to the great queen. Nicòla stood with the ladies, their heads bowed in prayer as Katherine professed love for her husband and daughter, for her role as queen and love of her adopted country. Her voice shook the whole time; Katherine was a pious woman, who knew her moment to enter paradise had come, yet fear still lurked deep within her. The illness she bore; whatever had Katherine in its dark grip, the time had come. As women around Nicòla wept, hearing the bishop's words of the last rites, Nicòla thought of Henry back in London, awaiting news of this death. How happy Henry would be, how Anne would no doubt fall to her knees in thanks to God. Yet this room held a reverence, a beauty and honesty Nicòla never saw in any palace occupied by the King.

As minutes passed, Katherine's breath grew loud yet shallow. When she ushered Nicòla close again, Lady Maria held of one of Katherine's hands, pressed warm against her chest. Katherine reached to her and Nicòla felt the weak shake of death against her skin.

'I must write to my Henry,' she wheezed, a shallow breath between each word. 'I must write and tell him that I forgive him for his wrongs, that I wish him to set upon the right path once more.'

Lady Maria put her rosary beads between Katherine's fingers, the beads entwined between their hands as Katherine closed her eyes. There would be no letter writing. All at once, the mighty Queen was ready to slip away. As her frail lips moved in a whisper, all her weeping ladies leaned forward to be close at hand for Katherine's final prayers.

'Anima Christi, sacrifice me. Corpus Christi, salve me. Sengis Christi, inebria me. Aqua lateris Christi, lava me. Passio Christi, conforta me. O bone Jesu, exaudi me. Intra tua vulnera absconde me. Ne permittas me separari a te. Ab hoste maligno defende me. In hora mortis meae voca me. Et iube me venire ad te, Ut cum Sanctis tuis laudem te, In saecula saeculorum. Amen.'

'Amen,' the room recited and they all crossed themselves, something Nicòla had not seen in some time.

Katherine prayed for the saints to come to her, to ease her pain, keep her safe from foes, to sanctify her and place her in the loving arms of Jesus. The tiny hand in Nicòla's loosened its grip, and Nicòla opened her eyes, still lowered in prayer, to see Katherine's pained blue eyes grow still, her whispering lips hang open. At once, Lady Maria let out a desperate wail for the soul of her friend, and fresh tears stained the ladies' cheeks, their whimpers strengthening with pain. The weeping bishop began to pray as the first tears of loss pricked Nicòla's eyes; tonight, she had witnessed the death of what could be the last great Queen of England. A woman who understood the plight of others. The greatest soul to ever grace England's shores. But Nicòla could write Katherine's letter to Henry for her, to remind Henry of all he lost.

My most dear lord, king and husband,

The hour of my death now drawing on, the tender love I owe you forceth me, my case being such, to commend myself to you, and to put you in remembrance with a few words of the health and safeguard of your soul which you ought to prefer before all worldly matters, and before the care and pampering of your body, for the which you have cast me into many calamities and yourself into many troubles. For my part, I pardon you everything, and I wish to devoutly pray God that He will pardon you also. For the rest, I commend unto you our daughter Mary, beseeching you to be a good father unto her, as I have heretofore desired. I entreat you also, on behalf of my maids, to give them marriage portions, which is not much, they being but three. For all my other servants I solicit the wages due them, and a year more, lest they be unprovided for. Lastly, I make this vow, that mine eyes desire you above all things.

Katharine the Quene.

Chapter 31 – January 1536
Greenwich Palace, downstream London

Lyes can expyre, but trouth cannote

The large turquoise stone wiggled upon Crumwell's finger as he rubbed the inside of the gold band, a constant distraction when he became lost in thought. The winter ground was so hard and cold at Greenwich Palace that the damp began to seep into his shoes. Jousting in January? Surely jousting in the summer was uncomfortable in the heat, yet in the depths of winter seemed utterly ridiculous. But the King was in a mood of utter celebration. His wife had begun the fourth month of her pregnancy, and mighty Katherine had finally fallen. From the moment Henry heard of Katherine's passing, he had rallied the court with wild celebrations. Anne came out in a flowing golden dress at a party the very night after Katherine died, and Princess Elizabeth matched her mother. Somewhere at Hatfield, the Lady Mary would be sleeping in a cold bed, grieving for her mother, while Princess Elizabeth was carried around court by Henry, shown off as the greatest jewel in his possession.

But jousting in January? Crumwell had no time to play glorified party planner. His bill to commence the closing of the lesser monasteries was only weeks away from entering parliament and that left little time for anything else. He still had to oversee Katherine's funeral and its costs, which Henry insisted on inspecting down to the final coin. Poor Katherine had only been dead a little over two weeks, and yet Henry partied and carried on as if a huge cloud had lifted. Yes, the threat of war with the Holy Roman Emperor was now dead with Katherine, but enemies could appear from anywhere, even from at home.

'Voglio avvolgere le mie braccia intorno a te.'

Only one person would wish to wrap their arms around Crumwell. With half a weary smile, Crumwell turned his eyes away from the tilt yard busy with preparation for the day's events, and looked upon Nicòla, who stood there with her hands behind her back and a playful smile upon her face.

'You are very well met,' he replied. 'Even when I sneak away from my office, you find me, even out hither among the workers.'

'Do you wish to lose me?' Nicòla asked as she stepped from one foot to another to stay warm in the weak winter sunshine.

'Never.' Crumwell glanced up and down Nicòla's crimson livery, which matched his own for the day. No black, that was Henry's orders. No black that may suggest mourning at court, mourning for the late Katherine.

'Are you wishing you could joust like the King today?'

'No,' Crumwell scoffed. ''Tis bad enough that Richard participates. At least Gregory shall never have a fondness for the occasion. The King is much too old for such behaviour, but he needs to feel young.'

'With a baby on the way, the King feels alive.'

Crumwell just shrugged his shoulders. As Chief Minister and Vicegerent, some days that meant being the King's nurse, as if he were still in the nursery.

'I wished to inform you that Henry Fitzroy, Duke of Richmond's household has sent word,' Nicòla's smiled dropped. 'The Duke is much ill.'

'Does His Majesty know?'

'I know not, but someone needs to tell him, and soon.'

'I can do it,' Crumwell sighed. 'He may be Henry's bastard son, but the King loves that boy.'

'He has been such a good friend to me, and I worry for him. Fitzroy is a fine possible successor, had he not been a bastard son,' Nicòla mused. 'Not to mention constantly ill, not unlike Prince Arthur all those years ago.'

Crumwell paused and held Nicòla's gaze. She would want to visit Fitzroy soon, their friendship ever growing. 'I shall ensure the best physicians are sent to the boy's household.'

Nicòla smiled again as she nodded in agreement. 'May I ask you to come to the King's tent and inspect that all is well for the tournament this afternoon?'

'Do I give off the appearance of a party planner?' Crumwell gruffed as Nicòla turned in the direction of the royal tent, which sat behind the thrones set up in preparation for watching the joust.

'You give the best parties at court, you serve the best meals, you give the finest gifts, so naturally, Thomas Crumwella's eye is the one everyone needs.'

Nicòla pulled back the entrance to the tent, to find the room dressed magnificently for Henry and Anne. Silk floated around tables and chairs, candles laid out, the finest silver plate ready to serve. Not a person stirred within.

'All looks well enough. What do I need to check?'

Nicòla grabbed Crumwell by his crimson overcoat and pulled herself against him, her lips keen to feel his. Since returning from Kimbolton Castle almost two weeks past, Nicòla had seemed more affectionate, yet quiet as well. She climbed into Crumwell's bed every night; he often woke in the darkness to find her huddled against him like a kitten seeking protection.

'What be all this?' Crumwell said the moment she let him take a breath. 'Can you imagine the uproar if I was seen kissing my attendant?'

'No one shall come to the King's tent while the King is not yet ready to attend. Everyone is busy with their own work.' Nicòla continued to hold onto the edges of his coat. 'I received a letter from Rome. Alessandro tells of the Emperor keen to renew his alliance with London and complete his daughter's marriage. So, my annulment shall be granted with all haste. With Katherine now passed from this world, our mission to create an alliance between Rome and Henry is easier. The news about Katherine has surely reached Rome by now. Alessandro can remarry in the summer and my marriage to him will be forgotten. My identity as a woman will be forgotten from the world and I shall be truly free at last.'

'Shrug off not all your womanly aspects,' Crumwell replied as he wrapped his arms around her little frame. A sense of urgency ran through his body as they kissed again, something Crumwell had not felt since his illness so long ago now. Its return only made Crumwell feel more amorous towards Nicòla in the empty tent, for he had worried he may not be able to still satisfy a woman so much younger than him. Thank the Lord for such a beautiful moment.

~~~

One benefit of hosting a jousting tournament in the winter meant that the smell of horses did not stray as far. Flies did not buzz around everyone sitting in the hot weather. In truth, sitting in the tilt yard watching jousting was not all that exciting. When his friends were on horseback, certainly, but the days of riding for glory ended more thirty years ago for Crumwell, when he learned he had a mind worth nurturing rather than endangering. So Crumwell sat idly among the highest noblemen, enjoying the scent of Nicòla still upon his skin, rather than watching the entertainment.

The roar of the crowd woke Crumwell from his memory of the rushed encounter in the tent; the King was to joust. 'Who is facing Henry?' Crumwell asked, and frowned in the low winter sun.

''Tis Brereton,' Norfolk grumbled from his seat only a few spots away from Crumwell, seated with his brother-in-law and nephew, the Boleyn men. 'Brereton w-w-was the only idiot willing to t-t-take on Henry.'

'My days are long behind me,' the Duke of Suffolk mumbled close by. 'I have almost killed Henry twice with my lance; I shall never be so foolish again.'

'Do you suggest the King is foolish, Suffolk?' Crumwell laughed.

'You cannot hang me for treason, Crumwell,' Suffolk retorted. 'I am ennobled.'

No, but I could have you beheaded, Crumwell thought but did not even move his lips. Nicòla, who stood nearby with the other attendants, caught his expression and smiled. 'With some luck,' Crumwell continued, 'it shall be Brereton on his back in a moment.'

'Are you still mad at Brereton for having that Welshman killed a few years back? The one who was your friend?' came the voice of Henry Norris behind Crumwell, higher up in the less desired seating. 'Best to just leave it behind, for I know Brereton thinks not of the moment.'

'An innocent man was hanged because Brereton hid under Queen Anne's skirt after having killed a man loyal to me,' Crumwell replied. 'I shall never forget such a thing.'

Crumwell caught sight of George Boleyn throw him a disapproving gaze but paused at the trumpets; Henry was on his horse. The crowd of the court all cheered for their king, who did not have his wife close to give him favours and applaud his bravery. Anne had not left the palace to watch, indeed she and Henry had not spoken much in two months now. Henry seemed tired of her company, of her ideas. Even when they celebrated the death of Katherine weeks ago, they had remained apart at the party, talking in separate groups, silent when dining next to one another. Crumwell had a mind to plant Nicòla into the Queen's chambers a little more to see what the women thought of affairs. Jane Seymour remained in Anne's inner circle of ladies, so whatever notion Henry had of the blonde, none had spread to Anne's ears.

The sound of a wooden lance hitting armour snapped Crumwell from his thoughts. By some accident of God, Brereton's lance had struck Henry right in the chest. The saddle on Henry's magnificent beast slipped, pulling the King from the horse, the weight of the armour too much for any man to control. The poor animal twisted upon its own legs, landing on Henry just seconds after he hit the ground, his neck crashing into the sand a moment before his head and back. The crowd was screaming, gasping; all seemed distant to Crumwell as he moved as fast as he had as a fleeing soldier in Italy. He pushed through those seated about him, Nicòla close behind.

With wide steps through the sand, Crumwell reached the still King as the horse tried to stand, Henry's foot still attached to the animal. Nicòla struggled to pull Henry's twisted foot from the stirrup, setting the animal free. A lump formed in Crumwell's throat; he knew if Henry were dead, chances are he would sink from his own grand heights.

'Henry!' Crumwell screamed, his voice caught in the lump of fear behind his tongue. 'Henry, can you hear me?'

'I shall find the doctor!' Suffolk cried.

Crumwell noticed Suffolk had fallen to Crumwell's side, and a great number more men gathered around. Nicòla brazenly flipped up Henry's pivot visor to find blood running between closed eyes.

'Pull off the helmet!' Norfolk cried from the gathering crowd behind Crumwell.

'No,' Nicòla gasped and looked up to Crumwell. ''Tis like a dagger wound, when you release the weapon from the belly of your enemy, far more blood weeps. The helmet may be holding his head together.'

Crumwell's own blood pumped in his ears, making all sound so lost he started to feel dizzy. He watched Nicòla feel around Henry's nose for breath. 'He lives!' she cried, to the gasp of the crowd.

Dr. Butts pushed his way through to the King's lifeless body. 'Let us fetch the King to his tent at once,' he commanded the surrounding men. 'We cannot leave His Majesty to die like this.'

Crumwell grabbed Henry by the arm, as did Suffolk, the Boleyns and the privy chamber men Norris and Weston helped to lift the tall King in full armour, each man straining under the weight of a seemingly dead king. Crumwell found himself walking as if driven by God; each step continued onwards, though Crumwell's mind could not see what to do next. With a string of clattering, the long table in the King's tent was cleared; just hours ago Crumwell had seen the elaborate decorations while in a dalliance with Nicòla. Now, his precious patron slept in a state of near death on the very same table.

'Does his blood flow?'

Crumwell turned to find Nicòla at his side again. The tent filled with people; Suffolk, Norfolk, the Boleyns, Weston, Norris, a nervous-looking Brereton, Chancellor Audley, Ambassador Chapuys, Ralph and Richard had come in worry, and Richard Rich and Thomas Wriothesley clambered into the tent before guards closed it off from court.

'What?' Dr. Butts asked as several men began untying Henry's armour, shaking his limp body.

'Does his blood flow?' Nicòla repeated. 'Remember, the doctors who came from Brussels some months ago now, who studied the blood flowing about the body when Secretary Crumwella fell ill.'

Dr. Butts touched Henry's neck and took a pause. 'I feel signs of the blood moving,' he said. 'The King still lives.' He gently lifted the helmet while the others continued to relieve Henry of his armour. Crumwell saw a huge gash on Henry's leg, his leg crushed by the horse and cut open. He turned his mind back to the helmet as, coated with blood, it slipped from Henry's white face to reveal red and silver hair laced with the blood of an anointed king.

'Non so cosa fare,' Crumwell muttered, for it was true; he knew not what to do. Nicòla looked up to him. They shared a long glance, and Nicòla dashed to Rich and Wriothesley. With a hurried conversation, both men left the tent at once. Nicòla rushed back to stand beside Crumwell, but he could not take his eyes from the King's pale complexion. Henry was totally motionless, blood oozing from a wound upon his forehead which Dr. Butts desperately tried to stop with a dirty handkerchief.

'I have told Rich and Wriothesley to ensure Princess Mary's safety,' Nicòla whispered in Crumwell's ear. Her breath on his skin made him understand how hot he felt; the instant terror had lifted him from cold in the seats to boiling in panic. 'If the worst happens, so help us God, Mary must be safe from reformers who will want Elizabeth to reign. We must make sure the Catholics do not rally to Mary's cause.'

'You should all pray,' Dr. Butts said to all in the tent. 'For unless His Majesty wakes, there is little we can do now.'

Many fell to their knees, but old Norfolk threw his wrinkled hands in the air instead. 'Forget p-p-prayers! What shall happen t-t-to England if Henry does n-n-not wake?'

All eyes swept to Crumwell, who tried to clear the lump from his throat. 'The Act of Succession states… states that in the absence of a son, the first daughter of Queen Anne shall rule.'

'Hold the country with a baby girl, and another child in the belly of the Queen,' Audley added. 'Can it be done, especially when the Lady Mary is almost twenty years, old enough to rule alone?'

'You question the laws we created?' Crumwell cried and began to recite the Succession. 'And for default of such sons of your body begotten, and of the heirs of the bodies of every such son lawfully begotten, that then the said imperial crown, shall be to the issue female between Your Majesty and your said most dear and entirely beloved wife, Queen Anne, begotten, that is to say: first to the eldest issue female, which is the Lady Elizabeth, now princess, and to the heirs of her body lawfully begotten….'

'An Act that all have sworn an oath to uphold,' Thomas Boleyn said from the edge of tent where he stood with George.

'And you,' Suffolk spat to Boleyn, 'are you to be to be Lord Protector, king in all but name?'

'Tis treason to ask such things!' George Boleyn threw back to the distraught Duke.

'Arguing shall not save our king!' Crumwell said. Now his mind began to clear; he focused not on the mysteries of the body, rather he could focus on the laws he wrote, the country he controlled. 'All paperwork pertaining to ruling in Princess Elizabeth's name is clear. We shall have no worries. Parliament could gather and declare Elizabeth a queen within the day. Someone must return to the palace and tell Queen Anne of this accident before she hears it from some attendant charging to the pregnant woman's rooms with tales of ruin.'

'I sh-sh-shall do it,' Norfolk grumbled and turned away from the group in a moment. Neither of the Boleyns seemed eager to join Norfolk in visiting Anne; they wanted to see the moment they snatched power on Elizabeth's behalf, see the moment Henry breathed his last.

'Shall we call a priest?' Crumwell asked the doctor.

'Yes, send for one, for we know not if the King needs the last rites read in his name.'

At that suggestion, Henry Norris turned and left the tent, and Crumwell caught a glimpse of outside in the tilt yard; many of the crowd begged to hear news. Suffolk sat on his knees next to Henry, praying fervent Catholic words for life to return. Crumwell sank down opposite Suffolk and began to do the same from his reformist teachings. He should have gone back to his office, to hold everything in case of uprising in the name of Elizabeth or Mary, but he could not leave.

Nicòla rested her hand upon Crumwell's shoulder, a gesture to steady him as he began to pray. 'Most Merciful Jesus,' Crumwell whispered, 'lover of souls, I pray You, by the agony of Your Most Sacred Heart, and by the sorrows of Your Immaculate Mother, to wash in Your Most Precious Blood, and have mercy on the dying…'

'God be praised!' cried Dr. Butts.

Crumwell lifted his head to see Henry's eyes flutter as life returned to him. No need for prayer, Henry's strength instead brought him to life. Everyone crowded around to see the blue eyes of Henry open and blink a few times, confused by his surroundings.

'Your Majesty,' Dr. Butts said clearly, 'can you hear me?'

Henry turned to Crumwell, and his hand lifted from the table to grip Crumwell's arm. The King said nothing, and Crumwell took Henry's fingers in his own. 'Your Majesty, you fell from your horse. Fear not, for you will be well.'

Henry tried to lift his bloodied head and looked down upon himself, stripped of his armour, Francis Weston holding a handkerchief on the wound on Henry's leg. He appeared not to feel any pain.

'Can you speak, Your Majesty?' Suffolk asked his lifelong friend.

'Charles,' Henry whispered, and everyone finally took a breath. The King was safe.

Crumwell held Henry's hand tightly in his, their hearts probably beating as fast as the other. 'Praise God,' said Chapuys from the other end of the tent. 'It felt as if the King slept for two hours!'

Ralph ran from the tent, and Crumwell heard him cry out of the King's safety, to the powerful cheers of the crowd. Without a word, Henry looked up to Crumwell and closed his hand against his. Crumwell simply nodded as tears formed in his eyes. It was Crumwell who could convince Henry all was well; for without Henry, England could surely dissolve into war at the prospect of being ruled by the infant of Anne Boleyn, the great whore. God had surely shown that England needed a male heir.

Chapter 32 – January 1536
Greenwich Palace, downstream London

Lyes can hurt even when the lyar means no harm

'I thought the plan was to remain calm,' Nicòla said as they whisked along the hallway to the King's chambers, Crumwell just ahead of her.

'Yes,' Crumwell said slowly, not looking back.

'Then stop walking so fast, Tomassito! For you move as if Jesus is due to return to Earth and scorch us all!'

Crumwell eased his pace, his steps smaller, far easier for Nicòla. 'I mean not to hurry.'

'If Henry's accident must be an event not worth mentioning, not worth recording or discussing, then you must look calm, not filled with worry and regret.'

Crumwell slowed again in the hallway and looked to Nicòla. 'The King of England almost died three days ago, and I could not do a thing.'

'You are not a man of medicine. You cannot control everything. Only God could make the decision to return Henry to us,' Nicòla sympathised. 'Had the worst happened to the King, our laws would have held England steady.'

'Perchance. I know the commoners are angry at the changes to the monasteries. They could revolt against the crown, with Lady Mary as their leader, and hang us all.'

'We could all be hanged or beheaded any time, for that is the life we have chosen,' Nicòla replied as they reached the doors of the King's rooms, the eldest Seymour brother standing with the guards.

'Master Seymour,' Crumwell said, and Edward nodded hello. 'Shall we find the King in much cheer?'

'No, you take a risk,' Seymour replied, 'for Her Majesty is currently in Henry's privy chamber. They are not speaking, or rather, His Majesty shall not speak to Anne.'

'Does Queen Anne speak of your sister Jane?' Nicòla asked.

Seymour narrowed his eyes. 'My sister is at the palace to assist the Queen, as she has for many years now. We must accept that Henry chooses to share his affections with Jane.'

'And how does the Lady Jane respond to these affections?' Crumwell asked.

'Jane does not push away the King. He wishes to write to her, to speak with her, all in the presence of members of the family. But with the Queen waiting to bear Henry's child, Jane is careful to keep her distance. Her Majesty is not well.'

Indeed not. The moment the Duke of Norfolk, the uncle Anne hated, burst into her rooms and informed her that Henry had fallen from his horse, Anne had not been well. She appeared with pale skin, her eyes showing signs of no sleep, her back hunched, her smile faint. If Lady Jane Seymour made trouble for the Queen and her baby, half the court would vilify her, the other half ready to embrace her.

'What brings you to the King's chambers?' Crumwell asked Seymour. 'I hope no trouble.'

'Indeed no, instead I wait for Sir Nicholas Carew. We are to ride out together this afternoon.'

Nicòla watched Crumwell stare his golden gaze at Seymour, who stood tall, his nose tilted upwards, ever the man of high standing. The brother of the woman Henry lusted for was riding with a man of the court who hated Queen Anne. That was no simple ride; both Nicòla and Crumwell knew so.

A simple farewell to the tall Seymour brother and Nicòla followed Crumwell through Henry's presence chamber into the private rooms. Announced by the chamberlain, Nicòla stood behind Crumwell, to see Henry lying on a day bed by the window, blankets covering his whole body. Anne stood by the fireplace, and Nicòla swore she saw the stain of tears on the Queen's cheeks. Anne looked not at all well, and Henry was laid back to help with his leg pain. His head rested upon pillows, helping him to sit and pretend to be well after his fall. Word had been spread that all was well with the King, to ease Henry's embarrassment. The man who unseated Henry, Sir William Brereton, seemed suspicious by his absence from the chamber.

'At last, some company I wish to enjoy,' Henry said and tried to sit up a little. Henry Norris jumped forward to help the King and was shoved away.

Crumwell bowed to the King and Nicòla copied. 'Good morrow, Your Majesty,' Crumwell said. 'I am sorry to break your time with Queen Anne.'

'Anne is leaving,' Henry said, and threw a dark look to his wife, whose gaze appeared ready to throw daggers back at her husband.

'Perchance I could assist Her Majesty back to her chambers?' Nicòla offered.

'Splendid,' Henry barked, and with a wave also dismissed all the servants in the room. Anne turned and shuffled from the King, less of an angry gesture, more of a defeated retreat. Nicòla ran to open the door for Anne to the private entry to the queen's rooms.

'I need you not, Frescobaldi,' Anne snapped.

'I wish to serve Her Majesty in any way I can.'

Anne stopped in the short panelled hallway, not yet at the rooms where her ladies would be waiting. 'You know the gossip and idle talk of all in England,' Anne replied in the darkness. 'There is no one Crumwell does not spy upon, even among my own ladies. Tell me, what news of Jane Seymour and my husband?'

'I swear upon my life I have never heard His Majesty speak of, or meet with, the Lady Jane,' Nicòla replied honestly.

'But someone has seen, certainly.'

'Secretary Crumwella has never laid eyes upon Lady Jane in Henry's presence.'

'Be plain, Frescobaldi! I am your queen!'

'The Seymours are intent on making themselves more beloved at court, to rise in favour. They have paired with Sir Nicholas Carew and the Duke of Suffolk. Neither have ever been friends to you, Your Majesty, or Secretary Crumwella. How they mean to use Lady Jane with the King, I know not. They may not even know. For one, Lady Jane is a mere fool among a pack of wolves and would have no plan of her own.'

'Now you speak some truth.' Anne paused and cupped her hands under the small bump of her belly. 'You bring me good news, even if I do not have the will to express any happiness.'

'Please, Your Majesty, you must rest. You carry the golden child of England, and you seem not at all yourself.'

'Since the moment Henry came from his horse, I have been in nothing but agony,' Anne said with a fresh burst of tears. 'I am tired, I am weakened; I feel as if the world begins to close in on me as I desperately try to bear the new ruler of England.'

Nicòla rushed to the next door and opened it for Anne. The light of the Queen's privy chamber showed Nan Cobham, Anne's closest lady-in-waiting, who ran to her ill queen.

'I shall not lose my saviour,' Anne muttered, her hands upon her stomach again as Nan took her arm. 'Please be my eyes, Frescobaldi.'

Nicòla bowed as another of Anne's ladies closed the door once more, and she turned on her heel to scurry back to Crumwell. She found Henry still upon his day bed, Crumwell seated close by, leaning in to hear the words of the King. Nicòla stood to one side in the far corner, to await instruction.

'Tis I who came from my horse these days past,' Henry gruffed, 'and yet Anne comes hither, complaining and saying my jousting caused her much distress! She, who sits idle all day! I am the King and I cannot stop appearing before my people, whether that be upon my throne, or upon my horse!'

'We are not young, Your Majesty,' Crumwell replied, his voice gentle, to not anger Henry further. 'I am sure you could privately agree that our bodies do not act as they once did.'

'I must admit I remember little, none, of what happened to me. I remember getting upon my horse, and I remember waking in bed with a sore leg.'

'You clung to my arm, Your Majesty, upon waking.'

'Yes, you were there, I am told. You spoke of what my realm would suffer if I died, that is what Suffolk told me.'

'Only to answer other people's fears, Your Majesty. But also, to calm myself. I believed not in your death and wished wholly for your survival. But knowing we could save all you have built brought me comfort.'

'I heard the Boleyns worried not, indeed seemed only worried with who would be Lord Protector.'

'I am sure as a worried grandfather and an uncle to Princess Elizabeth only.' Crumwell would not believe his own words, Nicòla knew so.

'If Anne were not with child...' Henry sighed and looked out at the cold rain beyond the window.

'But, to our delight, and God's mercy, Anne is with child,' Crumwell replied. 'Inside her belly could be the son you have wished for since the moment you were crowned so many years ago.'

'Not that many years,' Henry snapped back with a grin. 'God's blood, almost thirty years ago. And now Katherine is lost to me. I am blessed to have Katherine and her family no longer fighting me, but she was once the most beautiful woman I had ever seen. Those early years of marriage were the greatest time of my life, with many babies, if not lost. We were both young, active, ready for battle in the field, and in the bedroom. How goes Katherine's funeral planning?'

'All complete. Frescobaldi has done much of the work on my behalf. St. Peterborough Cathedral is ready for the ceremony and interment. It shall be a simple affair and shall be attended by no members of the royal household, as requested. Tis not the funeral of a queen, but of the wife of the late Prince Arthur. She shall not even receive the grandest burial at the cathedral, indeed some bishops have received grander burials there. Costs are minimal, Your Majesty.'

'I just need it over, I just need Katherine gone from my mind, my burdens. For I cannot bear any more pain.'

Nicòla thought of Katherine on her deathbed, wanting to write the letter to Henry. Nicòla disguised her handwriting when she instead wrote to the King. Henry had taken the letter and said he would not read it, but rumours said he had. Rumours said Henry had shed true tears upon reading the words of "Katherine", words of undying love and fealty, to honour the time of their lives together and their daughter. Even Crumwell did not know the letter came from Nicòla's hand, not Katherine's.

'Now that Katherine has departed this life, could it be possible to furnish myself with a new wife?' Henry asked.

'Your Majesty?' Crumwell gasped.

'Look not so stunned, Thomas, for we have spoken of such before. Yes, Anne carries my child, but for how long? If she bears me a son, then she shall be my wife forever, lavished with the greatest of honours. I shall honour her by taking mistresses more discreetly, and Anne can live out her days in any palace she chooses as my son is raised in my image. But if she does not…'

Anne spoke the truth; she did carry her saviour inside her womb. Anne Boleyn had risen to the height of queen and was closer to losing her world than she knew.

'The laws we created, to make Anne the Queen of England, are clear,' Crumwell explained. 'The Oath, which all must swear, that Anne is your wife, and Elizabeth your rightful heir, is so strong that men have died for refusing the Act.'

'In God's name, I know all this, and I sometimes regret killing Thomas More. Perchance you speak truth, Thomas. Perchance I cannot take a new wife, perchance I shall feel happier with Anne in times to come. But there must be a son.'

'I pray for the same every morning and night, Your Majesty.' Crumwell looked up and glanced over in Nicòla's direction; his face spoke of cold fear. Wolsey had died trying to gain Henry a new wife, and Crumwell could face the same fate if Henry turned away from Anne for good. God bless the child in her womb.

Chapter 33 – January 1536
Greenwich Palace, downstream London

Lyes do not end love affayrs, the trouth does

King Henry slowly tapped his fingers against his desk while he read. Crumwell stood on the other side of the paperwork as he waited for Henry's word.

'You think Sir Nicholas Carew should be given the Order of the Garter?' Henry asked and looked up from the papers.

'It would make good on a promise given to the French king some years ago, Your Majesty.'

'As if I wish to appease the French,' Henry scoffed and gently leaned back in his chair, careful not to move his sore leg. 'I gave them my favourite sister many years before, and my patience came to an end with all of France long ago.'

'The other option is to appoint George Boleyn to the Order of the Garter.'

'Has that family not yet gleaned enough from me?' Henry threw an angry look at Crumwell, a stern brow to match.

'We shall wait to decide, Your Majesty.'

'And the bill to close the lesser monasteries?'

'But weeks away from passing in parliament. Then we shall set up the Court of Augmentations, which shall take the land and wealth of the closed monasteries and you can distribute them as you see fit. All monies shall go to the crown, and land and buildings can remain in your hands, or be given to others. Many are already sending me notes, requesting they be given, or purchase such lands and monasteries, for personal use.'

'I shall leave all those decisions in your hands, Thomas. You decide who gets what, and how much they pay. I can trust you to bribe all those we need appease, and tax all those we do not like.'

Crumwell's smug grin ran over his lips. 'Naturally, Your Majesty.'

Henry gazed at the window close to his desk, the faint winter sun falling upon the desk. He sighed but said nothing for a moment. 'Today is the funeral for Katherine, all but one hundred miles north,' he mumbled.

'As you wished, and kept within the budget you wanted, Your Majesty.'

'Do you think I treated Katherine harshly, Thomas?'

Crumwell knew not the right answer. Henry had been terrible to his wife of twenty years, who loved him freely, who obeyed, said nothing of mistresses, raised an army against the Scots on her own, acted as a peacemaker between England and Spain, and between England and the Roman Empire for years… Henry had been hateful to Katherine, England's true queen. But her Catholic heart meant Crumwell had no choice but to ruin her on Henry's orders. 'You needed a new wife, Your Majesty, for the sake of continuing your family's line. And remember; the Church found your marriage to Katherine illegitimate. You had to do as your conscience told you, and that was to install a new wife by your side. Queen Anne makes you happy.'

'I am glad of my new marriage, and taking authority from the Church has gained us so much money over these past years. It is you who has helped me, Thomas. You have brought taxes during peace time to the fore. A brilliant plan! You have given me the right to decide on religion in my country. Anne… she has given me Elizabeth, and I love her so, yet the happiness has weakened over time.'

'Perchance this is common in marriages of love?' Crumwell shrugged.

'Was your first wife not a love match, Thomas?'

'I liked Elizabeth, trusted, respected her. Love can grow with time.'

'Yet it was not lust which brought you to her.'

Crumwell shifted his feet spread apart, which ached in his shoes after yet another long day.

'Ha!' Henry smiled. 'I have made the infamous Thomas Crumwell uncomfortable with talk of lust,' he jested. 'Come, Thomas, for you are married to a young woman dressed in men's attire! You clearly do not feel devoid of lust or love. Does your love weaken over time, as mine with Anne, like a candle worn down to the end of its wick?'

'No, Your Majesty. While I was working to secure you an annulment and a new bride, I was not able to legally do that for myself. My marriage is valid in your eyes only.'

'What other eyes do you need?' Henry asked and raised his palms in the air, as if to display his own wonder.

'Indeed, Your Majesty.' Now was not yet time to propose an alliance with Rome, as the Emperor wanted. Crumwell would have to heartily pray for forgiveness for such greed, pushing a country to support another for his own desires.

'Do you know why I like you, Thomas?'

'Because my turquoise ring controls you through witchcraft?'

'I had forgotten that one,' Henry laughed. 'I like you because you have not yet asked me how my leg is healing.'

'I believe you to be a healthy and strong man.' Henry yelled for days, at any person who dared ask after his health.

Without warning, one of the doors to Henry's privy chamber burst open and Crumwell spun to admonish whomever appeared foolish enough to do so. But there stood Nicòla, panting with worry, her green eyes searching the angry faces before her. 'I humbly beg for forgiveness, Your Majesty,' Nicòla said as she bowed. She swiped off her hat, but dropped it on the floor, making a struggle of her respect to the King she just invaded.

'What on God's Earth be all this?' Crumwell asked, annoyed at Nicòla. Henry was in a fine mood for the first time since he fell from his horse some six days ago, even on the day of his first wife's funeral.

''Tis the Queen Anne, she stumbled, and she bleeds! I was asked to send word.'

Henry jumped from his seat, bumping his sore leg on the table. He fell back into the chair with an angry scream. Crumwell grabbed Nicòla by the shoulders, too scared to approach the King. 'How bad is it? We need that baby!' Crumwell sneered at Nicòla, barely heard over Henry's painful cries.

Nicòla just shook her head. 'Ready His Majesty for the worst.'

'We will all be undone without a son!'

'And Anne knows that,' Nicòla hissed. 'She is holding herself, her hands covered in blood, desperate to keep her baby alive. I care none for men now!' With that, Nicòla disappeared from the doorway while Henry's gentlemen came in to move him to lie down and deal with his agony.

'I swear this!' Henry yelled at Crumwell as he pushed away Sir Richard Page's careful assistance. 'All shall be lost without a son by Anne! I mean not the end of my child, but the end of my love, the end of all you ever built!'

Crumwell hurriedly excused himself from the warm room filled with men desperate to appease their injured monarch, and he hurried through the private hallway from Henry's rooms into Anne's. He burst into one of the presence rooms, to see Nicòla standing in the distance beside the doorway to the bedroom. Women rushed past towards the tearful cries of Crumwell's queen. Nicòla rushed to Crumwell's side, but her eyes, glistening with tears, told of a broken dream. This was not the first child lost by Anne, nor the first witnessed by Nicòla.

'I dare not enter the room,' Nicòla hushed. 'A man close to the Queen in her state? I was questioned over the last miscarriage. Oh, Tom, all is lost…'

Crumwell looked up over Nicòla towards the bedroom. One of the ladies slammed the door shut, but Anne's screams, not of pain but of loss pierced every ear near the bedroom.

From the other side of the room, in skidded George Boleyn and his father. They saw Crumwell and Nicòla there, and their faces fell. 'What news?' George cried. 'Why are you hither?'

'I come on the behalf of Henry,' Crumwell replied. 'I wish nothing more than total health for Anne and the future King of England.'

The bedroom door opened once more, and George's wife Lady Jane appeared. Blood smeared her hands and silver dress.

'We are doomed to hell!' the elder Boleyn yelled, veins in his throat throbbing with every word. 'Stupid girl!'

'The child,' George sneered at his bereft wife.

'Tis no good,' Jane despaired. 'Anne gave birth to a tiny boy, three, perchance four months, along. A tiny, perfect, dead prince!' Jane burst into heavy tears, but George had no desire to comfort his wife.

Nicòla muttered a quiet prayer while everyone stood in stillness. Anne was far from favour and now she had lost a son.

'I shall not share the news with Henry,' George said, shaking his head, bouncing his dark hair. 'Jane, you saw the mess. You tell the King.'

'No, I shall tell the King,' Crumwell said. 'I am not afraid.'

'We should all be afraid,' Boleyn scoffed.

'Tarry hither for now,' Crumwell whispered to Nicòla. 'Wait. Listen, aid in any way you can. I shall go to Henry. Make sure the child is not destroyed.'

Crumwell scurried along the private hallway back to Henry's rooms; his feet felt so heavy, as if wearing Henry's armour at the joust last week. While the King needed to know of this failure, Henry's mood could be one of wild temperament. Henry glanced up once more when Crumwell entered the privy chamber in silence and clasped his hands together. England's great king stood slowly from his chair, his attendants parting like clouds in a steady breeze. With a hand he dismissed them all, the men of the privy chamber gone in a moment, yet not slow enough for Crumwell's taste. He could have waited forever to speak the truth that the world had stumbled.

Words did not form upon Crumwell's lips, the same way they would not form upon Henry's. The King's red eyelashes batted his cheeks gently as the moments ticked past, neither daring to speak or move, except for Henry's blinking eyes. Crumwell thought for a moment, of Nicòla losing their children, of the horror of their first son, Nicòla close to death. Then, another son lost by God's choice, and Crumwell himself caught far away on his own deathbed. To think of Nicòla alone in that moment, separated from the man who got the child upon her; Crumwell did not wish that for Anne.

'Your Majesty,' Crumwell spoke with a cough, and steadied his feet further apart for confidence. 'I am sorry to report that Her Majesty Queen Anne has delivered a child, three, four months old, and male.'

Henry clutched at the edge of his fur-lined coat, his blue eyes tender, innocent. He probably looked the same when he learned of his mother's death when he was but a boy.

'A son.' The whisper passed Henry's lips, barely reaching Crumwell's ears. Henry's weight stumbled under his legs, tumbling the already injured man to the ground, his leg coated in blood. Crumwell dashed forward without a word, and Henry grasped Crumwell's legs, his hands pulling at the black of Crumwell's clothing as the great monarch began to cry. Henry sobbed, wailed for all that was lost. For all the battles endured, by sword, by word and by quill, Henry had endured too much for any man to bear. His father had needed an heir, only to see his precious prince die young. Henry endured Arthur's death to become an heir, only to see his mother die in her quest for another son. Katherine had borne Henry six children, five dead in their arms. Henry's precious sister Mary was gone from this world, his life with his sister Margaret was troubled, Katherine was dead, and now a third dead son from Anne's prized womb. All the dreams Henry held, and the dreams of his father, the dream of holding the throne of England in peace shook like a violent storm overtaking the land, all trapped inside Henry's heavy heart.

Henry wailed and bawled like an orphan in the gutter, the air filled with the anguish of the Tudor men and their quest for power and peace. No one dared to come to the privy chamber; for whom could ease such pain? Who could offer words of hope or comfort? Until Henry eased in his cries, his tears beginning to fall in silence on his ageing cheeks, could Crumwell offer a prayer for the child.

'To You, O Lord, we humbly entrust this child, so precious in Your sight. Take him into Your arms and welcome him into paradise, where there will be no sorrow, no weeping nor pain, but the fullness of peace and joy with Your Son and the Holy Spirit forever and ever.'

'Amen,' Henry whispered and wiped his nose upon his coat. He looked up to Crumwell, who offered the bereft king a hand. Henry took it without a word and pulled himself up against his chief minister.

'I would have made that child the King of England,' Henry whispered, his gaze at his feet beneath him, his sore leg trembling from the pain no doubt coursing through its weary veins. Crumwell fought his own feelings, for to weep would be weak, foolish. The loss of a child was sad, yet did not tug at Crumwell's heart as such, it was the loss of a certain future that hurt so much. Without a Tudor man on the throne, England would surely be at war once more.

Henry made for the door to Anne's rooms, and Crumwell followed several paces back. Through the hallway came the sight of Anne's ladies, eight of them standing in the presence room, Nicòla stolen away in one corner by the window, her eyes near the bedroom, as instructed. No one spoke when the King entered, though the sobbing ladies all bowed slightly. Henry stalked through the group, past the Boleyns and into Anne's room.

Crumwell stopped close to Nicòla, who stood with her arms folded tightly. Indeed, her hands appeared almost white as she held herself so firm. From their position, Crumwell could see straight into Anne's rooms, where she slept on the bed, folded up under covers, two physicians close at hand. Anne appeared to turn her head slightly to Henry when he approached, and yet they both froze, no words spoken.

'Where is the child?' Crumwell whispered in Nicòla's ear.

'Still in the room, watched over by the doctors,' Nicòla replied. 'They have been afraid to allow any person to view the boy.'

Henry stepped close to the bed and Anne looked at him, her face red with grief, not unlike her husband. 'I shall speak with you when you are up,' Henry mumbled and turned away at once. He left the room, Anne left upon the bed with her sickening face of grief. Henry brushed past Crumwell, just the faintest hint to bid him follow.

Crumwell fell in behind his king, knowing Nicòla would attend upon the Queen and the child not ready for this world. Crumwell closed the door into the privy chamber once more, the room still in silence, the fire not making a sound as it burned gently beneath the mantle. Henry carried on, towards the largest window in the room, the sun beginning to set in the distance far beyond the grounds of Greenwich Palace.

'I see God shall not grant me male issue,' Henry finally found his voice. Crumwell had no words for such a moment. Perchance Henry spoke truth; for it indeed seemed as if God no longer wanted Henry's line upon the throne. Crumwell could almost hear the laughter of Chapuys now, writing to the Emperor, telling him of England's fate. All of Anne's enemies would be raising a glass to the death of her child. Gertrude, Marchioness of Exeter, wife to Henry's cousin, Henry Courtenay, was probably getting prophesies at this moment, saying the Marquess of Plantagenet blood should be on the throne instead of Henry. All those against the dissolution of the monasteries would be rallying, thinking this sign from God would halt the Reformation. But woven in with all those things upon his heart, Henry's words shocked Crumwell.

'There is only one man who would know the words to soothe this,' Henry uttered as he turned from the sunset. 'Old Wolsey would know what to say.'

Wolsey? Henry dared to mention Wolsey now? The cardinal, the friend, the ally and the most loyal man to the King for twenty years, the man who died trying to evade Anne Boleyn was the man to soothe Henry's fears? All these angry thoughts and Crumwell could not utter any of them.

'Your Majesty, indeed, Cardinal Wolsey would say the time is not right for a king to be born, that God would bestow the child upon the royal couple at a better time.'

Henry half-smiled at Crumwell words. 'Indeed, he would have said just that. You are a comfort, Thomas. I should think of Anne, and yet, I think of Katherine. Is that a sin?'

'Indeed not, Your Majesty. The woman you believed your lawful wife is to be laid to rest today.'

'Katherine lost our first daughter, and one year later, to the day, she delivered of a son, named for me. For six weeks we were the happiest couple in England. Even after the loss of that child, Katherine led an army with a child in her belly, killed a Scottish king in my absence. Anne cannot even hold a child for me for several months! Be there no end to God's cruelty? Am I to be given barren women? Why do you get a son and I do not?'

The comment about Gregory threw Crumwell's calm. 'My first two sons were named Henry and Thomas, the eldest named for you, Your Majesty. But both were in the grave after a week of life. Gregory survived, only for another Thomas to die at birth, and then another son stillborn last year. Two of my three daughters are both in their graves, alongside their mother! I know pain!'

Henry just shook his head and turned back to the window. 'I wish to be lonesome, Thomas,' Henry barked, though Crumwell knew tears streaked his bearded cheeks once more. 'Order all to leave me until I call upon them.'

Crumwell bowed in silence to Henry's turned back and left the room. A quick word in an usher's ear, and Nicòla was fetched from Anne's rooms. Crumwell could not bear to enter the Queen's rooms himself. Nicòla appeared from Her Majesty's rooms into the public presence chamber where Crumwell waited after only a minute.

'What news?' she whispered as she stood before him, her face pale and worried.

'No news,' Crumwell shrugged. 'There is nothing to say, to do, to report. Anne is lost of her saviour, and I fear so are we.'

'There could be more Boleyn princes,' Nicòla replied. 'This is not the first loss.'

'But it is Henry's last loss, I can promise you. For His Majesty's heart and kingdom can bear simply no more pain. He shall turn to stone before he endures this again.'

Chapter 34 – March 1536
Whitehall Palace, London

People lye when they are afrayd of the trouth

'I received a visit from one of the Seymour brothers.'

Fitzroy's comment gained Nicòla's full attention, lost in the view of the river. Despite the cold in the air, the pair wandered the garden close to the Thames, keen to gain a little peace from the palace.

'Edward, I presume,' Nicòla replied as she looked up to him, their slow steps in time along the path.

'Indeed, for Thomas has gone to visit their brother, Henry, at Taunton Castle. Edward wished to know my mind about his sister, Lady Jane.'

'Henry and Anne grieve the loss of a son, yet men are still eager to ensure Henry has a new mistress.'

'But Jane Seymour?' Fitzroy frowned. 'She is so dim-witted, hardly a match for my father in any respect. After the love of a woman such as Anne Boleyn, how could His Majesty possibly be satisfied with someone so dull?'

Nicòla let out a little laugh. 'Perchance your father needs a little peace.'

'This past month, I have not seen Queen Anne in my father's rooms once,' Fitzroy continued, and flicked a wisp of blonde hair which had fallen from beneath his blue cap.

'Does he speak of Anne? The child?'

'Father weeps at times, though for Anne, I cannot be sure. Did you hear His Majesty sent gold coins to the Lady Jane?'

'I heard it not. Why?'

'A gift. Father wrote a letter to accompany the gold coins, one of hope and courtly love.'

'When?'

'Just this evening past,' Fitzroy replied, and looked around to ensure nobody listened to the garden conversation. 'Lady Jane is welcome entertainment, I fear. Anne is cast away, grief making talk between our sovereigns too much to bear. The King's leg has healed, but he is still not himself.'

'Secretary Crumwella has spoken of the same,' Nicòla answered. 'He comments on His Majesty's headaches, his forgetful natures, and of a pitying that will not yield.'

'Yes, I too have seen these and they worry me. Now, any man could easily force his sister under my father's nose for his own ends.'

'You think Edward Seymour has dishonest plans in pushing his sister's match for His Majesty's bed?'

'No man could deny the opportunities in pushing forward a sister or daughter.'

'And your father?'

'You know His Majesty as well as any person. One day he can love Queen Anne most heartily, the next be so angry he cannot bear to place his eyes upon her, to hear her tone. His Majesty has been attending parliament with us, has been completing his duties.'

'Secretary Crumwella is as busy as ever,' Nicòla nodded. 'From a political point, the King is in fine spirits.'

'His Majesty is tired of Anne. She has not delivered upon the promise of her womb. Father holds me by the shoulders and speaks of how he shall have no sons but I.'

Nicòla bit her lip for a moment, her eyes straight forward as they walked together. 'What if the King was to make you his heir?'

'Princess Elizabeth is the heir. There is also Lady Mary, daughter to the mighty Queen Katherine, God rest her immortal soul.'

'Girls.'

'You know how I do not prefer the company of women,' Fitzroy smiled. 'But they are daughters by anointed queens. Lady Mary may hate me, for the position of my birth makes us natural enemies…'

'And once, possible spouses.'

'Lady Mary is my half-sister. I had nothing but respect for the Queen Katherine. I respect my father's decision to marry Queen Anne, and recognise Princess Elizabeth as my half-sister and heir to the throne of my country. I am but a duke. I seek no crown.'

'England could do worse than have you serve as Henry the Ninth. As Machiavelli said, "how laudable it is for a prince to keep good faith and live with integrity". You could be a great heir for your father.'

'That is treason, Mr. Frescobaldi,' Fitzroy teased with a wide smile. 'No, I seek no glory, nor shall I ever be a true prince. My mother may have been mistress to the King for some eight years, but that is all the glory my family needs.'

'Do you see your mother often?'

'Never. She has three healthy children, two boys and a girl by her first marriage. She married again last year, and is expecting again, so she writes. We live fortunate lives, you and I, Mr. Frescobaldi.'

'Indeed, we do.'

'Is Secretary Crumwell with the King at present?'

'Yes, talking of a most serious issue.'

'The passing of the bill worrying the monasteries?'

'No, that is well in hand. It is another matter.' Nicòla paused for a moment; none walked near the pair in the gardens in the weak sunlight. 'Crumwella speaks about a proposal to bring His Majesty closer to Rome, to the Emperor and the Pope.'

'But why, when the Reformation is going so well? We are free from the idolatry of Rome.'

'An alliance with the Emperor would bring lasting peace. Yes, Queen Katherine, God rest her soul, is gone from this life, so the Emperor has no need to fight on her behalf. Yet Anne still sits upon the throne. We seek not to end the Reformation; we seek to bring the parties closer to form safety, to prevent fighting amongst ourselves, and if France causes trouble, we will have an ally on our side.'

'But how?' Fitzroy frowned.

'Ambassador Chapuys, a man you know and trust, thinks it can be done. He and Crumwella have attempted to be friendly of late.'

'And you seek my company to be on your side?'

'No, I only seek your company and friendship,' Nicòla smiled.

'An invitation to walk and speak is welcomed, for I shall return home tomorrow.'

'St James' Palace but a mile away,' Nicòla laughed. 'You can visit any time, and you attend parliament so very often.'

'Indeed, yet as Lord-lieutenant of Ireland, I am busied of late. Crumwell's help in the running of the country is much needed, so I shall never be far away.'

'No visit to see your wife? Does she reside at one of your estates?'

'Mary? No, she is currently at Kenninghall. The Duke of Norfolk can tarry with her for a time, though the manner between father and daughter is not a happy state. Mary's mother, Duchess Elizabeth, is living destitute, and Mary seeks to win favour for her mother. Norfolk's mistress, Bess Holland, is of course still attending upon Queen Anne, so Mary hopes her mother can return to Kenninghall as the rightful Duchess.'

'I find that unlikely, for Norfolk is never a man to back down on any matter,' Nicòla scoffed. 'If he wants his mistress at Kenninghall, not his wife, then that shall be.'

'Quite true. I have written not to Mary; I heard all this from her brother.'

'How is the Earl of Surrey?' Nicòla asked with raised eyebrows. All knew Fitzroy's relationship with Henry Howard to be the important one in his life, not that of his sister.

'Surrey does quite well, working on his poetry as always. He and Sir Thomas Wyatt have been working together of late. Surrey has done his duty by his wife and Frances gave birth to a son not one week ago. Baby Thomas shall be the Duke of Norfolk after his father passes.'

'Henry Howard has a son, a grandson for the old Duke?'

'Surrey is best pleased. He and Frances have had a strained marriage, but they are settling into their lives.'

'And you and Surrey?'

'We shall always be the closest of allies,' Fitzroy grinned at the mere mention of his special friend.

Footsteps behind the pair caused them to turn, to see one of the Crumwell Chambers gentleman-ushers there. 'I see time for pleasure is over,' Fitzroy said and placed a large hand on Nicòla's shoulder. 'I dare say we will meet soon when Crumwell's new bill is passed.'

When Nicòla entered Crumwell's private office, he was pacing slowly around the Turkish carpet on the floor. Nicòla closed the door and folded her arms over her doublet. 'Where have you been?' Crumwell asked, still pacing.

'I took a turn in the garden with the Duke of Richmond. He prepares to leave for St James' Palace.'

'And?'

'And he is worried over his father's health since Queen Anne's miscarriage.'

'We should be worried. Word of the miscarriage shall have raced across Europe now. I put to the King that we should favour an alliance with the Emperor and Pope,' Crumwell continued and rubbed his chin. 'His Majesty sees the benefits and feels the ills of the past all too keenly.'

'We all do,' Nicòla shrugged.

'If the Emperor wants peace with England, we must make it so.'

'We serve the King, not the Emperor. We must do what is right for England,' Nicòla warned.

'Would it not be good if we could serve England and get your divorce signed by the Pope?'

'I have been married six years, Tomassito; we can live happily without a divorce. Do not pressure the King into an alliance with his former enemy to serve my needs.'

'What good is power if you cannot serve yourself?'

'Fitzroy tells me that Henry sent a gift of love letters and gold coins to Lady Jane Seymour.'

'Yes, and when I went into the privy chamber, that gift was returned. Jane sent it back as a signal of her virtue. It only served to make Henry like her more.'

'Should we be worried?'

'My queen is on the throne. I defeated Queen Katherine to get Anne on the throne and us into power. Now Edward Seymour seeks to supplant Anne with his boring sister. Sir Nicholas Carew is coaching Jane to be a better mistress.'

'What an awful thought,' Nicòla shivered.

'Henry is tired with Anne, and a docile, chaste blonde is being waved under Henry's pitying nose.'

'If he wishes to stop the pity, he should align with the Emperor. Or soon enough the Marquess of Exeter will seek to take Henry's throne. Courtenay is Henry's cousin and would be next to claim.'

'I would see Fitzroy on the throne before the Courtenays,' Crumwell scoffed.

'What is made can be unmade.'

'I know. I made Queen Anne, only I shall unmake her.'

'Do you want to play Queenmaker again?'

Crumwell threw his hands in the air, the black sleeves on his coat billowing. The pacing increased in speed. 'Chapuys has been in my ear. Talking about new brides for Henry. French brides! No, I shall never make a French princess.'

'It is for Henry to decide,' Nicòla shrugged.

'Jane Seymour is for the old faith, the old ways and thinking. We do not wish to have her on the throne.'

'Jane Seymour is dim-witted. Pretty, charming, but boring. She would not cause you trouble and her family are easily bought. Rome would love Lady Jane, a Catholic.'

'Are we truly discussing the downfall of Anne Boleyn?' Crumwell frowned to his secretary. 'The way in which Henry loves Anne…'

Nicòla waited for Crumwell to continue, but he said nothing. She held out her hands to prompt him. 'Only my love for you surpasses Henry's love for Anne.'

'That is fine for the purposes of courtly love notes, but love does not speed this country's reformation.'

'But England needs an heir.'

'Changing wives and wombs did Henry no favours before, so why now?' Nicòla asked.

'We are to parliament in a week, so let us see that through, no more talk of replacing the Queen. I have no reason to unmake Anne, no matter her failure in the childbirth bed,' Crumwell replied.

Nicòla nodded as Crumwell finally sat down at his desk. 'Can a marriage survive such heartbreak?'

'Ours has.'

'Our illegitimate marriage,' she sighed. 'We should worry about saving Henry's marriage to Anne, not worry about a younger blonde taking her place.'

Chapter 35 – April 1536
Whitehall Palace, London

Everyone drinks sweet lyes, but only sip bitter trouths

'The dissolution of the monasteries will be the biggest challenge we face,' Chapuys said as he leaned back in the chair across from Crumwell at his desk.

'The bill passed some two months past,' Crumwell replied. 'I shall not relent in reforming the monasteries.'

Crumwell flicked a quick glance at Nicòla as he spoke. The meetings with Chapuys became more common these past weeks, as keen for an Anglo-Imperial alliance as Crumwell. But by Crumwell's own admission, he was on his own; the King had no idea of how Crumwell planned to reach to gain an alliance without any royal order. The situation found itself where enemies could be friends – Chapuys, once ousted from Crumwell's company, now visited almost daily. All these years, and yet Chapuys still had not come face to face with Queen Anne. If Chapuys had his way, the concubine would be out, with a French princess in her place.

Chapuys noticed the gentle look between Crumwell and Nicòla, and turned in his chair, to where Nicòla sat perched at her own desk. Chapuys knew, all of Europe knew, the Duke of Florence wanted an annulment to marry the Emperor's daughter. Only a few knew the Duchess of Florence sat in Crumwell's office, and Chapuys was one of them.

Chapuys turned back to Crumwell. 'The Emperor shall be happy to make peace with England after many years of disquiet, yet there are conditions that must be met.'

'Indeed, I am sure the Emperor will want England's support against the French in the war over Milan,' Crumwell replied and leaned forward, resting his clasped hands on the desk. 'And if war breaks out between the Empire and Ferdinand of Hungary, England shall be expected to rally, no?'

'Ferdinand may be Charles' brother, but yes, support shall be needed, as the French are no allies,' Chapuys sighed. 'And that does not begin to cover the threat from the Turks.'

'The Emperor needs England,' Crumwell said with a smug grin.

'But the Emperor will not favour England until King Henry makes peace with the Pope. Emperor Charles can only do so much to smooth the way with the Pope, but it is your king who must relent for this plan to work.'

'What are the Emperor's final terms?' Crumwell asked, and clicked his fingers twice for Nicòla to make notes, which she readied out of his line of sight.

'Henry must acknowledge the supremacy of the Catholic faith and that the Pope is the sole head of the Church,' Chapuys said. 'The Lady Mary, Princess Mary, must be returned to the line of succession. While the Queen Katherine is no more, the Emperor wishes to see his cousin Mary treated well by her father.'

'And of Queen Anne?' Crumwell enquired.

'Charles is happy for Anne to remain on the throne. If Anne is married to Henry, then Henry is off the marriage market and less likely to make an alliance with France.'

'Do you favour an alliance with France?' Crumwell interrogated Chapuys.

'I must serve my master first.'

'I have written to Bishop Gardiner many times, who remains in France, and there is no love for Henry there. A French princess on the English throne would be unlikely,' Crumwell replied. 'So, the Emperor will allow Anne on the throne?'

'I think all of Europe would like to see the great whore step aside, but for now, the Emperor shall relent.'

'If Anne were to step down as queen, she would still be the Marquess of Pembroke and remain hither at court, and so would her base,' Nicòla interrupted. 'I have gone over the laws many times, and even divorce would not relieve us of Anne.'

Chapuys acknowledged her words with a gentle nod and turned back to Crumwell. 'If we write out a formal agreement, we can begin talks with the King.'

Nicòla sat at her desk as Crumwell walked out of the office with Chapuys and she glanced down at the small chest beside her. With the top open, inside the red and white ivory chess set gleamed; it had belonged to Queen Katherine. Henry did not want it, and yet did not offer it to Anne, as if she were not worthy of any more of Katherine's possessions. Nicòla desperately wished to send it to the Lady Mary, to have something of her mother's. Letters between Crumwell's office and Lady Mary were constant, and Nicòla could not bear to see the young woman so mistreated. Queen Anne would be livid if she knew.

Crumwell returned to this office and did not close the double doors. He stood with his hands on his hips and Nicòla rose for her next instruction. 'A messenger just spoke to me of George Boleyn, who is in dark spirits,' Crumwell said. 'He was heard muttering that he believes Henry is God's enemy.'

'That sounds most treasonous,' Nicòla frowned, and Crumwell nodded.

A bang of the main doors to the Crumwell Chambers heralded muffled voices and pounding footsteps. Crumwell took a few steps backwards to look through the doors, and his face went pale.

'What?' Nicòla asked.

'I demand to see Cremwell alone!' came the voice of Queen Anne from the antechamber.

Crumwell rushed forward and pushed Nicòla low. 'Get under the desk,' he hissed.

'What?' Nicòla whispered back, and Crumwell pulled away her stool. He pushed her into the space under the desk and covered her mostly with the stool and the chest filled with the chess set.

As Crumwell rose to his feet, Anne slid into the room, gentleman-ushers closing the doors behind her. She stood tall in a golden gown, her hair pulled back tightly, her black eyes wide and angry. 'Your Majesty,' Crumwell said and bowed deeply. 'How may I serve you?'

'I thought us friends, Cremwell,' Anne said as she moved her eyes over his desk. 'I saw you as the path to making me a queen. I know many call you the Queenmaker as if it were you who decides who the King marries, as if I play no real role, simply a toy.'

'I do not believe that to be true, Your Majesty. Had His Majesty loved any other, he would never have broken the Church to wed them. You are the only woman he truly loved.'

'Loved? As if he does not love me now?' Anne spat back. 'You think I do not hear the rumours that Henry talks with my own lady-in-waiting, Lady Jane Seymour? That he writes to her, sends her gifts? Or you think I do not hear the talk, that I am merely a grieving woman, in need of entertainment? But I come neither to discuss you making queens, or the Seymour girl, Cremwell. I want to discuss the dissolution of the monasteries.'

'Oh,' Crumwell paused. 'As you wish, for Your Majesty may know all.'

'People talk of me fighting with my Henry. They talk of my grieving as if nothing is sacred. They talk of a new woman in my husband's life, and as all this entertains many, I wish to know more of the torture you seek to unleash on England.'

'What do you wish to understand, Your Majesty?'

Anne continued to walk about the room and Nicòla prayed she did not wander close enough to see her bundled under the wide desk. Nicòla watched the hem of Anne's golden gown ambling about the room. 'There be 850 monasteries in this country, Master Cremwell,' Anne said, not referring to him as Secretary, 'and you shall close 560 of these lesser monasteries, is that right?'

'Her Majesty understands well. All have been inspected and found unfit for representing the Church. Some are in disarray, some are crumbling, and some are heavily in debt.'

'And yet they shall be emptied out of all the people and their possessions, and their lands and wealth shall go to the King.'

'Indeed, Your Majesty, as the King wishes.'

'Would that money not be better spent? For indeed, monasteries teach children, they take in the sick and they feed the poor. Monks give treatment to the people of England, who have no other access to help. Monasteries help every community, from nourishing bellies and souls, healing the ill, taking in travellers. All this shall be gone, and nothing shall take their place?'

'I intend to look at new measures…' Crumwell began.

'You do no such thing,' Anne hissed at him. 'You shall set up the Court of Augmentations to move religious revenues to Henry, and it will sit in His Majesty's Exchequer, or it shall serve as bribes. Buildings will be destroyed or given away to wealthy men. I hear, of the 560 monasteries caught in this initial clutch of greed, that 123 are already sold, as the new owners bribe you directly!'

Nicòla had spent some time calculating the many bribes which came Crumwell's way. He already had prized lands in this possession, or in the hands of his friends, and soon also with those Crumwell needed to bribe. Twas a busy project, with hundreds more monasteries needing to be destroyed.

'Your Majesty, all works are happening with the King's consent, all done the way he wished the dissolutions to proceed.'

'I am your queen and I demand more for the people of England!' Anne cried, and stomped one of her feet on the carpet she stood upon. 'It is bad enough I have been forced to lose my precious son! I know the Lady Mary still walks the Earth and wants to destroy me! I must endure gossip over my husband's eyes watching Jane Seymour! But I shall not have the women and children of England starving and uneducated because you have destroyed the monasteries.'

'I work at the King's command!' Crumwell rose his voice. Even from her hiding spot, Nicòla knew he would be in a panic; no one could yell at the Queen.

Anne wandered to Crumwell, her face close to his. 'There are some 7,000 monks, 2,000 nuns and 3,500 laymen who shall be homeless and without their religious guidance, and all shall be harmed by the dissolution of the monasteries, to say nothing of the commoners who shall be affected. You push too hard for the Reformation, Cremwell. And you could not have the Reformation without me upon the throne.'

'Do you know the story of Icarus, Your Majesty?' Crumwell asked quietly. 'Icarus, a common man, was given wings to escape imprisonment, but was giddy at his new-found power, and flew too close to the sun. His wax wings melted, and he drowned in the sea.'

'You dare threaten me, Cremwell? You, a commoner? For I am the Queen, married lawfully. You created the laws that made my place on the throne and by Henry's side. You should watch yourself, Cremwell, for I could have your head at any time. Perchance I should ensure you are parted from that resplendent head of yours, should you dare to disagree with me on any matter.'

With a swirl of her gown, Anne pulled open the doors and was gone in an instant, a whirl of movement as she left the Crumwell Chambers. Only once Crumwell closed his doors did Nicòla crawl out from under her desk.

'Anne means to kill you,' Nicòla said.

'Yet another reason to be sure this Imperial alliance is firm, which makes Anne safe on the throne,' Crumwell swallowed hard. 'That shall appease her.'

'All are talking of Henry abandoning Anne. Even the King himself has mentioned it to you. You made a queen, Tomassito, you can unmake her. Especially if she means to have you dead.'

'Anne threatens with the fancies of a woman.'

Nicòla folded her arms. 'Nothing is as powerful as the fancies of women.'

'We are to Greenwich again this week. Let us be calm for now.'

'I could not dare see you harmed.'

Crumwell turned to Nicòla and smiled his smug grin. 'Worry not, Nicò. I have planned for this situation before, and I shall be ready if Anne comes for me.'

Chapter 36 – April 1536
Greenwich Palace, downstream London

When people lye, it means you are not worth the trouth

Crumwell felt Anne's eyes upon him as he sat in the chapel. She naturally sat in front of him but continued to turn and look to him and Nicòla, who sat beside him, rather than with those of her rank. The grumblings of those who disliked Crumwell's prized Waif had long passed now – and yet Anne appeared to want the scorn of Crumwell's creature to return, complaining that the Waif rose too high at court. Crumwell knew Anne did it solely to anger him, so he could not to look at Her Majesty. There was no need to play games to upset Anne. Just the day before, Sir Nicholas Carew, the newfound ally of Crumwell, and enemy to Anne, was ordained as a Knight of the Order of the Garter. This hurt Anne, not just because Carew was a strong Katherine and Mary supporter, but also because Anne wanted her brother George to be ordained; yet Henry chose Carew instead, without mentioning anything to Anne or George, who were forced to watch proceedings. The space between the King and Queen seem to widen all at once, which only served to make Crumwell's alliance with Rome seem close to becoming real, more so than he could have dared hoped just a month ago.

Crumwell's eyes crossed the aisle and noticed Cranmer steal a glance in his direction. Cranmer had written to Crumwell, rather than coming to see him, to say he supported Queen Anne and her desire to disperse the wealth of the monasteries to the needy. The notion! Crumwell only carried out Henry's orders. And yet Cranmer suddenly decided he would support Anne instead of Crumwell and the King himself! Cranmer, the reformer to beat them all, knew nothing of Crumwell's alliance plans.

Almoner Skip's prayers began, but Crumwell listened not, rather bowed his head and looked to Nicòla's little hands now brought together in prayer.

How he missed being so powerful and free to do as he pleased, rather than plagued by whispers of his queen's downfall. He spent years destroying one queen to make another, and to lose all now seemed too hard to bear. How he missed those earlier days, after Nicòla first came home to England, with baby Jane strapped to her body like a peasant woman, easier times when he could lie in bed at night and touch Nicòla's rose-gold hair, playfully kiss her, feel her slender fingers on his skin when he tried to sleep.

Nicòla's leg moved a little and bumped Crumwell from his dreams. He glanced at her, not daring to move his head. She shot a worried expression back, she too wishing to seem calm, though her face said something else. Her green eyes looked to Crumwell and then shot to Skip at the altar, back and forwards, so Crumwell returned to listening to the morning prayers.

'These are times when a man must stand up,' Skip said, passion in his tone, 'stand up and defend the ancient ceremonies of the Church. None here need to be reminded of the sacred traditions of the faith which lies in our hearts and souls.'

Crumwell's ear heard the faintest whispers behind him but thought not of them. 'Now be the time, pious ones, to rise and defend the clergy against defamers, and from the immoderate zeal of men. These men, they hold up faults in single clergymen, and yet put these faults to the public as if they are the fault if every man of the Church.'

Crumwell again heard a whisper; Skip was talking of Crumwell himself, and the whole congregation knew. The faults of the clergy had spread far and wide since the inspection of the monasteries; no man in the Church was safe from speculation now.

'Hither in England we have a wise king,' Skip continued. 'The people of England are in need of a king who is wise in himself and can resist the evil councillors who seek to tempt him into taking ignoble actions. We all must condemn these evil councillors who dare to alter the established customs of the Church.'

Anne turned her head just enough to glance back to Crumwell, a smile on her face, as the whispers in the chapel grew louder, all shocked to hear that Anne had instructed her almoner to slander Crumwell himself in church. For everyone still thought of Crumwell as Anne's man, as she had so often said at the beginning of her time upon the throne.

'Calma,' Nicòla whispered.

But how could Crumwell be calm? He turned slightly in his seat to see many hundreds of eyes upon him, some talking behind their hands, others too nervous to look him in the eye. He looked forward once more to Cranmer who looked to his feet rather than the faithful of the Greenwich chapel.

'Let us remember the story of Haman, the evil enemy of Queen Esther. Esther was the loved wife of Ahasuerus, and she replaced his first wife, who was not as faithful as Esther. The King took wise counsel from many, but lurking within was the evil Haman, who showed no respect for Esther, or indeed any person, including the King's other advisors. Haman sought to slaughter all the Jews in Persia and confiscate their lands and possessions. Haman sought to destroy Mordecai, the Queen's most trusted advisor, and have him beheaded for being a Jew. Haman was cunning, he was greedy, and he was faithless. But Esther threw herself at the feet of her king and master, begging for the lives of all Jews, even admitting her own Jewish blood. Haman begged at Esther's feet for forgiveness, but the King pulled Haman away and had him beheaded on the very same scaffold that Haman had built to kill Mordecai. For Queen Esther was faithful, showed resolve, mercy, caution and courage. She could reign at the King's side and served to aide her son when he took the throne. Evil, such as Haman, can always be toppled, always be defeated by those with God on their side.'

Crumwell needed no more time for thought. He stood from his place and stepped into the aisle of the chapel. Without a word nor a look, he stormed from the chapel, his eyes directly on the doors, which opened for him by two guards eager to serve. Hushed voices accompanied his long walk of shame out into the halls of the palace, but Crumwell heard none of the worst. His blood pumped so strongly in his body he felt a little faint. He stopped and leaned back against the cool stone wall and closed his eyes, desperate to catch his breath; he had stormed from the King's chapel without permission and seen by all who heard the words of his own humiliation. Nicòla had not followed him, which seemed for the best, yet all he wanted to do was hold her close to calm himself, if even only to stop him from doing something ridiculous.

Crumwell opened his eyes to see a handful of his personal guards there, waiting patiently for their instructions. 'Two of you, stay hither, make sure you see Master Frescobaldi is accompanied to my offices the moment he leaves the chapel. The rest of you, wait for Almoner John Skip to finish his vainglorious sermon, and then see to it he is brought directly to one of the cells beneath the palace. There he may wait until such time I am ready to inspect his conscience. I, as Vicegerent of England, demand his arrest.'

With nobles in the chapel and their servants about their work, Crumwell stalked unseen back to his chambers, where gentlemen-ushers opened the doors and fetched food and ale. Crumwell brushed them aside with a double click of his fingers, and dropped into his high-backed chair behind his desk, his head in his hands, his headache refusing to abate. The Queen of England wanted his head.

Time passed, Crumwell knew not how long, but his pains persisted when Nicòla flew into the office also, her pace at a run when she charged in and pushed the doors closed.

'You are not the sole man to leave the chapel this morning,' Nicòla said as Crumwell looked up at her, his eyes only half open. 'For the King himself left at an angry pace. It seems Anne first had you attacked from the altar and then had Skip move on to Henry! Skip told the story of Solomon, who lost his true nobility towards the end of his reign due to his sensual and carnal appetites. Henry's face was reddened with great anger as he stormed from the chapel, and poor Jane Seymour looked most ashamed at the reference to Solomon and his concubines! Naturally Chapuys is loving such twists and turns. I left the moment I could, escorted to see you. I left both Rich and Wriothesley to listen for the gossip of the courtiers, so we shall know all minds before the sun gets too high in the sky.'

Crumwell rose from his desk and pulled Nicòla into his arms, his lips desperate to touch hers. He kissed her deeply, as desperate to hold her as a dying man may seek water in the desert. Her little hands, so pious at prayer, rested upon his cheeks as he drank her in, happy to be devoured, to be pulled tightly in a long kiss searching for relief. Lust had barely entered Crumwell's mind since his mystery illness one year past, for neither time nor events permitted such thought.

'Remember me like this,' he said as he pulled her against him, one hand on her back of her head, her soft cap warm in his palm.

'I have no need to remember, for you are before me,' Nicòla said as her hands whispered around his waist. 'I shall you remember fondly in many ways, as will all the world and history. The Queen shall not defeat you, Tom. For you are not alone.'

'Be it true that any person would wish to aid me?' Crumwell scoffed.

Nicòla pulled herself gently from his arms to look upon him. 'The Exeters and the Poles have Plantagenet blood in their veins and want Anne gone. Lord Lisle is the King's bastard uncle, another Plantagenet who seeks change. If we keep them on our side, they shall not seek to usurp the throne, rather sit happily with Henry as their king. Norfolk is disquiet with his niece as queen. All those who support Lady Mary, and they are in their thousands, would support you if you were kind to her. Catholics would weep with joy to see Anne dethroned. Sir Nicholas Carew and Sir Francis Bryan are lifelong friends of Henry and would back your endeavours, and both men have the ear of the Duke of Suffolk. As for the Seymours, Edward has long been a kind friend…'

'To do this would simply align me with the men so opposed to my ideals, especially the Catholics.'

'We must move swiftly to protect you, Tomassito.' Nicòla paused as she rubbed her hand on his arm, as if soothing little Jane when she tripped in the garden. 'For now, we align and plot a safe course through Catholic waters. To be aligned with the Roman Emperor sees us aligned to the heart of the Catholic faith. Yet your Reformation continues to sweep this country, so we must be prudent, we must stay this course with careful guidance.'

'I must ask a favour.'

Nicòla stepped back, no longer the lover but the servant. 'What is your wish?'

'Your rooms hither at court. I wish to move into them. Naturally you will be there with me, but we shall hold the pretense you sleep elsewhere for now.'

'Why shall we not preside in your rooms? My room is but a bedroom, a place for servants to place my clean clothing, a place to store shoes, to dress, to bathe…'

'I am happy to be in that one tiny room with you, Nicò. For I shall give my large rooms, presence rooms, bedrooms, washrooms, all to the Seymour family. A room for Edward, Thomas, and old Sir John if he visits. And he shall visit, if Lady Jane is to become the King's new love.'

'Queen Anne shall breathe fire to learn that Lady Jane and her family have rooms that connect directly to Henry's privy chamber!'

Only now did a smile grace Crumwell's lips. 'When it comes to parties, I am king, not Henry. Say, four nights from now we hold a party. We have Chapuys hither, ready to talk real terms of an Imperial alliance with Henry. We must have the French ambassador here too, and show that France is not an ally, and that we need Rome. We bond to Rome, gain that alliance, gain your annulment from the Pope, and make Anne appear to be completely forgotten, as if she were never an influence at court. We must denounce her in subtle manners.'

'How?'

'First, we have Chapuys finally meet Anne. Chapuys will not like it, but we shall have to deceive them both for the meeting to occur. That shall vex Anne, throw her from her confidence, as she knows of Chapuys', and Emperor Charles', hate for her. Then, my alliance with Rome shall be submitted to Henry, then we seek to divorce Anne from her crown. We have destroyed a royal marriage before, and we shall do it once more.'

'And Almoner Skip and his words?' Nicòla asked.

Crumwell shrugged lightly. 'I shall speak with Henry at once, for he shall be most vexed over proceedings, as am I. Skip is but a puppet for Anne's words and ambitions.'

'To do what you say, to bring down Anne Boleyn, that is treason, treason by your own laws,' Nicòla warned. 'All involved could be killed, like all those quartered monks, or old More and Fisher on the block.'

'Either we topple this queen, or we go to the block. They are the only choices now.'

Chapter 37 – April 1536
Greenwich Palace, downstream London

Lyes are beautyful when dressed as promyses

Nothing more than the early morning stirrings fluttered in the hallways near the mighty Greenwich chapel after morning Mass. Naturally Almoner Skip did not oversee proceedings, even though his detainment and interrogation by Crumwell was short. Skip had been sent from court for a while, removed from Queen Anne's circle of allies. Cranmer himself had overseen all in church for the past few days, a man Nicòla never thought she would have to keep her thoughts and plans from – for he and Crumwell has been almost brothers in years past. Now, Cranmer sided with Anne on all matters, and Crumwell was determined to serve only his king.

Nicòla stood humbly alongside Ambassador Chapuys, the pair always catching the gaze of any person at court. The exciting gossip of Nicòla punching Chapuys at Austin Friars still delighted those with weak minds and loud mouths, and only time could possibly end that story. Chapuys was Europe's biggest gossip, and yet even he did not write about the incident, so surely the story would fade.

Chapuys stood, his ageing hands ever clasped before him, resting upon his dark grey fur, and turned only slightly to Nicòla, looking down to her face. 'I can presuppose that Secretary Crumwell has all in hand for this evening?' he muttered, his thin lips barely moving, his voice barely rippling the quiet of the gallery.

'Yes, for no issues have set themselves against us,' Nicòla replied. 'Tonight, the King shall enjoy the party and agree formally on an alliance with the Emperor. You shall have both his word and his signature on the terms.'

'I never thought I would see the day when Crumwell agreed to an alliance with my master,' Chapuys replied and turned his eyes to the gallery before him, people talking quietly. Crumwell stood on the other side of the wide room, in deep discussion with Lord Chancellor Audley. 'I met with the Seymours yesterday, as you surely know,' Chapuys continued. 'The rooms that Crumwell gave to the family are most excellent, lavish and well-positioned. The Lady Jane can catch the King's eye any time of the day… or night.'

'I thought you wanted Jane on the throne not on her back,' Nicòla retorted.

'Come now, Waif,' Chapuys chided, 'God willing, Henry shall have Lady Jane for both and we can have an heir, one with a mother of the true faith.'

'You stand in a country swept by reformation, Ambassador,' Nicòla reminded him. 'On my master's orders.'

'We both know that this country will sway in whatever direction Henry's bedfellow directs him.'

Nicòla sighed, averse to agree, but so much truth swirled in Chapuys' words. If tonight, at the party, Henry held discussions with Chapuys, there could be, in writing, an alliance with the Holy Roman Emperor. Crumwell would be paid, by Charles, with an annulment of Nicòla's marriage to Duke Alessandro, straight from the Pope's office. King Henry would never need know that Crumwell formed an Imperial alliance to suit Nicòla's personal needs.

'I must say,' Chapuys said, the slightest hint of laughter in his tone, 'many at court have been keen to see the end of Anne Boleyn for some time, and we never thought we would have Thomas Crumwell on our side. It had been thought we would first need to destroy Crumwell to rid ourselves of the false queen.'

'Be advised,' Nicòla said coolly, 'in this English court, we all know that when we wake in our beds each morning, and go to prayer, by the end of that day, any of us could have our heads on a spike on London Bridge. That is the game we play, the price we pay. You shall never defeat Secretary Crumwella, Ambassador Chapuys. We all have secrets.'

'Crumwell and Cranmer have been close for these past years,' Chapuys replied. 'Now Cranmer has openly supported Anne over Henry, so would Crumwell destroy him?'

'We have enough gossip on Cranmer to keep him on our side.' Nicòla paused and thought of Cranmer's pregnant wife Margarete, endlessly moving between Crumwell's estates to remain a secret. 'Just as we could have you executed for treason for these very conversations, Ambassador. Your closeness to the Lady Mary could be used against you also. She may be declared a bastard but she is still the King's daughter.'

'I know you also wrote to the Lady Mary,' Chapuys sneered. 'I know you personally send her monies, that you supported Queen Katherine even while sitting in the whore's rooms and laughing with her. You have the heart of a woman, "Master" Frescobaldi.'

'To think the heart of a woman is weak would be a fatal move on any man's part.'

Groups of talking nobles slipped aside for the solitary figure of Lancelot de Carle, the young Bishop of Riez and secretary to the French ambassador. He walked with his head down, his white vestment hidden under a black cassock cut too long for him, dragging on the stone floor. The purple cincture about his waist caught the light coming from the window across the gallery.

'Bishop de Carle,' Nicòla said and stepped forward and bowed slightly in politeness. The gentle poet and scholar did not often stop to talk.

'Ambassador Chapuys, Master Frescobaldi,' he said, his French accent chewing Nicòla's name.

'I understand that Ambassador de Castelnau shall attend the evening's festivities,' Nicòla continued.

'Well indeed.'

'Might I seek an audience with your master in the afternoon?'

'His Excellency shall be in his rooms. I shall tell him to expect you, or shall it be your master, Secretary Crumwell?'

'Just me, kind sir.'

With a single nod, de Carle disappeared into the group of people standing around after Mass, lost in a moment.

'You seek the French ambassador? He would be most pleased to see a waif like you in his rooms. Be careful,' Chapuys snorted.

'We must all play our part.'

Chapuys opened his mouth to reply but his lips screwed up at the sight of George Boleyn. Boleyn caught sight of the disdain and trotted over to the pair in the corner.

'Old Chapuys gathering in dark corners with the Waif,' Boleyn said with a tease, his hair not covered by a cap like most in the gallery.

'Lord Rochford,' Chapuys curtly replied as Nicòla bowed slightly in acknowledgement.

'Surely even you have not been distasteful enough to attend Mass when under the influence of too much drink?' Nicòla eyed Boleyn up and down; he did indeed sway a little on his feet, his hair messed, no cap, his dark eyes reddened.

'The night was indeed a long one,' Boleyn said under his breath. 'You know Lady Margery Horsman, mistress of the Queen's wardrobe? She has been at court almost ten years and has been as tight as a nun! Will the women of the court ever loosen up?'

Nicòla could not hide her distaste for Boleyn's choice of words. 'Oh, did you rather not enjoy that story?' Boleyn laughed, louder than the hushed conversation needed. Several heads turned in Boleyn's direction. 'You, Chapuys, trusted ear to nobles across Europe, ordained and blessed by the Pope, and you, Frescobaldi... well, no one knows what you enjoy.' Boleyn laughed loudly again, attracting more attention this time, including Crumwell and Audley's.

The foolish Boleyn fell into disarray as the gallery hushed and bowed for the Queen herself, followed by her ladies, who entered through a hallway leaving the chapel. In an instant, Chapuys turned to disappear. He never attended Mass when Anne was close; he had never met the Queen in all the years he had lived in England. Nicòla prayed he did not suspect that Crumwell asked him to attend chapel this morning, so he could accidentally bump into Anne; the alliance with Rome needed Anne on the throne, at least for now.

Boleyn grabbed Chapuys by the shoulder. 'I think you should find it in your heart to pay respects to your queen,' Boleyn uttered through fetid breath.

'As I just said to you,' Nicòla said as she jumped before Chapuys, blocking any escape, 'we must all play our part.'

Queen Anne stopped in the centre of the gallery, where Boleyn had dragged the ambassador by the shoulder. Chapuys barely made eye contact with Anne and bowed deeply. Anne nodded her head in respect to him as her ladies bowed gently in their matching blue gowns. With a swish of her pale gown, Anne pushed passed Chapuys, who scuttled out the way of Anne and the ladies who bobbed their way from the gallery. In a moment all was done; the ambassador of the Holy Roman Emperor had acknowledged Anne Boleyn as the Queen of England. Without a word, Chapuys stormed from the gallery and down another hallway, no doubt livid at having to come face-to-face with the concubine after all his years of loving Katherine and Mary. Once Chapuys recovered himself, he would be angry enough to start a war, so Nicòla moved in an instant not to be caught near him, and away from Boleyn's stench. Audley spun away from Crumwell to leave the gallery and Crumwell's eyes landed upon Nicòla with great delight.

'Twas almost too simple indeed,' he said as he rubbed his hands together, his golden eyes sparkling.

'Contain such open displays of joy, Master,' Nicòla said with a smile. 'You did not plan Chapuys to acknowledge the Queen, remember? It was an act of mere surprise.'

'Soon we shall have England turned from France and in an alliance with Rome. Your annulment shall be assured.'

'Are we wrong to deceive a king this way? For you work so openly without the blessing of the King. All so the Pope shall sign a parchment to end my marriage? We could end up at war with France or sending men to fight the Turks due to this alliance.'

'All shall benefit. You spoke to the French ambassador's secretary? Are you to meet with Castelnau?'

'As you commanded,' Nicòla smiled. Crumwell's grin of delight at their plan caused her own smile to grow. 'I can threaten the man with such subtly and ease.'

'Are you certain you wish to do this task? For I could send Rich. He is a great lawyer and liar both.'

'No one can lie better than I, Master. My lies have got me before the greatest men in Europe.'

~~~

The French ambassador's apartments smelled of oranges, which sat in a bowl in the afternoon sun upon Castelnau's desk. The round bishop sat upon a cushioned chair and watched a servant pour wine into two cups before them. Nicòla only watched the boy through the corner of her eye, while Castelnau's quiet secretary closed the door upon the conversation.

'I was most joyed to hear Crumwell wanted to send a messenger to my rooms,' Castelnau said as he waved the servant away. 'Rumours swirl of an alliance with the Roman Emperor.' He spoke in French with much pace, and Nicòla thought perchance Castelnau hoped to confuse her with his language, yet Nicòla could keep up with his gently smug voice.

'Can England not be in alliance with all the countries of Europe?' Nicòla replied and resisted the wine before her.

The old bishop leaned back in his chair, his ring-laden fingers rubbing the knobs of the armrests either side of his ageing waistline. The way he delicately touched them made Nicòla discomforted at once. 'We are at war over Milan,' Castelnau continued. 'England would need to side with one or the other, as an alliance with a nation would need reinforcements in any war.'

'Perchance your nation could leave the duchy of Milan alone,' Nicòla shot back as Castelnau licked his lips. 'I come today to seek of your thoughts on the Queen Anne, as your country has always been something of a home to Her Majesty. I come in search of your king's private thoughts on Anne.'

With one hand still rubbing the knob of the chair, Castelnau used his other hand to wave to Nicòla, as if swishing her words in the air between them. 'Tell me of you, Monsieur Frescobaldi,' he answered. 'You are the brother to the Duchess of Florence, no?'

'Well indeed.'

'It is well known that your sister is something of a recluse, for none see her at her husband's side in Florence or any of the Medici estates.'

'I can assure you that my sister is the wife of Duke Alessandro.'

'I doubt it not, but the Duke is well known for his mistresses and his appetites.'

'Men must satisfy their appetites,' Nicòla answered, watching Castelnau's hand rubbing the knob. Something about the way he touched it quite unseated her.

'I heard the Duke Alessandro sometimes enjoys the company of men as well as women.'

'I cannot give you an answer to such sinful thoughts, for I spend little time in the company of my sister's husband.'

'I hear the Duke of Florence wants an annulment, so he can marry the Emperor's bastard daughter? Is it true? Is your sister to be abandoned? On what charge? For there is a child, no? A child between the Duke and Duchess?'

'A daughter, Giovanna,' Nicòla paused and thought of her precious daughter Jane, whom she had not seen in weeks. 'As the Medici family has the friendship of the Pope, all remains for His Holiness' ears only.'

'A curious choice,' Castelnau said, still avoiding Nicòla's questions about Queen Anne. He could not be fooled into saying something treasonous if he continued to ask about Nicòletta Frescobaldi. 'Why would the Emperor want to give his bastard to Alessandro de'Medici?'

'The Duke is a wealthy man.'

'As was his current wife, your sister. So, you too have a fortune? Is that why Crumwell enjoys your company? Why is a man like you hither when you could live the life of royalty in Italy?'

'As I said, all men must satisfy their own appetites,' Nicòla half-smiled.

Now Castelnau stopped rubbing the chair and rose his heavy frame from his chair. Nicòla too stood in politeness for the ageing ambassador. She noticed sweat running alongside his ear, his balding head unable hide his discomfort in moving about freely.

'I like you, Monsieur Frescobaldi,' Castelnau said as he rounded the desk towards Nicòla. 'You intrigue many at court, as you know. You spend much time with Sir Thomas Wyatt, and the musician boy that dances about the Queen.'

'Mark Smeaton,' Nicòla replied. 'I dare call them close friends.'

Castelnau stood before Nicòla and looked her black doublet and hose up and down a few times. 'Crumwell dresses you well. You are secretary to a rich man, and a rich man yourself. All at court wonder about the Waif; I do not escape hearing the English rumours.'

'There is little to know of me.'

Castelnau grabbed Nicòla by the shoulders as she gasped. 'So gentle of voice,' Castelnau said of her cry. Despite his age, Castelnau had the advantage of weight. He pushed himself against Nicòla, which her frame could not hold. The pair fell to the floor in a moment, Castelnau's lips against her face, trying to find her lips as she struggled. Nicòla could feel a wayward hand fumbling between her legs, searching for something the ambassador would never find under her hose. Castelnau's heavy hand continued to caress between Nicòla's thighs, but his hands slowed as he could not find the part he longed to touch. They locked eyes for a moment, as if the Frenchman found shock in the lack of manhood in his hand.

The door to the office opened to the sight of Bishop de Carle accompanied by George Boleyn. The pair gasped at the sight of the wide ambassador on top of Nicòla, the pair squirming upon a rug. At once, Castelnau rolled off Nicòla, landing on his back with heaving, desperate breaths. The flustered de Carle ran to his master, and Nicòla leapt at her feet in a moment, her clothing rumpled about her form. She moved for the door and Boleyn relented in a moment, so she could leave the sad scene.

'What was that?' Boleyn called as he followed Nicòla through the ambassador's presence room and out into the hallways of the palace. His own reasons to see Castelnau were forgotten; indeed, all he cared for was gossip he could spread in minutes around the warrens of Whitehall.

'Lord Rochford, I must ask you to desist!' Nicòla said as she scurried around the hallways, rather bare of others on a quiet afternoon.

'The appetites of the Bishop of Tarbes are well known,' Boleyn continued, only one step behind Nicòla.

'Yes, he spoke lustily of appetites.'

'Did he rub the knobs upon his chair?'

Nicòla stopped and eyed Boleyn. 'Ask me not of the scene.'

'Do I see tears in your gentle eyes, Frescobaldi?' Boleyn asked with a smile. 'Did you gain more favour than you sought with the ambassador?'

Nicòla swallowed hard and did not respond. Her clothing kept her feminine frame from the hands of men. She looked either way along the hallway, yet none walked the space, no guards, no one.

'Everyone wonders what lurks beneath your doublet, Frescobaldi,' Boleyn continued. 'My question is, what did the ambassador hope to find?'

'The body of a man surely,' Nicòla replied and took a deep breath. 'For I am a man, the brother to the Duchess of Florence.'

'I am close to my sister,' Boleyn said and tilted his head sideways as he examined Nicòla. 'My sister knows all about you and Crumwell. And my sister is angry at present with your master... and lover.'

'I am no man of carnal appetites such as yourself.'

With a sudden movement, Boleyn thrust his hand between Nicòla's legs. A painful reminder of the meeting just moments before, his fingers grabbing hard, looking for a body part never present. Nicòla jumped from Boleyn as he began to laugh, and she shuffled from the man, who dared not follow. Crumwell could be tainted if Nicòla's sex was ever revealed. Nicòla herself would be imprisoned, or sent home to her life in Florence, one of grave uncertainty once the Medici divorce reached the Pope. Gossip to threaten the French ambassador with had come from the meeting, but at great cost. With luck, God's grace, or even just chance, the ambassador would assume he simply did not grab Nicòla rightly and think nothing of her gender. Boleyn however knew all, as long thought, and could speak up at any time. His hand was a threat, almost a promise, that she and Crumwell could be destroyed at any moment. Tonight's meeting and the alliance formed between England and Rome simply had to pass, or the power of the Boleyns would surely destroy everything.

Chapter 38 – April 1536
Greenwich Palace, downstream London

Lyes will scream when they are forcyd into the lyght

'Would it be best if I leave court?'

Crumwell ceased his pacing at the question. Across his office stood Nicòla, dressed her best new doublet and hose, in aid of the King's party. Even Crumwell wore something special, silver rather than his usual black, while Nicòla sparkled in pale blue, her favourite fabric from Italy. She protested that all was well after her moment with the French ambassador and then with George Boleyn, yet when Crumwell observed her, Nicòla's eyes were not upon him, and her hands shook with fear. He had placed his precious Nicòla in a place of great harm; it had been her legal mind which was to draw the ambassador into a place of disgrace, not her body. Crumwell sought the French ambassador to be brought low due to sharing treasonous words against the King or Queen, to make an Imperial alliance appear more enticing to Henry. Yet Castelnau had acted in a way even Crumwell had not foreseen, for the ambassador's leanings were mere rumour until today.

'If you leave court, it says you have done something wrong, or that the ambassador discovered a secret about you,' Crumwell said. 'If either Castelnau or Boleyn seek to out your fair sex now, you running from court only endorses their words. No, you must tarry hither, and act as if nothing is wrong.'

'Boleyn has known the truth of me for years,' Nicòla argued. 'He had no reason to bring us low until now.'

'But he will if his sister is constantly angry with me,' Crumwell shot back. 'No, we simply push ahead. Tonight, Henry and Chapuys will formally agree to an Imperial alliance, the Emperor will be joyous, and the Pope shall sign your annulment. We all win. Besides, trade between

England and Italy will flourish, and for merchants like ourselves, the money will be beneficial. There are no losers in this arrangement.'

'Except France, who will be seated between two enemies in an alliance together.'

'France made their choice the moment Castelnau threw himself upon you.' Crumwell paused and pulled at the collar of his new linen shirt. He employed only the best tailors and seamstresses and yet the shirt still felt wrong. Perchance it was his mood that ill-fitted, as he felt ready to fight any man who came near him.

A knock on the office door heralded Ralph, who sported a white feather in his soft black cap. He had picked up the habit from Wriothesley. 'Master, it is time to enter the main hall, for the King is almost ready to begin.'

'Any news on the French ambassador? Shall he attend tonight's festivities?' Crumwell asked as he fetched his cap from his desk.

'Indeed no, Ambassador de Castelnau has become ill with much haste. He sends his secretary, Bishop de Carle in his place this night,' Ralph said, knowing none of the day's events in the French apartments.

Crumwell shot a stern look to Nicòla. 'That is our major adversary gone from the night. God willing, I shall achieve one of my greatest laws yet, an alliance with the Holy Roman Emperor.'

'They are the words I long to hear,' came the voice of Chapuys, and Crumwell turned to find the ambassador behind him. 'How fortunate our French counterpart could not make it tonight.'

'No one shall miss Castlenau,' Crumwell said, and dismissed Nicòla with a click of his fingers.

~~~

'Is it true, Secretary Crumwell, that the French ambassador once called upon you at Austin Friars, only to be turned away, even though you were in the garden playing bowls?' Chapuys asked.

'Well indeed.' Crumwell sipped his wine as he stood among his party in the great hall. 'Such is my confidence that I can deny any person I please, and my servants are endlessly faithful.'

'You are a king yourself in England.'

'Treason, Eustace,' Crumwell laughed. 'Say no such things in my company, nay any person's company.'

From the far corner of the room, Crumwell noticed the hand of Thomas Audley wave to him. 'Come, Eustace, we are to dine with the King, the Lord Chancellor and Lord Rochford in the presence chamber, away from this festivity.'

'Be there any way to say no?' Chapuys replied.

'None, for tonight we shall seal our legacy.' Crumwell thought of the papers on his desk, letters from the Roman Emperor himself, written to Crumwell. The Emperor wrote to him, such a man of low birth. Crumwell would not confess it openly, but he had kissed the letters in reverence to the moment he became powerful enough to converse with the King of Spain and Emperor of the Holy Roman Empire.

In the presence chamber, a dining table had been laid out, enough to seat some thirty men, yet only the King and George Boleyn sat there as Crumwell, Audley and Chapuys were shown to their seats by a gentleman-usher, who was waved away in a moment, along with the servants laying food before Henry. The King sat crooked in his chair at the end of the table, one elbow balanced on the wooden arm of the seat. All three bowed to Henry, who barely acknowledged them as they sat down to dine.

'There be much talk at the party tonight,' Henry said, a smile growing upon his face. 'Indeed, it is a fine night to enjoy the company of so many at court.'

'I so agree, Your Majesty,' Crumwell said and folded his hands together upon the white tablecloth. He would make this one of the greatest nights at court in some time.

'First,' Henry replied, and ran a hand over his lips, 'tell me of talk which has been reported. That men in the German States and the Low Countries are talking of a potential alliance between England and Rome.'

Crumwell watched Audley shift awkwardly in his seat. Audley of course knew much of the plans; he and Crumwell had spent many a night talking of the benefits and law changes needed to create an alliance.

'It appears my own envoys have been moving on England's behalf to consider an Imperial alliance,' Henry continued, and Boleyn nodded with the King's words.

'I would be ready to forfeit my head if anything was said in those countries that went to His Majesty's prejudice,' Crumwell said.

'We wish for an alliance, Your Majesty,' Chapuys announced with great confidence. 'As Secretary Crumwell has your government in hand, he and I have spoken at great length about a potential alliance, and the terms needed to make the nations stronger together. Indeed, much work has been done on your behalf, Your Majesty. Emperor Charles is ready to make overtures to His Majesty at once, with terms between your countries settled.'

Chapuys grinned to Crumwell and he grinned in reply; they had worked endlessly on such an alliance and were confident. For all their previous dealings, now they could create a legacy of peace.

'George,' Henry said, and glanced to Boleyn beside him at the table. 'Please excuse us.'

Crumwell noticed Henry's blue eyes follow Boleyn, who slunk from the room in silence. Henry burst from his chair, enough to throw the heavy seat crashing to the floor. 'How dare you!' Henry seethed, his face reddening as Chapuys turned white with worry. 'How dare you come in and tell me you have sorted an alliance without me, without my express command!'

'Your Majesty,' Chapuys said as he, Crumwell and Audley all stood from their seats, 'we dared not put down anything in writing.'

'Without my express command!' Henry repeated slowly as he stepped towards Chapuys. Henry stopped just inches from the ambassador, who looked down in submission. Crumwell could not believe Henry's sudden anger. Surely an alliance would be nothing but helpful, even if just to end the Empire as a threat after years of panic.

'Your Majesty…'

Henry silenced Crumwell with a single hand raised in his direction. Yet the King's eyes stayed firmly upon Chapuys. 'They speak of an alliance throughout Europe, so that means for months there have been letters sent, opinions sought, papers given and received. Without my express command, you have sought your master's mind yet not told me?'

'Your Majesty,' Chapuys said, still looking to his feet. 'The Emperor gives you good terms for such an alliance. The Emperor can ensure you are not excommunicated from the Catholic Church. The Pope is ready to halt all his plans to excommunicate His Majesty and England. The Emperor wants peace with you, and peace between you and the Pope. The Emperor shall recognise Queen Anne as your lawful wife.'

Crumwell noticed Henry flinch. Those words either excited Henry or made him foul of mood.

'Why?' Henry asked, his voice deep and tempered.

'The Emperor believes such an alliance…'

'No,' Henry cut off the ambassador. 'Why accept Anne as queen? Why not want a Catholic bride on the throne?'

'You have married Queen Anne…'

'And yet the Empire never acknowledged my marriage,' Henry said as he steadied his feet wide apart. 'But now they shall keep my name in the Catholic faith and accept my marriage to Anne. What do they want from me?'

'They wish for your support against the French in Milan, and they want Lady Mary restored in the line of succession.'

'I have just spent a year ensuring everyone acknowledges my Elizabeth as successor!' Henry yelled with enough power to make Chapuys lose his footing, and he fell against the dining table, knocking over several glasses of wine. The entire party outside would have heard the words. 'I am married to Anne, according to the religious law of England!' Henry screamed. 'The succession is clear! Katherine was never my true wife!'

Audley shot a quick look to Crumwell – something had gone horribly wrong. Perchance it was pride, perchance Henry wished for no alliance other than one he sought himself. Perchance either his wife, or his new love Jane, had hurt the King's mood. For all the planning and preparation, Henry's feelings were about to swiftly bring the whole plan into the dust.

'If,' Henry said slowly, finally bringing down his voice, 'I order an audience with Charles, whose Empire would not be as large as it is without my help, it shall be based on alliances and plans written in the past. Plans written expressly between myself and the Emperor. Only I forge laws in this country, Chapuys. I am the King, and without my permission to create an alliance, you would all have your heads on spikes.'

'I seek not to meddle with your authority, Your Majesty. We would not harm you, not for all the gold in England! We seek good terms as honest men.'

'You seek to claim my authority over my realm!' Henry spat and stumbled back a few steps from Chapuys, as if repelled by his very notion. 'You seek to make decisions over me, the anointed King of England, the Defender of the Faith, the Supreme Leader of the Church of England! You dared to ask your master if he shall accept Anne as my wife? I need no such acceptance! You seek to tell me who shall be my successor, as if you are willing my death? You expect me to fight the French in Milan, as your master needs? The only treaty that shall ever be made shall be discussed by myself and the Emperor, and no mere mortal shall ever expect to be part of discussions! We are anointed kings! You have gone against the men that God has placed at the head of great realms. You seek to go against God!' Henry's spittle landed firmly in Chapuys' face with every outburst.

The ambassador had shrunk, cowering before the great King, his face reddened with his anger. Crumwell could not be sure who would stumble first; Henry from rage or Chapuys from fear. The room fell silent for a moment and Henry's eyes swung at Audley.

'Lord Chancellor, how much have you planned in this treason?'

'Your Ma…Ma… Majesty,' Audley stuttered in panic, 'there is nothing in writing, so my official capacity has been nonesuch.'

'Lord Chancellor, please escort the ambassador back to the party, as I wish for all to see his much-diminished status at this moment,' Henry said through gritted teeth.

At once both Chapuys and Audley bowed in reverence and fled from the room. All fell silent again, the sounds of voices in the distant party to be heard through the open door. No doubt hundreds had heard the screaming just now; the entire court would know of the feud within minutes. The doors to the presence chamber closed and Henry took a deep breath. But as Crumwell dared to relax his stance, Henry's angry gaze turned on his most faithful servant.

'I must make a confession,' Henry quietly began, his eyes firmly upon Crumwell. 'Never have I looked upon a man who has committed treason against me. Always, the men are captured far from my chambers, be them a noble, a peasant or a clergyman, and never have I looked them in the eye. Those moments when I find out who disgraced themselves and their family, their honour, I have someone else arrest them, question them, destroy them. You know this, naturally, Crumwell, as sometimes it is you who sees out my plans, my arrests, my executions. And yet, this night, I am forced to look upon a man who wished to take my place as the ruler of this nation.'

Crumwell fell to his knees in a moment. Not once he had considered this result. Countless times he brought laws and changes, proposals and policies to the King's ear, always listened to, his words considered or reformed, or simply just agreed to in good faith. All Crumwell wanted was a treaty signed, bringing benefits to the King, to England and to Crumwell himself. There was to be no one harmed in such an endeavour. 'Your most gracious Majesty…' he begged.

'You dare to interrupt my words?' Henry spat over Crumwell's tone. 'Are your words worth more than mine?'

Pain swirled within Crumwell's stomach. So much wine had been consumed that day. First over anger at the fight in the French ambassador's rooms, then in nerves over the evening's proposals. All now appeared determined to return to his mouth. The dizzy humours not felt since Crumwell's illness suddenly returned to his mind, now swimming in its own fear. Henry's chest swelled with rage and Crumwell did his best to steady himself upon his knees for the tirade about to bear down like a winter storm.

'If you were but a candle, I would order you blown out!' Henry screamed. He kicked Crumwell, finding him firmly in his swirling stomach, but Crumwell did not dare to move. 'You, Crumwell, were the one man at court to challenge me in wit, and yet now you are an enemy! You are but a groundling, swimming in the mud of the Thames! You are the fool, hated and jeered by all at court! You are a snake, unfeeling and greedy, you are a rake fire, outstaying your welcome in my court! Admit it! Admit you acted alone without my authority!'

Crumwell let Henry catch his breath before he dared utter response. 'Your Majesty,' he whispered, 'I acted alone without authority, to impress you with my reach on the matter.'

'Why?' Henry threw his hands in the air. 'We seek no treaty with Rome! You have defied me!'

Hot prickling tears balanced in Crumwell's golden eyes. A man of some fifty years, reduced to tears. But even when on his knees, weak, threatened and humiliated, the chance to escape appeared from the echo of a cheap comment made by Nicòla months past.

'Your Majesty, you said I could accept incentives and bribes, provided I gave the crown ten percent.'

Henry shook his head in confusion, his fists clenched so hard his skin looked pale around each golden ring. 'Are you quite out of your senses? Are you to say you were bribed by the Holy Roman Emperor? You are but a peasant, a commoner!'

'The Emperor wants to marry his daughter to the Duke of Florence. My secretary is married to the Duke. I wanted Frescobaldi to receive an annulment.'

'You could not receive an annulment for me!' Henry shoved Crumwell and he fell hard to the floor, flat on his back. 'I had to destroy the entire Church because YOU failed to get me an annulment! Yet you tell me that you have defied me for your own creature's annulment?'

'I was offered a swift annulment in return for an alliance. I did not seek the annulment, it was offered as payment. The Emperor needs you. I thought that would give you comfort, pride even. The Pope has offered lack of excommunication. You would be the proudest, most powerful king in Europe, safe from Rome and welcome in both the Catholic faith and within the Reformation sweeping the people. No one would have power like you, Your Majesty. If the Emperor needs you, wants you, and accepts Queen Anne, all kings would surely follow. Charles is the Emperor and the King of Spain, the leader of your biggest enemies. France across the sea would be no threat ever again, surrounded by this treaty.'

'If your plan was so prosperous, why not bring it straight to me?'

'Because I was desperate and wanted all done swiftly. I wanted the bribe, and the Emperor's acceptance of Anne, and to make you a favourite of Charles and the Pope.'

'Greed is a sin. As is lust and pride, all sins committed by you.'

Crumwell nodded as Henry stood over him, but he felt his heart blacken, not for his sins, but because Henry dared to say such, when the destiny of the kingdom depended on Henry's lust and pride and greed. 'Why would I need you to convince kings to bow to me? I am the King of England! You suggest I am not all powerful? You break your own treason laws! Not only do I desire to take your head, but my most beloved queen shall also wish to see your head on London Bridge!'

Crumwell knew not to move as Henry forced his heavy foot hard into his stomach. He had to endure Henry's wrath, for to fight back would be treason, more added to his torture. Henry kicked him several times as he cowered on the floor. Henry gave up his angry domination and stood back, as if to admire his work.

'Be gone from my chamber, and you would do well to be gone from my sight, lest you not live long enough to see the annulment of your Waif. With one utterance, I could expose the both of you and have your heads!'

Crumwell rolled and pulled himself upright using a chair, eager to appear beaten. It was no lie, for the pain kept him doubled over. As Crumwell opened the presence chambers doors, through the pain he stood upright and smoothed his hair and adjusted his cap, for no man or woman at court could witness his destruction.

The party stood in total silence, the screaming heard by all. Crumwell felt the eyes of court upon him as he walked slow and steady through the crowd, seeing Chapuys in a far corner, whispering in Edward Seymour's young ear. He continued walking through to the far end of the room, where gentleman-ushers pulled open the doors to the hallways back to Crumwell's offices. No doubt Nicòla and Ralph would soon follow, but they needed to give it time; not just to look less suspicious in their quick departure, but also to give Crumwell a moment to cry in private. He was beaten for the first time. The King was no longer Crumwell's closest friend and ally, and without Henry, he had nothing. Already Anne had turned against him, meaning the entire Boleyn clan and allies would be the same. All the nobles despised him, and even Cranmer, one of his dearest friends and colleagues, was confused over the dissolution of the monasteries. Everything was ending. Nothing could stop Crumwell's tears as he limped into his small bedroom, which truly belonged to Nicòla, and only an important shift in politics would save his head.

Chapter 39 – April 1536
Austin Friars, London

Lyes are like fyres, they could warm you or burn you

Nicòla sat on a wooden bench in the back garden, her eyes on the short grass by her feet. Jane played nearby, chasing one of her mother's beloved peacocks, but Nicòla paid little attention. A trance stung at her, rendering her body lifeless, as if a strange paralysis set about her. She took gentle, shallow breaths under her heavy fur coat, but her stillness conveyed none of her mood. Nicòla was angry, afraid, disillusioned for the first time in so long. She felt this way in the days after her father's murder outside Florence, and in the early days after marrying Alessandro. But never like this in England, the land of her freedom.

The attack in the French ambassador's chambers hurt her more than expected. Nicòla knew men like Castelnau, a powerful man who would paw at her in such a manner; though her dress usually allowed Nicòla to escape such behaviour. The King's rejection of the carefully planned alliance with the Emperor hurt less; it was Crumwell who desired Nicòla's annulment.

What also hurt was Crumwell's behaviour since fleeing the King's court. Three days passed and still he had not risen from his bed. Yes, Nicòla went to him in the night when the house slept, but in the day, he refused to rise. Such weakness had never instilled itself in Crumwell and now he slept in bed when he needed to plan his next great conspiracy, lest he be the court's next victim.

'Nicòla?'

The voice broke Nicòla's stillness, but only just. She tilted her head, her eyes barely seeing past the soft edge of her black cap. The voice she knew well, for there stood Ralph over her shoulder. 'We did not have you installed in the King's privy chamber for you to return home once more, Ralph…' Nicòla turned on her chair to see Ralph not alone. 'Mr. Sadler, you bring a guest,' she added as she stood to bow to the lady at Ralph's side, her blonde hair still covered by the soft red hood of her coat.

'Mr. Frescòbaldi,' Lady Jane Seymour said as Nicòla stood straight once more. 'I hope I am welcome at Austin Friars.'

Nicòla glanced up to the third level of the manor, to the window of Crumwell's bedroom, where she saw him not. Her eyes shot back to Ralph, who swallowed hard. 'What brings you to Austin Friars, Mistress Seymour?'

'Mr. Sadler agreed to accompany me when I wished to visit you.'

'Me? Not Secretary Crumwella?'

'Uncle Ralph!' little Jane cried when she saw the new arrivals. She charged over to Ralph, and he scooped her up in his arms. Since the departure of Ralph's wife Ellen and their children to the newly built Sutton House four miles away, Jane missed her family. The poor girl would certainly have no siblings now and Gregory remained in Stepney.

'Perchance you could spend time with your… niece?' Lady Jane said to Ralph, who without a word, took Jane from her mother's sight and into the house.

Nicòla gestured to the slightly damp bench seat. 'I am happy to aid you, Mistress Seymour, or would you rather sit in the house?'

Lady Jane sat down, and smoothed her hands over the silver gown under her coat. She gestured for Nicòla to sit beside her. 'I love how you pronounce my name,' Jane began.

'I must ask you to excuse my accent, for not all words come from me quite right.'

'No, I quite enjoy it. I have never been a curious woman, never the prettiest girl, the exotic beauty, or the well-connected lady's maid.'

'You have served two queens, Mistress Seymour.'

Jane turned a little on the seat to Nicòla. 'Let us speak plainly, Mr. Frescobaldi. There are rumours throughout court about your master.'

'I hear all, even if I am serving my master at Austin Friars. Secretary Crumwella has always been a man of rumour and scandal. No man born low can ever hope to raise high without attracting enemies.'

'You are not noble, Mr. Frescobaldi.'

'No, but born wealthy enough to have advantages in Florence and Rome.'

'You sister sits as Duchess of Florence, married to a Medici?'

'Indeed.'

'Your reclusive sister, whose bastard child lives hither as Crumwell's adopted daughter?

'Young Jane is my niece, yes. My sister, Duchess Nicòletta has always been reclusive.'

'Because she hides under the garments of a man?'

'You must excuse me, Lady Jane…'

Jane raised her hand to stop Nicòla. 'It is known the French ambassador supports Queen Anne. There are whispers that something happened between you and the French ambassador, and you are lacking the... the part that Ambassador de Castelnau is known to enjoy.'

'You speak with great candour!' Nicòla admonished. 'No woman would ever dare say such things.'

'I am no ordinary woman,' Jane replied as she took her hood from her long blonde hair. 'My brother Edward likes to speak for me, for our family. My father was part of a scandal in years past, and Edward is now the head of the family. I am just property.'

'What do you want, Lady Jane?'

'I like you, Mr. Frescobaldi. I always have. You have a subtly to you that no man at court possesses. I have noticed this about you. I too am one to stand in the shadows, for I am considered the plain sister of my family, of a family not noble enough to be of any great importance. My sister Elizabeth is always seen as the beautiful one and has already borne two children to her dear departed husband. My youngest sister Dorothy is pretty and haughty, my brothers are well-liked and intelligent. But I, I have always stood in the shadows. And I see others that do the same, like you, with your watching eyes, with your shining rose-gold hair that captures attention even though you do not seek it. Then I heard this preposterous rumour about you and the French ambassador...'

'I seek nothing from the French ambassador, Lady Jane,' Nicòla interrupted without thinking.

'I know, and none believe the rumours. You are the Waif; the creature Crumwell keeps. Some say you are his lover, a gentleman. But while your mind speaks of being a man, your presence portrays a woman.'

'You mean to threaten me, Lady Jane? My master is not in the King's favour today, but I am no victim ready to be plucked.'

'Forgive me, Mr. Frescobaldi, for I come not to threaten. I came to say, that I wish there was a woman in the court who knew my mind, a woman who could help me, rather than be steered by an army of men in all my dealings.'

'If you came to hear me say I am a woman, Lady Jane, I fear you shall be disappointed.'

'I wish not to hear such things,' Jane said with a delicate wave of her hand. 'You appear to have the heart of a woman, Mr. Frescobaldi. You have raised yourself high, and your sister even higher in your homeland, as a duchess.'

'My sister may soon lose that title as the Pope shall annul the marriage.'

'I heard so,' Jane replied. 'I am of the old faith. As an Italian, where does your faith lie, with the Catholic hearts of your homeland, or with your master and the Reformation?'

'My heart shall always lie with God.'

'I come in search of an ally, Mr. Frescobaldi. I want to stop men from ruling me.'

'That is a desire all women seek, but it is not God's will.'

'Quite, yet we can seek guidance from women, can we not? I ask you not to say you are a woman, but I feel you can be the ally I need.'

Nicòla knew not how to reply, for she would not admit her sex to any person, no matter how desperate they were for female companions. 'I know my sister's mind, Lady Jane, and perchance that means I can be an ally.'

'I want to be a queen, Mr. Frescobaldi. I want to rise all the way to the King's side, rise the way your sister did in Florence. Henry writes me letters of love and I believe he likes me a great deal. Anne does not comfort him any longer. There, I have made all plain. My brothers and my father have been looking for support on my behalf, as I ask them to do. Sir Nicholas Carew and the Duke of Suffolk are on my side, as are the Poles and Exeters, the last Plantagenets on Earth. I support the Lady Mary as heir to the King, the daughter of the great Queen Katherine.'

'You speak treason, Lady Jane, to oust an anointed queen, the only queen crowned in the Bury St Edmond's crown,' Nicòla said with a panic. No one ever spoke so plainly, especially no woman. Jane was the leader of the plan to oust Anne, not her brothers.

'The Pope would like a Catholic queen in England. It would make the Holy Roman Emperor happy, as no French queen would sit in England.'

'Why see yourself down such a dangerous path, Lady Jane?'

'Because I love Henry. Have you never loved, Mr. Frescobaldi? You have no women at court.'

'I dedicate my time to serving my master, and His Majesty.'

'Your master has no women either, despite all his titles, his power, his parties and charm.'

'You spy on us, Lady Jane?'

'It is well known Crumwell is the master of secrets. But words travel about the court.'

'I deal in politics and law, Lady Jane, not idle talk.'

'Make I speak with plainness? My brother, Edward, wants to see me on the throne of England. He wants me to be at the King's side, though will sell me as a mistress if that is all I can be. If I am to be a pawn in such a manner, I want some control. If I cannot be a queen, I wish to be a wife elsewhere, not a mistress. While many women are content as mistresses, I cannot be one.'

'A quality I admire, Lady Jane. Your brother does not get to decide who is Queen of England. It is treason just to say such things. Idle talk it may be, but treason as well.'

'The only person who gets to decide on a queen is Secretary Crumwell.'

'His Majesty decides on who is his queen. God joins a marriage and that is the end of any matter.'

'Poor Queen Katherine.' Jane paused and crossed herself. 'I hear rumours, Mr. Frescobaldi, that you pay money to Lady Mary, which would anger the King. You pay the girl's costs and send her items belonging to her mother. I wish not to report such rumours as you may find yourself in trouble.'

'You seek to threaten me now? After uttering such treason, hither in my master's garden?'

'Henry would not believe you. I have watched you since you first came to court, Mr. Frescobaldi. I remember the first time I noticed you. You came to Queen Katherine's chambers in the night, prayed with her, spoke to her in her language. I know not what was said, but it was clear that Katherine trusted you, liked you. I come hither today to speak to you for one reason. It is Secretary Crumwell who holds the power in this kingdom.'

'And he creates that power on three things, Lady Jane. First, Secretary Crumwella's ability to enrich His Majesty. Second, because Crumwella can aid His Majesty in controlling his realm through religious means. And third, because he was the man able to create a marriage with Queen Anne. The laws made by my master cannot be unmade.'

'Unless Secretary Crumwell unmade them,' Jane replied. 'It is well known you have a hold over Crumwell. Where Crumwell goes, you go too. No one, not even Mr. Sadler does so, and Sadler is considered a son of Crumwell. Crumwell adores his Waif, his creature. I am being pushed to be the King's next love, and if this is to be, I wish to have control. I want the control you have – you stand in Crumwell's shadow, yet you have so much influence. I want to know how you do that. We can be much alike, Mr. Frescobaldi.'

'Do you read Machiavelli, Lady Jane?'

'I confess I cannot read.'

'If you hope to be beside a king, you may wish to change your habits. Machiavelli says, non possiamo attribute alla fortuna o alla virtù ciò che si ottiene senza. We cannot attribute to fortune or virtue that which is achieved without either. If you see me as an evil presence in court or a fool at the Queenmaker's side who can give you a quick way to the throne, you are much confused. I have seen enough evil things done in the name of power and seek to do none to England or His Majesty.'

'I ask for no such thing, Mr. Frescobaldi,' Jane said as she stood and pulled her hood over her blonde hair once more. 'On the contrary, I seek to do as little harm as possible.'

'To be queen, you must destroy Anne Boleyn. She is an anointed queen. Her father is the Lord Privy Seal, her brother one of the King's most trusted attendants. Anne's uncle is the Duke of Norfolk, one the King's longest-serving friends. Her Majesty is educated, charming, intelligent, beguiling, beautiful and strongly for the Reformation. With respect, Lady Jane, you are none of those things.'

'I am peaceful, I am quiet, obedient and respectful of faith. The opposite of Queen Anne. Have you not thought I am precisely what His Majesty seeks? His Majesty's eye chose me. I wanted to speak with you, as there is a great change coming at court; the King has asked for more than courtly love from me, but only marriage shall tempt me. I thought, with Secretary Crumwell on my side, it would make things smoother, safer and kinder. I want everyone's safety.'

'Except for Queen Anne's.'

'I shall take my leave, Mr. Frescobaldi. Remember, I have much on my side, many of Crumwell's enemies. He could make them allies by coming to my camp.'

'No one at court shall ever respect Secretary Crumwella, and he knows of that, Lady Jane.'

'Ideas change, politics change.' With those words, Jane Seymour turned and walked away from Nicòla back towards the house where Ralph stood, minding his own thoughts. It seemed foolish that another queen could sit on the throne.

~~~

The whole bed shook in a violent shot and Crumwell opened his eyes. At the foot of the bed stood Nicòla, her arms folded. Indeed, she had said little during the time of his melancholy, but her face spoke of disquiet.

'Get up.'

Crumwell blinked a few times as he sat up in the bed. Nicòla never spoke in such a tone, but she felt a fire in her belly. 'Nicò?'

'You call me your wife, not your secretary, so I shall speak to you as a wife. Get out of bed. You are being as lazy as a fool, weak as a woman. Get up.' Again, she kicked the end of the bed to shake him from his slumber.

'Can a man not rest?'

'A simple man, yes, but you are no such thing. You are the King's Chief Minister, the Vicegerent of England! The realm could fall at any moment and yet you lie in bed. I have had children ripped from my womb, God rest their souls, and spent less time in bed.'

Crumwell rubbed his face and said nothing. His palms slipped from his cheeks, and Nicòla softened her stance a little. 'Have you never wished to throw it all away, Nicò? Have you never thought to give up, take what you have, and settle for what you have left once the dust of battle has settled?'

'Yes, I have thought that. I thought that after giving birth to our daughter. I thought perchance I could tarry in Florence with my husband, or Rome with the Pope, God rest his immortal soul, and I could be a duchess and a Medici wife. But instead, I smuggled my babe aboard a ship and came back to England in search of you. And it is time I said this – you could not be the Queenmaker without me. You would not have England in the palm of your hand without me at your side.'

'Why this sudden anger, Nicò?'

'Today, while you laid in bed, surrounded by your soft cotton and feathered pillows, soft velvets and silk, tapestries keeping in the warmth of the fire, Mistress Jane Seymour visited me. She is making a play for the throne, aided by her brothers, all while you sleep the day away! She is being used as a tool and is standing at the front of the coming tide of change, while I sit in the garden because my master cannot rise above his weak humours!'

'Jane Seymour came here?' Crumwell blinked a few times, shocked by the change. 'Henry is happy with Anne. That is why he was so angry at me, for daring to say he needed Rome's approval of his marriage.'

'I have had messengers coming and going from the palace all day,' Nicòla fought into the pocket of her coat and tossed them on the embroidered bedcovers. 'Ralph brought Lady Jane. Already she has written to the Lady Mary, expressing her support for the girl, saying she should be Henry's legitimate heir. Other messengers say they have seen Lady Jane in the King's privy chamber, letting him touch all manner of parts, while saying she is chaste and innocent in public circles. Jane Seymour is no innocent fool as we suspected. She is not smart like our Anne, not beautiful like our Anne, but she has all the things Anne lacks, and Jane knows that, and is ready to play the role of meek mistress while Anne is the disquiet wife.'

'Anne is my queen,' Crumwell said as he pulled the bedcovers away and swung his feet to the floor. Nicòla rounded the bed to stand before him, her face still in a frown. 'Henry could love Anne one day and then Jane the next. I would never dare turn away from Anne, Nicò.'

'Anne has turned from you; my messengers tell me so. Chapuys has written no less than seven times in the last two days! There is news that Stephen Gardiner is to return from France, hoping England can ally with the French, not Rome. Some suggest the Exeters are planning to smuggle Lady Mary out of England to Spain where she can be married and return with a Spanish army to claim her father's throne! Others report Henry has spoken of legitimising Fitzroy and making him an heir, which I would never refuse. But I am just a humble secretary to the Chief Minister of Staying in Bed!'

Crumwell leapt to his feet and swiped the messages from the bed. 'What of Anne?'

'Queen Anne is angry with you. She has spoken to Henry for days about her hate for you. Cranmer is no help, staying at Lambeth Palace and saying nothing. No one is there at court, fighting in our corner, Tom. Anne wants you ousted for your plot to align England with Rome. Everyone has a plan and we are doing nothing while London burns! Do not let this country become what Rome became to me.'

Crumwell paused, to think of Nicòla, much younger, dressed in rags, hiding from soldiers in Rome as the city fought itself. He thought of himself as a boy, running from home in the night, getting aboard a ship to France, starving and desperate. They had come so far, only to be undone by one alliance plan. Crumwell towered over Nicòla and smoothed his night clothes. 'We need to make peace with Anne.'

'Even if it is not real peace.'

'You want to destroy Anne, Queen of England?'

'We cannot rush into another divorce. The laws you created for the royal marriage are so tight we shall never untangle such webs. Look at the pain of the first divorce. It could take years and Anne will have your head before then. We have enough work to do running this country and dissolving the lesser monasteries. Besides, you wrote up patents, so Anne is the Marquess of Pembroke; she could be the old wife of the King and still live at court!'

'Nunnery?'

'Anne Boleyn? In a nunnery?' Nicòla choked with laughter. 'Understand this; I love Queen Anne. I think she deserves Henry's love. I wanted Katherine on the throne, the true queen. I came to this country expressly to save Katherine. But Katherine is dead, and I stood at your side as you chose Anne as your queen. I care nothing for the truth, that the people of England hate Anne.'

'Anne could be put aside if someone accused her of treason.'

'Treason? Anne?' Nicòla squinted.

'There are many ways to accuse someone of treason, for there are many ways to commit treason against the King. I wrote the laws,' Crumwell replied. 'Lack of a male heir is not enough. Wishing the King's death seems unlikely from Anne...'

'Adultery.'

Crumwell's golden eyes settled on Nicòla's gaze and they remained silent for a moment. 'Adultery? Anne is loyal.'

'We lie. We set up men, create the evidence. The right bribe can make any person say anything. If Anne is accused of adultery, thus found guilty of treason, it annuls the marriage. Henry could commute the sentence of death to life in the Tower,' Nicòla suggested.

'Yes. We cannot have Anne beheaded for treason. She is an anointed queen. I would never dream of killing Anne even if she wanted me dead.'

'And she does, we know Anne wants you dead, Tom. It would be easy enough to do. I am in the Queen's chambers often, I see who is there, what they say. Norris is there constantly, as is Weston. They both laughed, stating that they are there to seek the love of their queen. Wyatt and Smeaton are there constantly, so they could be innocent witnesses.'

'Weston and Norris were witnesses at Henry's private London wedding to Anne,' Crumwell said as he thought. 'Who else came with us that night?'

'William Brereton, that old toad.'

'Yes, Brereton. If we shamed those three men with adultery, they too could be jailed and silenced. That will be revenge upon Brereton for his actions in Wales, defying my authority and killing poor John ap Griffith Eyton. Anne brought two of her ladies to the ceremony.'

'Yes, Margery Horsman. She would make an excellent witness. The other woman present was Nan Bray, Baroness Cobham. And let us not forget Elizabeth Somerset, Countess of Worcester. She is Anne's attendant yet visits Henry's bed,' Nicòla told him.

'But what of the rest of the Boleyns?'

'They shall be diminished once Anne is discredited. The Boleyns have few allies at court. We have an alliance forming between the Seymours, with the Poles, Exeters, the Lady Mary supporters, the Catholics, Suffolk, Carew and the Katherine supporters. We must be on both sides if we are to be safe. We take Anne to trial for treason, and she is imprisoned, not executed, or mayhap banished like poor Katherine.'

'You speak as if this would be easy.'

'I have a message, from the Queen's own chamber, written by Mark Smeaton himself! He says Anne was in a mood and yelled at Henry Norris. Anne claimed Norris "looked for dead men's shoes" because he looked to have Anne for himself if the King died! That could be evidence.'

'That is treason!' Crumwell cried.

'Weston laughed at the argument and said Anne should be his love, not Norris', and that he wanted her.'

'Is it that simple, to try a queen for treason?'

'You created a queen; why not break one down as well? You defeated Katherine of Aragon, so Anne Boleyn would not be so difficult. Henry can have Anne or Jane, whatever he chooses. Fitzroy can become the heir. Lady Mary would be happy to see the end of Anne Boleyn. We could have peace and continue with the Reformation.'

'Have you heard of a commission of oyer and terminer? It is an obscure law made 300 years past, where a court is set up, a special grand jury, held in the county where the crime is committed. Oyer and terminer courts only deal with serious cases. If Audley can organise this, with the permission of the King, we could see a queen before a court. But we shall need witness statements, whether real or paid for, victims set up, times, places, dates, and we must arrange everything, then make sure the judges have no choice but to find in favour of the result I desire. We must set up the court in secret, so Anne has no time to win Henry's love, and we can fill the judges' seats with men angry at Anne for various reasons. We must do all before Henry and Anne leave for Calais for their scheduled trip in early May.'

'That trip is but two weeks away,' Nicòla replied. 'Can we achieve all in two weeks?'

'Do we have a choice? We plan and then return to court. People shall think we are at Austin Friars as I sit away from Henry's temper. It is not entirely untrue, but they shall not learn of our plan. We must recall my nephew Richard at once, for he shall be part of this plan. He is a member of Privy Council and beyond reproach. God bless you, Nicò, for you have given me a reason to live.'

'Planning to frame a queen for treason to have her imprisoned for life is a reason to live?' Nicòla frowned.

Crumwell grabbed Nicòla by the shoulders and kissed her. 'I am hated by the nobles for being low born and hated by the commoners for discovering how to control them through tax and religion. I might as well go down fighting, either die or live to see an anointed queen imprisoned. That is something history can remember me for, do you not think?'

Chapter 40 – April 1536
Stepney, outer London

You can lye to yourself, but you myght not beelieve yourself

Retreating to Stepney was a move of genius. Now Crumwell was outside London, "scared to return to court," or so everyone thought. Everyone gathered at Greenwich Palace, ready for the May Day celebrations, but the King had scared Crumwell, the Chief Minister, away from court, now hiding with his son Gregory. That was the story spun by Ralph, a rumour which soared around the thousands at court within hours. The truth bore a different likeness; in the countryside peace, Crumwell could plan the downfall of his own queen. Letters came and went from court, giving little pieces of news, all the false rumours written up in Nicòla's hand on Crumwell's orders.

For all the work needed to make Anne a queen, it took precious little to remove her. Any woman slandered with adultery had no chance to recover from such shame. To take down a great queen such as Queen Katherine needed Crumwell to fight the Pope, take on God himself, yet for Anne, it took a mere rumour. Anne, for all her education and her attention to politics, she lacked so many skills Katherine possessed; for one not born to rule could never see all the tiny details needed to make a great monarch. For Crumwell, as a commoner born, a commoner always, all he needed was the law, and people prepared to lie for his cause. Those people, those he trusted, were all summoned to Stepney, so planning remained as quiet as possible in a sea of gossip, idle minds and talkative wastrels.

The library, home to a rounded table, was where Crumwell seated his allies. Normally a place for Gregory's education, today he sat outside with his tutors, little Jane alongside them; the visit to Stepney needed to be a family occasion rather than a plot to destroy a sitting queen, a plan that would see all at the round table attainted for treason if they failed.

Crumwell looked up from his papers. To his left sat his nephew Richard, his hands clasped upon the dark table top. A man of the Privy Council, Richard Crumwell was a man of high standing, a man who would soon play a keen role in the governance of England. Beside him sat Thomas Wriothesley, the arrogant lawyer desperate for Crumwell's favour. His ginger-tinged beard needed a trim, so unlike Wriothesley, such a vain man. Beside him sat Nicòla, dressed not in her glowing colours today, her glorious hair pinned up under her soft cap, wearing the plain black livery of the Crumwell household. She leaned back in her chair, her little hands on the armrests, most comfortable for someone who had helped create such a powerful plan in a matter of days. Next to Nicòla sat Sir Richard Rich, an immoral man even at his best. He was ready to sit at the head of the Court of Augmentations, which would oversee the dissolution of the monasteries. At his side next to Crumwell himself sat Ralph, his son in all but name. Ralph knew more of the plans than the others, who were in the dark about proceedings, except Nicòla. But there were things even Nicòla knew not; for Crumwell could only trust himself in this most dangerous of plans. The conversation over the early afternoon meal had been one of the most awkward the group had ever shared, and now in the library, over wine, things had taken a serious tone. Now Crumwell was ready to share.

'Gentlemen, I bring you hither due to my keen need for family, friends and allies.'

'If you need fealty, uncle, you need not ask,' Richard replied. Other heads around the table all nodded.

'I do, I need fealty most keenly,' Crumwell admitted. 'For in this court, trusting friends can be difficult, hard to understand and dangerous to respect. I bring you hither to tell you of a most heinous crime committed, and I fear, if I am not believed, my head shall part my body. Chancellor Audley has issued me with a commission of oyer and terminer. We shall set up grand juries in Middlesex and Kent where crimes were committed.'

'Oyer and terminer? They are ancient court rules,' Rich commented. 'I have never heard of them ever being used, surely a grand jury has not been used in one hundred years or more.'

'I have serious crimes to investigate,' Crumwell replied. 'While the local sheriffs could have selected jurors in a trial, I can appoint nobles as the oyer and terminer jury, to ensure a favourable result.'

'Commissions of oyer and terminer are appointed after someone arrests an accused,' Wriothesley added. 'Whom do these courts judge?'

'There have been no arrests,' Crumwell replied and shifted in his seat. 'No part of the case has precedent. We have all studied the law and need to be prudent in this case.'

'Leave us not with secrets,' Rich said. 'Tell us all, for you have caught my intrigue.'

'First, Sir Richard, I wish to make it known you shall soon be sworn in as Speaker in the House of Commons, besides being the Solicitor General. I also want you to oversee the dissolution of the monasteries, which shall make you a wealthy and well-respected lawyer.'

'I shall do anything asked of me,' Rich uttered in surprise.

'Remember such words.' Crumwell turned to Wriothesley. 'Thomas, if you continue to serve me, I shall ensure you soon receive a knighthood. You are Clerk of the Signet and I will appoint you ambassador to Brussels, where you can represent the crown's merchant dealings.'

Wriothesley nodded in surprise and silence. Crumwell could almost see gold coin reflected in his greedy brown eyes.

Crumwell shifted in his seat again. 'Now, gentlemen. I must share with you the gravest of news. An indecent and profound crime against our most glorious Majesty. To say such words out loud grieves me so.'

The moment the words entered the ears of any person other than Nicòla, there would be no going back for Crumwell. 'Some say that Queen Anne, our gracious King's wife, has committed the offence of adultery.'

Crumwell waited in reply. No yelling occurred, no shock, no anger, only silence. Ralph and Nicòla shared a look; Richard stared at his uncle with a frown. The mouths of both Rich and Wriothesley hung open.

'Has the King said such words?' Richard asked. 'Is this so Henry can make Mistress Seymour his new wife?'

'The King knows nothing of this, and yet he must be informed, but only if we can gain evidence,' Crumwell instructed. 'We cannot act without evidence or a confession.'

'Who would dare confess to such things?' Wriothesley scoffed. 'None would admit to such a crime, and we could torture no nobleman.'

'We can torture a man close to Anne, who is not noble.'

'If we rack a man in the Tower for adultery with a queen, then everyone shall know in moments,' Richard said with a shake of his head. 'No one could keep that secret after such an act.'

'Rather than using torture, or seeking Anne's confession, we must gain witnesses. Queen Anne has many ladies in her chambers, all of which know every detail of her life. They have seen all, heard all,' Nicòla said as she laced her fingers together.

'Who would trust the word of a woman?' Rich asked with a gentle laugh. 'They will say whatever their families instruct them to say.'

'I know, but women can be tormented, frightened into saying something that fine legal minds can craft into evidence,' Crumwell replied.

Nicòla's gaze fell to the tabletop while the others nodded. Crumwell felt pain for saying such a thing before Nicòla's ears, be it true in cases of the other women.

'Mr. Frescobaldi, you have spent much time in the Queen's company, at her request. You were present during several miscarriages, were you not?' Rich asked. 'You would make a fine witness, with the trusty reputation of any man.'

'We could torture you for a confession,' Wriothesley laughed.

'No man shall place a finger upon Mr. Frescobaldi,' Crumwell shut down the gentle laughter.

'Who committed such crimes?' Richard asked.

Crumwell looked to the papers before him and pulled one from its hiding place in the centre. All names were written in Nicòla's fine hand. Crumwell caught Nicòla's gaze again. This was the list they had come up with over earlier days; men who could be trapped into crimes, with others innocent, to make the hunt look if it were real and not planned from a fantasy. 'Sir Henry Norris, Groom of the Stool in the Privy Chamber, Keeper of the Privy Purse, Gentleman-Usher of the Black Rod, Chamberlain of North Wales and Constable of Beaumaris Castle. 'Tis noted Sir Henry is courting Margaret Shelton and spends much time in the Queen's company.'

'Anne accused Norris of looking to have her after the King's death just days ago,' Ralph reported. 'And His Majesty knows of this.'

'Anne and Norris?' Rich frowned. 'I suppose it could be true…'

'Sir Francis Weston,' Crumwell continued over Rich. 'Gentleman of the Privy Chamber, Knight of the Bath. The young courtier spends much time with the Queen for no obvious reason other than to spend time with Anne, rather than attending to the King, or at home with his wife and newborn son.'

'Young, handsome, appearing innocent,' Nicòla said. 'I have heard him speak at length of his fondness for Anne.'

'Sir Richard Page, Gentleman of the Privy Chamber,' Crumwell continued. 'Sir Richard is a supporter of the Queen, ever since he abandoned working in Cardinal Wolsey's household to support Anne. He is Captain of the King's bodyguards, giving him special access to Anne.'

'Page is not a young man,' Richard replied. 'His wife is mother to Lady Anne Stanhope, Edward Seymour's new wife.'

'Just because Page is related to the Seymours does not mean we can discount his involvement in this scandal. We also cannot overlook Sir Thomas Wyatt,' Crumwell continued and saw Nicòla wince. She did not wish to question her friend Wyatt but had little choice. 'Wyatt has loved Anne since the time of their childhood. We have confirmed no rumours, but we still must investigate.'

This time the table fell silent. All liked Wyatt, a sweet man, a friend to many. Only Crumwell and Nicòla knew Wyatt would be found innocent.

'There is also Sir William Brereton, younger than Norris and Groom of the King's Privy Chamber. Anne has told me of her trust in Brereton. Brereton is an awful man, a man who abuses the powers of his royal grants in Cheshire and the Welsh marshes. That man could go to any lengths for his desires. Let us not forget Sir Francis Bryan, a skirt chaser of a great number, and always friendly to the Queen. Anne may be his cousin but still… Bryan could be a good ally, for he shall cry his innocence. Bryan would admit to bedding any woman with joy, but he would never admit to defiling the King's wife, his own cousin. His mother is raising Princess Elizabeth and raised Lady Mary and Henry Fitzroy. Bryan would do anything to clear the family name. Bryan's sister, Elizabeth was the King's whore at age thirteen, sold off to be Nicholas Carew's wife and now only an occasional mistress to the King now…'

'And now Carew, Knight of the Garter, would do anything to oust Anne,' Rich said with a grin. 'I see this plan. Guilt is unnecessary, only the assumption of guilt. I care not if Anne is innocent or guilty. I shall help you in this endeavour, Secretary Crumwell.'

'Good. Let us not discount William Latimer, a priest close to Anne. To debase herself with a priest, her own cousin, and one of Henry's longest friends? This shall bring down the King's moods and we must be careful, but also get through this,' Crumwell instructed. 'The King is to leave for Calais with Queen Anne in a few days, so we must move fast, and…'

The sound of distant voices cut short Crumwell's words. Someone had arrived at the house and Crumwell's worries jumped in his stomach. This was the moment Nicòla would turn from the whole plan.

'I pity the man who takes the news to the King,' Rich commented.

'That shall be you, Richard,' Crumwell turned his nephew. 'A man whose name is honourable, whose reputation is exemplary. Devise to give His Majesty the news in public where he dares not lose his dignity.'

'But how shall we gain any confessions on this most grievous of crimes without awakening suspicion?' Rich asked. He appeared almost excited to find evidence of a crime which had never occurred. How easy it was to find accomplices for such a lamentable act.

A brisk knock and one of the house's young servants appeared. 'Secretary Crumwell, your guest has arrived.'

'Most excellent, show him to our table. We shall need another chair, and wine for our guest. Have you the bag I requested?'

The young man stepped aside and in came Mark Smeaton. The young musician, the envy of many at court, had dressed in his finery, a most beautiful red doublet and hose, glittering in fine detailing. In one hand he held his lute, the other a beautiful red velvet cap. 'Secretary Crumwell,' he said with a wide smile which spread through the group. 'How nice of you to invite me to your home. I see you are having a private gathering ahead of the May Day deliberations tomorrow. I adore invitations to Stepney, for I have never visited this most delightful country home! I saw Gregory and baby Jane in the garden. How splendid your family has become!'

Nicòla rose from her seat to embrace her dear friend while the others moved their chairs to accommodate Mark, sitting beside Crumwell.

'We do so miss you at court,' Mark continued as a servant poured wine in everyone's glasses.

'I have missed your fine company,' Nicòla replied.

'Close the door behind you,' Crumwell instructed the servant without looking their direction. He knew it rude, but Crumwell was fixed on what was about to happen. 'No one is to enter this room, regardless of any person's opinion, is it clear?'

The young boy bowed and closed the door, and Crumwell waited until he heard footsteps trail along the hallway again. 'Thank you for coming, Mr. Smeaton, for I know you are most busy in preparations for tomorrow's feast.'

'I shall always play in your home, Secretary Crumwell, for I have done so many times, and always find it an honour to see close friends such as Nicòla and Ralph... all of you.'

'You come upon us in such a grave state, I must say, Mr. Smeaton.' Crumwell paused and looked at Nicòla, who fell into a dark expression. Crumwell never called him Mr. Smeaton, for he was Mark, a dear friend. 'Mark,' he added to keep things calm. 'We were discussing important legal matters.'

'Shall I leave? For I wish not to trouble you,' Mark replied, his wide smile still splashed across his face.

'I feel you can help us. You have eyes all over the court, Mark. I feel you could answer questions, questions which vex us all.'

Ralph and Richard shared a look; for they understood. Rich and Wriothesley knew all about interrogating a criminal or witness; they leaned forward, their folded hands on the tabletop, as if leaning closer to the coming ruin. Nicòla said nothing, moved none, perchance she hoped she was wrong. Innocent Smeaton looked around the table at each of the faces turned in his direction.

Crumwell noticed a sudden change in Smeaton's stance. Fear threatened his usual cheery mood. 'I am no legal mind, nor one of your most excellent spies, Secretary Crumwell.'

'I need neither from you, Mark. Tell me, you dress most excellently. You seem to make a large sum of money for a talented, yet lowborn, musician.'

'I feel praised by such an assertion,' Smeaton replied. 'For you, Secretary Crumwell, are of low birth and yet look as fine as any nobleman. All but Mr. Frescobaldi at this table are not of wealthy birth, and yet we sit in the rooms of kings.'

'Tis true, Mark, yet I am the King's Chief Minister, and you are a musician of the court.'

'You brought me hither to see my clothing? Have I broken a court rule in what I wear, how I live my life? I have tried to follow all the court rules,' Smeaton frowned and looked at Nicòla.

Crumwell had to act fast, so Nicòla did not rise to Smeaton's defence. 'Mark, I commend your finery, I do. It seems you have spent quite a sum in readiness for the festivities of May. I hear you have several servants in your employ now, to help you with your music, your clothing, your lodgings. Is this so?'

'Yes, Secretary.'

'Yet, as the Keeper of the Exchequer, I know that your court salary is but one hundred pounds a year.'

'I earn fees for my music from courtiers, including yourself, Secretary Crumwell. Mr. Frescobaldi rewards me handsomely when I am in need.'

Crumwell looked at Nicòla, who frowned in anger. 'Indeed,' she said to the group. 'I have furnished Mark with items a great number of times, as a friend.'

'May I ask why I am being questioned in such a manner?' Smeaton asked Nicòla, ignoring all the others around the table.

Crumwell rose from his seat and gathered the bag given to him on Smeaton's arrival. He pulled out a rope filled with knots, and a wooden cudgel tied to one end. At once Smeaton jumped to his feet, his chair tumbling onto the floor behind him. Nicòla too jumped up at the sight of the simple torture device, not out of fear but out of defence of her friend. Crumwell had no choice, the only man he could torture in this case was Smeaton; common, lowborn, without safety or allies. They could touch no nobleman, and Smeaton was the only man allowed Anne's presence who was not high born, other than Nicòla herself. Crumwell knew he could do this; for he had hurt, interrogated, killed even. But seeing Nicòla there, standing before Smeaton in defence of her gentle friend broke Crumwell's confidence. He knew Nicòla would respond poorly.

There Crumwell stood, taller than all the men in the room, now all on their feet against Smeaton, a slender man of delicate sensibilities, and Nicòla, who simply presented the form of a man, her heart and mind of a woman ready to stand up for one of the few at court who knew and trusted her for the creature she was.

Rich took the rope from Crumwell's hands. 'Allow me, Secretary,' he said, wrapping the rope around his hands. Smeaton bolted for the door like a frightened horse, but Ralph and Richard blocked his way. Wriothesley, the widest of all the learned men in the room, grabbed Smeaton by the shoulders and forced him to the ground, which allowed Rich to knell over him. Despite Smeaton's flailing, Rich got the rope around Smeaton's head, one knot placed over his right eye.

'Fermare tutto questo ora!' Nicòla screamed.

Crumwell thought not of her cries to stop as Smeaton's struggles and pitying wails began. Rich held the rope around his head while Wriothesley held the musician's kicking legs, Ralph and Richard each holding one of his arms.

'Turn the rope,' Crumwell instructed.

Rich pulled the rope and twisted it around the small cudgel. Instantly the knot dug into Smeaton's eye, causing terrified screams.

'Where did you get the money from, Smeaton?' Crumwell asked as he stood over the fighting group.

'I swear,' Smeaton screamed, 'I swear to you that I got it for services rendered!'

Nicòla grabbed Crumwell by the arm, but he set his resolve; his stiff stance was too much for Nicòla to move. 'I can check financial records,' Nicòla pleaded. 'I can see his accounts, I can decide where the money came from, Tom.'

Crumwell licked his lips and thought not of her request. 'Did the Queen give you money?' he asked.

'Yes,' Smeaton whimpered.

Crumwell gestured to Rich to lessen his grip, which allowed Smeaton to catch his breath.

'Why does the Queen give you money?'

'She gives favour to all in her apartments,' Smeaton whimpered. 'I saw her give £100 to Lady Worcester just last week, even though she is one of the King's mistresses!'

'Elizabeth Somerset,' Crumwell said, and Nicòla nodded. 'Henry Somerset's wife, and sister to William Fitzwilliam. Ralph, set forth a message at once; we shall need to seek with Fitzwilliam today. He must come hither with all urgency.'

Ralph got to his feet, and Smeaton had an arm free, which he used to move the rope from his eyes, but Rich held him tightly, and Richard held the frail arm by the wrist.

Crumwell waited until Ralph closed the door again and then crouched low to Smeaton. 'Tell me more, Smeaton.'

'Lady Worcester is with child and close to her time,' Nicòla said in a flurry of words. 'That will explain the payment.'

'Lady Elizabeth is wife to the Earl of Worcester. She needs no money,' Crumwell argued. 'Perchance Lady Elizabeth received the money as a bribe, to hide certain details about Her Majesty.'

'I know not what you mean,' Smeaton replied, as he moved his head, trying to work out where everyone was around him, like a blind mouse.

'There are rumours, Mr. Smeaton, that the Queen has lovers about her chambers. Are you one of them?' Crumwell asked. He had a surge of confidence all at once, having reached the point of the meeting.

'What? No! Never on my life!'

Crumwell nodded to Rich, who turned the rope again around Smeaton's eyes and his shrieking grew louder by the moment.

'Come hai potuto fare questo? Mark è nostro amico!' Nicòla cried over Smeaton's screams of pain.

The knots dotted around Mark's head dug in all the way around, including right into his eye. Crumwell grabbed Nicòla by the shoulders and shoved her across the room away from the scene. 'I know he is our friend. I know we welcomed him into our home. How did you think this would end, Nicò? We are bringing down a queen.'

'Torture? Are we to be this base? Mark was not even on the list of suspects I created! Now, without even a request or hint, you have Rich trying to kill the man over nothing!'

Crumwell let Nicòla go and returned to the scene. Sweat ran along his hairline, fearing the wrath of Nicòla more than the guilt over hurting poor Smeaton. 'Are you the Queen's lover?' Crumwell yelled to the screaming man at his feet.

'No, I swear before God!' Smeaton wailed.

'Do not slander God in my home, Smeaton,' Crumwell sighed as he bent down to the screaming musician once more. 'You have received monies from the Queen as you are her lover. Perchance Lady Worcester knows and was paid to be quiet.'

'The Queen never paid me for anything but music.'

'Again.'

Rich pulled the rope tighter and the screaming only increased. Crumwell glanced at Nicòla, but she was missing. The screaming was so loud that Nicòla had exited the room with no one noticing. It would be for the best; her female disposition could not cope.

'You shall lose that eye should you not give me the answer I need,' Crumwell sighed to Smeaton.

'Sir Secretary, no more, I will tell you the truth!'

Rich let go of the cudgel and the rope loosened around Smeaton's head. One of Smeaton's eyes was so squeezed and swollen he may never see again. Nicòla would be furious. 'Do you use our queen like a whore, Smeaton? Does she pay you for services rendered in her bed?'

'Let me disclose all,' Smeaton moaned.

'Who else is in bed with the Queen? How vile have you been, Smeaton? What sins have you committed against God and our king?'

'I love Her Majesty,' Smeaton replied as blood dripped from his eye.

'So, you admit it?' Crumwell asked.

'No, I admire Her Majesty.' Smeaton paused as he coughed, the screaming, the struggle for air, the pain all taking their toll. 'I would never touch Queen Anne!'

'Rich, please put the rope back on,' Crumwell said and stood up again. Smeaton let out a horrific scream as he fought to stop Rich getting the rope around his head again. The noise had become so extreme the children would hear the events.

'Stop,' Crumwell commanded. 'We need to move him into a cell in the Tower where he can be interrogated properly.'

'Please,' Smeaton gasped through his own blood, 'please, no more, sir. I will tell you everything.'

'Most excellent. But we shall still move Smeaton to the Tower as I wish not to have this mess in my home where my children live. I need details before the King by midnight.'

Wriothesley stood up from holding Smeaton's legs and rubbed his forehead against his sleeve. 'Smeaton committed the adultery, did he not?'

'Let us hope so, or we shall all go to hell,' Rich added.

'I shall attend the Tower with Smeaton.' Crumwell looked at the crying wretch lying on the carpets, clutching at his bloodied face. The plan to attaint people and have them imprisoned had already gone wrong.

Chapter 41 – May 1536
Greenwich Palace, downstream London

Thyngs fall apart easilie if they are hyld togythyr wyth lyes

Nicòla tapped her gloved fingers against the back of her other hand. She stood, fixed upon the spot, both hands resting on her right hip, as her father taught her when first becoming a man. Her silver doublet and hose glistened in the late spring sunshine, but her heart felt frozen. Crumwell was gone, at the Tower, where poor precious Mark was tortured for a confession. Mark would be the first to confess to a crime never committed. Crumwell mentioned no use of torture, never any use of Mark, whose desires never seemed to grace men or women. But he got close to Queen Anne and was low born, and no one would come to his defence. Even Nicòla had to admit she did not fight for him, rather stood in the background as Mark got loaded into a carriage and taken to London like a beast caught in the King's forest. Crumwell had a plan, and nothing could stop him now.

'Mr. Frescobaldi.'

Nicòla turned to the unfamiliar voice to find William Fitzwilliam, one of the King's most popular courtiers, and Treasurer of the Royal Household.

'Sir William,' Nicòla replied and bowed a little in deference. Fitzwilliam had once worked under Wolsey with Crumwell, before betraying the old cardinal at the first opportunity. Nicòla knew Fitzwilliam was not to be trusted, so Crumwell seldom worked alongside him until now.

'I read the letter you gave me from Secretary Crumwell, instructing me to aid you in bringing ladies of the Queen's court to London.'

Nicòla nodded and looked out at the noisy scene before her. The first day of the May Day tournaments, and hither in the grand arena set up in the grounds of the palace, Henry sat with Anne on the royal viewing platform, the pair resting on their high-backed thrones, surrounded by their closest friends, all the nobles dressed in their finery. Crumwell begged Henry not to joust this time, not after January's accident, and the King had relented to the request. Jane Seymour sat below Anne, only a few seats along from the Queen, no doubt to be close to the King.

'You spy on Mistress Seymour,' Fitzwilliam replied as he towered above Nicòla. 'I heard she gave the King a favour for today, even if he does not plan to joust.'

'I fear for Mistress Seymour,' Nicòla sighed. 'But I also fear for the King.'

'Why so?'

'Women can appear demure but be deadly.'

'You speak as a man recently out of courtly love,' Fitzwilliam jested. 'I wondered if you ever dallied with women.'

'I have had my share of dalliances, Sir William, and I am certain you know what trouble that brings.'

Fitzwilliam slapped Nicòla on the shoulder, a gesture of manly friendship. 'Good for you, Frescobaldi. What are women for if not to be played with and enjoyed?'

Nicòla held her tongue for a moment. 'Your sister, Lady Worcester, needs to be removed to London as soon as the King leaves Greenwich.'

'I am ready on Crumwell's orders, but why my sister? Is she to be the King's whore again? What of Lady Jane?'

'We need your sister for services other than those on her back, Sir William. You know which other ladies you must escort?'

'Lady Cobham, Lady Shelton, Lady Horsman and Lady Rochford. Why would old Crumwell need so many women? He is the man who arrests other men for vice yet does not commit sins.'

'You have not been invited to gambling in the Crumwell Chambers then,' Nicòla scoffed.

The sound of the trumpets heralding the next joust quietened the conversation. With a polite nod, Fitzwilliam left Nicòla where she stood far back from the joust, to join other courtiers partaking in the entertainment. Queen Anne sat in her seat beside the King, no idea that precious Mark had been arrested and taken away. Crumwell himself had travelled to the Tower to see to the prisoner. Nicòla had no wish to speak to Crumwell, perchance never trust him again after seeing how all the men in the room turned on an innocent man. Yet if Nicòla lost Crumwell's favour, those same men who turned against Mark would turn on the creature that was Nicòla.

Henry, for his part, having seen a message written by Crumwell the night before, hinting at Anne's adultery, seemed to enjoy himself, his wife by his side. Richard went to the King before he retired to bed, giving him a note suspecting Mark of receiving monies from Anne as a secret lover. Henry seemed content to lie, to pretend all was fine, to prepare for further evidence of such a heinous crime. How people could lie; yet Nicòla was no innocent when it came to lies. She once suffocated a cardinal and pretended he died of sickness, so her soul would be beside the English court in hell.

Joust after joust continued, with men from different teams sparring against each other, but Nicòla cared not, she could not even stand still. People came and went, beautifully designed flags waved, women threw favours, men cheered between bouts, but Nicòla only woke herself from her thoughts when she spotted Crumwell, in the far distance across the arena. He stood with several of his personal guards, all in riding clothes, standing to attention. In a sea of bright clothing and levity, Crumwell stood in his usual black, like death come to a party.

From his spot across the jousting, he beckoned Nicòla, easy to spot wearing silver shining in the sun. As she moved through the crowds behind the seating areas, Nicòla's heart pounded. Two things could happen – the plan could work, and the world would change forever. Ruin could strike and leave them trying to explain why a musician disappeared. No one seemed to notice Mark was not at the joust, despite spending on the event.

Nicòla stopped; between rows of seating, she watched Crumwell climb the few stairs of the royal viewing platform. Few could do so, and it was the first time he had seen the King since their fight. But time had passed since the argument over the Imperial alliance, and the King leaned as Crumwell bent to whisper in Henry's ear. The King's blue eyes continued to watch the joust while Crumwell spoke, the King's expression not changing. Anne appeared not to notice Crumwell's presence at all.

Nicòla continued fighting between the crowds, past the tents and servants rushing to attend their masters when the crowd fell silent and rose to their feet. The King was on the move. Nicòla pushed all the way to the royal platform where Henry appeared, Crumwell right behind him. Nicòla fell into a deep bow as Henry rushed past and Crumwell pulled her upright by the shoulder.

'We are leaving for the Tower. Have you discussed all with Fitzwilliam?'

'Yes, a barge will wait for him and his charges as soon as he can get them to the river,' she replied. Fitzwilliam was probably in a bluster at this moment, no doubt realising something serious was occurring.

'I shall travel with the King. Take my barge back to London. Guards shall escort you.'

'Why would I need guards to escort me?' Nicòla frowned. 'I shall take Fitzwilliam and the ladies-in-waiting with me.'

'Protection, Nicò,' Crumwell said as he rested his hand on her shoulder, a strange display of affection for a public setting.

'Crumwell!' Henry barked, and they turned to see him nearby, a gentleman putting on the King's gloves. 'We ride for London. Who rides with us, Thomas?'

Crumwell stood tall, and all looked at him with surprise, for why would the King be taking instructions from any person? 'Edward Seymour, Sir Henry Norris, the Duke of Suffolk, Sir Thomas Heneage, the Duke of Norfolk and Sir Nicholas Carew…'

Through the growing group of servants waiting to attend on the King, Thomas Boleyn appeared. He pushed past Nicòla, shoving her hard as he passed. 'What be all this?' he demanded. 'Your Majesty, are you to joust? As the Lord Privy Seal…'

'I shall hear none,' Henry interrupted.

'We do not need you, my Lord Wiltshire,' Crumwell added. 'The King is to leave at once.'

'What? Your Majesty, Queen Anne is waiting to see George joust, he is up next, and…'

Without a word, Henry turned, and his men trailed behind, several scrambling away to find the men Crumwell listed. From now on, Henry had to be surrounded by men who would back Crumwell's plan to topple Anne. Any person loyal to Anne could plead her case once the story of adultery spread. Hours from now, everyone would know the happenings inside the Tower.

'You have the horses ready?' Crumwell asked.

'Yes, stabled with the King's horse,' Nicòla replied. 'I did so this morning.'

'Good. Get Fitzwilliam and the ladies on the barge and straight to the Tower. Make sure the ladies speak to no one before they leave.'

Crumwell turned away and headed after the King and Nicòla stood still for a moment. He would not look Nicòla in the eye while they spoke, which never occurred. But there was no time to wonder why Crumwell had been so cold; it was time to bring down a queen.

~~~

Darkness blanketed the Tower when the barge arrived in London, the warmth of the spring day gone from the air as they floated through Traitor's Gate. None of the ladies accompanied by Fitzwilliam spoke a word on the five-mile barge ride, and Nicòla blamed them not. They knew not why they were in London, pulled away from their mistress, unwilling witnesses to crimes not committed. How she and Crumwell were to interrogate ladies for crimes not committed, Nicòla knew not. Somewhere in the Tower, Mark would be imprisoned, and only God knew what had happened, what Mark had said. The King appeared to know what was said when he left the joust in such hurry, so Henry and Crumwell now knew far more than Nicòla. She and Crumwell had only spent one night apart and already Nicòla felt like she was losing him in this mess of their own making.

Had this plan to discredit Anne not been her idea? Had Crumwell not been languishing in his bed while Jane Seymour influenced the King into leaving his wife? Now Crumwell had taken Nicòla's plan to accuse people of adulterous crimes and turned it into torture. Things progressed at a speed Nicòla had not foreseen.

Nicòla found Sir William Kingston, Constable of the Tower, waiting for the barge to arrive, standing stiff as usual as they tied their boat for the ladies to disembark. Lady Rochford looked ready for tears at the thought of getting back on land.

'Mr. Nicòla Frescobaldi,' Kingston said as he leant a helping hand for her stepping onto the cold stone. 'It has been some time.'

'Leicester, November 1530,' Nicòla replied, her voice cold. The same man who had been escorting Wolsey to the Tower for what would have been his execution, had Nicòla not suffocated the old man in his bed. 'I trust Secretary Crumwella has informed you of what needs to happen.'

'Quite. We have guards to help Sir William take the ladies to their rooms where they shall reside. I am charged with taking you to a room where Secretary Crumwell awaits your arrival.'

Nicòla left Fitzwilliam with his sister Lady Worcester and the others and began her ascent through hallways and staircases of the poorly lit Tower. Where was Crumwell? Were they still in the tower where the prisoners were kept? Was he preparing for the ladies' interrogations already? It would be wise to interview them at once. By the time they reached a small wooden door, Nicòla had quite forgotten her way through the Tower. Kingston opened the heavy door, to the sight of Crumwell in a large cell, candles lit about the room, the last of the fading sun coming in a small window which overlooked the river. The cell had a large bed, fresh linens adorning it, wine and food laid out on a table which had several chairs about it. Not a dirty cell like the one Nicòla sat in years before, this was ready for a noble prisoner.

'Thanks be to you, Sir William,' Crumwell said as Kingston closed the door, but not before giving Crumwell the key. They stood in silence for a moment to let Kingston's ever-listening ears leave the hallway.

Nicòla stood stiff, recalling Crumwell's ease of instructing the hurt on Mark the day prior. 'I have removed the ladies-in-waiting to the Tower as you instructed,' Nicòla said, her eyes at her feet, her shoes damp from the barge ride.

Crumwell brought his hand to Nicòla's chin and tilted her face up to his. He smiled a little as he watched her cold expression. 'I am aware of your anger, Nicò,' he whispered. 'I only wished to frighten Smeaton yesterday.'

'If I wished to torture friends, I would sooner tarry in Florence with my husband.'

'I wish you could call me husband.'

Nicòla just shook her head, unwilling to have that discussion yet again. 'What of the King?'

'Smeaton confessed to sleeping with the Queen. He also told us of others who had committed such crimes.'

'But we know it not to be true.'

'Smeaton confessed, to not be harmed any further. I have ordered him removed to a cell where he might recover. I said they cannot put him to the rack.'

'How much pain have you already inflicted on Mark? You stood there, watching him in agony, confessing to crimes which never happened!'

'Smeaton said what we needed. I need a confession to convince the King, and threats provided the confession. I shall not have Smeaton harmed again, Nicò, I promise you. But Smeaton said just what we needed, that he had been with the Queen several times, and that Norris and Weston both did so. I wrote Smeaton's confession and he signed it.'

'Does Mark know what he signed?'

Crumwell let out a heavy sigh but said nothing of poor innocent Mark. 'On the ride to London, Henry asked Norris if he had slept with the Queen. Naturally, Norris denied everything.'

'Surely Norris thought it a jest.'

'The allegation confused Norris. Henry said he would spare Norris' life if he confessed and named others who had been in the Queen's bed.'

'Spare his life? None are to die for this lurid plot!'

'Calm, Nicò, calm. We shall get their lives spared. But Norris shall not confess without fear.'

'Norris shall never confess, not without torture.'

'Smeaton has confessed, and the King is ready to believe any news I report. He has quite forgotten our fight weeks ago. I can now arrest any man I wish as we investigate Smeaton's words. Anne's ladies will offer much detail, so I can craft more allegations.'

Nicòla narrowed her eyes. Crumwell seldom spoke in such a way. I can, I wish. 'You speak as if I am not part of the plan I devised to discredit Anne.'

'Much is progressing, Nicò and the situation changes by the moment. Norris has been imprisoned, and the King has settled in his private rooms hither for tonight. With God's fortune, we shall be able to make further arrests in the morning.'

'The lies told cannot be too lurid, for otherwise, the King might not be merciful, or easy to convince to have Anne imprisoned while we annul the marriage.'

'I am having Mistress Seymour brought hither by her brother as we speak. Henry shall agree to annul his marriage if I discredit Anne. Anne bore no son, and she is ready to topple me. I must see this plan to its end.'

I am, I will, I must. 'Tis commonplace to worry.'

'Anne's chamberlain, Edward Baynton, has been so helpful. He came to the Tower and was helpful with questioning Smeaton and will now also help with the ladies he knows so well,' Crumwell explained.

'I too know the ladies of the Queen's chamber. I have been a man close to the Queen for some time.'

Crumwell pulled Nicòla into his arms and held her tight against him. Perchance he felt more grief for his actions than Nicòla could see. 'I love you with all my heart, Nicò. I wish this could be different. I must ask you a dear favour.'

'I shall not torture a friend.'

Crumwell took Nicòla's face in his hands and kissed her lips. 'I need your rings.'

Nicòla looked to her hands as Crumwell took them in his own. 'You want my rings?' she looked back up to him while his tender expression turned to woe. 'One is the turquoise, the symbol of us, the other the ruby of my father. These never leave my hands.' The last time Nicòla went anywhere without her rings were in the early days of living in England when the guards of the Tower took her ruby after her first arrest. A shiver ran through her body, like a sharp knife of ice hitting her chest. 'No.'

'I am sorry, Nicò…'

'You are not sorry!' she cried and pulled her hands from his. 'You are not sorry for any of this! We wanted to discredit people's reputations and after one day look at what you have become!'

'This is for the best.'

'Best?' Nicòla cried as she clasped her hands over her rings. 'Is this to be my cell or shall you throw me in a cell below ground? Tossed back to the tiny cell of my first imprisonment? Shall you torture me like you did to Mark?'

'This shall be your cell, Nicò.'

'You may not call me Nicò any longer!' Nicòla cried as she pulled at her turquoise. She threw the heart-shaped ring at him, which fell to the stone floor.

'Nicòla, I beg you, listen…'

Nicòla forced her precious ruby from her hand but refused to throw such a priceless trinket. She thrust it against Crumwell's chest, hard enough to knock him off his footing. He fought none of her anger.

'When Anne discovers our plot, she will attack me. She, and her family know you are… of a…' Crumwell stumbled.

'That I am a creature.'

'Whatever you present yourself as, whatever we accept you as, Nicòla, you are a woman. If others discover you, who knows your fate? If you get locked hither, under suspicion of adultery with the Queen, then no one will believe Anne accusing you of being a woman.'

While Crumwell's idea had merit, he had planned Nicòla's imprisonment behind her back. 'You seek to lock me away like you do your queen? Will it be you and Henry with new women in your beds?'

'I lied to the King for you!' Crumwell screamed at her. He turned and swiped the turquoise from the floor. 'I call you wife! I swore to God you were my wife, Nicòletta! Yet you are the wife to a duke, thousands of miles away who cares not for you! He seeks to belittle you with annulment, and I wanted the easiest solution for you, and tried to create an Imperial alliance! I want to call you wife! I wish to have a wife at court like all the ministers I rule! And yet I am the King's henchman still, still after all these years, sneaking and lying and being disrespected at every turn! No more shall this be! I make laws, I destroy queens. If Henry wants Jane, he shall have her, and I shall create her! I order you, as my servant, as my wife, to be locked in this cell until such time I see it safe to release you!'

Nicòla took a few steps back and bumped against the edge of the bed. She fell back to sitting, relieved by the bed's comfort. 'Perchance I deceived us both, Master. For I thought myself safe. For I thought myself valuable. But I have done little but scurry about like a rat, doing your bidding, and being a weight about your neck. If Nicòla Frescobaldi is to live through this interrogation, perchance it is time he returned to Florence to be with his sister. The young Jane, Giovanna, can go back to her home.'

'Jane is my daughter.'

'Jane is also my daughter.' Crumwell could say anything, do anything, but he could not take Jane from her. 'The truth of Jane's parentage would shame you if all knew you kept a creature who bore your children, who gave you a bastard daughter and two dead sons...'

'Enough,' Crumwell snapped. 'If I am to arrest the Queen tomorrow, I must away. These words of anger must stop.'

Without another glance from his golden eyes, the King's Chief Minister left Nicòla's room, locking the enormous wooden door. Nicòla could not even hear footsteps in the hallway. The candles about the room flickered from the sudden movements, the only light left in Nicòla's life.

Chapter 42 – May 1536
The Tower, London

A half-trouth is the weakest of all lyes

George.
But George is her brother.
With her brother.
With George.
George.
When Crumwell said his morning prayers, not one moment of rest had come to his weary body. He prayed for rest; he prayed for Nicòla; he prayed for God not to send him to hell for the lies he told. Crumwell prayed for Mark Smeaton's broken body in his cell, he prayed that his children never learned the truth about his life. He prayed that everyone aware of this conspiracy remained faithful, so Henry did not part Crumwell's head from his shoulders.
George.
She calls him Georgie.
Lies on the bed with him.
Always touching, embracing.
They disappear for hours.
Crumwell sat on the small boat which edged its way to the Tower gate, the oars skimming the water under in the spring sun, words turned in his mind. Next to him sat Lord Chancellor Thomas Audley, who looked as confused as an orphan. The Duke of Norfolk, a man with no time for Crumwell, sat close by, looking out over the water at the city where the river turned towards Whitehall Palace, not that they would reach that far. Archbishop Cranmer sat beside Crumwell, in total silence.
Countess Worcester was the most helpful of the ladies; someone asked her for rumours, and she had gossip ready. No doubt her brother

Fitzwilliam had aided her. Elizabeth Somerset had spent a winter as the King's whore, and when admonished, commented that she was no worse than the Queen. Perchance Lady Elizabeth meant that Anne spent so long as a mistress before being a queen. Perchance she meant that the Queen was a whore. Crumwell could use that as evidence, and let the Countess go, as she was with child. But first Lady Elizabeth stated that George Boleyn slept in his sister's bed. What they did would never be known, and it frightened Crumwell to think of the Queen engaging in incest with her brother.

Lady Rochford was equally useful. She was a mild, weak woman, who would tell Crumwell whatever he wanted. She would not condemn her husband George, yet she would not defend him. Lady Rochford spoke of how Anne would laugh that the King's virility was poor, no doubt to scare Mistress Seymour away. To speak of such things was treason, and Jane Boleyn was easy to fool into saying anything. Poor Margery Horsman seemed happy to denounce all Boleyns. She told stories of how Sir Francis Weston spoke of his love of the Queen, and how Henry Norris fawned over Her Majesty daily. They did not need dates, details and places, for Crumwell could create those for court papers. The ladies' words were all he needed for arrests. Baroness Anne Cobham, known as Nan, was the Queen's closest friend. The pair were always together, and Crumwell expected Nan would be difficult to interrogate. As expected, it was Nan who refused to give up on her queen, yet gave answers which played into Crumwell's plans. She named both Norris and Weston as in Anne's constant presence, and she spoke of how Anne would tease Mark Smeaton when he came to play in her rooms. Nan confirmed Anne's discussions of Henry's impotent nights, and Anne's angry words about Henry on a regular occurrence. Nan confirmed the angry fight between Anne and Norris, discussing dead men's shoes. The ladies were so easy to intimidate. Nicòla would never have stumbled under that pressure, she would have shown her experience, her education, while these were scared women.

Norris, meanwhile, said nothing and spent the night in a basic cell. Nicòla remained in her cell, and perchance could look down upon the river at this moment. And what a moment. As they drifted along in the boat, under the Court Gate into the Tower, Cranmer turned in his seat and looked Crumwell right in the eye. They had shocked Cranmer when men arrived at Lambeth Palace on Crumwell's orders. All for their other guest on the boat. Queen Anne sat in the centre of the boat, flanked by the men charged with her care. They loaded the Queen onto the boat at Greenwich where palace guards, under Crumwell's orders, arrested the Queen in the King's name. The most powerful men at court sat in the boat with Anne as they took her to the Tower, where she would spend a long time if Crumwell had his way.

'Your Majesty,' Cranmer said as the boat floated its final stretch where Sir William Kingston and Sir Edmund Willingham, the Lieutenant of the Tower, awaited.

'Waste none of your time,' Anne interrupted her archbishop. 'I have not wronged my king. His Majesty has tired of me, as he once did with Katherine.'

'Please, Your Majesty,' Cranmer protested, 'we have discovered your vile acts!'

'The King has fallen in love with Jane Seymour. It has fallen upon Crumwell to get rid of me.' Anne paused and turned to her uncle Norfolk. 'You came to me during a tennis game, with Sir William Paulet, and accused me of adultery with Norris and Smeaton! You believe this shall rid the King of his lawful wife?'

The boat came to a stop, and they helped the Queen from the boat. Only Crumwell disembarked as the others were to return for interrogation another time. As Kingston and Willingham lead the Queen away, Crumwell took a glimpse of Cranmer in the boat; Anne had damaged their friendly relationship. The Archbishop had a grave face but nodded just once in farewell as Crumwell followed Anne, a nod which gave Crumwell hope of saving their friendship.

'Mr. Kingston,' Anne said, and the Constable turned to face her, 'shall I go to the dungeon?'

'No, madam,' Kingston said with a gentle shake of his head. 'You shall have the Queen's rooms hither in the Tower, where you stayed during your coronation.'

'It is too good for me,' Anne wept, 'Jesu, have mercy on me.' Anne fell to her knees as she cried and both Kingston and Willingham jumped to help. But Anne just laughed, as she so often did when in anger. Crumwell had seen her do it many times. 'Mr. Kingston,' Anne said again as tears streamed about her cheeks, 'I need the sacrament in the closet of my chamber, so I might pray for mercy. I am the King's true wife and free of the company of sin and men. Tell me, for I am to be accused of sin with three men, but I know of only two charges. Smeaton accuses me? Norris accuses me? My mother shall die of sorrow. My dear friend, Lady Worcester, she shall worry about me, and she has a child in her belly. My father, have you seen him? Surely he looks for me? What of my brother? Is the King hither, does he look for me? Am I to receive justice, Mr. Kingston? Even the poorest man deserves justice.'

'Your Majesty,' Kingston began, and paused for Anne's laughter again, and Crumwell knew this time it was fear, not anger, that caused Anne's laugh.

'Take me to the Queen's Chambers,' Anne said as she stopped her laugh. 'Mr. Kingston, Mr. Willingham, I allow you to show me to my rooms. Crumwell, leave me; I cannot answer your questions.'

Crumwell bowed. 'Your Majesty,' he said as he stood. 'I shall leave you for now. But I can answer so many of your questions. The King resides with Mistress Seymour at present. Your father remains at Greenwich Palace. Your brother shall be hither soon, for he is the third man with whom you are accused.'

Crumwell turned away as Anne screamed at him, a vile, unholy scream of a wronged woman. Crumwell left the doorway where Kingston and Willingham looked to steer the Queen, and he hurried away toward Nicòla's room. The way Anne screamed told Crumwell he had done the right thing by Nicòla with her "arrest," as Anne would hurt Nicòla to harm Crumwell's reputation. Already Smeaton, Norris, Frescobaldi and soon George Boleyn himself would be locked in the Tower.

But as Crumwell headed along the hallways towards his Nicòla, his confidence faltered. He had arrested a queen for the most hated act against God and law, conspiring against an anointed king. Yet to face Nicòla the day after arresting her for adultery with the Queen was too much to bear, but Crumwell risked losing all to keep Nicòla safe. Crumwell turned the corner and neared Nicòla's rooms. All sat silent, as the surrounding rooms stood empty, awaiting other men accused and arrested. He wondered what Nicòla was doing; reading, praying, watching the river? Did she see Crumwell bring the Queen to the Tower? Would she see George Boleyn arrive, who would be arrested by Richard and brought with palace guards? What did Nicòla think of the plan so far? Crumwell could not ask, for he doubted Nicòla would see him. Palace rumour would now know Anne got arrested for incest, and for adultery with Smeaton, Norris and Frescobaldi. While Anne laughed and cried at her situation, Crumwell felt a deep shame that would never abate.

Instead of seeing Nicòla, Crumwell turned away from her room and headed again for the barge to take him to Whitehall to continue his work. The King needed to stay away from everyone, locked away where no one could petition on Anne's behalf. The only company for His Majesty could be Jane Seymour and her family. The Seymours wanted a queen and Jane would happily play her part in this vile masque.

Two days passed before Crumwell set foot in the Tower again. Two more days he did not see Nicòla, did not hear her sweet accent, nor hear her educated opinion. Ralph took care of everything while Crumwell focused on the adultery and incest case. Seeing Sir William Brereton arrested and sent to the Tower warmed his heart, for it had been years since Brereton had his old friend John ap Griffith Eyton murdered in Wales.

Brereton had long gotten in Crumwell's way, refusing the dissolution of the monasteries. Brereton's uncle was a better man, a reformer who could take over and allow Crumwell to better control North Wales and Cheshire with ease. Yes, everyone at court seemed stunned by the arrest of Brereton, but he was guilty, perchance not of adultery, but it was a great opportunity for Crumwell to rid himself of the stubborn old man.

Sir Francis Weston was also taken that day, an arrest which brought no surprise. Anne's ladies had pointed to him, and he was long known to be a companion of Queen Anne, constantly praising her beauty. Crumwell took Brereton and Weston both to the Tower and waited. Richard had gone to Sir Thomas Wyatt's home to arrest him on adultery charges. Nicòla would again be livid, for she, Wyatt and Smeaton had long been close.

Crumwell stood with Kingston as the boat with Richard and Wyatt arrived. Wyatt even dared to smile when he saw Crumwell waiting for him.

'Could all this be so?' Wyatt asked in his gentle voice as Crumwell helped him from the boat.

'I am afraid I must question all in this grave matter,' Crumwell said as he bid his friend hello.

'They have arrested even Nicòla for adultery? Your own secretary?' Wyatt frowned.

'All those close to Anne, those who spent time in her chambers. You are childhood friends with Anne, and I am sorry for this, Sir Thomas, I am.'

'I had the Duke of Suffolk come to visit me, to say someone would arrest me for adultery with England's queen. The man has an evil will towards me.'

'I am sorry for it, Sir Thomas, but I cannot change laws now,' Crumwell replied as they walked inside to Wyatt's cell, right next to Nicòla's. 'You know well the love I bear you, I would cut out my heart if you were guilty of the crimes thrown against your name.'

'I would never wrong the King, not even in thought!' Wyatt said as they began climbing stairs, Kingston before his prisoner, Crumwell and Richard close behind him. 'I cannot deny my boyhood love for Anne, but it was love pushed aside when His Majesty took Anne's heart. I feel as though the safe land I could count upon has been ripped away, and I am left in an ocean of lies.'

'I shall personally see to your interrogation,' Crumwell replied. 'Fear not. And I shall write to your father with all haste to comfort him that you are cared for hither. You shall receive no dungeon cell, but instead a fine room with all care. I promise no harm shall come to you.'

'I hear they tortured Smeaton,' Wyatt replied as they squeezed around a narrow hallway.

'A fate you shall never have to consider as a nobleman.'

'And Frescobaldi, our sweet Waif? What shall become of him as a common born… man.'

Kingston showed them into the room and Crumwell paused; would Nicòla hear their voices through the wall? Most likely not in this part of the Tower, fortified with thick walls. 'No, there has been no need to torture Frescobaldi, for he has answered all our questioning.' Nicòla was not asked a single question; no one visited the Chief Minister's secretary.

'I dare say all is most confusing,' Richard commented as the three sat down in chairs about a short table and Kingston left them to talk.

'It surprised me not when Suffolk came to me to say I was accused of adultery with Anne,' Wyatt sighed. 'For I have written many a love poem about Queen Anne. I have always loved Anne. But I have never touched her, nor ever wished to do so. We know Anne for her virtue, her honour, her privacy and her honesty. Henry craved all those things, that is why he has loved her for the last ten years. Henry defied Katherine for Anne. You, Crumwell, have turned England upside down due to Henry's love for Anne. Can that be undone so fast?'

'Jane Seymour sits on Henry's lap now, with her youth, her flowing blonde hair, dim conversation and ripe womb. Pure love can turn to pure hate.' Crumwell paused and thought of Nicòla once more.

'Little Jane Seymour?' Wyatt scoffed.

'Little Jane Seymour is ready to be a queen, so doubt her not,' Crumwell replied as he leaned back in his seat. 'Soon we shall bow to little Jane Seymour if she has her way. We may know her as meek and mild, and while she may not read or write, she can conspire.'

'Are others being arrested?' Wyatt asked.

'I still have Sir Francis Bryan, Father William Latimer and Sir Richard Page to arrest,' Richard replied.

'What do you intend with this plan, Crumwell? What you accuse the Queen and men of is punishable by death.'

'Fear not death, Thomas, for that shall not be a result for any,' Crumwell tried to calm his newly arrested friend. 'I shall have you released in due time.'

'Is Queen Anne well, is she well attended?'

'Anne is in the Queen's rooms, not locked in the cell like a common thief. Ladies attend her, for Kingston's own wife is there, and two of Anne's aunts, Lady Anne Shelton and Lady Elizabeth Boleyn. Lady Stoner, mother of the maids is there, and Sir William Clifton's wife Margaret. All fine older women to soothe and consul the Queen.'

'And report to you?' Wyatt offered.

'Naturally, for no one is above scrutiny in matters of adultery, not even the Queen.' Crumwell paused for a moment and felt his confidence grow. 'I shall leave you and perchance you can answer questions Richard has, so we can quicken your release. I must away.'

'Thank you, Secretary Crumwell,' Wyatt said as he stood up again next to Richard, who accepted his uncle's embrace.

'Be well, Sir Thomas, for you will be safe in our care.' Crumwell turned on his heel and gestured to a guard to open the door. He waited in the dark of the hallway as the guard locked Wyatt and Richard in together. 'Please allow me to see Master Frescobaldi in the next room,' he instructed.

Nicòla jumped from a seat by the window when the door unlocked. Her fear turned to anger when she saw Crumwell enter the room. Neither spoke until the guard again closed the door.

'Have you come to tell me of my daughter?' Nicòla challenged.

Crumwell felt taken aback by the coldness in her voice. 'Jane is fine, safe at Austin Friars, as always with her nurse and tutors.'

'She is not tortured by the screams at Stepney?'

Crumwell sighed. 'I am sorry for what happened at Stepney. Would I want torture in my home? No, I am not Thomas More. I do not wish such behaviour close to Gregory and Jane. Nicò, please.'

Nicòla unfolded her arms, her shoulders loosening, and her eyes softened towards him. Nicòla knew him better than that. 'When will I be interrogated?'

'I have no plans to send any interrogators.'

'Who else is arrested? I saw Anne arrive several days past. George Boleyn?'

'I have not spoken to Boleyn, for we are to wait before questioning. All of Anne's ladies rounded upon Boleyn in a moment, so we have all the evidence we need. Wyatt is in the next room, is safe and will not be questioned, as planned.'

'Smeaton was not to be imprisoned or questioned either,' Nicòla shot back.

'Brereton put up a fight when arrested and is in a small cell at present. Weston came quietly and has denied all, begging to return home to his new son, Henry. Latimer, Bryan and Page will be here in a few days' time, all planned by us. I am following the plan.'

'I feel abandoned in here.'

'I feared so. All the court is gossiping. Anne has muttered that you are a woman, and the new ladies I appointed to wait on her laugh.'

'Will my name be blackened by the scandal?'

'Henry knows you are innocent, but I told him you are being questioned because we believe in total honesty and have to arrest and interrogate every name mentioned. Having you here makes Henry convinced I am doing the right thing and being honest. You are safe hither, and Henry is at Whitehall in private rooms with the Seymours. I have contacted Henry Percy, who is now the Duke of Northumberland. He is in very ill health but shall travel to London to say he was pre-contracted to Anne back in 1523. Everyone knows Anne loved Percy. He shall travel to London and if his health permits, I shall get him to sit in the council of jurors who shall try Anne for adultery. Their pre-contract shall render her marriage to the King illegitimate.'

'Is that what Henry wants?'

'Henry very much wants away from a woman like Anne now she is tainted by scandal.'

'A scandal we invented,' Nicòla replied. 'Was it not you, so many years ago, who told Percy to shut his mouth about any pre-contract with Anne, so she could marry the King? Now you ask him to say the pre-contract was real?'

''Tis the way this has worked,' Crumwell shrugged. 'But fear nothing, as the plan is working out well.'

'Not for Mark.'

'If not Mark, it could have been you tortured, Nicò, so I am not sorry.'

'Is this to be our lives, forever doing evil deeds to serve a king?'

'Is there any other kind of life for people like us? We can only pray to God for forgiveness. What I want is your forgiveness.'

'It was me who came up with this adultery plan to slander the Queen,' Nicòla said. 'While you stayed in bed filled with woe, and Jane Seymour casually threatened me in my garden, I came up with this plan to attaint Anne. But I wanted no one hurt.'

'I shall try to make sure that no one gets hurt from now on,' Crumwell said. 'You must admit that having you arrested was a goodly plan. I am sorry to surprise you with it, but if you appeared not shocked, not angry, then suspicion would creep into the plan.'

'I shall admit to the good ideas in your plan, Tomassito.'

Tomassito. Perchance Nicòla's mood had cooled. 'Cranmer is attending Anne, so she might pray. I can arrange Cranmer to pray with you as well.'

'Have you spoken with Cranmer?'

'Barely; he believes in Anne's innocence, but was swayed by the evidence I continued to create.'

'Cranmer is a good man and seeks only peace. Yes, I should like to pray with him, for we are all bound by God, our families and our service to our king.'

'I will save us, Nicò, I swear before God. I swear I shall do everything to see this plan have a smooth result.'

Nicòla walked to Crumwell and slipped her arms around him, her arms wrapped inside his warm black overgown. The relief made Crumwell fold himself over her small frame, so they could both have a moment of respite in the hell of their own making.

Chapter 43 – May 1536
The Tower, London

When you lye to the world, the world will lye back

Without a clock in the cell, Nicòla had no idea of the time, though the bell over Westminster Hall helped. But nothing had rung today, a day she perceived to be May 12, if she remembered rightly. Was this day twelve of being locked in the Tower? Crumwell had not come in a week, no doubt distancing himself from his secretary, accused of being in carnal lust with the Queen. No one else came either. Cranmer never came to pray with her. Neither Norfolk nor Fitzwilliam nor any person came to question her. The guards allowed her to pass letters to Wyatt in the next room, but he too knew precious little. England was on fire with the royal couple in turmoil, yet the silence of Nicòla's cell told none of the sordid tales.

The sun had not met its full height when the Thames seemed to fill with more barges than usual about Westminster. Nicòla watched with keen curiosity but was too far away to see any detail, her view obscured by the curve of the river and the small buildings on the bank. Further along at Whitehall, Crumwell would be in his office, without his secretary. Ralph probably stood in Nicòla's place once more. All they would have to do is "lose" the key to Nicòla's cell and it would be as if she never came to England at all.

The bang of her cell door tore Nicòla's eyes from the tiny window, and she turned, for it was not time for someone to bring a meal. Instead, a friendly face appeared from behind the bored guard. 'My Lord the Duke of Richmond!' Nicòla exclaimed as she bowed.

Henry Fitzroy gleamed a wide smile as he strode across the room to embrace his small friend. The King's own bastard son visited; surely that was a good sign.

'What brings you to the Tower from St. James' Palace?' Nicòla said as she offered him a seat. 'I must confess I cannot host you in the manner you deserve.'

'I care not, I only care to see you,' Fitzroy said as Nicòla sat in the sole other comfortable chair in the room which sat beside the cold fireplace. 'I see your lodgings are at least enough.'

'I am fortunate to have a large room with a real bed. I have paper and ink, books, and the food and wine is constant. They even send me water for bathing. Many endure far worse in the Tower.'

'I came to see for myself, though Secretary Crumwell assured me of your comfort. To see Crumwell stalking the palace halls without you coming behind him is quite a sight, as if the man has sustained an injury and lost a limb. Everyone asks after the missing Waif, and he scurries away like a wounded animal. Crumwell is a man bereft.'

'They have accused me of a crime which shames my master.' Nicòla thought of Crumwell alone in the thongs of vile people which occupied court.

'I come to tell you the news. Can you see much of the Thames from your window?'

'A little only.'

'Today there shall be a trial at Westminster Hall. Secretary Crumwell shall be there in his finery, and the jury shall hear evidence against four of the accused – Smeaton, Norris, Weston and Brereton.'

'Already?' Nicòla croaked. 'They got arrested but a week ago.'

'Father is pained by all this news, as you can imagine. It shocks His Majesty that his wife, the woman he loved for ten years, would betray him so. To commit adultery, to say that the King is not virile enough to satisfy a woman, which shames Father... they have instructed Crumwell to move this along with all haste. I am to be in court, so everyone might see me as a symbol of the King's virility.'

'A symbol all sons must play to powerful men,' Nicòla commented. For she would not be as a man if not for her father's desire for a son. 'My father paraded me as his precious bastard heir for years.'

''Tis my purpose in life,' Fitzroy jested. 'I hope I can do the task, for I feel not well.'

Nicòla noticed the rings beneath Fitzroy's usually shining blue eyes. 'Have you been ill?'

'A cough, perchance a little tired,' Fitzroy sighed. 'Nothing of worry.'

'Should you not be at Westminster to hear the evidence now? Does Crumwella have a strong case against these four men?'

'I must confess I do not find the evidence convincing. Norris, Smeaton and Brereton all strongly deny the claims of having carnal knowledge of the Queen. The places, the times and dates do not match rightly what the

Queen and her household were doing on those days. It claims Anne took Norris to bed while still recovering from birthing Elizabeth. Brereton has precious little to do with the Queen and has cried of his innocence. Weston seems to have become almost as if in a false sleep, for he says almost nothing, silenced by the entire charge. But there is evidence of Anne speaking in treasonous terms against His Majesty, and there are witnesses, her own ladies, to Weston professing love to the Queen, to Norris wanting Anne, and of discussing the King's death. They are witnesses to Anne and Smeaton talking in dark corners.'

'Smeaton has talked in every dark corner with every member of the court, including me,' Nicòla said with a sigh. 'Smeaton is a popular man.'

'That may well be his undoing. The judges to hear the case are who you would expect. I feel grateful not to be part of such a scandal. Crumwell is the sole lawyer who shall speak at the trial.'

'Crumwella can handle the entire case on his own. Who shall sit on the panel of judges? Howard? Percy?'

'Indeed, the Duke of Norfolk shall be the Lord President who shall preside for the trials of Anne and George. Percy shall give evidence to Archbishop Cranmer stating pre-contract and shall annul Anne's marriage. The judges for today are quite a group. You know Sir William Fitzwilliam, of course, and he took all four men to Westminster Hall this morning and claims Norris confessed all to him, though I know not who shall believe it. The foreman is Edward Willoughby, a man from a Katherine-supporting family, and he owes William Brereton money, so seeing Brereton guilty will be beneficial to Willoughby. And Sir Giles Alington, Lord of the Manor of Horseheath, will preside.'

'Alington, Sheriff of Cambridgeshire, who married Alice, Sir Thomas More's stepdaughter?'

'The very same, and you know how strongly that family hates Queen Anne. Another bitter enemy is Walter Hungerford, son-in-law to John Baron Hussey, who hates Anne.'

'Hungerford is a man who desires other men and is unduly brutal to his wife. She petitioned Secretary Crumwella for a divorce. Hungerford is desperate to regain credibility and will do whatever Crumwella tells him.'

'I know of William Sidney, he is a friend of the Duke of Suffolk, so he hates Anne with a passion also,' Fitzroy said. 'Also, Sir Thomas Palmer, the lawyer who is close friends with Father.'

'Palmer was helpful in Parliament in getting Crumwella's treason bills passed.'

'And there is Sir Anthony Hungerford, who is good friends with the Seymour family. He is another of Crumwell's friends in Parliament and is looking to buy some closed monasteries. Do you know of William Musgrave?' Fitzroy asked.

'Oh yes, he is one of Crumwella's hostile debtors. Musgrave was charged with gaining a treason charge against Lord Dacres in the north and failed. Musgrave owes Crumwella £2,000, a loan which can be recalled at any time, so he will do Crumwella's bidding, I can assure you.'

Fitzroy nodded as he took in the details of this severely compromised jury. 'There are several religious figures, William Askew, a strong supporter of Lady Mary. Sir Robert Dormer, an esteemed lawyer, MP and Catholic supporter, and Sir Richard Tempest, another Yorkshire man and MP, a man looking to gain respect and hates the Boleyns. Sir John Hamden, a relative of Sir William Paulet, has been a Catholic supporter. Crumwell has chosen the jury wisely.'

'Do the men know what they shall be accused of?' Nicòla asked.

'Smeaton shall plead guilty to three charges of carnal lust with the Queen, in hopes of gaining mercy. The others shall plead not guilty to charges of adultery with the Queen, and to plotting the King's death in Norris' case. Crumwell has been quiet on the details and evidence, but all shall be ready in court today, no matter how vile, how crude or how treasonous it may be. There shall be thousands present to hear what has become of Father's beloved Anne.'

'Do you believe any of the charges against Anne? What does your father believe?'

'I am hurt by the allegations, no matter how much Queen Anne detests me. Father is much hurt, and suspects it involves perchance witchcraft, for that is how Anne kept him so in love for all this time. We are fortunate that, while creating their marriage was a long road, dissolving the marriage shall be simple. When Father annulled his marriage to Katherine, the country rose up her defence, God rest her immortal soul, but with Anne, there is no one who cares.'

''Tis a sad occasion,' Nicòla sighed. 'His Majesty believes Anne committed adultery?'

'I do not know for certain.' Fitzroy coughed, a wet cough that sounded worse than earlier claimed. 'Father is angered such things would happen, but it attaints Anne as deceitful while His Majesty is not sullied. He is in love with Mistress Jane Seymour, a kind and devout woman. Already Lady Jane has written to Lady Mary, my half-sister, to be kind to her after years of sorrow. Lady Jane even came to me, so our friendship may develop. She is a good woman.'

'Your father wants Anne guilty, so he can be with Lady Jane. He has spoken to Crumwella about this before.'

'I want peace and my father happy. Perchance even a legitimate son. The men today shall be found guilty and sentenced to death, but Crumwell says he shall have that commuted. They shall confiscate their lands and their money belongs to the crown. Their families are disinherited and shamed. Crumwell wants no killings.'

'I am pleased to hear these words. What of the Queen and her brother, and the rest of us?'

'They shall try Queen Anne and Lord Rochford in a few days' time, as they deserve to be judged by their peers in a separate hearing. Crumwell shall be the lawyer to prosecute again. George Boleyn is not coping well and stunned that his wife sends him food but no tokens of love or a desire to fight for his good name. Boleyn will never be freed from prison, and Anne may tarry hither, or be banished to another prison or a nunnery. We know not. Sir Francis Bryan shall be released today, as will William Latimer, due to lack of evidence. Sir Richard Page has been vexing to Crumwell, as he tells me, so they shall keep him for a month or two before being released. Much attention is on Wyatt, due to his love of Anne, but they shall release him after the trials and sentencing, for his own safety. I am hither today to tell him such, and that the King remains firm in his trust.'

'And me?' Nicòla dared to ask.

'I must confess your fate has not been decided upon yet. From the way Crumwell spoke, he seems desperate to come to the Tower, yet does not wish to be seen favouring a prisoner. He must maintain his honour and remain in the King's trust if he is to have all these people found guilty of treason, adultery and incest.'

'I understand, though I worry.'

'I am certain they shall release you, Nicòla,' Fitzroy said with a smile. 'There is no hint of evidence, no mention of you in paperwork, and no one has uttered your name.'

'I am the Waif creature of the court, Crumwell's fool. I am forgotten by all.'

'In some ways, perchance that is God's will, to keep you safe.' Fitzroy gave Nicòla a smile of comfort. 'I fear I must go, for I have more messages to deliver before I head to court. I am to dine with Father and Lady Jane tonight and it shall be a most vexing day, I fear.' Fitzroy stopped to cough again.

'Please care for yourself, and I know many fine doctors if you need care,' Nicòla said as she stood and helped Fitzroy from his chair.

'Fear not, Nicòla, I shall be well. I look forward to a trip to your home country. Father has approved my travel and study in Italy for several months!'

'I am so pleased for you! Oh, how I wish I could come. You could one day be King of England, Your Grace.'

'I imagine no world without my father on the throne.'

'I think everyone in England keenly knows of your father's power, His most gracious Majesty.'

Fitzroy embraced Nicòla once more before he bid her farewell and left her sunlit cell. One of the greatest trials ever to be held in England would begin three miles west of the Tower and Nicòla would be powerless to see the moment. Somewhere close by, Anne would be in her chambers, wondering what would be said, what would happen. Nicòla's plan to sully reputations had instead become a fight for people to keep their heads. God have mercy on them all.

Chapter 44 – May 1536
The Great Hall of the Tower, London

If you love your lyes, soon you will live inside one

'O God set our minds on You. Let us not be conformed to this world, but be transformed by the renewing of our minds so we may prove what Your will is, that which is good and acceptable and perfect. Amen.'

Crumwell opened his eyes once more to the sounds of the barge readying itself for the ride to the Tower. Crumwell travelled to Anne's trial with the Duke of Suffolk, away from the palace where thousands gathered to hear the fate of their queen.

'Crumwell.'

Crumwell turned to see Henry himself standing in the doorway, too wary to step out from the privacy of the hallway into sight where Crumwell stood by the boat.

Crumwell bowed low to the King. 'How may I be of service, Your Majesty?'

'Go well today,' Henry said and gestured Crumwell closer. 'Do you believe in these charges?'

'I believe in the evidence,' Crumwell replied, not a real lie to his king.

'I want a new wife, Thomas. I have wished that before and you delivered me a queen. But that was wrong, I should not have married Anne. She must have used witchcraft against me! I want a virtuous woman, a pious and calming woman like the Lady Jane. How she could have graced the halls of my palace all these years and I knew not that Jane was the perfect queen for me.'

'I shall do all you command, Your Majesty.'

'You shall see Anne found guilty, Thomas, I command it.'

'As you wish, Your Majesty, for I have already ordered an executioner. There is a Frenchman, the official executioner of Saint-Omer, his name is

Jean Rimbaud, I believe. He can travel from Calais to execute Anne once the trial is complete. I sent for him several days ago.'

'Many thanks be to you, Thomas. For all that has occurred, we crowned Anne as a queen, and I cannot have her put to death in a common manner.'

'The Frenchman shall do the work, as he is a fine executioner.' Crumwell looked to his feet as he spoke. 'But we need not discuss sentences today, Your Majesty.'

Henry wanted Anne dead. Crumwell had planned to have her found guilty of adultery and treason, a sentence of death then commuted to prison once Crumwell sat and spoke with the King. Sending for the French executioner was just a bluff; he would never kill Anne. But Henry had now decided.

'What of the rest, Your Majesty?'

'Behead the men at the Tower. I never enjoyed the sentence of hanging, drawing and quartering. We are not barbarians, even to our enemies.'

Nicòla supposed no one to get hurt. 'As I say, there be no need to worry yourself with such matters today, Your Majesty.'

'I wish to be formally betrothed to Lady Jane within the next few days.'

'Archbishop Cranmer shall annul your marriage based on Anne's pre-contract to Henry Percy; we shall do that within days. Queen Anne's sentence will have no effect and you can announce your engagement. May I be first to congratulate His Majesty on his new marriage?'

Henry raised just half a smile. 'There are no others, no more guilty men?'

'No, Your Majesty. We found no evidence on any other names given, so we shall need no more trials after today.'

'Your Waif?'

'Frescobaldi shall get released soon, along with Sir Thomas Wyatt. Sir Richard Page shall get released in the future.'

'How could our perfect world end in this way?'

Crumwell stepped close to his king. 'Your Majesty, the perfect world has not yet arrived. Perchance that better world shall come with Lady Jane.'

'My perfect world came twenty-five years ago when Katherine delivered of a healthy son named for me. God took the child and perfection has not reappeared in all that time. Now I only hope for peace.'

Crumwell bowed again as Henry turned and headed back up the stairs away from the barge. What a revelation. This whole plan to free Henry would put blood on Crumwell's hands; but if he stayed honest to himself, it troubled Crumwell not that the days of Anne Boleyn were gone.

~~~

Voices of the thousands trying to get into the Great Hall hushed as Crumwell walked up the aisle between the men gathered for the trial of Queen Anne and her brother. The event boasted memories from those earlier days when Wolsey held a trial to get Henry an annulment from Queen Katherine. But this was different; for few in the crowd cared for Queen Anne. No one wanted Anne on the throne, many died for refusing to sign the Oath of Succession… God's blood, they would now have to change the succession. Princess Elizabeth would become a bastard. Men like Sir Thomas More and Bishop John Fisher died for not signing the Oath. Those laws would mean nothing with a new queen.

Silence befell the Great Hall behind Crumwell as he stood before the platform built for the jury to sit in judgement. First came the stuttering old Duke of Norfolk and his son, Henry Howard, Earl of Surrey. Norfolk appeared most happy to sit as Lord Steward of a trial which would see his niece and nephew convicted of treason and incest. Norfolk cared more for gaining power for the Catholics, not his family. Charles Brandon, the pompous Duke of Suffolk came in next, a man who spoken not a word on the barge ride from the palace. After all the anger between Crumwell and Suffolk, they now stood on the same side to bring down the Queen, and Suffolk's hate for Anne would serve Crumwell well today.

Henry Courtenay, Marquess of Exeter, and Henry Pole, Lord Montagu, the King's Plantagenet cousins came in next, eager to see the end of Anne, and Lady Mary back in her father's favour. Henry Percy, the Earl of Northumberland, a sick man, dragged his feet soon after, the once lover of Anne who now seemed happy to destroy her. The men muttered between themselves as noblemen whispered throughout the hall.

Crumwell continued to stand as the jury came to sit. Friends to King Henry, Ralph Neville, the Earl of Westmoreland, and John de Vere, the Earl of Oxford arrived together. Oxford had carried the crown at Anne's coronation and now sat in judgement for her life. Next came the Earl of Worcester, who would sit in judgement, listening to the evidence of his wife Elizabeth Somerset. He would be in good company, for George Brooke, Baron Cobham, would hear damning evidence against the Queen given by his wife, Nan Cobham. Also, there was the father of Jane Boleyn, George's wife. Lord Morley would have no trouble condemning his son-in-law and his sister. The others all were Henry's longtime friends, the Earl of Rutland, the Earl of Sussex, Lord Windsor, Lord Sandys, Lord Mordaunt. Lord Dacre from Yorkshire, who spent years bringing trouble, was in London and keen to gain the King's favour. Suffolk's sons-in-law, Edward Grey, Baron Grey of Powys and Thomas Stanley, Baron Monteagle, both came to sit in judgement, alongside Lord Wentworth, Jane Seymour's great uncle. Lastly came Lord Clinton, husband of Elizabeth Blount, young Henry Fitzroy's mother. None could be considered more loyal than Blount and her husband. Not one of these men would do anything but see their foe Queen Anne sent to her death.

Crumwell stood to one side of the platform where the judges sat and noticed many high-ranked nobles in the crowd, London's mayor, the French ambassador and his secretary. Curiously, Eustace Chapuys was not there. Perchance he had already fled London to wait with the Lady Mary. Norfolk rose from his seat and straightened the white ermine collar. 'Bring in the accused,' he boomed through the Great Hall.

More whispers gave way to silence as Sir William Kingston entered at the far end, and in came Anne Boleyn. She walked with her head held high; she held herself with great honour and appeared fearless in her walk towards her disgrace. Her black velvet gown moved silently along with her, her shoes not making a sound on the ground. Anne stopped before the panel and bowed three times to acknowledge the entire group. She even turned to Crumwell and gave him a bow which he returned, after all, Anne was still queen. Anne went to sit on a platform placed close to the lords where all could see her poise and calm demeanour. She clasped her hands on her lap and awaited the words of the lords, as if she were ready for a moment for conversation rather than defeat.

Crumwell gestured to Sir Christopher Hales, the Attorney General, to set forth and read the charges against Anne. 'Anne Boleyn, wife of His most royal Majesty, Henry the Eighth of England, you are charged with the crimes of incest, adultery, promising to marry Sir Henry Norris after the King's death, conspiring the King's death and laughing at the King and his dress. How do you plead on these charges?'

'I am not guilty, Your Graces and Your Lordships,' Anne addressed the panel, ignoring Hales.

The evidence Crumwell was forced to present seemed so feeble, but it was all he had to condemn a woman for crimes never committed. He stood before the court, before the Queen, before God, and read out the lurid details, either made up or made from comments from my Anne's ladies, twisted to sound lewder than they ever were. Crumwell read through his papers as if he were there in body, but not in his soul. His soul yearned to be away from his mess, for they would behead the beguiling and educated Anne for this, something Crumwell never wanted. But Henry needed such so he could have a new start with Jane Seymour.

'Frail and carnal lust... inserting her tongue into her brother's mouth, and he in hers... vice provocations... crazed with lust... bedding Norris just six weeks after the princess' birth... bedding Weston and giving him money... carnal appetites to seduce a musician thrice...' Crumwell rattled away all these accusations about imaginary events, along with dates in 1533, 1534 and 1535... suggesting her pregnancies resulted from men other than the King... accusing the Queen of acts in places she did not visit, with men who were not present. Yet no one on the jury questioned anything, for they all sat there so Henry could have a new bride. Every lord asked questions of Anne and every time Anne could give a calm, composed and logical explanation, but it mattered none, for the executioner had sailed from France. Henry was a fool to dismiss a woman like Anne Boleyn.

'Lady Anne,' Norfolk addressed his niece without her royal title, 'do you wish to s-s-peak to the court?'

Anne looked straight to the judges. 'I confess I did not always give the King the humility to which was owed, considering his kindness and respect he bore me. I took it into my head at the time to be jealous of His Majesty, but with God as my sole witness, I did no other wrong by my husband. I regret that such person's names hither today are to die for sins abused by my friendship and fealty, for those men die for me most unjustly.'

Norfolk paused in his seat; the jury did not need time to consider a sentence, as Crumwell had prepared all with Norfolk, wrote out the words of the sentence himself. But Norfolk wiped a tear from his old cheek. 'Anne Boleyn, because you h-h-have offended against our sovereign the King's Grace, b-b-by committing treason, by committing adultery and incest, w-w-we attaint you of these crimes. The law of this r-r-realm stands you deserve death, and the j-j-judgement is you shall be burned here in the Tower of London or t-t-to have your head smitten off, as d-d-decided at the King's pleasure.'

Sick Henry Percy cried in his seat and slipped, landing on the floor in a panic as servants struggled to collect their sick master. Crumwell heard a woman cry out in the crowd, no doubt someone who knew Anne well. He turned back to face Anne, and she stared right back at Crumwell, her black eyes calm. But she turned away again and faced her tearful uncle as he urged the crowd to be silent again.

'My lords,' Anne said, and the crowd fell silent. 'I will not say your sentence is unjust, nor presume that my words shall change your convictions. I believe you have your own reasons for what you have done; but you have removed those reasons from what you said in this court, for I am innocent of the offences. I have been a faithful wife to the King. I confess to jealous fancies and suspicions of him, and I did not use discretion and wisdom always. Think not I say this to prolong my life. I know these, as my last words, will award me nothing but I wish to defend my chastity and honour. I would willingly suffer many deaths to deliver my brother and the other men from their sentences, but as it pleases the King, I shall willingly go with these men in death. I shall lead an endless life with them in peace and joy, where I will pray to God for the King and for you, my lords.'

As the voices in the Great Hall rose again and Norfolk struggled to establish order, Crumwell turned away and headed out through a small side door. He needed not to see Anne dragged away by Kingston again, and he still had to see George abused and sentenced to death. The plan had always been to get the death sentences commuted. Henry had no such desire to being merciful. Nicòla may soon get released from the Tower, but her dear friend Anne Boleyn, and many others, like sweet Smeaton, would all be dead by the time Crumwell's love breathed fresh air outside her cell. Years of service, hard work and determination to gain Anne as the Queen had all come undone with an adultery charge, undoing the royal marriage in only two weeks. Crumwell knew he had scant chance to convince Henry to allow them all to live, but he had to try. Try just one more time to appeal to Henry's soft side, which once adored Anne.

Chapter 45 – May 1536
The Tower, London

Aftyr the fyrst lye, nothyng will be believyd

'O Lord, Jesus Christ, Redeemer and Saviour, forgive my sins, just as You forgave Peter's denial, and those who crucified You. Count not my transgressions, but, rather, my tears of repentance. Remember not my iniquities, but, more especially, my sorrow for the offences I have committed. I long to be true to Your Word and pray that You will love me and come to make Your dwelling place within me. I promise to give You praise and glory in love and in service all the days of my life. Amen.'

Nicòla sat on her knees of her cell, her eyes closed, with her hands together before her face while she prayed. Night had long fallen; midnight must have passed. The night felt much harder than the day, where she could see people, the sun moved in the sky. Once night fell, the despair of being locked away without any company made the hours seem unending. Wyatt in the next cell knew precious little, but both had a window out to the green within the Tower grounds and had seen a scaffold being erected on the grass over several days.

The plan was to discredit the Queen and most of her faithful followers. But the plan had not at all gone the way Nicòla expected; Crumwell had pushed it all further than she expected. What of the King, what did he think as news of his wife's adultery no doubt made him feel belittled, not even manly enough to satisfy one woman?

The sound of a key in the door brought Nicòla to her feet in a rush. She pulled her warm overcoat from the bed and thrust it over her nightclothes. Could this be it? A late-night interrogation? But the weary face which appeared told a different story.

'Sono così content di vederti!' she cried.

Crumwell waited until the door locked again. 'I feel pleased that you feel pleased to see me!'

Nicòla threw herself against Crumwell, an embrace so tight that Crumwell would have felt her loneliness and desperation just in the way her hands grabbed at him, how tight her arms wrapped around him.

'Do you plan to let me go?' he asked.

Nicòla shook her head, her face buried in his neck, sweet relief found in the smell of a man against her. Crumwell lifted her off her feet and shuffled towards the bed where he sat her down, and sat beside her, taking her hand. Nicòla could not bear to touch his face; Crumwell's bottom lip fat and split, the skin of his cheek bruised and raw.

'The King?' she asked.

Crumwell brought his hand to his face, and Nicòla noticed his fingers were red from a fight. 'Indeed, His Majesty did not like a proposal I put to him.'

'What proposal?'

'That we spare Anne and the traitors the sentences of being burned or hanged. I begged Henry not to execute Anne, regardless of the crime.'

'And Henry beat you?'

'Shoved me to the ground and kicked me. Henry said Anne has tried to destroy his manhood and he must punish her, for it is Anne's fault that England has no heir.'

'No male heir.'

'Henry walks the garden daily with Jane Seymour and her family. Spends all his time with them. If I am to survive, I am to encourage this new pairing, and announce their betrothal forthwith.'

'The scaffold?' Nicòla gestured to the window.

'I ordered it built a few days ago, once Henry commuted the traitors' sentences to beheading. He beat me yesterday but sent for me after dinner and repeated that he wants them all beheaded hither in the Tower, not quartered over at Tyburn. I believe Henry wants it done; they are no longer trusted friends and courtiers, but enemies and tyrannous snakes to be removed from this Earth for their crimes.'

'Were you tempted to tell Henry we made up the adultery charges?'

'What would you have me say? I lied about the whole thing, Your Majesty? He might like that, for now he can have a new wife. It removes the Boleyn family and all their supporters. If I create Queen Jane, then I will return to favour. Had we not come up with this plan, it would be my head on that scaffold tomorrow, or your head. We had to choose, and I believe in what we did, even if I want no one to die.'

'Do you regret all of this?'

Crumwell turned to Nicòla and looked at her in the eye for a moment 'No. I regret nothing, for we all knew what could happen when we came to court and made our lives hither. I felt I had to shake the throne, and I have done so. I am sorry for Mark Smeaton, I am, but I needed a commoner no one came for, asked for, begged for, and Smeaton was perfect. Weston's father, Sir Richard Weston, offered me some £100,000 to spare his son, though I know not how he would come up with that money. Weston's wife has sent men on Weston's behalf to plead his case, but all is of no use, for nothing can change now unless Henry pardons the men. Weston has debts of almost £1,000, enough to destroy his wife, so I have ordered that debt wiped, to spare her any further pain. I spoke to Weston just now, to tell him Henry changed his sentence to beheading, and he cried, thinking he had many years left to play the courtier and raise a family.'

'You spoke to Weston yourself?'

'I have spoken with each of them, as Henry sent me to tell them of their sentences myself. I think he did so to inflict more pain upon me. But I did my duty. Brereton spat in my face, Norris would not share his last words, and Smeaton, I sat with him for some time.'

'Can I see Mark before his death?'

'No one else is to see the prisoners, and I am sorry for it, Nicò.' Crumwell sighed. 'I know you cared for Smeaton, and I told him so, but I cannot allow you to see him, on the King's orders. I spoke to Wyatt just now and made sure he is being treated well. I will release you both in coming weeks.'

'I am to be released?' Nicòla said, her voice almost a whisper in surprise.

'Yes, as there is no evidence against you or Wyatt, two men caught up in the mess. The King approved your release.'

Nicòla could hold it no longer; she burst into tears and hunched over on the bed, relieved to hear the news she could go home, see her daughter, live her life once more. Being separated from Jane made Nicòla want to be sick. Queen Anne would feel the same over Elizabeth.

'I went to see Queen Anne too.'

Nicòla sat up and Crumwell wiped tears from her cheeks with his reddened fingers. 'Her Majesty wished not to see me, instead wept when Kingston told her of my arrival. But she sent me a message – that she chose not to destroy the Waif, for the creature's punishment shall be an eternity by my side.'

'Condemned to be at the side of the man who framed a queen for incest and treason,' Nicòla sniffed. 'That is a harsh punishment.'

'Is it a burden you can bear?'

'It is as you said – either Anne and her supporters fall so low, or we do. Still, to think they shall condemn her…'

'I tried to have the sentences commuted, though I cannot say I feel sad to see most of the men gone, though Smeaton was your friend. Every day at court is a struggle for survival. It pleases Henry that I ordered a French executioner ahead of time.'

Nicòla shook her head as her tears stopped. 'The King has become something of a monster. Once a man so in love has become a cruel, vainglorious tyrant.'

'We can only pray now, pray for a calmer world. I will risk Henry's wrath once more and beg for Anne. But think of what we did to Katherine, move her from manor to manor, slowly reduce her income, her household, until she grew sick and died alone. Is banishment any better than execution? Both are deaths, but one is quick.'

'Yes, but banishment offers the chance of a pardon.'

'When Henry marries again, there would be no hope for Anne Boleyn, but Henry's temper would flare knowing she still walked the Earth. If Anne dies, we are safe. We can move on with the Reformation and worry no more over the Oath, or about the question of which princess is more legitimate than the other. We only need to hope Jane Seymour bears a son. Henry said he was happy to spare Anne's life if I put my head on the block in her place. Most assuredly that is a threat I take with all seriousness. If Henry can turn so coldly away from Anne, he can even more easily turn away from me. I must do everything to make Jane a queen, and a loved queen.'

'Can we hope to survive to create yet another queen? We shall be queen killers, queen destroyers, not Queenmakers.'

'I will do everything in my wide powers to ensure we see a new queen on the throne and all will soon forget the reign of Queen Anne.'

Nicòla nodded in agreement as she studied the lines of Crumwell's face. He bore tiredness not seen since his brush with almost fatal illness. This trial and illness were not that far removed, for in both cases, death sat just outside the door. 'Gli uomini dovrebbero sia per essere trattati bene o schiacciati,' Nicòla quoted Machiavelli. Men should either be well treated or crushed.

Crumwell raised just half a smile. 'Perché possono vendicare le ferite più leggere, di quelle più serie che non possono.' Because they can avenge the lighter injuries, more serious ones they cannot. 'May I tarry hither tonight?'

'Hither, in my cell?' Nicòla scoffed. 'Why would any person ever wish such a thing? I have been in this room for weeks, locked away from the world. Am I forced to watch executions from my window tomorrow?'

'It is a hard truth, but yes, as will Anne and George from their windows.'

'Anne is right now in her royal rooms,' Nicòla commented. 'But the others destined to die await close by in the Beauchamp Tower I believe.'

'No one locked hither in Bell Tower shall be harmed,' Crumwell said, but Nicòla could not raise a smile.

'If I am to witness the deaths of Lord Rochford and the other men, all because of my planning, I wish to watch it hither with you. Perchance we can get the guards to allow Wyatt in here tomorrow as well. For your safety, we cannot allow your release tomorrow, and I fear for my safety in public tomorrow. We have defeated the Boleyns, but we are not safe yet.'

'Perchance we never will be safe.'

'Do you know who else is imprisoned in this tower? Sir William de la Pole, nephew to the old King Edward. Pole's father was the second Duke of Suffolk, his mother Elizabeth Plantagenet, sister of King Edward and King Richard. They have imprisoned him for as long as you have been upon this Earth, Nicò. His claim to the throne is stronger than...' Crumwell's dipped his voice to a whisper... 'stronger than King Henry's.'

'Whisper no such treason, for spies lurk in the walls,' Nicòla replied.

'I know, for most of them are in my employ,' Crumwell said with a wry smile. 'And for tonight they can report that I left the Tower after failing to obtain an audience with Anne Boleyn.'

'You should leave while you have the chance, for Henry may change his opinion at any moment. What if Henry regrets his decision to execute Anne? He shall come for you.'

'Henry is planning every aspect of Anne's death while planning his future with Jane Seymour. It is Henry who wants Anne's head, not me.'

'Tom, remember you are the one who imprisoned me hither. I could hold an anger towards you, for the lies, the deceit, the torture of my friend Mark.'

'Let me spend time curing you of that anger.'

'I am so lonely, Tomassito, and that loneliness, the confinement, is stronger than any anger. You must kill Anne to stay alive and I am on your side.'

Waking up in a bed next to a warm body reminded Nicòla of being a person, not just a prisoner. It would be a gruesome morning for May 17. The sun would not shine in the sky, as if even the weather felt sorrow for the day ahead. Nicòla woke before dawn and watched Crumwell sleep beside her. He turned and fussed all night, unable to ease his mind into a state of calm. In the next tower, the prisoners would wake to a day of executions. Poor Anne would wake to the day she watched her brother beheaded. George Boleyn was never part of the plan; he was to just fall from favour once they attainted his sister. It had been the ladies of Anne's chambers who hinted that Crumwell should also take down Lord Rochford. The Earl of Wiltshire would see his daughter and son executed, but walk away from court with his life, back to his wife at Hever Castle. Mary Boleyn was far away with her common husband, and her most recent child, a daughter named Anne. Mary seemed wise to tarry far from the court.

Anne's uncle, the Duke of Norfolk, had disappeared from court too, so Crumwell had said. But the pompous Duke of Suffolk stayed to see Anne die, and with much joy.

A bell tolled in the distance, loud enough to wake Crumwell beside her. He brought Nicòla into his embrace, unwilling to wake.

'We cannot ignore this day, Tomassito,' she whispered in his ear.

'I know,' he replied with a groan like a schoolboy who did not wish to attend his lessons.

'Be it true I can see Wyatt today?'

Crumwell opened his eyes and sighed. 'I must away. I shall see if Kingston will allow the three of us together for the executions. Norfolk was the Lord Steward of the trial, not I, so I cannot decide about release. Norfolk ordered they could not release you or Wyatt until after Anne's death.'

Crumwell, who slept in his clothes, gave Nicòla a long kiss goodbye before he climbed from the bed and banged against the door for the guard to come. 'Prepare for release,' he ordered Nicòla from across the room. 'I have already made sure they give you and Wyatt the best food and that they clean your cells for you. Dress in case I can get you released today.'

The sound of the key echoed, and the guard appeared, who seemed unsurprised of Crumwell's presence in the room.

'Arrivederci, amore mio.'

'Arrivederci, cara, Tomassito,' Nicòla called back from the bed, hidden by the half-open door, out of sight of the guard.

~~~

Dressed and readied, Nicòla sat by the small window of her room. The scaffold was complete, and a crowd formed before it, ready to watch death's exhibition. The wind blew off the Thames, over the walls and onto the green between the Bell Tower and the stronghold White Tower in the centre of the fortress. Nicòla watched women hold their billowing gowns and men hold down their soft caps as they stood in the cool breeze of the cloudy day. She recognised many people as suspected; the Duke of Suffolk was there, as was Nicholas Carew. Courtiers poured onto the green, though Eustace Chapuys was not present. The Lady Mary most likely needed his company in Hertfordshire, some twenty-five miles north of London. Half of Nicòla wanted to hide away from the frightful mess too, but this was her idea, to discredit the Boleyn supporters. This resulted from her idea, the result of the threatening meeting with Jane Seymour three weeks ago. Just three weeks ago.

The heavy door opened, and Nicòla jumped up, her black Crumwell livery looking as fine as possible in a cell, and there stood Kingston. 'Mr. Frescobaldi, I must ask for your total discretion.'

'I am at your command, Sir William,' Nicòla said as she got down from the ledge by the window.

'I have spoken with Secretary Crumwell. Crumwell proposes he, yourself, and Sir Thomas Wyatt attend the executions from the rooftop walkway which leads from Bell Tower to Beauchamp Tower. As I have not gotten word from the Duke of Norfolk that they can release you today, this is all I can do without being accused of letting prisoners roam.'

Nicòla allowed Kingston to chain her at the wrists, and the constable led her from her cell and along the hallway for the first time since her arrest. Through narrow walkways, Kingston led her out onto the top of the fortified wall which connected the two strong prisoner towers on the east side of the castle. Guards stood ready all the way along the wall, but there stood Crumwell and Wyatt, who also had his hands in irons. Nicòla walked as fast she could without appearing to try an escape, and embraced Wyatt, the pair a mess of bound hands trying to embrace one another, to Crumwell's laughter. All manners were gone, for both had spent weeks locked away, knowing none of events, scared during every minute God gave them.

'I must go down to the scaffold to bear witness,' Kingston said. 'Guards shall escort you back to your rooms in a moment.' A moment, for that is all it would take.

'I fear we are shaking the throne today, Secretary Crumwell,' Wyatt commented as the three of them stood above everyone gathered by the wooden scaffold. They watched Kingston push through the crowds to stand where the executioner had arrived to do his duty. The crowd was ready, almost restless at the wait.

'If today shakes the throne, then tomorrow shall threaten to destroy it,' Nicòla noted as the sound of the crowd grew. The prisoners were being led out of the ground exit of the Beauchamp Tower.

The three leaned over the edge of the wall to get a glimpse of the men walking towards the scaffold. They stopped all but George Boleyn, who, according to his rank, would die first.

'I cannot believe such a thing could occur,' Wyatt said. 'Forgive me, Mr. Secretary, but George Boleyn's guilt cannot cross my thoughts. He is a gentleman, a scholar, a diplomat.'

'None of the female witnesses spoke well of him,' Crumwell replied. 'Quite the opposite. They spoke of lewd behaviour.'

'We all make blunders with women.'

'And that is what women described, so for him to have carnal knowledge of his sister is not too hard to believe.'

312

Boleyn, dressed in a white linen shirt and black hose, climbed the few stairs of the scaffold to the jeering crowd. They quietened as Boleyn came to address the world of the living for the final time. 'Christian men, I am borne under the law, judged under the law, and die under the law, and the law has condemned me... Masters all, I am not come to preach, but to die, for I have deserved to die, for I have lived more shamefully than can be devised... I am a wretched sinner, and I have sinned shamefully. I have sinned so openly it would be no pleasure to you to hear them, nor for me to repeat them, for God knows all... Masters all, I pray you take heed by me, and especially my lords and gentlemen of the court, take heed by me and beware of such a fall... I pray to God, the Father, the Son, and the Holy Ghost that my death may be an example to you all. Beware, trust not in the vanity of the world... and especially in the flattery of the court. I cry for God's mercy, and ask the world's forgiveness, as willingly as I would have forgiveness from God... If I have offended any man that is not here now, either in thought, word or deed, I pray you to heartily, on my behalf, pray them to forgive me for God's sake. I say you all, if I had followed God's word in deed as I did read it and set it forth to my power, I would not have come to this. I read the gospel of Christ, but I did not follow it; if I had, I would be among you now: so, I pray you... masters all, for God's sake, stick to the truth and follow it, for one good follower is worth three sinners, as God knows.'

Boleyn gently knelt to the block as the crowd fell as silent as the tears upon his cheeks. Standing all close together, Nicòla took the chance to take Crumwell's hand, his billowing black overcoat shielding their hands from the guard's eyes. The executioner took a heavy swing, struggling a little with the strong wind. With a thump, the axe fell upon Boleyn's neck, yet it did not sever his head. As people shrieked in the crowd, the axeman swung quickly again, this time missing the head, hitting the shoulder. As the body, still moving, blood spilling, slipped away from the block, he swung his axe once more, this time the head coming from the body in the black pool of blood. Crumwell held Nicòla's hand tight and Wyatt did his best to rest his bound hands on Nicòla's shoulder, to comfort her and himself, from the vicious execution.

The crowd moved like the choppy Thames in the breeze, all stretching to see the twitching body pulled to one side of the scaffold, the head of Boleyn tossed into a large basket. A servant tried mopping up some blood, but the man fought a tide of red.

The noise of the crowd rose again as Norris approached the scaffold, pushed up the stairs by the guards. More people jeered and booed at Norris, his lower rank giving him less protection. He too addressed the crowd as they quietened to hear a dead man's words. 'I think no gentleman of the court owes more to the King than I do or has been more ungrateful than I have. But I loyally believe in my conscience, I think the Queen innocent of these things laid to her charge; but whether she was, I will not accuse her of anything. I will die a thousand times rather than ruin an innocent person.'

Nicòla felt Crumwell squeeze her hand again as Norris raised his hands to pray. Beside Nicòla, Wyatt cried.

'Most Sacred Heart of Jesus, I accept from Your hands whatever kind of death it may please You to send me this day with all its pains, penalties and sorrows; in reparation for all my sins, for the souls in Purgatory, for all those who will die today and for Your greater glory. Amen.'

Norris dropped to his knees at speed, like a final angry gesture to the world. He placed his face in the blood of George Boleyn and laid down his arms. With a single stroke, the man of three and fifty years was dead. The crowd talked among themselves as they pulled Sir Francis Weston to the scaffold.

'I feel saddened for the Weston family,' Crumwell commented. 'They so desperately petitioned me, but we had witnesses talking of Weston's love for the Queen.'

'Was Weston, or any of these men, guilty of these crimes?' Wyatt asked, tears on his face.

'They are all guilty of something,' Crumwell replied. 'We are all guilty of something.'

Weston, a man only half the age of Norris, whose blood he stood in, his bare feet red with his coming fate, seemed confused by his surroundings. He had written goodbye letters to his family and begged forgiveness from his young wife Anne. Crumwell had promised to pay his debts on his family's behalf, at least giving Weston a little comfort after living a life of waste. Tears rolled down Weston's gentle cheeks, pooling somewhere in his short dark beard.

'I had thought to live in abomination for another twenty or thirty years, and then to have made amends... I thought little I would come to this. Everyone, you would do well to take the example of this, and to live clean lives under God.'

With those few sentences, Weston knelt in pools of blood, whose blood no one could quite be sure, and laid his head. With one swipe of the axe, Weston's head fell into the basket, blood spraying the nearby observers. Nicòla silently prayed in thanks to God for allowing Crumwell to elevate her above the killings, for it made them all separate from the truth. Standing in the crowd would be too much to bear as her plan made all of this happen.

Up next was the final man of the nobility, Sir William Brereton. Brereton walked alone after pushing the guards away with angry turns of his shoulders. He stood before the crowd on the scaffold, now a mix of shock and horror at the sight of piled up bodies to one side, heads tossed in a basket. The wood of the scaffold now looked black with the blood of the three men who came before him. Brereton looked out over the green and its crowd, his face appearing angry.

'I have offended God and the King; pray for me!' Brereton yelled as loud as any frightened man could. He stood defiantly on the scaffold, as if he could fight destiny with an angry face. 'I have deserved to die if it were a thousand deaths, but the cause whereof I die, judge me not. But if you judge, judge the best. But if you judge, judge the best. But if you judge, judge the best. But if you judge, judge the best!'

Nicòla had less fear of watching Brereton die. He had been a cruel man in the lands of Cheshire and the Welsh lands where he ruled. He took bribes, he had men killed. Yes, he was innocent of sleeping with the Queen, but he was no innocent young man like Weston.

'I have committed the goods, chattels, rents and fees of Brereton's lands to his widow, so she can raise her son,' Crumwell commented as they dragged Brereton's heavy body onto the pile, which oozed blood over the others. 'Even though Elizabeth Brereton's sister-in-law was one witness who spoke against Brereton, his wife still thinks him a good man.'

'I knew Brereton the least,' Wyatt replied, 'but many spoke well of him. But none of us are innocent men.'

The crowd rose again, making angry noises, of booing and hissing. It was time for Mark Smeaton, the commoner, to die. Tears dripped from Nicòla's eyes at once; she had no warning, they plucked themselves from her eyes with a hot terror against cold skin. Wyatt too wept for his dear, dear friend. Nicòla, Wyatt and Smeaton had spent much time together as close friends, different in their own ways, all outsiders at court since Nicòla first came to England. Wyatt fell to his knees as he cried, only his face peering over the wall. Nicòla placed one hand on Wyatt's shoulder, unable to do any more to comfort her friend as she watched their companion being dragged to the scaffold.

Smeaton got to the stairs and paused. Two guards grabbed him by limp and bruised arms and pulled him forth to the block. Mark's clothes were filthy; the white linen shirt he arrived in at Crumwell's Stepney house now stuck to his bloodied skin, his beautiful curly black hair matted with blood. Bruises circled around his eyes from the frightful torture at Crumwell's demands. Nicòla could not dare imagine what else had befallen sweet Mark in the Tower. Nicòla sobbed aloud like Wyatt, as Smeaton, still held by guards, lifted his weary head to speak.

'Masters, I pray you all to pray for me... for I have deserved the death... I shall be justly punished for my misdeeds and my lies.'

'His only lie was his false confession,' Nicòla sobbed as Wyatt nodded his head.

The guards stepped back for Smeaton to fall to his knees by the block, so thick with blood it no longer resembled wood. Before he rested his head, Mark turned and looked right in Nicòla's direction. With a wail of tears, Nicòla reached out her hands down to him, bound tightly together. Smeaton raised one hand in her direction for a moment before a guard pushed his young head to the block. Nicòla heard the thump of the axe but saw it not as she buried her face against Crumwell's shoulder and he wrapped his arms around her, holding her to standing as she gave way to the horror. She and Wyatt both wailed openly, Crumwell silent. It made no sense to cry on the shoulder of the man who arranged the killings, but Nicòla had no choice in this incredible defeat.

Wyatt found his voice after a minute, and as the crowd dispersed, he pointed to the pile of bodies. 'Where, Mr. Secretary, shall they be buried?'

'Hither in the churchyard of Chapel of St Peter ad Vincula. Boleyn shall receive his own plot, and they shall bury the others in pairs, their heads included.'

Nicòla lifted her face from Crumwell's shoulder and stood on her own. It was time to return to their cells. She could not bear to look at Crumwell, for he was the master of this plan, and yet the only source of her comfort, all in one man. God could be cruel.

'This is all my fault, in wishing to condemn one woman, I have killed five men,' she sniffed.

'What do you mean?' Wyatt sniffed as guards came to fetch him.

'I spoke against Anne in the first after Jane Seymour threatened me. God have mercy on my soul.' Nicòla let the guards take her by the arms and drag her away from Crumwell, who stood helpless to stop her and Wyatt from being removed to their cells. The worst was still to come the following day, when Anne Boleyn took the scaffold to be reviled and humiliated for all time.

Chapter 46 – May 1536
Greenwich Palace, downstream London

One syngle lye can distroy a hole reputaytyon

'But how could that be?' Crumwell yelled at the messenger, knowing it was of no use. But the King would accept no excuses. Weary humours after a night praying rather than sleeping made everything harder. The Seymours still occupied Crumwell's magnificent apartments, so that left Crumwell in Nicòla's tiny room, which she used as a dressing room when court stayed at the palace. If only today would end; if only the Queen was dead.

'Weather becalmed the ship in the night. She was not docked at dawn as planned, Sir Secretary,' the messenger replied.

'Do you know when the ship shall make land?' Crumwell asked, one hand over his eyes.

'Perchance this afternoon, Sir Secretary.'

'We are executing the Queen of England at nine o'clock this morning and we have no executioner? We have no executioner! How could that ship not arrive from Calais?' Crumwell screamed.

The messenger stood before Crumwell's desk and knew not what to say. 'Go to the dock and wait for that ship,' Crumwell said through gritted teeth.

The messenger ran off and Crumwell fell into his seat. Jean Rimbaud had not landed in England. He ordered that French executioner for Anne as soon as possible and yet the weather had thwarted the whole plan. Nicòla would have got that executioner to England on time. She could have organised everything while Crumwell told his lies in court. But Nicòla was still locked in the Tower to save her from a disgraced queen and vengeful king. To see Nicòla's face as they pulled her and Wyatt back to the cells yesterday, tears staining their cheeks over what had happened… Crumwell knew not the agony they shared. He shared none of Nicòla's guilt, for he wished to remove the Boleyn faction from court for his own safety, to be in

317

the right side of the coup, and it was Henry who ordered the death sentences. Crumwell wanted no one to die, but he could admit in solitude that having George Boleyn and his supporters dead made life easier. All they needed was to have Anne removed, and now that could not happen.

Crumwell found Henry in his rooms after morning prayers, sitting at his desk. The chamberlain allowed Crumwell into the privy chamber where Henry sat, not willing to look up from his reading when Crumwell stood before him. 'Your Majesty.'

'Not now, Thomas, for I am busy and have much to attend. Surely you have the same level of work.'

'I do, Your Majesty. But…'

'And we shall announce my betrothal to Lady Jane this morning. Is she not the most kind, most virtuous lady at court, Thomas? Is she not gentle, and honourable, and of good breeding, for her parents had ten children, so I am bound to gain a son. After the wedding, I wish to give out new titles and honours, and I shall need your help in bestowing those awards.'

'Of course, Your Majesty. But I have news, the ship from Calais has not arrived and…' Crumwell stopped at the sight of Henry's angry stare which lifted from his pages to his Chief Minister. Crumwell moved from foot to foot, ready to be chastised for the problem.

'This has to end. I cannot stand any more of Anne!' Henry screamed. He stood up from his writing table, knocking everything on the floor. Henry grabbed Crumwell by the shoulders and shoved him to the ground, Crumwell unable to defend himself, for to resist would be treason. 'Everyone who attended my wedding is now dead, except for the bride, Thomas. You and your Waif were outside the door. I have pardoned the ladies who attended the wedding; they gave the evidence we needed, but you and the Waif have done nothing.'

'We sold our souls for you!' Crumwell screamed.

Henry stood back from Crumwell on the floor and wiped the spittle from his lips. Never had Crumwell spoken back to Henry during his anger. 'I want Anne's head! I want Elizabeth declared a bastard. I want this done!'

'Archbishop Cranmer has declared your marriage to Anne illegitimate, Your Majesty. You know that occurred yesterday after the executions. Cranmer is at the Tower, hearing Anne's last confession and taking the Eucharist before her death. You can marry Lady Jane no matter where Anne is now.'

'I want her gone!' Henry screamed. 'Look at me!' Henry paused as tears ran down his cheeks. 'My son should be the one getting married, expecting the birth of his sons. I should have a household full of sons securing my father's legacy, securing our nation's safety. Yet here I stand, at my age, still looking for love, still waiting for a son.'

'You are loved by our whole country…'

'No, I lost the love of my people when I married Anne. I lost their love when I removed Katherine. Well, I am the King! I rule the Church of England and they shall bow in fear if not in love. I want Anne dead!'

'I have messengers waiting on the road from Dover, Your Majesty. The executioner may not be here until nightfall.'

'Shall we get another executioner then? Shall we have her hanged at Tyburn? Shall we throw her in the Thames?' Henry cried.

'We shall wait for the executioner to arrive and have the Queen executed with great dignity because you are King Henry the Eighth, a king not a tyrant.' Crumwell surprised himself at his confidence while lying flat on his back before Henry once more, but if the King wanted to act like a child, then Crumwell would speak to him as one.

'Get up,' Henry barked, and Crumwell jumped to his feet as fast as his tired body would allow. 'Postpone proceedings. As soon as the executioner arrives, then get the job done. Do not dare to enter my sight until Anne is dead. I know they call you the Queenmaker, Thomas. Put your queen in the ground. I have a new queen to wed and have more jovial plans than you. Be gone, unless you desire to substitute Anne's head for yours!'

Crumwell moved without a word and rushed out of the chamber. One day more and all this would be over. Just mentioning Anne and the Boleyns was banned throughout the court, and all discussed the virtue of Lady Jane, who had whisked away to Wulf Hall, some seventy-five miles west of London during the executions. Soon that woman, a woman who portrayed herself as kind and meek, who threatened to tell everything of Nicòla's true being, would be in Anne's place.

~~~

Steven Vaughan, one of Crumwell's oldest friends, tried to call on him at Austin Friars. So did his nephew Richard running the Rolls office, as did many of Crumwell's staff. Thomas Avery, who helped Ralph run Austin Friars, tried to talk with him, and Ralph wanted to leave Greenwich Palace to be with his adoptive father. But Crumwell wanted to see no one that day, instead only lock himself out in the back garden of his favourite manor and talk with Gregory, play with Jane. What did they think of their father having a queen executed? What did it mean for their futures? Poor Anne would be in the Tower, going wild at the change of days for her execution, terrified that Henry was trying to hurt her further. What if she believed the stay of execution meant they could spare her? The executioner would kill Crumwell's queen in the morning.

Crumwell retired early to his rooms, hoping to find solace from the world on the final night of Anne's life. So, when someone dared to knock on his bedroom door, he barely had the energy to order them away. But the door opened after being told to leave the third floor, the most private part of the house.

'Perche 'mi mandare via?'

Why send me away? Crumwell spun his chair, spilling wine on his doublet, not that he cared. Nicòla came into his room in a run, the first smile Crumwell had seen in some time. Nicòla threw her arms around his neck, her feet leaving the ground as she latched upon him.

'Whatever are you doing here?' he asked, breathless at the shock of her appearance.

'I was to get released after Anne's execution. They delayed the execution and yet they did not change the date and time of my release, nor that of Wyatt's. I know not why, perchance it was just forgotten. But we could go free as it was not our fault something delayed the Queen's executioner from Dover.'

'Wyatt, is he well?'

'He has gone tonight to his private residence, where Lady Elizabeth Darrell is waiting for him. But tell me, how is my daughter? And Gregory, too? I expected you to be at court.'

'Jane is well and Gregory also, but I came hither this morning after being dismissed by Henry, and his anger over the execution.'

'That surprises me none. Queen Anne's response is a strange occurrence also, as Archbishop Cranmer told me.'

'You spoke to Cranmer?'

'Cranmer took Anne's last confession his morning before they told her of the executioner's delay. She spoke of how she had only a little neck and the executioner has an easy time of it all. I have always liked Anne, Tomassito. I wept for the loss of her departed children. Anne has been used cruelly, and I know she turned against us, but it still hurts me dearly.'

'You are home now, and importantly, you can be with me.'

'I confess I first went to Jane's room, but she sleeps. I held her sleeping body, thanking God for the chance. If the servants are still working, I should much like a bath, and I can tell you all my thoughts, and of Cranmer with the Queen. Anne spoke of me in her rooms, so Cranmer shared.'

'And said what?'

'Anne told Cranmer she was not angry with me over this whole affair and sought not to harm you by revealing my secret, or our marriage that night in Calais. A woman should not be harmed to attack her husband, Anne said. We have cut her down to make Henry happy, but Anne would not act in the same manner. I think Anne understands that Henry could not let her live. She fears for Princess Elizabeth, and I wish to look out for the girl, as she shall have a difficult life, and is only a few years younger than our Jane. I am tired, Tom, of hiding the secret of being a woman.'

Crumwell frowned at her words. 'You may leave court if you wish, I can release you to live with Jane.'

'I know not what the answer may be to my weary soul, but it is my fault Anne is to die, and I cannot sit quietly in the garden. I must suffer forever.'

~~~

Even with Nicòla safe at Austin Friars, Crumwell could not sleep easy. Perchance he never would again. But as the sun rose, and he dressed for his day, there would be no more delays. A messenger had come in the night; the executioner had arrived, and Kingston at the Tower had seen to the Frenchman and all would be ready. It was said this Jean Rimbaud had a technique of distracting his prisoner, so they turned away from him when he swung his beautiful sword, and he executed them in confusion, never knowing their moment had come. Rimbaud would need to do fine work to earn his £20.

Quite a crowd gathered to see the demise of Anne Boleyn, supporters and enemies alike. They had draped the scaffold in black for the occasion, the only proper colour, for once again the late spring sun did not dare shine on such a day. Those gathered on the grass on the western side of the White Tower waited in the gentle breeze of the early morning. Crumwell walked in with Nicòla and Gregory, who begged to come to the occasion. Ralph and Richard too came from their positions to join the mourners and revellers of the day.

The first person to dare talk to Crumwell on this fateful day was the pompous Duke of Suffolk. 'Ah, the Waif is out of his cell, I see,' Suffolk said as Crumwell stood with his family.

Nicòla turned to the Duke but said nothing in reply. 'Your Grace,' Crumwell said, 'good morrow and well met.' Just one of many lies told in the last week.

'I have long awaited this day,' Suffolk said and rubbed his hands with joy. 'My dear late wife hated Anne with all her wits, a woman who could never compare to the real queen, Katherine. My new wife agrees.'

'Your new wife should still be in the nursery,' Crumwell mumbled. He glanced around Suffolk to see Henry Fitzroy join the crowd.

'Your Grace, the Duke of Richmond,' Nicòla said, and Fitzroy gave his friend a hearty embrace before politely saying good morrow to his father's oldest friend, pompous Suffolk.

'A sad day for us all,' Fitzroy said. 'I much confess I never supported Queen Anne, but executions are never a good occasion.'

'Anne so often wished you dead,' Suffolk commented to Fitzroy.

'Out of love for her daughter, who is my half-sister,' Fitzroy replied.

'You should be pleased with yourself, Crumwell,' Suffolk continued. 'For Henry shall be most pleased once you deliver this news back to him at Greenwich. The Seymours have already left Wulf Hall on their return to the palace for the wedding. Did you know Henry decided upon their wedding day last night? They shall announce the betrothal tomorrow, and the wedding shall take place ten days later.'

'The King is to marry this month?' Nicòla asked up to Crumwell.

'We do the King's duty,' Crumwell mumbled.

The sound of the trumpets heralded the coming moment, and the large crowd hushed itself into silence. From the Queen's apartments, Anne would have walked past the Great Hall, through the Cold Harbour gate and out to the green. Through the crowd, Crumwell spotted Kingston leading the Queen, dressed in a grey damask robe trimmed with ermine, which only queens could wear. She hid her hair under a gable hood, followed by her ladies, a silent parade between the guards which led Anne to the scaffold. What would go through Anne's mind? Was she free of judgement upon those who condemned her? Did she accept her fate? Her walk suggested so, for Anne looked as formidable today as the day she walked into Westminster for her coronation.

Kingston stopped and allowed Anne to climb the black stairs of the scaffold. Anne stepped forward and her eyes crossed the crowd. She stopped when she saw Crumwell there, looking back and she held his gaze, no expression on her face. She looked to Nicòla, to Suffolk, to Fitzroy, going over everyone whether they came to cheer or cry.

Queen Anne took a deep breath. 'Good Christian people, I have not come to preach a sermon; I have come hither to die. For according to the law and by the law, I am judged to die, and so I will speak nothing against it.' She paused as she continued to look about her. Whatever she wished to see, she could not find it. 'I am come hither to accuse no man, nor to speak of that whereof I am accused and condemned to die,' Anne continued, her voice gentler than before, 'but I pray to God to save the King and send him long to reign over you, for a gentler nor more merciful prince was there never, and to me he was ever a good, a gentle, and sovereign lord.'

The wind grew a little stronger, enough to cause a chill in Crumwell's spine. The hood Anne wore moved a little on her small head as she took a deep breath. 'And if any person will meddle of my cause, I need them to judge the best. And thus, I take my leave of the world and of you all, and I heartily desire you all to pray for me.'

The crowd stood in utter silence as Anne's ladies stepped forward to help her. There were only four, and none of them the faithful women who had been her companions for years. Lady Kingston was there, tears already on her face, Margaret Coffin, Elizabeth Stoner and finally Anne's aunt, Lady Elizabeth Boleyn. These women had been fine spies for Crumwell in the Tower, but over the weeks had become loyal to the woman they watched, convinced of her innocence.

The wind caught Anne's dark hair for the final time as she removed her hood to wear a simple white cloth cap for her final moments. Lady Kingston slipped Anne a small bag which held the money that Anne paid to her executioner, the sword of Calais, who had already covered his face. The Frenchman bowed to Anne to beg forgiveness, which only made her ladies cry more.

Crumwell turned to Gregory, stood stiffly beside him, Ralph close next to him, Richard right behind him. Nicòla stood with her hands clasped beside Crumwell, the members of the Crumwell family lined up in silence, though Nicòla's cheeks were already wet with tears.

Anne knelt, and a few gasps escaped from the crowd while her ladies fixed a white blindfold on Anne, her black eyes hidden for the final time. How strong Anne looked, how steady and calm in the face of such a cruel end.

'O Lord have mercy on me, to God I commend my soul. To Jesus Christ I commend my soul; Lord Jesus receive my soul,' Anne mumbled to herself, barely loud enough for Crumwell to hear. The crowd in the front knelt as Anne prayed, and one by one, more sank to their knees.

Gregory looked to his father, but Crumwell shook his head, for if Henry heard they knelt for Anne, there would be punishment. Nicòla knelt beside Crumwell and he could dare not pull her up, for her womanly feelings defeated her on this awful day, and she had been a friend with Anne over many years. Soon the entire crowd sat on the ground, praying in whispers alongside their queen.

Crumwell looked out across the crowd. Suffolk and Fitzroy had not knelt, further along, Chancellor Audley had not either. Chapuys was gone, and Cranmer had fled the Tower for the Lambeth Palace in severe melancholy over the whole affair. The Duke of Norfolk did not attend, nor Thomas Boleyn; Anne's beloved father had left London in disgrace.

Crumwell looked to his queen one more time as the Sword of Calais lifted his beautiful blade, causing cries from the crowd, especially from the women. On her knees, Nicòla leaned against Crumwell, still offering prayers.

Anne turned her head towards the executioner, no doubt in response to the gasp of the praying crowd. Crumwell silently begged Anne to keep still, for all the hate she bore him, he wanted her to suffer no more. In his strong French tone, Rimbaud called out to his young attendant, and Anne turned her head to where all the attendants had been standing upon the scaffold.

This was the moment; Rimbaud lifted his singing sword and with one silent stroke, he cut through Anne's little neck. People cried out as Anne's head fell to the black scaffold, and it appeared her lips kept moving in prayer as it fell to its end. Anne's small body fell in a heap upon itself next to her head, the blood all tipping towards her ladies. It was over, the reign of Anne Boleyn had come to a sad end on a cold day.

Crumwell took Gregory's hand for a moment, his son terrified at what he witnessed. All watched as Lady Kingston did her best to gather Anne's bloody head into a white cloth bag, the other women too upset to help.

'There's no coffin,' Crumwell muttered aloud.

Nicòla stood up from the ground as many others too finished their prayers and returned to their feet. They watched the four women on the scaffold look at one another as blood soaked along the hems of their gowns, no idea what to do with their murdered queen. Nicòla left Crumwell's side and headed to the front of the crowd. She looked left and right around the yard and ran toward the White Tower.

He spotted what she had seen; a wooden box. Nicòla pulled it open and pulled bow staves from it, tossing them on the ground. Nicòla dragged the box along the ground towards the scaffold which caught the eye of several of the ladies, who went to Nicòla's aide, and together, they pushed the makeshift coffin to the scaffold. Several guards lifted the box up the few steps, and Nicòla stepped forward to help lift Anne's blood-soaked body into the box.

But Lady Kingston turned and shoved Nicòla hard, and cried out, 'no man shall touch Queen Anne!'

The cry was enough to frighten Nicòla off the scaffold, and all other nearby attendants and guards moved away while the weeping women went about their work.

Sir Francis Bryan appeared at Crumwell's side. 'I understand you are to tell the King the good news,' he said. 'I am to see the Seymours and tell Lady Jane of the events. I shall do you a favour, Crumwell, and not tell them that your Waif was so loyal to the last moment.'

Nicòla came back over to Crumwell, who stood still with Gregory as the crowd swirled about them, heading away from the awful scene. Nicòla's hands showed the blood of an anointed queen. This was the England that Crumwell created as Queenmaker, as Chief Minister. Any person could die at any time, even the King's most beloved wife.

Chapter 47 – May 1536
Whitehall Palace, London

Ther be goode reasins to tell lyes and the trouth

'I received a letter today describing quite a scene.'

'One of many I presuppose.'

Crumwell stood with his arms at his sides as Nicòla brushed his new red velvet doublet, making the fabric shine. He hated the colour on him, much to Nicòla's enjoyment. The King instructed his minister sharply not to wear black, so Nicòla had ordered cloth in the reddest of shades she could find in London at such short notice.

'The letter,' Crumwell continued, 'stated that eleven days ago, when Anne Boleyn died, the tapers at St Peterborough Cathedral lit themselves.'

'And they believe the spirit of Queen Katherine lit the tapers as someone killed her enemy?'

'That is what they claim.'

'Just one many of lies we can vanquish as we close monasteries and abbeys around the country. There.' Nicòla stopped brushing and ran her hand over Crumwell's chest. 'You look fit for a royal wedding.'

'I am glad for it.' Crumwell pulled Nicòla towards him for a kiss, his private office door closed. 'Why are you not wearing this horrid shade of red?'

'You mean the red rose of your sovereign's royal house?' Nicòla smiled. 'I am but a servant and only permitted to wait for my master as he attends the King's wedding today. I have no need for ceremony. You are one of the chosen few.'

King Henry had been engaged but ten days and today would marry Jane Seymour, for he wished to wait, not to be seen to be rushing into marriage again. But Anne Boleyn was dead; had been for eleven days now, just long enough for everyone to stop being haunted by her beheading for every waking second. Well, at least it haunted Henry none.

Crumwell kept his arms around Nicòla as she fussed with his ever-greying hair. 'I am not much for weddings myself,' Nicòla continued. 'As a bride, I have never enjoyed them.'

'Now we will have good terms with Rome with this new marriage, I shall have you annulled from the Medici family soon enough.'

'Whatever would the world do if women did not have to marry to be safe?' Nicòla sighed.

'Women are mothers and wives. There is no other life.'

'Other than the heretical one I lead.'

Crumwell kissed Nicòla again and let her go. 'Jane Seymour is a fortunate lady. Jane is colourless, from her pale skin, to her lack of wit, to her haughty nature. Jane is a bore, cannot read nor write beyond her own name. Her features are sharp and mean. I have seen letters written to Chapuys stating that no man in Europe can understand Henry's mind. People write that her secret parts must have magic to them.'

'Jane Seymour has been at court for almost ten years and no man had need of her secret parts, as you say. I have many worries, but none relate to any secret part.'

'I worry Jane bears no son and they shall force me to behead another bride! Come, let us away.'

Nicòla opened the doors of the office, though the other rooms were quiet, none of the clerks yet at work. But several guards and gentleman-ushers milled about, so Nicòla turned to Italian for their walk to the Queen's rooms, as she and Crumwell so often did to cloak their conversations in solace.

'I have worries of my own,' Nicòla said, her voice lowered despite being in a language most never learned. 'I fear that Lady Jane courts Lady Mary's favour most heartily, as Mary is the King's daughter. But what happens once Jane has power of her own? Shall she toy with poor Mary and then toss her aside once she has her own child?'

'Jane Seymour shall do whatever her family tells her, by Mary supporters, by Norfolk, Suffolk, Carew, Exeter, all their supporters, and any of the Catholic nobility,' Crumwell replied.

'Let us not misunderstand Jane — for she will marry a man that ordered last his wife dead eleven days ago. She is not pious or meek as she claims to be.'

'Jane is ruthless, and she is being taught by those who want Lady Mary back in the line of succession. I feel for Lady Mary, I truly do, separated from her father for five years, her mother now in heaven. But I will reform this country and Mary is opposed to all I believe in; I shall never allow her back into the line of succession.'

'But how would you keep her out? Mary is the King's daughter, and the King decides who is the heir.'

'No, the law decides who is the heir. I shall ensure Parliament passes a bill that declares neither Mary nor Elizabeth are in the line of succession. I have a plan and it shall bring Henry into my hands, so worry not.'

'Can we not just make Henry Fitzroy legitimate, for he would make a marvellous king.'

'I know,' Crumwell groaned. 'We are so close to having a fine heir and yet I cannot make Fitzroy legitimate. But fear not, perchance parliamentary reforms shall see our dear friend on the throne one day. I feel pleased that Cranmer granted the dispensation for this marriage. Henry and Jane are not close cousins, but still family through Edward the Third.'

'How is Cranmer?' Nicòla asked.

'The Archbishop is not at his best. He is about to marry his king to a devout Catholic woman and is scared that now we have lost Anne, our Reformation shall stall. I have tried to soothe his doubts, but he is not to be swayed. Cranmer is still much dismayed by Anne's death.'

'The King shall marry today in private ceremony in the Queen's closet; a closet another queen occupied which just weeks ago. Even Henry must worry, for he has made no announcement of the wedding.'

The conversation paused as they entered the Queen's apartments, where all hints of Anne Boleyn were removed. The rooms were bare, furniture and tapestries moved, items in chests, no doubt Jane's belongings being readied. Several people waited in the Queen's presence chamber, messengers, courtiers, servants, where Nicòla too was to wait while the royal marriage took place.

Crumwell noticed Ambassador Chapuys there and continued through the guarded doorway to the private rooms where the wedding would take place. But Nicòla had no such luck, and Chapuys moved to her side in a moment. He too wanted to speak in Italian, which he seldom did at court.

'Good morrow, Ambassador Chapuys,' Nicòla mumbled. 'I see you are returned to court.'

'I have been with the Lady Mary these past weeks,' Chapuys explained. 'It has been a difficult time for the girl.'

'No longer a girl, but a woman of twenty years, ready for marriage long ago.'

'Indeed, and the time has come for Lady Mary to be restored to her father's favour. I think the King has always loved Mary, I do. But he sees her as a threat to his throne as a successor.'

'How is Lady Mary?'

'Mary asked after you, Mr. Frescobaldi, and says she has not had a letter from you in some time. Do not worry, I have told no one of your letters and gifts to Mary over the years. Mary wished to write to her father, as she has had many letters from Mistress Seymour. Our new queen, a devout woman, wants Mary returned to court.'

'And the succession?'

'Naturally, for Lady Mary is the King's daughter and should be his heir,' Chapuys said.

'Have Mary write to my master. Secretary Crumwell likes Lady Mary, so perchance he could intercede with the King for her.'

'I will not lie, Mr, Frescobaldi; I am happy the great whore is dead. I am pleased we have a new queen, as are most back in Rome. The Emperor is pleased to see a Catholic woman at the King's side once more. Many great things could happen in England now that the concubine is gone, and Lady Jane is in her place.'

Nicòla sighed openly. 'Anne Boleyn was an exciting woman, she was educated and talented. Anne could talk politics with the men and sew and dance with ladies and outwit the lot. She made Henry love as he has never loved, fight like he has never fought, brought him happiness a heart can only be so lucky to find on this Earth. Anne was a reformer, yes, but a smart, pious woman. Jane Seymour is boring.'

'Jane Seymour is quiet, yes, but the King is tired of fighting, tired of factions between friends. Jane Seymour is perfect because she is not Anne Boleyn. Jane is pale, Anne was dark. Jane is silent, Anne was loud and intemperate. Yes, Anne Boleyn was beautiful, and Jane Seymour is not attractive and not young either. But it must be God's will! Jane loved Queen Katherine, served her honestly and faithfully.'

'You speak of nothing but flattery,' Nicòla commented, 'so no doubt you have written to the Emperor to talk of Jane's many qualities.'

'It is hard, for Jane is a woman who barely speaks, but is that not what men look for in a wife? I personally took holy orders and shall never marry, but if I were to marry, I would not want a woman meddling in my affairs. But yes, I am filled with flattery for Jane as I believe she shall be nothing but good for England.'

'Crumwella instructed we were to speak ill of Anne and talk of little but Jane's virtue, of her chaste and pious nature, so people can be ready to embrace her. We went to oversee work on Hampton Court Palace; They are replacing at the "A's" at court, throwing "J's" over them, so the HJ symbol is everywhere. Greenwich is mostly complete, and Whitehall as well. Hampton Court looks rushed, and many other royal houses are being restored now. All the while, Jane Seymour has been taught on how to be the perfect royal bride by Sir Nicholas Carew out at Sir Thomas More's old Chelsea manor.'

'We must have faith that the difficult times of the court are now over, and put our personal feelings aside,' Chapuys said as Nicòla nodded in agreement. 'It matters not who we loved or hated, for this is a new time and we must make sure we are in everyone's favour. I know you and I, and your master and I, have not always been friends, but perchance we can build a new world.'

Nicòla waited only a short time before Crumwell reappeared from the wedding, along with the Duke of Suffolk, Sir Nicholas Carew, Henry Fitzroy, Thomas Audley and Thomas Cranmer, all the loyal men around Henry. They sent messengers and servants off to tell of the news, though there was no public announcement. Crumwell wished to set off back to his offices, not letting Nicòla talk with Fitzroy for long.

'How was the ceremony?' Nicòla asked as they moved down hallways filling with people beginning their day.

'Brief,' Crumwell said. 'Jane promised to be buxom and bonny in bed and board. God let the woman do nothing but lie on her back until a child comes. Henry is taking her to his bedroom as we speak.'

'Not something I wish to imagine.'

'We have no time to waste on the King's amorous intentions. Queen Jane shall sit at Henry's side at dinner at Greenwich in two days' time, and on June 4 we must have Jane attend Mass at Greenwich where she shall receive the treatment of a queen and walk in the royal procession. We have many vacancies to fill in the King's rooms with the executions, and Queen Jane needs ladies-in-waiting. We must be very careful about whom we choose. I have a list.'

'I am certain you do,' Nicòla smiled as they reached Crumwell Chambers.

'Queen Jane shall sit beneath the cloth of estate at Greenwich, less than five weeks since Queen Anne did the same,' Crumwell shook his head. 'And we must smile and pray for a royal son to come soon.'

'Seven years to annul Henry's marriage to Katherine, and less than seven weeks between Anne's fall and today's wedding,' Nicòla commented.

'From today we must never mention Anne or the Boleyn family. It is Queen Jane now. With good fortune, she is the last queen I create. Now please help me out of this awful red doublet and hose.'

'Can I have it altered to fit me?'

'Whatever your little heart desires.'

~~~

The week seemed to go smoothly; the stories of a secret wedding spread among the court and everyone bowed to Queen Jane as if there had not been another queen only weeks earlier. An enormous party was in the planning, to be held at Chapuys' country home along the banks of the Thames between Greenwich and London. The Lady Mary wrote Crumwell, and while Henry was flushed with new love, and appetite in the bedroom, while adoring Jane's quietness and ignoring her looks, Crumwell gently asked Henry to write to his daughter, much to Henry's preferment. In a matter of weeks, they had erased the royal marriage, had a new marriage sworn before God, everyone seemed happy and Lady Mary looked to be reconciled. If only the ease could have come at a cost that was not Anne Boleyn's head.

Nicòla trailed behind Crumwell as they moved through the palace to the King's presence chamber, where they would award honours to Edward Seymour, now the older brother of the Queen. The Seymour family was not well ranked within the nobility; and had few lands until Jane's wedding gift of 104 manors and their surrounding estates, with enough profit to pay for her household. Today was the day to change all that.

'Ah, Thomas,' Henry said as he watched Crumwell and Nicòla come into the room and bow to His Majesty, who sat upon his throne, two velvet-covered steps above everyone else. Nicòla scurried out of the way to where courtiers often waited in the corner. But now Smeaton would never be in the King's rooms, and Wyatt had vanished. Norris was dead, Weston was dead. But at least Ralph was there, along with several new faces, all men desperate to gain Crumwell's favour.

'Your Majesty,' Crumwell replied as he handed Henry the patents needed to give a new title to Edward Seymour. 'I trust you are well this morning.'

'All is well when there's a new bride in bed,' Henry laughed, and Crumwell smiled. Any person in the room could see Crumwell had no desire for the conversation. 'Let us move quickly so I might enjoy the day with my new family, Thomas,' Henry said as he stood up and watched Crumwell prepare his sword. 'I am certain all other matters of running the realm can be left in your hands?'

'Always, Your Majesty,' Crumwell smiled at Henry's side. 'Edward Seymour,' Crumwell called to the antechamber where the Seymours waited. Seymour, dressed in a fine gold doublet and hose, came in and bowed low to the King and sank to his knees.

Henry took the sword from Crumwell. 'Edward Seymour, of Wulf Hall, I name you Viscount Beauchamp of Hache.' The King placed the sword gently on each of Edward Seymour's grateful shoulders. 'You shall review a sum of monies and lands owing to you, as stated in the patents drawn up by Secretary Crumwell.'

'Thank you, Your gracious Majesty,' Seymour muttered.

Nicòla sighed; Edward Seymour was a boring man, much like his sister, and to top it off, Seymour had married Anne Stanhope, an awful woman who had leered at Crumwell near and far.

'My brother-in-law deserves the title,' Henry said as he stepped down to embrace Seymour. 'We are to hunt today, Thomas,' he said to Crumwell, who at once stepped down away from the throne, so to not stand above the King. 'Shall you join us?'

'Alas, I have much to ready for Queen Jane's procession down the Thames tomorrow, Your Majesty.'

'Thomas, I know you are a busy man, scurrying about with your spies and your many roles in the court and parliament, but please tell me you shall enjoy the party in honour of Queen Jane tomorrow night?'

'I promise to enjoy myself.'

'Perchance even find you a woman,' Seymour jested, and Henry laughed.

'Thank you, Lord Beauchamp,' Crumwell replied through gritted teeth.

'Thomas,' Henry said, and placed one hand on his shoulder, 'a solemn marriage, lawful in England and officiated with God's blessing is a beautiful thing. I urge you most heartily to choose someone who can give that to you. Hold not onto old ideas.'

Nicòla narrowed her eyes. After all this time, Henry thought Crumwell needed a woman, after years of supporting the creature who followed Crumwell everywhere?

'One other thing,' Henry said, his hand waving in the air, 'we have no Lord Privy Seal at present. I want to elevate you, Thomas, to that position.'

Crumwell fell to his knees in a moment. 'I humbly thank you, Your Majesty, for such an honour.'

'Come,' Henry said and let Crumwell take his hand, 'you all but run this realm for me, so you as Lord Privy Seal makes sense. Leave your work, come hunting, I command you.'

'Congratulations,' Seymour added, though Nicòla heard his tone fill with envy. 'Such a pity we cannot call you Lord Crumwell.'

'Lord Privy Seal is a great honour,' Crumwell replied. Indeed, it was, for now, he could write on the King's behalf and use the wax seal of the King himself. All those Imperial alliance negotiations had not soured Henry's love for Crumwell. The beheadings probably helped that cause.

Nicòla waited until Henry ushered his new brother-in-law from the room to head out hunting before she ran over to Crumwell with a wide smile, one of many keen to congratulate him on his new title.

'Lord Privy Seal!' Ralph said as he embraced Crumwell.

'Yes, that is precisely how you are all to address me from today,' Crumwell laughed. 'It makes sense I would hold the title and run the Privy Council. We need new people in old roles. It is a new world. Let us away, for I have to prepare for a hunt.'

Nicòla smiled, but the King's words stuck in her mind. A solemn marriage, lawful in England and officiated with God's blessing is a beautiful thing. I urge you most heartily to choose someone who can give that to you. Hold not onto old ideas. Was Henry about to eject Nicòla from the court, for being part of the old world?

Chapter 48 – June 1536
Westminster, London

Half-trouths can be worse than full lyes

Queen Jane stepped from the royal barge to wide applause. The most impressive members of the royal court stood upon the grass along the Thames outside Chapuys' country manor, hundreds of people clapping with joy over their new queen consort. Henry held Jane's hand as she stepped onto dry land, gesturing at her as if she were the latest jewel he had purchased. Perchance that was the best way to describe Jane. Chapuys stood there, eager to be the first to bow and flatter Henry and his new bride, with many a number of courtiers eager to do the same. All the world now knew King Henry had married yet again.

'Whilst I know that His Majesty is happy with Jane,' Cranmer said as the Crumwell faction stood together beside a banquet tent emblazoned with the Holy Roman Emperor's arms, 'I do so worry for you.'

'Worry not, Archbishop,' Richard Rich said as he adjusted his golden cap. 'As chancellor of the new Court of Augmentations, I shall see that we destroy the monasteries and abbeys. We shall remove Catholic preaching at once, no matter who is queen.'

'I fear if a Catholic woman sits by Henry's side, all our work was for nothing,' Cranmer replied and turned to Crumwell. 'We have lost too many lives, too many sacrifices made to stop and be ruled again by the Catholic men of Rome.'

'Fear not, for Henry shall never wish to relinquish his role as Head of the Church,' Crumwell replied.

'Our heads could all be next for the block,' Cranmer muttered.

Crumwell held his tongue, for Cranmer worried so often but saw nothing of plans in parliament. He paused as the King and Queen approached, and all bowed low to their masters.

'My Lord Privy Seal,' Henry called to Crumwell and slapped his shoulders with a hearty grin. 'You wear royal blue tonight, and in satin! Glad to see you embracing the celebrations. And just look at your Waif, dressed in red! What a pair you make!'

Behind the King stood many of the men of the privy chamber, Ralph in among them, dressed in green. Ralph held his cheeky smile, as he often teased Crumwell for his usual boring fashion, for Crumwell had chastised young Ralph so often for dressing in a sumptuous manner. Now Crumwell stood in royal blue, sewn in silver thread with pearled buttons, the gold Collar of Esses draped upon his shoulders. Nicòla bowed again as the Queen moved toward her, and Jane frowned at Nicòla.

'Sir, you have a curious pectoral cross about your neck. I heard it belonged to the former Pope?' Queen Jane asked.

'Yes, Your Majesty, Pope Clement willed it to me.'

'I find you and I could be friends, Mr. Frescobaldi, for we believe in many of the same things.'

Nicòla nodded politely as Henry and his new prize drifted along a sea of flattery and vanity. But Crumwell stood in place with Nicòla, Richard, Cranmer, Rich and Audley, all watching from afar as Chapuys fell over himself to impress the royal couple while the rest of the court flittered like moths by candlelight.

'Little over a month ago they would have flocked like that to Anne, had there been some benefit,' Audley sniffed.

'The Catholics have won back the crown,' Crumwell whispered to his group, 'and now all the people who taught Jane, who pushed her, cajoled her, displayed her will want something in return. They want Lady Mary as the heir to the throne, Catholic rule once more. They will try to stop our Reformation and expect Jane to provide a son to make all their dreams happen. Fear not, for none of this shall happen, lest it is my head on the block.'

'We have worked hard to ensure your head was not the one on the block, uncle,' Richard said. 'Never, never laugh of such things, we all beg you!'

The conversation broke off, for the four hundred guns shot from the Tower down the river. The country had a new queen, and everyone for miles could hear it.

~~~

'We cannot have men such as Ambassador Chapuys lament on the human cost of the dissolution of the abbeys,' Crumwell said as he stood in parliament. The lords sat in peace, all looking weary in their seats. Not so for Crumwell; he was back right where he belonged, the centre of attention, which remained crucial to his plans for England's future. 'I proposed the Beggars Act, which I intend to pass hither today. We have 376 smaller religious houses to be closed, and eighty more spared. This shall leave twenty thousand monks and nuns who know not how to live. This shall be on top of the homeless beggars who litter our country. These people shall be restricted to their home villages and towns, and the parish or municipality shall assume full responsibility for these people. Work must be given to these people and children must be educated, and those who refuse shall be whipped until they bleed. Each parish shall also need to raise funds to provide for the sick and diseased. This gives each local area control over their people, caring for those who need help to be Englishmen and women.'

Crumwell knew little argument would come through that law. No one liked the poor, and this act stopped the lords from needing to do too much personally to control the people. Crumwell himself had been a beggar once; to rely on the village for support was a luxury few received until now. Now, the sick and poor would be housed, fed and healed for the betterment of themselves and their village. The needy could be warm, dry, safe, and have work and food. Children could learn to read, no longer only a luxury for the rich.

'But, Your Majesty,' Crumwell gestured to the King high above the seating, 'your noble lordships, we are gathered hither not only to ensure we seize the wealth and control of monasteries and religious offices, we will ensure the second bill for the Act of Succession. I ask you to vote on this bill to legislate that King Henry's first two marriages are invalid and that his marriage to Queen Jane is lawful. Therefore, all male children born to Queen Jane, or any future wife His Majesty may have, shall be the only heirs to the English throne.'

At once, pompous Suffolk rolled in his seat, from sitting back calmly to suddenly upright. 'What of the Lady Mary, Crumwell?' he called.

'The Lady Mary is an illegitimate daughter of the King,' Crumwell said and looked to his papers. 'Shall the King himself remind you of such?'

Suffolk rose to his feet. 'I need no instruction, common Crumwell,' he said coldly. 'The King's family is my family.'

'I have read a letter which Lady Mary has written to her father, His most gracious Majesty, and Lady Mary has accepted her father's authority, has rejoiced in his new marriage to Queen Jane. Just as all of you did so last night. None can disagree with the state of England now.'

Crumwell glanced up into the gallery again where the King sat, with a greedy smile. As the nobles mumbled amongst themselves, discussing this new act would not restore "their" heir Mary, as Queen Jane had promised to do, Crumwell knew he would make even more enemies pushing this law through. So be it, for none had the power of the King on their side.

Crumwell could behead queens, so he could decide who would inherit the throne. Power meant nothing if you could not use the law.

'Thomas,' Henry called from where he stood in his privy chamber. Queen Jane sat nearby, taking in the sun through the window out onto the Thames. Crumwell had been in his chamber dining room beside Nicòla, drinking wine with their friends after a good day when Henry summoned him.

'Your Majesty,' Crumwell bowed, holding his papers to his chest. 'How may I be of service?'

'I wished to thank you today, for you pushed a bill through parliament in a single day, and so my Jane's children shall be my heirs.'

'The Act of Succession is of the utmost importance.'

'I got a complaint about you, Thomas,' Henry said as he fetched his wine glass from a nearby table, 'from my dear cousin Henry Courtenay.'

'Yes, the Marquess of Exeter was unhappy with the bill today, but he submitted.' And it felt so good. Courtenay had a terrific claim to the throne, with his Plantagenet blood, championed by his overly ambitious wife.

'Many in my court, many in parliament, feel they may tell me who my heirs shall be,' Henry said. 'I am glad for the law tonight.'

'We have filled the court with changes and new alliances of late, Your Majesty.' Crumwell paused; had he spoken too closely of Anne's death? Henry said nothing, perchance the mention troubled him not. 'Some feel they may speak their truths as if the treasons laws shall ease.'

'That shall never happen,' Henry said. 'I have total control over my country and the Church!'

'Until the new Act of Succession is complete and signed by all, Princess Elizabeth remains the heir. We need to fix this and change the law to ensure you can choose your heir, legitimate or not. You could even choose the beloved Fitzroy as an heir if desired.'

'My love,' Queen Jane spoke from the corner. Crumwell had almost forgotten the tone of her voice as she spoke so little. 'Surely it shall be Lady Mary who shall be the heir?'

'She is a girl and a bastard,' Henry snorted. 'You should speak only of your own children.'

'But Mary has agreed to make peace with you, Your Majesty,' Jane said as she stood up from her seat. Her blonde hair was now under an English gable hood. Jane had banned French fashion from the court. Not as meek as she claimed to be, stamping out signs of Anne Boleyn in such a way. 'You have agreed to meet with Mary for the first time in five years,' Jane continued as she walked to the King. 'Mary had a fine Catholic mother, and while they led you to believe your marriage was legal...'

'I was not led into anything!' Henry cried at his wife. 'I am no fool!'

'Of course, Your Majesty, but...'

'But nothing, woman!'

Crumwell stood still and bit his tongue.

'I am sorry, Your Majesty. I thought as Mary is so loved by the Emperor, and England would trust...' Jane continued.

'Lady Mary has not even signed the Oath of Supremacy, has she, Thomas?' Henry turned to Crumwell with wild eyes. 'Mary has not acknowledged me as Head of the Church in England. She has not accepted her mother's marriage was unlawful, that she is illegitimate. All Mary wants is to overthrow me! She is no better as an heir than my son, Henry Fitzroy, the finest of men.'

'Indeed, Your Majesty,' Crumwell added. 'Fitzroy is the finest man at court and has sworn the Oath.'

'But Mary is the daughter of Katherine,' Jane said as she took Henry's hand. 'She believes in the true faith...'

'True faith?' Henry spat in his wife's face as he pulled his hand away, strong enough to knock the new queen back a few paces. 'Hear this from me, wife,' Henry seethed. 'I am in control, not the snakes in Rome, do you hear me?'

Crumwell tried not to smirk his greediest of grins. Henry would never give up the power and money of the Church. The Reformation seemed safe at this moment.

Henry swung back to Crumwell, still inflamed. 'I want Mary to sign the Oath of Supremacy, and if she says she shall not, then she shall be charged with praemunire. Remember what happened to Thomas More for this crime!'

'Yes, Your Majesty, we shall have a copy for Lady Mary to sign.'

'Do you know what Norfolk said today?' Henry continued. 'He said if Mary were his daughter, and to be so obstinate, that he would beat her head against a wall until it became as soft as baked apples.'

'Lady Mary is a strong and stubborn woman,' Crumwell replied. Even if she would not sign the Oath, Crumwell never considered harming the girl. 'I can have a letter written up, in my own hand, stating Mary's conformity to your will, Your Majesty. She can rewrite in her hand and sign it, and along with the Oath of Supremacy, and I can give the papers to you. I think now that we have a good new queen, Lady Mary shall sign.'

'Mary shall never sign,' Jane replied. 'She is of the old faith, steady in her belief...'

'Oh, shut your mouth, woman!' Henry screamed at Jane, who fell back into a chair. 'If you had a mind, you would use it shut your mouth and stop telling me what to do with my daughter!'

Henry swung back to Crumwell. 'I want you to go to Mary at dawn and get her to sign.'

'With respect, Your Majesty, some in the court gossip I should marry your daughter to make my children kings. While this is preposterous, a lie made in jest, if I were to fly to Mary's side, it may disgrace her poor name to be associated with me.'

'You, marry my Mary?' Henry laughed, and Crumwell joined him. 'These nobles can be of the worst minds. Then I shall send Norfolk and a group of his men, and he can threaten Mary's head with baked apples. But, I want you to send your Waif.'

'The Waif, Your Majesty?'

'Yes, as a show of fealty. Ensure your Waif gets Mary's signature. Send the Waif and I shall know you mean nothing but good for myself and my heirs.'

'As you wish, Your Majesty. I shall inform Norfolk.'

'No, I shall do it myself. He is hither at court and I shall inform him. He is probably in the company of those two young ladies I saw earlier. Perchance I married too soon,' Henry chided in Jane's direction, who sat in the chair, her dull eyes filled with tears. 'Ready the Waif, for I expect great things, since you and Frescobaldi both owe me so much.'

Chapter 49 – June 1536
Hatfield Palace, Hertfordshire

Lyes can mayke great promyses

God must have been on Nicòla's side, for they met with hard rain as they rode north to meet with the Lady Mary. If rain lashed their faces, no one wanted to talk on the ride. To be riding north again; Nicòla had not done so since her visit to the great Queen Katherine upon her death. Now she was threatening the Lady Mary with the Duke of Norfolk and Ambassador Chapuys, who came more out of pity than as a threat, for Chapuys adored Mary like a daughter of his own. Nicòla let herself rock in the saddle for the 25-mile journey, glad to be free of London for a while. Her master held the entire country of England, and Wales, plus most of Ireland, in the palm of his hand yet they seldom left the confines of the palace walls.

The morning after their late arrival, Lady Mary appeared from her private rooms, looking every piece the royal daughter. A beautiful twenty-year-old woman, Mary should have been the prize every prince in Europe fought over, remained an outcast in the countryside, like her charming mother in her final years. Mary's hair shone a brilliant auburn, like that of her parents. She bore her mother's eyes, and Katherine's powerful stature and confidence.

'My Duke of Norfolk,' Mary bowed gently.

'My Lady Mary,' Norfolk said and bowed in his green doublet, something he had not been slim enough to fit in some time. Norfolk stepped aside and Chapuys stepped forward, and Mary allowed him to kiss her hand. Her eyes lit up at the sight of the ambassador, one of the very few friends she still had on this Earth. The pair exchanged genuine kindness and Nicòla felt relieved Chapuys had come, for Norfolk, with a group of courtiers on hand to strengthen his confidence and anger, would have met this poor young woman on less friendly terms.

'Mr. Frescobaldi,' Mary said as Nicòla bowed low. 'I am much surprised they sent you to see me. Are you Crumwell's spy in my household?'

'His Majesty sent me,' Nicòla replied as she stood up straight. 'I confess I was surprised, but His Majesty made the decision with my master.'

'Why did the King send you, in your words?'

Nicòla paused and looked Norfolk and Chapuys, who both narrowed their eyes. 'Lady Mary, we came for a very specific purpose and I believe His Majesty wished the party that met with you appear as a range of different opinions and backgrounds. That way, it shall not appear that we threatened you write what we demand today.'

'You dare demand of me?' Mary scoffed. 'I have had many kind letters from both yourself and Crumwell. Why threaten me now?'

'We need you to sign the Oath of Supremacy, Lady Mary,' Norfolk gruffed behind Nicòla. 'You must sign it today as we shall return to London to present the papers to the King. From there, the King shall have a view to meet with you, and one day return you to court.'

'Me? Back in court?' Mary asked. 'That is my prize for selling my soul and defying God?'

'No, my Lady Mary, it is not that simple…' Chapuys began.

'I shall meet with each of you privately. My Duke of Norfolk, I am sure you wish to threaten me with signing and you may do so before my ladies and myself. Then I shall talk to my dear friend Ambassador Chapuys, and then Mr. Frescobaldi.'

'You want to converse with the foreigner and the commoner?' Norfolk barked.

'Frescobaldi is the commoner who sits at the side of the man who wrote the document you wish me to sign!' Mary admonished the Duke. 'He is also the commoner who sat at my mother's bedside upon her death! Do not presume to tell me who I may speak with, Your Grace!'

Nicòla and Chapuys left Mary with Norfolk, but stood outside the door of the parlour, unsure of their next move.

'Did you hear what Norfolk said of Mary?' Chapuys asked Nicòla as they stood by a large window which looked down at the stables.

'That he would bash her head until she became soft like boiled apples? Oh yes, Crumwella told me.'

'What shall you say to Lady Mary?'

'I can only beg her,' Nicòla explained. 'My master has done all he can to make the letter Mary must write to the King appear gracious, but she must also sign the Oath. I fear what would happen to Mary if she does not. You did not see Anne's head smitten off.'

'His Majesty could never hurt his daughter in the way he hurt the concubine.'

'There are many ways to hurt a woman, Chapuys, some are with a sword, others are slow and painful.'

'For my part,' Chapuys said with a sigh, 'I can only beg Mary to sign and then beg God for forgiveness later, as so many have already done in England. But Mary's integrity is perfection, and to get her to sign the Oath and go against her mother is a tough choice for the girl to make. But we must accept the truth – while the whore was queen, the Roman Emperor and Rome were ready to fight for Mary. But now a Catholic queen is at Henry's side, and the Emperor no longer feels any anger towards Henry, who has remarried to a virtuous bride. Lady Mary no longer has the support of Spain and the Empire.'

Hours passed before Nicòla got a turn to see Lady Mary, leaving her weary. One of Mary's ladies let her into the parlour but left them alone. Mary's eyes were red from crying; which of the two men made her cry, Nicòla knew not.

'Please sit down, Mr. Frescobaldi.' Mary sniffed as she sat in a chair in the stale room and dabbed her face with a white cloth.

'You appear pale, my Lady, allow me to get you something,' Nicòla said.

'No, please sit and speak with me.' Mary took a deep breath and rested her hands on her lap. 'Have you ever been harmed by those you trusted, Mr. Frescobaldi?'

'A great number of times,' Nicòla almost scoffed. 'Faithless men are everywhere and faith in each other can be lost.'

'Did you know my cousin, the Holy Roman Emperor, is no longer ready to fight for my cause as heir to the throne?'

'Ambassador Chapuys spoke of such, yes.'

'I am so alone now. I have Norfolk saying he shall hold me down to sign the Oath, and I have Chapuys begging me to sign for my safety, at the cost of my soul.'

'I was one of the first to swear the Oath, my Lady,' Nicòla explained. 'My soul is no worse for it. I believe your father rules this country. The Pope is still the head of the Catholic Church while the King rules the Church in England. God anointed your father to rule this realm. I do not feel it damages my soul, I assure you.'

'My mother made me swear, above all else, to never turn from God.'

'You never shall turn from God, Lady Mary,' Nicòla implored. 'We never wrote the Oath to turn people from the Church, I promise you. We spent many months drafting the Act of Supremacy, and many more revising and voting on the issue, with scholars of all kinds throughout Europe lending their opinions. We did not create the Act lightly, I swear.'

'I would have to swear that my mother's marriage was unlawful, and I am a bastard. My mother words, with her dying breath, were that she was a lawful queen.'

'I heard those words, my Lady, and it grieved me, I promise you. You do not have to swear that your father's marriage to Anne Boleyn was lawful, nor swear that Elizabeth shall be the heir to the throne.'

'What of Princess Elizabeth?' Mary asked. 'Is she still a princess?'

'She is, as the bill to make her illegitimate has not passed in parliament yet. Elizabeth shall be a bastard, like you, in a few months.'

'She is still my sister,' Mary replied. 'Who shall care for her now? Does Lady Bryan still care for her?'

'Yes, and Lady Bryan writes to Secretary Crumwella and asked him for money for the little princess. Crumwell obliged, from his own purse, with a promise to keep the money a secret.'

'Why would he do such a thing?'

'Elizabeth is only a few years younger than Crumwella's adopted daughter, Jane. I persuaded Crumwella to think of Elizabeth as he does Jane and see her needs and her innocence.'

'I hear the ward Jane is your niece, Mr. Frescobaldi.'

'Yes, my sister's daughter. I brought young Jane to England when my sister married a duke and could not keep her child.'

'I heard a rumour that Crumwell is the girl's natural father, for she carries his golden eyes.'

'Another rumour is that you are to marry Crumwella, Lady Mary, so perchance rumours are not helpful,' Nicòla replied.

Lady Mary let out a little laugh. 'What fun, perchance Crumwell can be my valentine,' Mary smiled. 'Is Crumwell on my side?'

'Secretary Crumwella is on no one's side, if I am plain with you, Lady Mary. He serves only the King. In all honesty, Crumwella wants you only to sign the Oath to make your father happy. Many at court want you to be the heir to the throne now Queen Jane sits at your father's side. Crumwella wants you close to your father, safe from any outside plots.'

'You mean the plots to overthrow the King and put me upon the throne?' Mary admonished. 'For no such thing would occur. I am no threat to my father. Perchance the only thing for me to do is dress as a man, and pretend to be my father's son.'

Nicòla's eyes met Mary's and Mary stared back at her, neither speaking for a moment. 'Could you imagine doing such a thing?' Mary asked.

'I can imagine a father greedy enough to do that to his daughter.'

'Would it be so bad though, to hide as a man and truly live?'

'They chide and ridicule my whole life as an effeminate man, my Lady, and I can assure you there could be no joy in such matters.'

'I wrote my mother when His Majesty banned such activities. The letters were smuggled and destroyed after reading. We spoke mostly in Spanish and in a code we developed. My mother once mentioned you as a person in great trust to the old Pope.'

'Indeed, Pope Clement was close to my heart, and I to his.'

'Your sister married the Pope's bastard son, did she not?'

'Indeed.'

'Is it true you are half a woman and half a man, and you married the Pope's bastard son?'

'Is that what your mother wrote to you?' Nicòla frowned.

'No, that is my claim. My mother said you held a deep secret that allowed you to be a man of great tolerance to the needs of women.'

'Because I am half a woman?'

'That is what I believe she was telling me. The letter is long burned, I assure you, but I remember everything my mother wrote. I know people call you Crumwell's creature, the Waif of the court, that they question your effeminate natures. But no man will strip down another man at court for the sake of such talk.'

'Good!'

'Why should I not tell all you are a woman, have you killed, and have Crumwell brought so low he may die also?'

'The same thing Queen Jane threatened me with, my Lady. Allow me to tell you one thing. Anne Boleyn could have destroyed Crumwell with rumours of me but did not. Because Anne believed we should not use a woman as a weapon against a male enemy. I am safe, my Lady, regardless of my gender, because His Majesty knows the truth about me, in all openness and plainness and accepts I am not against God's law. I am a creature, yes, but to denounce me would go against the King's own knowledge and truth.'

'I knew this not,' Mary said. 'I am sorry. I only wished to seek the truth.'

'The truth is, Lady Mary, that the world is not a safe place for women, and the world is filled with men who only want sons. Queen Jane may bear a son for your father, and who your mother was, or whether or not you were born legitimate, will never matter. But you can go on, marry and live at court and be happy. His Majesty would never harm your mother, and would not harm you, but you know what he did to Anne Boleyn, so no one is truly safe. We must submit to His Majesty. I saw the Queen's head smitten off, my Lady. A day earlier I saw traitors' heads cut off, one of them a great friend of mine.'

'But was he not guilty of heinous crimes against the King and against God?'

'So the law claims, but it hurt me no less to see him die as he did. I saw Thomas More's head smitten off, and Bishop Fisher, both men who stood up for your mother. 'Tis better to be with the throne than against it, my

Lady. If the law changes that Crumwella has written are made official in parliament, then your father shall be able to choose his successor, rather than the order of birth. You could be a queen, Elizabeth could be a queen, even Henry Fitzroy could be a king. I ask you not to sign to choose earthly delights over your immortal soul, I ask you to sign the Oath as a means of safety. We mean to overhaul the Church and monasteries in England because they are foul and corrupt, and God's light is not shining through them. Your soul cannot be harmed by signing; both God and your mother would understand. You are doing your duty and serving your faith.'

~~~

Crumwell stood by the King's side in the presence chamber while Henry spoke on his throne, a few steps above all milling about the room. Norfolk walked in first, holding the letter written to the King, along with the signed Oath. Ambassador Chapuys walked one step behind the Duke, and Nicòla followed at the end. Both Henry and Crumwell looked up in surprise to their arrival, already back at court after only several days away. The three of them bowed together and Nicòla grinned at Crumwell as his golden eyes widened.

'Your Majesty,' old Norfolk said with hands out in triumph. 'Behold, the Oath of s-s-Supremacy signed by your daughter, the Lady Mary, and a l-l-letter to you, to say sorry for her stubbornness in s-s-signing, to say sorry for being a b-b-bastard, and for her sister Elizabeth f-f-for being a bastard. Lady Mary also states she is c-c-comfortable about having you as h-h-Head of the Church.'

Just like Crumwell had written for Mary to copy, word for word. Lady Mary gave in; while Nicòla knew not who convinced Mary to sign, the main goal of calming the simmering Catholics was done. Mary now supported Henry's reformation, in word and oath, if not in heart, not with faith. Now Henry could choose his own successor, all the heirs and their factions would be easy to control.

It was not like the King to order a meeting of his closest courtiers at such short notice. A grand banquet was ready for Henry Fitzroy's birthday, where he, the King and Queen Jane would sit in the Grand Hall before their favourites, hundreds of people, all together to share in the occasion. But first, courtiers summoned had to gather in the presence room in Greenwich. Nicòla had no time to change from her riding clothes and scrub away the days on the road and dress in her best for the evening. Was Henry to announce Lady Mary's signing? Surely not, for Henry was a private man, but rumour had already spread and was probably working its ways through messengers across England at this moment. Nightfall soon passed when the group stood together in the presence room, knowing the main hall swarmed with the ladies of the court as they readied for a lavish evening hosted by the King and his new queen.

But Henry stood at his throne, wearing his ermine cloak, not something he often wore, and he stood with Suffolk and Norfolk, two arrogant faces as stone-cold as the other. Nicòla tucked herself to one side to see what was happening around all the much taller men at court. Around one hundred people gathered in the presence room, brought in at short notice to hear the King speak.

'I call upon the Lord Privy Seal, Thomas Crumwell,' Henry called out.

Crumwell had been standing to one side close to the King as he always did, ready to give Henry what he needed. Crumwell shot a quick glance over the crowd and caught Nicòla's eye for a moment. He had a look of surprise, but also of momentary excitement, a smile trying its best not to form upon his lips.

'Mr. Thomas Crumwell.' Henry said and gestured down to him. 'I wish to reward you for fine work done these past months. I stand hither, a man who is free of sin and closer to God. I have the religious houses of England in my grasp as we purge their corruption from this realm. I now have a lawful and loving wife, and the signatures of all who support me as Head of the Church.'

Crumwell bowed to the King and said nothing.

'No one could be more valuable in this court,' Henry continued. 'You are Vicegerent in government matters, but now I wish you to be Vicegerent and Vicar-general of spiritual manners in this realm. Under me, you the most powerful man in the Church of England, and this is a role you shall share with Archbishop Cranmer.'

Crumwell turned to see Cranmer in the audience, who must have known about this appointment, for he had been in a private meeting with the King for hours. Crumwell turned back to Henry. 'Thank you, Your Majesty, for the bestowment of your love.'

'Speak not so fast, Crumwell,' Henry laughed, 'for I have not yet finished my speech. I wish for you to have greater power in parliament. I appoint you the role of Receiver of Petitions in the House of Lords.'

Crumwell opened his mouth, but paused, for he could not argue with a king. Nicòla could almost see him relaying the laws in his mind, knowing that was the role he could not hold. Henry could see his secretary's worry as well. 'Worry not, Mr. Crumwell, as I know the Keeper of Petitions must be a lord of the house.'

Henry paused and gestured with a single finger to Suffolk, who produced the King's sword. 'I command you knell before me, Thomas Crumwell.'

Crumwell stumbled to his knees in what would be panic, Nicòla knew full well. Her own heart pounded with the surprise of the moment, all while the court murmured at the prospect looming over them all.

'Thomas Crumwell,' Henry said, and placed the sword on one shoulder, 'by letters patent, I name you Baron Crumwell of Wimbledon.' He paused and moved the sword upon Crumwell's other shoulder. 'Lord Privy Seal, Vicar-general, Vicegerent of the Spirituals, Chief Secretary, Chancellor of the Exchequer, Chief Minister… and all the other offices you hold,' Henry laughed, to the laughter of the audience. 'Please stand, Baron Wimbledon.'

Crumwell stood up to the reluctant applause of the court, Henry one of the few honest in congratulations. Nicòla thought of Machiavelli, of his prince. A prince should make himself feared in such a way that if he does not gain love, he at any rate avoids hatred. Crumwell may have inspired Machiavelli twenty-five years ago, but Crumwell did not yet succeed in obtaining England's love, love which he needed to stay in power.

Crumwell's golden eyes fell on Nicòla as she saw tears ready to form; for he was no longer the commoner of the court, now he was Thomas Lord Crumwell, Baron of Wimbledon, a member of the peerage. It may have been by letters patent and not birth, but no matter, for the court applauded Crumwell at the King's command. There was nothing left that Crumwell did not rule.

'Now,' Henry called out to quieten the crowd, 'as tomorrow marks the seventeenth birthday of my dear son, so Henry and I shall dine in private, but later, we shall join the party!'

Nicòla glanced over at Fitzroy, who also stood close to the King. For a young man of seventeen, he looked weary. His skin appeared whiter than ever before, his blonde hair oily on his head, his eyes dull. Fitzroy needed to lie down, not have a party in his honour. He may have been half Nicòla's age, but Fitzroy was still one of her closest friends now. Hopefully, the next time that Baron Wimbledon entered parliament, he could make Fitzroy a legitimate heir to the throne, and England could be at peace.

Chapter 50 – July 1536
St. James' Palace, London

Lyes cannot work all the tyme

'More wine, my Lord?'

Crumwell laughed as Nicòla offered him more wine, fresh from a ship from Portugal, which had docked only a day earlier. He happily took the new Murano glass filled with the sweet wine and leaned back, to feel the sable fur of his new coat tickle the back of his neck. It felt good to be a baron, a baron who could rejoice at Austin Friars and wear sable like a noble.

'Must we have parties so often?' Ralph asked, drunk on the wine. 'I am to be in the King's privy chamber now, but alas…' Ralph trailed off as he gestured to the wine in his hand, his cheeks pink with festivity.

'Have we not had a difficult year?' Richard asked across the dining table and Chapuys next to him nodded with his eyes closed, the wine too taking his thoughts. 'Why not celebrate?'

'We have celebrated for weeks,' Chancellor Audley replied with a mouthful of cheese.

'My father is a baron of England,' Gregory said as a servant also filled the younger Crumwell's glass. 'What can be wrong in celebrating for a few weeks before the work begins in earnest?'

'Right, my boy,' Wriothesley said across from Gregory as he brought his glass to Richard Rich's next to him. 'Are we not slandered at court as creatures, as men of common birth, with ideas instead of titles?'

'Excuse me, Wriothesley,' Rich said, 'for I am the Secretary General!'

'I am Lord Chancellor,' Audley added, 'Chapuys is an ambassador, Cranmer an archbishop. We have all the main titles.'

'You know what we need?' Chapuys said as Nicòla returned to her seat next to him, close to Crumwell's side. 'We need Stephen Gardiner to return from France.'

'Why would I want my enemy at my table?' Crumwell scoffed and sipped his wine again.

'You and Bishop Gardiner could not live without each other,' Nicòla said and patted Crumwell's hand on the table. Crumwell took her hand in his and held it, the eyes of the room be damned. 'You write to Gardiner weekly, and he to you in return!'

Cranmer raised his head from the opposite end of the table from Crumwell. His wife Margarete had retired to bed hours ago, likewise Ralph's wife. 'Baron Crumwell and Bishop Gardiner, from common men to leaders of the English court.' He raised his glass, and all did the same. 'To the Baron!' they all cried again and brought their expensive glasses together with laughter.

Crumwell sat back in his seat and glanced around the table; his son was sixteen years old now, old enough to sit with Ralph and Richard and take wine and laugh and talk politics. Gregory would now inherit a noble title. Cranmer, Audley, Chapuys, Wriothesley, Rich... all men who made something of themselves, men who once rode the wave of Cardinal Wolsey's prosperity and now ruled England themselves. Not one of them were born to power but had earned it.

The door to the dining room opened and Crumwell let go of Nicòla's hand on instinct. A gentleman-usher, looking tired in his new grey livery tunic, handed Crumwell a damp letter. 'With all urgency,' the boy said and excused himself. The conversation and jests carried on around the table continued as Crumwell unfurled the message.

Lord Crumwell

His Grace Henry Fitzoy, Duke of Richmond and Somerset, requests you to wait upon him at St. James' Palace with all speed. His health has declined at pace and needs your presence, likewise Archbishop Cranmer to give the last rites.

Norfolk

Crumwell looked up from the letter to Cranmer at the other end of the table. He caught Crumwell's golden glare and frowned, seeing the sudden serious expression on the new baron's face.

Nicòla too noticed Cranmer's face and turned to Crumwell. The smile fell from her lips. 'What is it?'

All silenced their discussion and looked to Crumwell. Everyone loved Fitzroy dearly, he would be an ideal reformist king for England.

'I must away at once,' he said. 'Cranmer, I beg you go with me.'

'But what has happened?' Nicòla asked again, everyone else frowning in panic. There would be no sense in delaying the news to Nicòla. 'It is His Grace, Henry Fitzroy. He is much ill and is calling for myself and Archbishop Cranmer.'

'What?' Nicòla cried. 'Fitzroy has had a difficult cough these past weeks, but it is summer! Even the plague has not been so bad in the city this season… surely you do not fear the worst?'

'I am afraid his attendants fear the worst. Ralph, you must away to court at once and tell the King that his son is ailing. The best doctors shall already be at St. James', but the King should know the truth. We have three miles to travel to Fitzroy's home, and we have not a moment to delay.'

Nicòla would not tarry at Austin Friars after the news; she rode the three miles to the palace beside Crumwell and Cranmer, a dozen guards about them in the warm London night air. The Duke of Norfolk stood in the main hall as the group arrived, and he grimaced at the sight of Nicòla behind Crumwell.

'My l-l-Lord, as I presuppose I must now pr-pr-pronounce you,' Norfolk said to Crumwell, and turned and bowed his head to acknowledge Cranmer. 'Archbishop, thank you f-f-for coming. My son-in-law has taken a s-s-serious turn.'

'I saw Fitzroy not two days ago,' Crumwell said as the group followed Norfolk up the main staircase through the palace, the red brick stairs and hallways mostly unlit, save for a few flickering candles in the cool air wafting through open windows. 'Fitzroy seemed fine, his usual cough, but nothing more.'

'The b-b-boy has coughed since the m-m-moment his mother bore him,' Norfolk replied as he walked on ahead on the party to Fitzroy's private rooms. 'I r-r-remember when he became a d-d-duke, a boy of five, coughing as the k-k-King awarded him some of the highest honours in th-th-the kingdom.'

'I remember,' Crumwell said. 'Cardinal Wolsey was Fitzroy's godfather, and I helped him draft Fitzroy's honours. Have you informed your daughter that her husband is most unwell? Where is Duchess Mary?'

'She is at the f-f-family estate at Kenninghall. While my daughter has n-n-never lived with her husband, she shall not be p-p-pleased he is ill.'

'What ills His Grace?' Cranmer asked.

'I know not, but p-p-perchance it is consumption, as the d-d-doctors say,' Norfolk said as they stopped at the door to what must have been Fitzroy's bedroom. 'But… if I am h-h-honest…'

'That would make a splendid change,' Crumwell shot back.

Norfolk pursed his lips for a moment. 'Let me be p-p-plain. The Catholic supporters at court have g-g-got their queen on the th-th-throne, and they mean their p-p-prize to be Lady Mary as s-s-successor. You, Crowmell…'

'Crumwell!' he altered the Duke's words.

'Y-y-you have made laws that shall prevent s-s-such. Meanwhile, laws are changing t-t-to suggest Fitzroy could b-b-be the next heir to the throne.'

'Making your daughter the queen consort,' Crumwell argued.

'I am the Duke of Norfolk; my grandfather w-w-was slain at Bosworth. My first wife was a York princess. My s-s-second wife is a daughter to the d-d-Duke of Buckingham. Be not amazed th-th-that I married my daughter to the King's bastard, f-f-for I know how one f-f-family can be legitimate one m-m-moment, attainted the next. The rules constantly change. But you have half the c-c-country wanting a Catholic heir, and another half who w-w-would happily see the King's reformist bastard take the throne. You h-h-have just blocked Lady Mary from the throne, and s-s-suddenly Fitzroy falls ill?'

'Poison?' Nicòla muttered behind the group.

'At least one of you un-un-understands, even if it is the w-w-Waif,' Norfolk muttered as he threw a look over Crumwell's shoulder to Nicòla. 'Though, Creature, I h-h-heard you were crying on your knees over my n-n-niece as they smote her head but weeks ago, s-s-so you are d-d-difficult to understand.'

'Let us see him,' Crumwell hastened Norfolk.

Norfolk opened the door to the enormous room, with Fitzroy in a large bed, the gold velvet curtains all drawn back, the boy atop his bedcovers, sweating in the room even though the windows were open to the night air. Norfolk's son, Henry Howard, Earl of Surrey, sat at Fitzroy's side, cradling his hand. The two had been friends most of their lives.

'Archbishop Cranmer,' Fitzroy said in a weak tone. 'I am so grateful of your arrival.' He paused to cough, and Crumwell cringed at the angry sound which came from the young duke.

'In times of great struggle, the Lord shall soothe our fears,' Cranmer said as he stood at the bedside.

'My new Baron Crumwell,' Fitzroy said and reached out for him. Crumwell took his hand, hot to the touch. The healthy young man of only days ago had gone. Poor Fitzroy was only a year older than Gregory.

'Your Grace,' Crumwell said as he held Fitzroy's hand. 'I come with all speed to do as you command.'

Nicòla pushed past both Crumwell and Cranmer and stepped to embrace Fitzroy on the bed, his illness and sweating be damned. Crumwell noticed relief in the boy's eyes to have someone hold him. 'We shall do anything to ease your discomfort,' Nicòla said while Fitzroy coughed in her face, yet she moved not. Instead, she reached for a cloth from the bedside cabinet and dabbed a touch of blood from his chin. Surrey dabbed Fitzroy's forehead with the wet cloth, allowing the water to roll along Fitzroy's pale and sunken cheeks. His eyes closed as he sat cradled by Surrey and Nicòla.

Norfolk gestured his head to Crumwell and Cranmer, who stepped away from the bedside to seats placed close to a cold fireplace. 'I have had the k-k-King's doctors hither, and they say Fitzroy shall not l-l-last the night.'

'Never,' Cranmer said in shock. He fumbled in a pocket inside his purple robes and pulled out a small trinket of Jesus which he often had in his hand when worried. Poor Jesus' face had just about been rubbed out with all Cranmer's worries.

'Just look at him,' Norfolk replied. 'I lost all f-f-four of my children by my first wife when they were young, a-a-and then my wife herself. You know the plague took my new d-d-daughter Katherine a few years back. Did not the s-s-sweating sickness take some of yours, Crowmell?'

'Two daughters, the summer of 1528, along with my wife,' Crumwell sighed, ignoring Norfolk saying his name wrong again.

'Then you know h-h-how this appears. You know when you look upon a p-p-person and they are lost to you. The k-k-King loves his son dearly, no matter how he was b-b-born to a mistress. Fitzroy is a good man, the s-s-same age Henry was when he took the b-b-bloody throne! His Majesty has been m-m-most erratic of late and this shall not c-c-calm the difficulties of court, I can assure y-y-you of that.'

'Thank you for the plain details,' Crumwell retorted. 'Can nothing be done? Where are the doctors, the servants to attend to Fitzroy's illness?'

'The doctor has gone to f-f-fetch a tool he needs. But Fitzroy wanted my s-s-son to sit by his side, his best friend. The Waif t-t-too seems to have won his h-h-heart.'

Norfolk paused as the three turned to the bed to see Fitzroy smile as Nicòla brushed his wet blonde hair from his forehead for him. 'He wanted you, Cranmer, b-b-because Fitzroy knows the end is coming. Crowmell, he knows y-y-you are close to the King, he wants t-t-to know you shall have all in hand upon his d-d-death; he wants certainty as he p-p-passes. Fitzroy wants you to t-t-tell the King of his son's d-d-death.'

'Could you tell him?' Crumwell argued. 'For you, Norfolk, you have been at the King's side for over twenty years!' '

Yes, but I came to h-h-hate Anne Boleyn, and yet the Seymours are f-f-far worse for Henry. Fitzroy knows m-m-my distaste for the c-c-court at present.'

'And a distaste for me,' Crumwell muttered.

'My lords?' Fitzroy spoke loud enough to pause the conversation.

'Yes, my son,' Norfolk said as he hurried to the bedside again, Crumwell and Cranmer close behind.

'I must speak with you all. I need you, l-l-Lord Crumwell.'

'Of course.' Crumwell sat down next to Nicòla. 'How can I serve you?'

'I have a secret I have been holding for a week or more now. 'Tis about Lord Thomas Howard.'

'Surely not me,' Norfolk said, 'the other Lord Howard, I presume.'

'Yes, the other Lord Thomas Howard, the Duke's brother of the same name.' Fitzroy coughed, and his breath seemed to make a noise like wind whistling through trees. 'Lord Howard is in love with Lady Margaret Douglas, daughter of Margaret, Dowager Queen of Scotland.'

'The King's niece is hither at court. Young Lady Margaret is safe under Henry's care,' Crumwell replied.

'But Thomas and Margaret have been in a love affair for some time, and one week ago, they married in secret. I was there as a witness, at their request.'

'What?' Norfolk cried. 'My idiot b-b-brother has married the King's n-n-niece without permission! God in heaven, if he has b-b-bedded the girl...'

'Howard bedded Lady Margaret before last Christmas,' Fitzroy replied. 'It was a secret I was ready to keep, but now, with Anne Boleyn dead and her daughter Elizabeth no longer a princess, Margaret Douglas, the daughter of a true Tudor princess, has jumped up in the line of succession.'

'Howard married his young mistress to get closer to the throne,' Crumwell mused.

'No, because Lady Margaret is with child.'

'In Jesus' holy name,' Cranmer muttered while Norfolk cried out in frustration and crossed himself.

'I do not want my father to be angry with Lord Howard,' Fitzroy whispered to Crumwell. He coughed, and his voice returned. 'Lady Margaret confessed to me, being my cousin, and she is happily married now she is with child. Please, see that His Majesty harms Lady Margaret not.'

'Lady Margaret and Lord Howard have committed treason, so there shall be punishment, but your father, in his kindness, would not harm a woman carrying a child, much less his own niece. I shall see her given the best rooms in the Tower, for her comfort.'

'My father will be angry when I die,' Fitzroy said as he closed his eyes, 'and my cousin should not be the one to bear the burden of his rage.'

'Your father will be sad if he were to lose you, Your Grace,' Cranmer said where he stood behind Crumwell. 'But by the Grace of God, we shall do all we can to heal you.'

'I want to take my confession, Archbishop,' Fitzroy said, his eyes still closed. 'I need time to make my peace with God.'

Norfolk led his son from the room, followed by Crumwell and Nicòla. They retreated into a quiet presence room off the bedroom where they would no doubt need to reside for some time as Cranmer soothed Fitzroy's sick soul.

'See,' Norfolk said the moment he sat down next to his son in a pair of matching soft chairs. 'I was not w-w-wrong in calling you and Cranmer together t-t-tonight, rather than waiting until m-m-morning.'

'Yes,' Crumwell said as he straightened his coat. 'Thank you, Your Grace, for this is a terrible night.'

'And you,' Norfolk gruffed at his teary son, 'Henry, you must stop s-s-sniffing like an infant who has lost its m-m-mother. You are a man of almost twenty y-y-years! I know it to be a shame Fitzroy is about to b-b-breathe his last, but you look foolish by crying at h-h-his bedside. I suppose you shall h-h-hurry off now to write more p-p-poetry?'

Crumwell glanced at Nicòla, a step behind him, who too had only just wiped her eyes dry. Norfolk never had a way with words.

'I could prove myself as able with the sword as with a quill if given the chance!' young Surrey cried. 'I will one day be the next Duke of Norfolk and I shall choose…'

'Stop!' Norfolk cried and turned from his son. 'I w-w-want none of your outbursts.'

'You did not raise me, so do not pretend you get to say how I am to behave,' Surrey told his father. 'The court raised me alongside Fitzroy. We have the same first name, learned from the same tutors, soothed by the same nurses, laughed with the same friends, shared the same servants, travelled the same roads, slept in the same beds. Tonight, I lose a brother, not just a brother-in-law.'

Crumwell shared a glance with Nicòla; for they knew the love Surrey bore for Fitzroy was more than just brotherly love. He and Fitzroy had been unnaturally close for years.

'I know all of th-th-this, Henry!' Norfolk spat as he fell back in his seat with weariness. 'How dare you dis-dis-disparage me before commoners?'

'Norfolk…' Crumwell began, to quieten the argument while Cranmer gave Fitzroy his last rites in the very next room.

'No,' Norfolk spat back. 'I am the Duke of Norfolk. I am de-de-descended from the Mowbray family, who were d-d-dukes, and before that, n-n-nobles who created the Magna Carta for this c-c-country hundreds of years ago! I will not be argued against by my s-s-son before the sight of commoners!'

'Yes, I am a commoner,' Crumwell replied and kept his voice low. 'Common as they come, and once, a common soldier. But now I am a baron, and one day, it shall be my children, and their children, and their children who sit high in society, just as your family does now. So, no admonishing me with the threat of being common shall ever hurt. You are angry, Norfolk, I know that, for I am angry as well. Fitzroy is the best chance we have at getting a king on the throne after His Majesty, and that chance is disappearing right before our eyes. Abusive tones upon your son who weeps for the loss of his brother-in-arms shall not restore what we are about to lose.'

Crumwell left the Howards to their argument and went to sit in the far corner in a window seat where Nicòla soon joined him. They sat in silence for a while; to think they had been at a party not an hour ago. The wine had drained from his body the moment Crumwell saw Fitzroy upon his bed.

'Ti importa?' Nicòla asked in a whisper.

'Do I care about what?' he whispered back in Italian, so the Howards did not hear the conversation.

'About Surrey's grief.'

Crumwell took a long pause before he answered. 'Death and grief are part of life. At court, we must sit high above daily life as we must be beyond normal thinking and learning. We must be stronger, better educated, swift in our response and strong in our convictions. 'Tis been a hard life at court of late, and it becomes easy to forget that while we make decisions that rule a realm, this is a moment of grief. I am sorry for losing an heir which could have ruled over England, and yes, I am sorry for people suffering grief for those they loved. I am sorry that I had to execute Anne Boleyn, but I have no room for grief. That does not mean you cannot grieve for the friend you found in Anne, or in Fitzroy. I am sorry to lose such a good young man such as Fitzroy, and I accept that people, like yourself, like Surrey, also suffer personal loss. Surrey is about to lose the love of his life and I do feel for him.'

'I would not swap my commoner for a thousand noblemen.'

Crumwell raised half a smile as he looked to Nicòla and caught Norfolk scowling at their Italian conversation. 'But never sacrifice a thousand noblemen to save me if we are ever at war.'

'My love,' she said to him, her sweet Italian words just a whisper, 'we have always been at war.'

Crumwell lost track of the time while Cranmer delivered the comforting words the Duke needed to hear from God. By the time he and Nicòla, plus the now silent Howards entered the bedroom, Fitzroy had declined even further. They took turns sitting by the bed as he dozed, the hours drifting by in a sea of tiredness and worry. But not long before dawn, something roused Crumwell from his gentle sleep in a chair. Crumwell woke to see Surrey and Nicòla sitting by the bed in tears as Cranmer prayed over Fitzroy. Norfolk too had dozed off in a chair nearby and awoke at his son's cries. Crumwell struggled to the bedside with Norfolk, and together they watched as Fitzroy's eyes fluttered, each breath long and whistling in pain. With Surrey embracing him, and holding Nicòla's hand, the King's precious son took a deep breath and let go, his face resting at once. The pain was at an end.

Cranmer leaned past Nicòla and closed the Duke's eyes. 'Saints of God, come to his aid. Come to meet him, Angel of the Lord,' Cranmer said softly. 'Receive his soul and present him to God the Highest. May Christ, who called you, take you to Himself; may Angels lead you to Abraham's side. Give him eternal rest, O Lord, and may Your light shine on him forever. Let us pray.'

The other four gathered their hands to pray, Nicòla and Surrey awash with tears, whether they be Catholic or Protestant, it mattered not as they recited a prayer they knew all too well, led by Cranmer.

'All-powerful and merciful God, we commend to you Henry, Your servant. In Your mercy and love, blot out the sins he has committed through human weakness. In this world he has died: let him live with You forever. Through Christ our Lord. Amen.'

They looked up again and Crumwell placed one hand on Nicòla's shoulder. She dabbed her eyes upon the sleeve of her coat and took a deep breath. Through grief, they had to be above it, for the sake of their work in the royal court. 'Eternal rest grant unto him, O Lord, and let perpetual light shine upon him,' Cranmer added. 'May he rest in peace.'

'Amen,' they all muttered.

'May his soul and the souls of all the faithful departed, through the mercy of God, rest in peace.'

'Amen.'

'What if someone has p-p-poisoned this poor boy?' Norfolk muttered, not filled with tears; he was angry.

'We must do an autopsy,' Surrey said as he slipped off the bed to stand by his father.

'We must go to the King and tell him of this at once. If this was poison, someone will burn for it,' Nicòla added.

'I can assure you of such,' Crumwell said. 'But we must wait until the autopsy before we tell any person of Fitzroy's death. But the King must know at once. We shall go to Whitehall and tell him all and then we shall prepare a grand funeral for the Duke of Richmond and Somerset. If this death is in revenge for cutting Lady Mary from the succession, all shall know. All shall be punished.'

Chapter 51 – July 1536
Hatfield Palace, Hertfordshire

Sumtymes you must lye to save yourself from trouth

Nicòla and Surrey walked rain-soaked behind a hay-filled cart in the night, which held Fitzroy's hastily-found coffin. They dumped the Duke, the sole son of the King, in a grave at Thetford Priory, eighty miles north of London. Nicòla could still feel the way she rocked in her saddle on the wet ride to Norfolk, poor Fitzroy's body wrapped in lead. He was supposed to be placed in a closed cart, but she and young Surrey could not find one. The whole ride, Nicòla could hear the echoes of King Henry's desperate wail as he lay upon the ground of his privy chamber, his fat hands grasping at Crumwell's dark clothes after receiving the distressing news. Finally, the grief of the past months flooded from the King, pouring out in desperate despair for the son who could never take the crown.

But facing death was something Henry could never take; no sooner than Henry knew of his son's death, he fell into his melancholy once more, and ordered Norfolk to hide Fitzroy's body. No announcement, no funeral, no burial tomb, and painfully, no autopsy. The truth was lost forever. A cart filled with hay carried Fitzroy to the Howard family tomb Thetford Priory.

Oh, how the rain poured; Nicòla could still feel the drops upon her shoulders. Surrey, deep in grief for the man he loved, walked with Nicòla at a distance behind the cart through the graveyard at Thetford, while rain hid the painful moment from the eyes of the world. The King had refused an autopsy, so if someone had poisoned the Duke, no one would ever know. What an awful, silent end to the mighty Henry Fitzroy, the never-King of England.

The ride seventy miles south to Hatfield hurt also; Surrey stayed behind with Fitzroy cold in the ground. The weather broke, allowing Nicòla to ride hard to Hatfield Palace, where Crumwell and the King awaited. Also waiting was a familiar sight; her precious Crumwell with a bloody lip. Crumwell appeared as soon as Nicòla dismounted her horse at Hatfield, her muddy riding boots glad to be out of stirrups, her back relieved to be out of the saddle. Crumwell must have waited for her by a window, a feeling which warmed every part of Nicòla's worn soul.

The moment servants of the palace were cast away, Nicòla fell into Crumwell's arms, tears pouring from her eyes in silence; for no one could hear Crumwell's secretary crying to him inside his private rooms.

'All shall be well,' Crumwell tried to soothe Nicòla as she wept against him. He pushed Nicòla's dirty hair aside to look upon her face, but Nicòla could not bear to pull herself from him, her face buried in his chest.

'I fear nothing shall ever be well again,' Nicòla sniffed. 'I have seen so many people die. Fitzroy was one of the greatest of men and he lies forgotten in the Howard tomb. He lies unmarked, only given the most basic of rites by the Priory monk. Smeaton is in pieces, not even given a grave of his own in London… bodies and souls depart one another with such a pace that I fear the golden world we dreamed of has fallen into hell.'

Crumwell rocked Nicòla the way she would rock little Jane after a bad dream. Nicòla dared to lift her face to look upon Crumwell's battered lip.

'The King?'

Crumwell nodded with a sigh. 'After you and Surrey left with Fitzroy's body, I was with Henry when old Norfolk came to see His Majesty. Henry flew into rage, of which I have never seen, nor Norfolk. Henry demanded to see his son's body, demanded there be a grand funeral in his honour in London. It was as if Henry forgot his own demands for Fitzroy's body be taken from London and forgotten, rolled up and hidden from the world. Henry screamed, oh, how he screamed at Norfolk, who has since ridden north in deep shame. Henry screamed at me, as if I were the one who ordered Fitzroy be forgotten. The entire court knows of Fitzroy's sad end, and yet no one can utter a word. We must act as if Fitzroy were never born. His wife, the Howard girl, shall receive nothing of her lands or estates as a widow, as the marriage was never consummated. Henry has remembered how dearly his son was loved by all, and regrets sending the body away. I was hurt in the battle of Henry's dark humours. Poor Queen Jane, for she was in the way also, but I stepped in front of her and got punched.'

'That is most kind,' Nicòla commented as she touched Crumwell's fat lip with her freshly washed hand.

'And now we are hither, at Hatfield. I must prepare, for the King has taken only a short break in his private rooms, and soon he shall meet with both the Lady Mary and the Lady Elizabeth. Both now are bastards, but Henry will see his daughter Mary for the first time in five years. None of us know how this shall go.'

'Pray that the loss of Fitzroy has some goodness, some light amongst the darkness. Henry may embrace his daughters once more, perchance learn the lessons so recently known by Fitzroy's loss.'

'We can but pray. Already Henry is worried he shall not get a son on Jane.'

'It is only two months since Anne lost her head,' Nicòla replied as she began to wipe away her tears.

'Henry worries…' Crumwell lowered his voice, despite being alone in the room, despite being so close in each other's arms, 'Henry confessed to me that he lately has trouble doing his duty by Queen Jane.'

'Henry spoke so plainly?'

'Indeed. We were playing dice in his privy chamber one night, and he asked me if I knew anything of the "problem." He feared God has brought this affliction upon him for what we did to Anne.'

'Perchance God has done much in punishment; we took Anne and God took Fitzroy from us in return. All we have now is Lady Mary and Lady Elizabeth. Mayhap what Anne said was true, that Henry could not satisfy a woman in the way he should as a man. The realm has never been more troubled.'

~~~

Nicòla awaited with Crumwell in the small room outside the royal couple's private chambers, their hands clasped before them as Lady Mary approached. Mary gained more of her mother's look with each passing month; her delicate features, her fiery auburn hair, her gentle grace and confident stride. Mary uttered not a word as her blue eyes gazed upon Nicòla and Crumwell, who bowed in reverence, but as Mary passed them, she asked the guards on the doors to leave the entranceway open and looked back to the pair. For the first time, Lady Mary sought comfort from Crumwell and Nicòla, as if having the doorway open for the meeting provided her with extra eyes and ears, the only way Mary could find any support in a world vastly against her for simply living. Nicòla knew not how she could help Lady Mary if the meeting with the King did not go well, and Crumwell would not be able to say much in Mary's favour either, but if Mary found comfort in their nearby presence, Nicòla knew there was nowhere else they could be at this moment.

Tears. Nicòla expected none from the King, and yet Henry wept openly as he pulled his daughter into his arms. They had not seen one another in five years, and now Mary was a woman of twenty years of age. She bowed low to her king, but easily gave way to the welcoming arms of her father. Queen Jane stood by with a grateful smile, finally being the one to reunite King Henry with the daughter of Katherine of Aragon, the princess born to the greatest royal couple of Europe. Henry and little Mary spoke to each other in a careful embrace, words unheard by any ears other than their own. Nicòla watched Henry bestow a gentle kiss on Mary's forehead, and Nicòla wished to cry all over again. How Fitzroy could have been comforted by the same gesture in his final moments, one which never came. Yet Queen Katherine's soul would rest easy, for Henry had once again come to learn just how powerfully he loved his daughter.

'My Baron Crumwell.'

Crumwell and Nicòla turned to the voice, to see Lady Margaret Bryan, Lady Elizabeth's chief nurse with her old lips pursed tight. Her graying hair had been pulled so firmly under a hood that her very face threatened to disappear up under the garments she wore. Nicòla stepped back and felt guilty to have been caught watching the King's reunion with his daughter.

'Lady Margaret, good morrow and thank you for allowing us to stay in the Lady Elizabeth's palace,' Crumwell said.

'We are not calling the girl Princess Elizabeth any longer, as you instructed,' Lady Margaret replied. 'It was my son Francis who wrote to me, telling me of your new title as Baron of Wimbledon.' The old woman paused and looked Crumwell up and down. 'Is His Majesty ready to receive the Lady Elizabeth?'

'His Majesty is speaking with Lady Mary at present, and Queen Jane has only just met the girl. But perchance now is the time to bring in Elizabeth, as the King is in his fine spirits for the first time in a while.'

'I must thank you, Lord Crumwell,' Lady Margaret spoke almost in a whisper. 'Thank you for the personal funds you send us to clothe and feed Elizabeth. She may be a bastard of Anne Boleyn, but she is still the King's daughter. All those lies saying Elizabeth is Mark Smeaton's daughter; anyone who sees the girl knows she is Henry's.'

The mention of Mark Smeaton made Nicòla want to be sick. But Lady Margaret spoke her name and Nicòla sucked back the need to cry. 'Thank you, also, Mr. Frescobaldi, as I know you given monies to both Mary and Elizabeth over the years, your own personal money.'

'It is a pleasure to help,' Nicòla managed to reply.

Footsteps echoed from behind the wide dark skirts of the royal nurse, and Lady Margaret turned to see Lady Elizabeth coming towards her through the dark hallway, followed by her other nurses. Anne Boleyn's daughter; Elizabeth had Henry's orange hair and her mother's beautiful black eyes. The girl did not pause to anyone standing in the hallway. She was a princess until now and bowed to no one. But Lady Margaret clicked her fingers and Elizabeth paused, for she was about to meet the King.

'My Elizabeth!' Henry's voice called to Elizabeth, who trotted in her little purple gown to her father, to be scooped up in Henry's arms. Nicòla wondered if Elizabeth even remembered her father, for he rarely saw her.

The daughter of Katherine of Aragon and the daughter of Anne Boleyn, alongside their father and his third wife. A sight no one ever could have foretold. Despite the need for a son, Henry loved his daughters. One look at Henry with Elizabeth in his arms told of his affection, no matter how much Henry grew to loathe Anne. The way he gently but desperately pulled Mary into his embrace spoke of an intense adoration for the sole surviving child borne to him by Katherine.

Lady Margaret dutifully closed the doors, for surely none, even Lady Mary, needed Crumwell and Nicòla now. Nicòla watched Lady Margaret and the nurses wander away and just smiled to Crumwell.

'Can we return to London with all haste?' Nicòla asked. 'As heartening as it is to have this reunion today, I want to hold my own daughter. Jane is all I have thought of since the moment I watched Fitzroy lowered into the ground. We have suffered enough for the royal family. Please, let us stop shaking the throne. Let us love Jane and Gregory while we can.'

'My heart aches too, aches for the chance to be happy once more, Nicò,' Crumwell whispered. 'Do we not deserve happiness?'

'I do not know the answer to that, but I shall become a thief and steal happiness if I must. Please, Tomassito, for if the King can be happy with his children, surely so can we.'

Chapter 52 – October 1536
Whitehall Palace, London

The trouth has legs, but lyes have wyngs

'A convocation headed by Archbishop of Canterbury, Thomas Cranmer, shall give a section to the "Ten Articles created by the King's Highness' Majesty to set up Christian quietness and unity." Five articles relate to the doctrines and five relate to ceremonies…'

Nicòla paused reading the papers in her hand as Crumwell crept up behind her and wound his arms around her waist. She smiled as he pulled off her soft cap and tossed it on the floor. 'My Lord?'

'Say that again,' Crumwell mumbled as he gently kissed her neck.

'We are not in the country any longer.'

'Let us pretend.'

Nicòla tried not to laugh as his lips tickled along her neck. Three weeks away in Northampton at the new manor gifted to Crumwell by the King had been the first time in years that any peace had come to the Crumwell family. Some three months after Henry Fitzroy's death, the world seemed to have calmed down.

'Article one,' Nicòla continued. 'Holy scriptures are the basis and summary of the Christian faith.'

Crumwell took the paper from the top of the pile and tossed it on his desk as he kissed her neck.

'Article two. Baptism is essential for both children and adults as it conveys remission of sins and the grace of the Holy Spirit.'

Crumwell also took that one and dropped it on the floor.

'Article three – penance is necessary for salvation. Article four – the body and blood of Christ is present in the Eucharist. Article five - justification is remission from sin but good works are necessary for reconciliation with God…'

Crumwell took those laws and dropped them as he turned her in his arms.

'I hope we locked the doors,' she commented.

'Oh yes, I am well prepared for what we are about to do.'

'Do you not wish me to learn the ten articles, as you have made it law for all in England to learn these laws, Tomassito. If we are to re-educate every church in England, I must learn the ten articles you and Cranmer made with the King.'

'We worked on these articles for months, why would I want to hear them again?' Crumwell said.

Nicòla read over his shoulder as Crumwell kissed her neck. 'Article six – images are useful in remembrances, but not objects to worship.'

'I can worship you,' Crumwell mumbled against her skin.

'Article seven – saints are examples on how to live a good life, and helpful in prayer. Article eight – saints are useful for remembering holy days, and article nine – ceremonies are to celebrate devotion and are reserved for their mythical significance.'

'Are you done?' Crumwell muttered against her neck.

'Article ten,' Nicòla raised her voice. 'Prayers for the dead are good and useful, but papal pardons and masses for the soul are not good and should not be offered at sites of worship.'

'Amen.' Crumwell lifted Nicòla up onto the edge of his desk as she tossed the last of the papers on the floor to let Crumwell kiss her.

'For a man reforming the Church, you like to sin often,' she murmured.

'What we are is not a sin,' he smiled. ''Tis too beautiful to be a sin. And you read the new articles; we can repent sins.'

Nicòla laughed as Crumwell brought his lips to hers again, his arms wrapping around her as she perched on his desk, her fingers carefully unbuttoning his clothes.

An offensive, intense banging came from the other side of the office doors and Crumwell's face turned to anger.

'Now?' he cried toward the doors.

'Lord Crumwell!' came the panicked voice of Richard Rich. Rich never panicked about anything.

Nicòla jumped from the desk and forced her hair back under her hat as Crumwell swiped up the articles from the carpets on the floor. He sat back down in time for Nicòla to unlock the doors.

Rich blustered past Nicòla in a second and stood at the other side of the desk. 'Lord Crumwell, I come with the most fearsome news. Murder and rebellion.'

'What?' Crumwell scoffed as Nicòla approached Rich, and she noticed sweat running down his forehead, his hat in his hands, wrung out of shape by nervous fingers.

'It started a week ago now when a man named Thomas Kendall did a sermon for the evening in Louth.'

'Where is Louth?' Nicòla asked.

'Lincolnshire,' Rich said, still breathless. 'Kendall spoke about how the Church is being destroyed and the people should rise to destroy Thomas Crumwell who is sending men to churches and monasteries to steal goods for his personal use. The next day, the commoners in Louth seized John Tenage, registrar to the Bishop of Lincoln, when he tried to read out your commission over the closure of their monastery. They burned all your papers, Lord Crumwell.'

'Arrest those responsible,' Crumwell shrugged.

'By the next day, 3,000 men had gathered in Louth and marched twenty-five miles north to Caistor and seized His Majesty's subsidy commissioners.'

'What in God's name?' Crumwell said as he sat up straight in his chair.

'That is when the trouble exploded. On October 4, the rebels captured Lincoln's Chancellor, along with one of his servants, a cook I believe, and both were murdered. The cook was hanged, but when the Bishop cried foul over the murder, he was wrapped in the hide of a freshly killed cow, and left to be attacked by dogs, as they stated that was what they wanted to do to you, Lord Crumwell.'

Crumwell jumped from his seat in wild anger, a kind Nicòla seldom saw in him. 'They killed two of our men?'

'Brutally,' Rich swallowed hard. 'These men are saying they are on a pilgrimage and we are the targets for their rage, due to the changes to the Church and the Statute of Uses bill regarding tax. The laws ruined their lives and they blame you, Lord Crumwell. Some say there are many as 10,000 men. It has taken days for word to reach this far south. Their leader is a man named Robert Aske, a commoner who has been speaking on behalf of these murderous men, and they are mustering men while marching upon York. Yorkshire is now in rebellion. They have dispatched word to the King as we speak.'

Crumwell shoved past Rich and he and Nicòla struggled to follow him as they flew down the hallway to the King's privy chamber. Crumwell burst through to find Henry and the Duke of Suffolk talking together.

'Look who is hither,' Suffolk said as he looked upon the three bowing in reverence.

'Your Majesty, I have just received word…'

'Yes, that half the country wants your head on a spike. As many as 10,000 men are fighting against changes to the Church and taxes. I am sending Suffolk north with an army to put down this rebellion.'

'Your Majesty, I believe…' Crumwell began.

'You do not get an opinion this time, Crumwell,' Suffolk said as he wandered over to him, a confident swagger in every step. 'I am to war with my own countrymen thanks to your new laws,' Suffolk said with a sigh. 'You may wish to think over your personal safety in case the rebels have sympathisers at court.'

'Charles,' Henry warned his best friend. 'Thomas is my Chief Minister and Lord Privy Seal. No man in this nation can threaten his life, as Crumwell speaks for me.'

'Your Majesty,' Rich gently said, 'the rebels have sent a six-point complaint against Lord Crumwell and the changes they demand.'

'Thomas writes my laws for my realm!' Henry screamed, which frightened the whole room. 'How dare they send me a list of demands?'

Rich pulled a screwed-up letter from his wrung hat and Crumwell snatched it from him and gestured for him to step back behind Nicòla, a step behind her master already. Nicòla watched him open the list, which looked crudely written by a simple man.

'What do they want?' Henry asked as he looked to Suffolk rather than Crumwell.

'Sheriff Dimmock in Lincoln states that the crowd, through a show of hands, want six changes. One – stop the dissolution of the religious houses and of the consequent destitution of "the destruction of the realm." Two – change the restraints imposed on the distribution of property by the "Statute of Uses," which is a law we put in place to help with taxes a year ago. Three – change the grants to the King of the first-fruits of spiritual benefices, so the monies can instead be given to the community.'

'They want my money and to change my laws,' Henry replied with a smug laugh.

'Four – stop the payment of the subsidy demanded of them.' Crumwell shook his head. 'Now they believe they do not have to pay taxes? Five – stop the introduction into the Privy Council of Crumwell, Rich, and other "such personages of low birth and small reputation," as decided by them.'

'They mean you, Frescobaldi,' Suffolk commented.

'I am not on the Privy Council!' Nicòla shot back, too worried to care what Suffolk thought of being addressed in such a manner.

'The final change,' Crumwell continued, 'to reverse the promotion of the Archbishops of Canterbury and Dublin, and the Bishops of Rochester, St. David's, and others, who, in their opinion, have "subverted the faith of Christ." So, they want me dead, all my men dead, and Cranmer and his followers brought down after all the work they have done to help the Reformation.' Crumwell screwed up the message and tossed it on the floor. Nicòla scooped it up in a hurry; they would need that later.

'I am to ride north and deliver a message to these rebels,' Suffolk told his king and closest friend. 'Shall I place the message on the end of my sword?'

Crumwell turned to Rich. 'Set forth for Lambeth Palace at once, as Archbishop Cranmer must know all of this at once.'

Rich bowed to the King and disappeared down the hallway to the Crumwell rooms and Nicòla waited for an instruction, which never came.

'I shall send those rebels a message,' Henry seethed. 'They think they can dictate laws? Take away things awarded to me in parliament? I never saw men committing to such treason! Suffolk, I demand you ride north at once, and take the Earls of Shrewsbury, Rutland and Huntingdon. All need to show their fealty. Lord High Admiral Fitzwilliam must go too, and I want 100,000 men sent north to quell this rebellion. No one rebelled against my father and lived to tell the tale, and no one shall during my reign!'

At once Suffolk bowed to his friend and disappeared from the room. Henry stood on the spot shaking his head, his hands on his hips.

'Your Majesty,' Crumwell said. 'It has been over thirty years since I fought in a battle, and I lost that battle. I would gladly take Suffolk's place if I thought it useful…'

'Half the men in your army would rebel and kill you, Thomas,' Henry replied. 'I am no fool; I know my favourite minister is not everyone's favourite minister. But I shall not turn against you in this, Thomas, so have no fear. I shall recall Norfolk from his home at Kenninghall and help to control the north.'

'Your Majesty, my nephew Richard is in Ware, thirty miles north, close enough to defend Windsor yet still on the main road north to Lincoln. I shall send him as many men as I can; I have eighty men working on Austin Friars. I have one hundred horses and can get handguns and arrows from the Tower…'

'Yes, send all to Richard at once. He is a member of our Privy Council and must be defended. I value Richard. I shall not lose my crown to rebels.'

'There is no need to worry about this, Your Majesty. I shall write up your words to the rebels, commanding them to obey their anointed leader on pain of death. This rebellion shall be broken apart in as fast as Suffolk can ride to Lincoln.'

'I lived through the sacking of Rome, Your Majesty,' Nicòla said. 'Likewise, the uprising in Florence born from Rome's uprising. I watched my father slain, his body burned. Even when society stumbles, Your Majesty, it is won back. Chaos cannot prevail for long.'

Henry nodded. 'You are a woman, Frescobaldi. Tell me, why is my new wife not with child yet?'

'I know not, Your Majesty,' Nicòla stumbled on the new subject. 'For I have only given Lord Crumwell one daughter and two dead sons.'

'As have both of my wives, and even more besides!' Henry cried. 'There shall not be a third wife who fails! My only son is dead, and I cannot mourn him openly as he was illegitimate!'

Nicòla looked up and down at the King, dressed all in mourning black. 'Many of us mourn Lord Fitzroy, Your Majesty. He is in our prayers.'

'I want guards all around the palace,' Henry changed conversations again. 'I need double protection for myself and for Queen Jane. I want Lady Mary surrounded always, for she could be a symbol of hope to these rebels. Arm yourself, Thomas. If we are to war against our people, we shall win.'

Crumwell and Nicòla bowed to Henry and started back to their chambers, Crumwell walking at a high speed, and Nicòla ran to keep up. 'We must get word to Austin Friars at once,' Crumwell said. 'I want all men in the household to be ready to defend the manor, and I shall have fifty royal guards to watch the place. Gregory and Jane shall move away at once, we shall send all their nurses and tutors with them.'

'Would they not be safer at Austin Friars, surrounded by people loyal to us?' Nicòla asked as they headed into the private office again. The Ten Articles of Christ remained jumbled on Crumwell's desk; the stolen kisses seemed forever ago.

'Tens of thousands of men are marching in the north to kill me. They want my head on a spike. Nothing is too good for the safety of Gregory and Jane. Stephen Vaughan is my oldest friend in the world and is staying in Calais. The children would be safe in Calais.'

'I shall not send the children to France!' Nicòla exploded, uncaring that all the clerks and ushers of the rooms would hear.

'You will do as I say. Gregory is my son and heir.'

'Gregory is almost a man.'

'I think we can both agree that Gregory is no great scholar or soldier,' Crumwell lowered his voice as he neared Nicòla, looking her right in the eye. 'He is a man of a...'

'Effeminate nature, like me,' Nicòla asked. 'A creature, a fool?'

'Say no such things about my son,' Crumwell hissed back.

'Jane is my daughter, and I will not put her on a ship due to an imagined rebellion of a group of village idiots from the north of England.'

'You could be upon the ship with them both,' Crumwell replied.

'If we were under siege, I would fight, I would never leave,' Nicòla scoffed. 'How could you imagine such things?'

'Imagine what they would do to a loyal servant of mine,' Crumwell said. 'Just think, Nicò. What if they were to discover your truth? I cannot bear to think what a mob would do.'

'I know what they do to women, that is why my disguise as a man came in so useful in Rome,' Nicòla said. 'I have seen all the worst that people can do. The King is sending Suffolk to muster 100,000 men and nobles will tell these rebels to desist under pain of death. They are marching north and are 130 miles from us at present. We do not need to fear.'

'We have to fear all at court, for any person could be a rebel from within. Everyone hates me for being low born and in power. Any person could knife you the moment you leave my sight. You must be guarded always, as do the children. If this rebellion does not disband when Suffolk reaches Lincoln, I shall take drastic action to protect my family, even if that means sending you all to Calais to face my fate alone.'

'I shall not leave London or you, Tom, not for anything, even if it means I die with an arrow through my belly. We have not fought so hard to change England to lose to rebels. Have all we done, all we have seen, suffered and inflicted been for nothing?'

'Not if I can help it. You may tarry in London for now. We have much to plan if we are to get 100,000 men to back Suffolk in the next few days. We must seek to gain everyone to our cause. If we are to die by these rebels, they will have to fight for our heads.'

Chapter 53 – October 1536
Windsor Castle, Berkshire

Lyes can rendar any man blynd

The Duke of Norfolk was now High Marshal, in command of the north while the Duke of Suffolk manned an army. Crumwell walked the palace hallways in London, flanked by ten guards to keep him safe from internal rebels. The dukes loved every second of the rebellion. Crumwell could imagine them sympathetic to the rebels and their cause, to fight the Reformation and stop Crumwell's rule. Along with Suffolk, the Earls of Shrewsbury, Rutland and Huntingdon were eager to prove their fealty to the King and were ready to fight the rebels too, as the gentry of the Yorkshire area could not, or would not, suppress the commoners and their marching.

Weeks had passed since the uprising by the time the King's angry reply to the rebels reached Yorkshire through Suffolk. Fresh news arrived at Windsor, where Henry and Jane were safe, and it was Crumwell who had to give the news to the King.

Flanked by guards, Crumwell approached the main entrance to the privy chamber where the King sat with his wife, and behind him, Crumwell heard Nicòla with a bag of coins. She was giving the guards extra money to remain faithful. All these years of hard work for England and this was the reward?

The chamberlain announced Crumwell's entry and Nicòla trailed in behind, carrying his books. Crumwell straightened the Tudor rose which hung from his Collar of Esses before Henry turned in his seat, where he sat by the window with Queen Jane. A fire had been lit nearby in the fireplace, just a little warmth in the autumn cool of the chamber.

'Thomas,' Henry said but did not rise from his seat. Instead, he gestured Crumwell to come over to him, leaving Nicòla by the doorway in silence.

'Your Majesty.' Crumwell bowed to the King and the same to Jane. But as he turned back to Henry, he noticed the pain on his face. Henry's cheeks were red, his eyes wet with tears. 'Can I be of service, Your Majesty?'

'Tis my leg,' Henry spat. 'Damned thing hurts again. I fell in the joust almost a year ago, so when shall this pain cease?'

'I can call for Dr. Butts, Your Majesty.'

'The doctor has been, Lord Crumwell,' Jane said. 'But the King needs rest.'

'The last thing I need is rest,' Henry shot back. 'Rebels are marching on my cities! What news, Thomas?'

Crumwell swallowed a heavy lump in his throat. 'We have received word, from Lord Darcy of Temple Hurst. He states that all of Yorkshire is up in rebellion, with plans to march upon the city of York. Both Sir George Lawson and William Harington, the Mayor of York, have asked for aid, as they face 40,000 men. Suffolk gave the leader of the rebellion, Robert Aske, your letter. They know their rebellion is contrary to God's law, as you are the anointed leader of England. To rebel against you is to rebel against England and against God. Parliament sets the laws and for the commoners to revolt is treason and they shall be subject to Suffolk's anger should they choose not to disperse.'

'They mean to take York,' Henry sighed and leaned back, a fear running across Henry's strained face. Jane held her hands together, unsure of what to say to her husband. 'There was rebellion when my father was king,' Henry said. 'My glorious mother kept us safe while my father fought the rebels himself. And Lord Darcy was one man who fought on my father's side. That same man is now elevated to great power in the north and I expected him to aid in ending this stupid affair.'

Henry paused as he cringed in pain. Crumwell dared to glance at the King's leg. Against the elaborate detail of his hose, Crumwell could see the dark stain of blood. Whatever the doctor was doing, it was not good enough for the King. 'I shall do anything you desire, Your Majesty, to bring this rebellion to an end.'

'Perchance I should cut off your head, Thomas, and then the rebels will go home.'

'And they shall also take your profits from the monasteries, will not pay their taxes, and no longer consider you the leader of the Church, Your Majesty,' Nicòla said from the other side of the room.

Crumwell turned in horror at Nicòla's outburst, but she did not shrink away; rather she stood behind her words. 'Those rebels wish to fight you, Your Majesty, and everything you have given them. You have presided over them and the lands you allow them to live upon. Do you muster armies, taking away their precious sons? Do you start wars and burn homes in unrest? No, you are the great king of England's peacetime. They think they know best about the monasteries and their abbeys. They are so fooled by the lies; they know no better. These rebels learn less in a lifetime than we educated men learn in a week. We are removing corruption from their lives and replacing it with the right to read and understand the religion which governs their souls and their lives. You and your father have given England great peace, and the commoners are taking that peace for granted. They fight due to a lack of education, Your Majesty.'

'You dare let your mistress speak in such tones?' Henry said to Crumwell.

'The Waif speaks the truth,' Queen Jane added. 'These men rise up from a lack of education. They have not the education of noble men and cannot understand the Reformation. They find solace in the old faith.'

'The Catholic faith lies and steals, Your Majesty,' Crumwell replied to her. 'I want better for England. I shall not steal the parish churches from the commoners, nor their riches; we shall use those churches to educate the masses, if only they listened to what I tried to teach them.'

Henry placed both hands on his aching leg. 'Should I offer these rebels peace and a pardon if they give up?' he asked. 'Is that what you think, Thomas?'

'It would be far cheaper than any civil war, Your Majesty. I would need 100,000 men ready to mount a war. A pardon would give the men a chance to disperse and take with them the details of the dissolution of the monasteries. I aim to educate all men in the English faith. Killing men in their thousands shall bring nothing but continued anger.'

'Can we not save the monasteries and abbeys?' Jane asked.

'Stop it, you stupid woman!' Henry cried at his wife. 'Lest you wish to be like my other wives!'

Crumwell stood back a few steps as Henry pulled himself to his feet. 'Send word north at once to Suffolk and Norfolk. I shall offer peace in return for the end to the rebellion. All shall be pardoned at once. But if not, Suffolk can slaughter every man, woman and child in the north until York is safe and my authority is safe!' Every word in Henry's voice grew louder.

Crumwell swallowed hard and bowed low. 'At once, Your Majesty.'

'If I must take heads from commoners, Crumwell,' Henry added, 'then your common head shall be first!'

Crumwell flew from the room without acknowledging his king, Nicòla trailing behind him. The slew of guards waiting outside the privy chamber assembled about the Lord Privy Seal and his secretary once again as he pounded the hallways to Crumwell Chambers.

'How dare you speak to the King in such tones?' Crumwell cried at Nicòla, given the space of private hallways, too narrow for any person to approach the wide group of black-clad guards.

'He threatened to take your head!' Nicòla yelled at Crumwell's back. 'I care nothing for the worry Henry suffers, and I care not for the pain in his leg. How dare he threaten you, threaten all you have done in his service, just because he wants to blame someone? The King wanted this reformation, he was the one who asked you to destroy the Catholic Church in England.'

'We only have to look around the court to know the Reformation is losing,' Crumwell replied. 'We only have to look at the blessings and ceremonies Cranmer is forced to perform in the court chapels, all filled with idolatry and pronounced in Latin. We must step up reform in England, and the King must understand this. If there is rebellion, nothing good will come of our work.'

'We know the Queen shall help us none in our quest,' Nicòla replied as they entered the offices.

Crumwell dismissed the guards at the front entrance of the chambers where the clerks worked in silence. They walked into the private office where servants were stoking a small fire to prepare for nightfall. Crumwell kicked them from the room with a click of his fingers.

'Never speak to the King without permission,' Crumwell reminded Nicòla. 'We have none of the constant openness that we had when Anne by Henry's side. The King has become as dangerous as the dragon on his father's banners. You are my only solace in the world, Nicò, and we know that one day the King could turn against his discretion towards our situation.'

'Perchance we should end our situation.'

'What do you mean? Not weeks ago, you swore that my idea to send you and the children to Calais was madness. Now you think we should not work this way any longer?'

'You worry too much on the issue,' Nicòla replied as she sat at her desk in the corner. 'Who would balance your accounts and monitor your gambling debts if I left you?'

Heavy footsteps yielded the face of both Wriothesley and Rich in the doorway. 'What?' Crumwell asked with a sigh.

'We have received word that the rebels in Lincolnshire have disbanded under the threats of Suffolk and his troops,' Rich said with a flourish. 'They are dispersing around the area with all haste. They fear Suffolk and his men may slaughter them.'

'They assume rightly,' Crumwell scoffed.

'I also have a letter hither from your nephew Richard,' Wriothesley added. 'Richard was to muster another 10,000 men to protect London from a base in Herefordshire, but now feels he has lost the opportunity to be a soldier, as the rebels are breaking up their units to return home.'

'I shall still send word to Suffolk that a pardon is possible if they return home and stop the violence against the men of the monastery dissolutions.

We shall threaten them with extreme violence if they do not. Some areas may be quiet, but I know Norfolk has been struggling with men on their march north as the weather is poor and moving the artillery has proved difficult in the mud.'

'There be many guards posted outside your rooms, Lord Crumwell,' Wriothesley commented.

'I am paying one hundred extra men out of my own pocket. Already I have had to melt gold plate from the King's Jewel House to pay extra salaries to Norfolk's men and must pay guards in the palace myself. I hope you men have enough protection?'

'The men you sent us are working,' Rich said and Wriothesley nodded. 'I know Cranmer is feeling safe.'

'How be the King?' Wriothesley asked.

'Angry either at the rebellion, his sore leg or Queen Jane. He fears for his crown, his tone and his humours prove so,' Nicòla answered. 'Rebellion is a betrayal to His Majesty.'

'They are not calling it a rebellion, but a pilgrimage, the Pilgrimage of Grace,' Rich replied. 'Our men commissioned to halt the monasteries and abbeys are under threat and in hiding.'

'The only pilgrimage will be of soldiers marching north to take lives,' Crumwell spat back. 'We must work at once, for much correspondence must reach Suffolk and Norfolk. The rebels in Lincolnshire may go home, but they could arm themselves at any moment. The Yorkshire rebels are two hundred miles north and want the city of York for themselves. Our messengers with the pardons and the threats of death must reach these men with all haste.'

~~~

Days passed but Crumwell focused not on the country. Men marched in their thousands to see him dead. There were no words to describe the pain of knowing so many wished him killed. No prayers to God could soothe his heart. The loss was so great; he had fought since childhood to be respected, and all had come to nothing. He sat, a man of fifty years, hated by a nation. The King hid away with Queen Jane, while all the courtiers dispersed to their estates to prepare for war, to prepare for sending their tenants to be soldiers against the north of England. At any moment, someone loyal to the Pilgrimage of Grace could burst into Crumwell's rooms and stab him in revenge for his desire to remove corruption from the Church. Crumwell had fought off a pope to make Henry the leader of the Church, had gone against the threat of war by the Holy Roman Emperor and King of Spain, just so Henry could take a new wife. Crumwell beheaded a queen with a torrent of lies at Henry's command. All the while, Crumwell tried to reform England for the better.

Crumwell looked up from his desk and looked through the open doorway. From his Windsor Palace office, a small doorway led to the presence room, just a few small chairs by a fireplace. There sat Nicòla, facing away from Crumwell, with baby Jane on her lap. Mother and daughter, both with their long rose-gold hair loose over their dark skin, Jane's golden eyes closed. Crumwell could not see Nicòla's expression, but she was talking in Italian to Jane, perchance singing a little tune. Gregory sat in a nearby seat; he sat upright with his young head on the back of the chair, fast asleep. They had made the thirty-mile ride from Austin Friars to Windsor, under heavy guard. Austin Friars was a safe place, for Richard, Ralph and Cranmer had their wives and children there. But Nicòla needed to see her daughter.

A delicate knock came upon the office door and with haste came Rich again, this time with a sullen face, his eyes red, no doubt from lack of sleep. 'I come bearing news, Lord Crumwell,' Rich said. 'It is from Lord Darcy at Pontefract Castle, only twenty-five miles south of York city.'

'What does he say?' Crumwell asked as he double-clicked his fingers for the letter. The clicking disturbed Nicòla from her song with Jane.

'The letter comes from Thomas Milner,' Rich replied. 'The King needs to know, and no one dares to do such a task.'

Nicòla appeared the small doorway, Jane left behind on the warm seat by the fire. Crumwell's eyes skimmed the words, but they did not seem real.

'What does it say?' Nicòla asked as she secured her long hair under her soft cap behind Rich.

'It says the rebels, numbering in the unknown thousands, descended upon Pontefract Castle, on Lord Darcy, Archbishop Lee of York, and many others of the local gentry. They are running low on provisions and cannot hold out against the rebels, who are on their way to York. Lord Darcy had no choice but to yield the castle to the rebels and has sworn allegiance to their cause, as has Archbishop Lee and all others present at the castle. Darcy would rather side with the rebels than with the King. Darcy now considers himself a leader of the uprising alongside Robert Aske. Darcy believes I am the sole target of the rebellion, and my head shall soothe the entire region,' Crumwell sighed.

Nicòla let out a whimper and Rich's head sunk in sorrow. The King needed to hear this at once. The way to end the uprising would be for Crumwell to let his head fall into a basket, just like innocent Anne Boleyn, not five months past. Crumwell rose from his seat as he folded the letter up once more, its creases coated in a layer of dust from the ride south.

'I can pray the King finds the kindness to allow me my head,' Crumwell added. 'Please leave us, Rich. You may share this news, for all shall hear of it soon enough.'

Rich bowed and closed the office door behind him and Nicòla just stood in the doorway. She had a look of loss, one he had never seen. Crumwell may as well have already been dead; but first, he knew what else he needed to carry out once they returned to London.

Chapter 54 – October 1536
Whitehall Palace, London

A lye is a betrayal that shall never be mended

'War is an impossibility in winter in the north,' Henry said to Crumwell.

The King stood in his privy chamber at Whitehall, back in the one room that the King could call home. Back at Whitehall, things could take a more serious turn. Henry stood with his arms out as servants brushed his long red sleeves, the fabric new and prepared for the coming weather. Whatever the doctors had done to the King's leg, God had directed their hands. Queen Jane had prayed fervently for the King's recovered honour, even though the bloodletting of Henry had been horrendous for the royal couple to endure. But now, Henry was in control of himself and wanted his country back.

'Who do these traitors think they are?' Henry spat as he shooed his servants away. 'To think they can demand my Lord Privy Seal's head! You are the Vicegerent of the spirituals, you are a member of the nobility now. These commoners and their traitorous gentry can all burn. The Archbishop of York shall see himself stripped of many powers, as shall all the bishops and priests who join this crusade against their king and their God.'

Crumwell smiled just a little; for the King did not want to stop the rebellion by cutting off his head. The King wanted blood, yes, but it was the blood of the commoners, of those who dared defy their anointed sovereign.

'The rebels wish to take London,' Crumwell replied. 'My nephew Richard is mustering men again to guard the roads north of the city, so the rebels will never reach this far. Both yourself, and the gracious Queen Jane shall be safe.'

'I will ride out and slaughter these men myself!' Henry cried. 'For I offered pardon to a great number and they still fight against my men.'

'Norfolk is near Pontefract Castle at present, Your Majesty,' Crumwell said as he looked at the papers in his hands. 'Norfolk complains he has around 6,000 men at his back, yet the rebels number some 30,000. But Norfolk's men are trained and equipped, and the battle would be a bloody affair. These rebels are not wise or learned men; they would be cut down almost at once.'

'Like you said, Thomas,' Henry said as he wandered to the fireplace to warm his hands, 'we would save much time and money if we did not have war with our own people.'

'Indeed, Your Majesty, and yet this treachery cannot go unpunished.'

'I shall ask Norfolk to go to Lord Darcy and to Robert Aske. You know how much I respect Darcy, for all he has done for me and my father before me.'

Crumwell also knew how Darcy was one of Cardinal Wolsey's best friends and yet turned against him without a thought. 'Yes, Your Majesty.'

'But we must ready for war hither in London. Do you think it wise to move Jane to the Tower for safety?'

'I do not believe that decision is necessary yet, but there may be many courtiers who ask for that solace for their families in coming days and weeks.'

'It should be your family who lives in fear more than mine,' Henry said without a moment of thought for how harsh it cut Crumwell's heart. Something drastic was needed and Crumwell knew just the ship leaving London which would do the task.

~~~

Crumwell walked into the main entrance to Austin Friars, to many welcomes from his household, clerks, maids and servants alike. All supported their master for the kindness he gave. Their fealty never wavered. Perchance retirement to Austin Friars to be a merchant once more was a better choice than life in the King's shadow. Everyone asked to gather was there, ready to discuss the war coming to London.

The parlour yielded Crumwell's closest family; Nicòla stood there with Gregory and little Jane. Richard had Frances with him, her own baby beginning to show under her gown. Ralph and his wife Ellen waited with their sons, and Cranmer awaited with Margarete, who, after many miscarriages, was large with yet another child.

'I am certain you know why we all gather,' Crumwell said. 'Richard, you are to use the military training you gained, for it shall not be jousting this winter, but a siege upon London. Tonight, a ship belonging to Stephen Vaughan shall leave its dock in London and travel to the Low Countries, with a stop in Calais. I have a manor there ready to receive all who wish to leave England to prepare for the war.'

Cranmer too had thought of this possibility. 'I should put Margarete on this ship at once,' the Archbishop said. 'I shall stay, as the loyal Archbishop of Canterbury. The Archbishop of York may have sided with the rebels, but I shall never fail to stand by my king.'

'Ellen, Thomas and baby Edward shall also sail,' Ralph said.

'I cannot leave Austin Friars!' Ellen cried. 'We should be at home.'

'You shall leave at once, Ellen,' Crumwell replied. 'You, Ralph's children, and your own older children shall all travel. And you, Frances, you and your soon-to-be born son. And Mercy, too. She is Gregory's grandmother and must accompany you, for everyone's safety.'

'Mercy would be a good companion for Gregory and Jane as they head for Calais,' Nicòla said. 'All the servants and maids and tutors shall go forthwith to make their journey easier. I promise you all, as part of the Crumwell family, you shall be safe in Calais.'

Crumwell turned to Nicòla and steadied himself. He felt pleased Nicòla had changed her mind and allowed Jane to travel to France, but it was not enough. 'Nicòla, I command that you also travel to Calais with Gregory and Jane.'

'What?' Nicòla almost laughed. 'I shall not run from a war. I fought in the sacking of Rome. I can fight, I can help prepare for all that we need in this most difficult time for England. I shall not flee when the fight for the Reformation comes to such a battle!'

'You shall, for I command you do so.'

At once Nicòla stalked from the room, past the glorious portrait of her father, Francesco Frescobaldi, which had hung for many years in that parlour. Crumwell followed her out to the back garden where she stood stiff, knowing Crumwell would follow. The sky threatened them, but Nicòla's anger was far more fearsome.

'I shall not leave you,' Nicòla said the moment he appeared behind her. 'I shall fight with you. What shall you do? Lock me in the Tower once more? So be it!'

'Jane and Gregory are our children, they need support.'

'Please do not make me into a mother. After years as a courtier and your secretary, I am no fool, Tom, so please do not treat me as one.'

'I love you, Nicò, and I want you safe. The place to be safe is Calais!'

'And what, leave you to be beheaded in London? For you to be hunted down by a treasonous courtier and killed by the rebels when they reach this far south? For Henry to get angry and order you dead in a rage like he did to poor Anne? No, I shall not leave your side for such things to occur.'

The pit of Crumwell's stomach hurt more than it had in years. 'I hear your words, Nicò.'

'You do?'

'You will come to the dock tonight though, to see the ship off?'

'Of course, I am sending my daughter to sea for the first time, so I shall be there, for it can frighten a child. I want Jane to know I am not abandoning her, only protecting her. Love and support will surround her and Gregory, so I can only hope that is enough.'

Crumwell smiled, and Nicòla returned it, but he knew the moment his world would end would come swiftly.

The pain throughout Crumwell's body spread while he waited upon the dock. The ship had to dock out with the evening tide, and the sun had almost set over London by the time all the chests were loaded onboard for the families to leave the city. This was what all his effort had come to, to send his family into exile in Calais in case a group of lowborn men, just like himself once, attacked the city and made Crumwell's family their victims. No one knew how many men would descend upon London, or once York was in rebel hands, the whole north could turn towards the capital city. They spread Suffolk's army, Norfolk's men, Richard's battlement north of London, across the lower half of England and ready to fight, but not as one large group. They could lose days moving in any direction in bad weather, and rumours of pestilence only hindered the risks of moving an army to defeat fellow Englishmen.

The air felt sharp as needles with its cold breeze as one by one, those of the extended Crumwell family boarded the ship for Calais. The captain, a regular used by both Crumwell and Stephen Vaughan, looked impatient to set off as they loaded their last-minute passengers. Crumwell thanked God for being able to fit so many people on board a ship in such a hurry. The commoners and the nobles alike would hate Crumwell more when they heard he had sent away his own family, as he now expected them to volunteer husbands, fathers and sons to fight to save his own head.

Women and children alike took their goodbyes with grace, tears for the unknown yet to come. Gregory embraced his father as he so often did, with the confidence of a man almost ready to make his own way in the world. Jane took her brother's hand as she took the careful walk up onto the ship high above the dock. Crumwell noticed two men come back down the steady gangway to the dock. This was the moment he dreaded the most.

Nicòla stood at Crumwell's side as she waved to her daughter up on board. He placed one hand on Nicòla's shoulder and she turned to him with a look of innocence.

'Nicò, you know I love you.'

Nicòla's beautiful green eyes narrowed as she gave him a confused smile. 'I know, as I love you.'

'I am sorry and shall pray to God for betraying you.'

'What betrayal do you speak of?' she asked and looked to Gregory and Jane on the ship once more. 'I feel sad to see the children go, but it is for the best. We can settle the rebellion without fear for our family.'

'That is what I want, so dearly.'

'It is as Machiavelli wrote; è necessario ad un Principe, volendosi mantenere, imparare a potere essere non buono, ed usarlo e non usarlo secondo la necessità.'

'It is necessary for a prince wishing to hold his own to know how to do wrong, and to make use of it or not according to necessity,' Crumwell repeated.

'Indeed, Tomassito, and on this occasion, we are not doing the wrong thing in sending the children away.'

The two men, men Crumwell did not know, came to him and stood with their large hands at their sides. One held a bale of rope between his fingers as requested. 'Lord Crumwell,' one man, the younger of the two, addressed him. 'We are ready for the prisoner.'

'Which prisoner?' Nicòla asked.

Crumwell took his hand from Nicòla's shoulder and stepped back from her. He gestured to her and the men nodded. 'Please escort Mr. Frescobaldi onto the ship. He is to be released once the ship is at sea, and trusted with the greatest care,' Crumwell instructed the men.

'No, I am not going to Calais,' Nicòla answered Crumwell, but both men took her by the shoulders.

'Be sure to tie Mr. Frescobaldi's hands behind his back, for he is a fearless man and a strong swimmer,' Crumwell raised his voice as Nicòla tried to fight off the much larger men. 'Frescobaldi has the strongest wit in the land and has powerful friends. He could talk the captain into turning the ship back to London if given the chance to speak with him. It is for the best that someone monitors Mr. Frescobaldi with all respect during the journey.'

'No!' Nicòla cried as one man held her tight, the other binding her thin wrists behind her back. She kicked the man who held her shoulders, and he stumbled away from her. 'I shall not leave!' she cried.

Ralph, Richard and Cranmer all stood close by, watching the scene unfold, the men all losing their families to Calais with their consent. Ralph covered his mouth in shock at Nicòla's desperate cries.

'You cannot send me away!' she screamed as the men tried to move her to the gangway. 'I am a free man and cannot be commanded!'

'I am your master and as the King's Chief Minister, I can order you on this ship and away from England,' Crumwell pleaded with her. 'Please, they packed all your personal belongings on board with the children's clothing. Please, Nicò…'

'Beg not to me!' she screamed as they dragged her up the gangway, her feet barely touching the wood. Her soft cap came from her hair, which flew about her anguished face. 'If you send me away, you shall never see me again! Nicòla Frescobaldi shall never return to England! You cannot make me leave you to die alone! You promised me, Tom, you promised I would be the last thing you saw before you died!'

Crumwell balled his hands into fists as he resisted the tears coming to his eyes. Nicòla was not begging; she was angry. 'This is not the end!' he cried over the sound of her shrieking as they pulled Nicòla aboard the deck.

The dock hands untied the ship from its moorings and Nicòla continued to fight the men appointed to care for her. Two more deckhands came along to subdue her, but she tried to kick them, spitting in their faces. The four men gripped her, her limbs all pulled to stop her fighting.

'I will never come back to you if you make me leave! You are not "The Prince" after all!' he heard her scream.

Jane and Gregory were both crying; Margarete Cranmer and Ellen Sadler stood nearby with the children, all weeping for Nicòla's state.

'In times of great struggle, the Lord shall soothe,' Cranmer said to Crumwell, and placed a gentle hand on his shoulder, his hand covered in a purple glove against the cold.

Crumwell bent down and picked up Nicòla's cap, which had fallen to the dock in the gentle breeze. Rose-gold hairs stuck to the satin lining. He looked back up as the ship slipped from the mooring, Nicòla still crying. They put Nicòla to her feet and tears streamed down her dark cheeks, no more screams but anguished crying instead. For she did not want to leave England in this time of crisis.

She just shook her head, her hair sticking to her wet face as the ship began its descent into the Thames and off towards the narrow sea to France. Even if Crumwell lived to see the rebellion defeated, Nicòla might not forgive him for this betrayal.

Chapter 55 – December 1536
Greenwich Palace, downstream London

once the lyes are all layd bare, the light shynes everywhere

'Sir, Your Majesty allows a tyrant named Crumwell to govern yourself.'
Weeks passed between Crumwell abandoning his family on a ship, and the rebellion leader Robert Aske stating such words before the King. Three weeks was a long time to go without Nicòla's comfort. Three weeks was an eternity of sorrow. Three weeks heralded only letters from Gregory, nothing from Nicòla. Crumwell had deserted his only true ally while he ended this rebellion, and yet it was Norfolk who prepared a truce between the rebels and the armies. Three weeks after sending his family abroad, the rebels came to London, but only in the form of negotiations while the disillusioned commoners returned to their homes under the watchful eyes of the King's armies.

'If not for Crumwell, I would not have the 7,000 priests in my company that are now ruined wanderers.'
Everything came down to how much the people of England hated Crumwell. He took the full blame; even though he wrote laws and pushed them through parliament at Henry's command. Crumwell's taxes were only created to satisfy Henry's greed. The rebels thought the dissolution of the monasteries was a cash grab rather than a chance to save English souls from the corruption and greed of the Catholic faith.

'It is you, Lord Crumwell, who is the original cause of this rebellion.'
The words said to his face, to the King's face, by the rebels cut through Crumwell. But Crumwell's heart hardened, and he had earlier beheaded a queen, so if the rebels thought they could break Crumwell's spirit and resolve, they made a large misstep.

'The blame lies on the King's councillors; all is run and started by Crumwell.'

The King, with his sore leg and the mood of a scared child in the face of rebellion, was easy to convince that the rebels were to blame. Henry would never relinquish control over the Church, not now he had fought so hard for it. Henry would not argue over the riches of the monasteries and abbeys, and how they would be in the royal exchequer with every commission undertaken. Henry promised a truce, a pardon for all the rebels if they downed their arms, put down the banners sewn in the shape of the five wounds of Christ, and returned to their homes in the frigid north. Henry promised to listen to all their complaints, to ratify all their pains and salvage all their losses. Not for one moment was Crumwell prepared to step down, and never once did the King ask him to make sacrifices. Crumwell had sent away his family, sent away his precious Nicòla, all for nothing.

The rebels finally signed the proclamation of peace by December 3, five weeks after the Crumwells, the Sadlers and the Cranmers went abroad. Groups disbanded, with Norfolk returning to Kenninghall, angry that Crumwell had not lost his head to the King's anger. Suffolk returned to London, smug that Crumwell was so hated right across the land. The court and parliament broke up for the celebrations of the season, with many laughing behind Crumwell's back. One moment a man could be the highest in the court, the next day he could take a boat ride to the Tower for execution.

All the panic and fear, all disarmed with a simple truce meeting. All the preparations, the tears and the worry, all gone in a moment, over in a single day.

'It seems, Crumwell, that the country does not know you as I know you, and whoever harms you harms me.'

The King's word at the official court gathering did Crumwell much good, but by then, the world had stumbled about him. A ship from Calais brought everyone home; Gregory leapt into his father's arms, pleased to be at home but also excited by the two months in Calais. The homecoming was bitter, for all on board and those waiting in London, for one reason.

'Thomas.'

Crumwell looked up from the fire. The King sat in the other chair across from him, the pair engaging in wine by the warmth on a bleak December eve. Henry felt like Crumwell's only friend at the moment. Indeed, he wished to speak to no one else. 'I am sorry, Your Majesty... I...'

'You are trying not to cry again. Like you have done all day, all week, all month.'

Crumwell blinked his golden eyes, for tears perched on his lashes. 'Your Majesty...'

Henry dismissed Crumwell's words with his hand. 'You do not place any coming policies before me, you do not discuss parliament, or plans to ensure the rebels do not rise again.'

Crumwell swallowed hard and looked to his mulled wine. 'I received a letter today…' he paused, his mind confused through his pain. 'I received a letter from Her Majesty's sister, the Lady Elizabeth Seymour. As a widow, she has no formal home for her two children, and seeks to acquire a monastery once it is closed, so she may turn it in a home for her son and daughter.'

'Is it true she once wrote to you, suggesting she would be a good wife for you?' Henry smiled.

'Indeed, when her husband first passed away.'

'I can tell with great certainty you do not wish to take Lady Elizabeth as a bride. She is much younger than my dear Jane and is fertile. Perchance she could marry your Gregory? He is of age now, is he not?'

'Gregory is seventeen,' Crumwell replied and placed his wine on a silver tray placed gently upon a table beside him. Marry Gregory to the Queen's sister? That would make his son an uncle to any royal children Queen Jane had with Henry. 'Do you think my son suitable for the Queen's sister, Your Majesty?'

'Your son shall be Lord Crumwell one day, in his own right. Elizabeth's first husband was only a knight. I trust your son is in your service at Austin Friars, and can be groomed to be a suitable match?'

'Yes, Your Majesty, most certainly! My son has lands and homes in his name at present, and could provide a home for Lady Elizabeth and her children.'

'You do not need to care for Elizabeth's previous children; just ensure your son can do his duty and give the girl more.'

Crumwell swallowed hard again. This was a wonderful match for his son; he would be lavished with titles and honours in the future, awarded lands and monasteries as a member of the royal family. But Crumwell knew Gregory to be a gentle man, and marriage would be a big step for him, and he still grieved heartily over the recent pain done to the Crumwell family.

'You would think I was asking for your head, not giving you a wife for your son,' Henry interrupted Crumwell's thoughts.

'It would be an honour for my son to marry Lady Elizabeth Seymour,' Crumwell replied. 'Mayhap in the summer?'

'If you wish to wait that long, so be it. Not ready to face a wedding?'

'I am hither and ready to serve in any way needed, Your Majesty.'

Henry leaned forward, careful not disturb his wounded leg. Blood often showed through his clothes now, for Dr. Butts could not stop the wound opening and seeping fluids of many shades. 'Thomas, the whole court talks of you.'

'Half the country wants my head.'

'They ask me, Norfolk, Suffolk and others, why I would continue to promote a man as weak as Thomas Crumwell, a man once so powerful, suddenly wrecked upon the shore of misery.'

'Have I failed in my duties, Your Majesty?'

'No.' Henry sighed and rubbed his tired face. 'I must talk about the Waif. I hear rumours, Thomas.'

'Nicòla Frescobaldi did not return to London with Gregory. The last words I heard from Frescobaldi were when the ship sailed for Calais.'

'No letters? She is your creature, surely she writes you. What does your son say?'

'Gregory farewelled Frescobaldi, who left Calais and sailed for Portugal, taking the child as well.'

'The girl you say you adopted.'

'Jane; Giovanna Frescobaldi also sailed for Portugal.'

'Your mistress has left you and taken your bastard with her, leaving you deprived of a woman you should call wife, plus your daughter, and indeed your master secretary.'

Crumwell nodded and said nothing. Nicòla's ship sailed for Portugal and no one wrote to England to tell Crumwell, not even Gregory. By the time Crumwell heard of this progress, Nicòla and Jane would have landed in Lisbon, and now could be anywhere, travelling under any name, on land or sea, with Nicòla's powerful fortune ready to move her through Europe. They surely had returned home to Italy, to Florence. Crumwell had so many spies in his employ reporting so many stories throughout Europe, from the opinions of the commoners to the movements of nobles and kings. But not a word came from Nicòla, nor any person who had conversed with her. Only time would allow letters to come to Crumwell through the slow channels of the winter months.

'It has been a difficult year, Thomas,' Henry sighed as he laid his head back against his soft chair. 'And through all of this, still, there is no child in my queen's womb.'

'The creation of a child is God's will,' Crumwell mumbled. 'If you feel I have offended God on your behalf, I shall stand aside, Your Majesty.'

'I could never bear losing you from the court, Thomas. I know I have threatened you in the past, but that was the pain of my leg, my worry over my country. Please think not of leaving. Though, without your Waif following you, you seem a man lost.'

'I am bereft, but every man must make his own way in the world, and that includes Mr. Frescobaldi.'

'But not a woman, indeed a woman who pre-contracted herself to you in marriage, and has your child at her side. Surely the Pope will annul her marriage to the Duke of Florence, so he can remarry the Emperor's daughter. The Waif could return to London, I would allow any passage into England if it means you can have your creature back again. You cured me of Anne and I can at least help you in this one way. For you made the same marriage vows that night in Calais, the same that bound Anne to me.'

'All matters not if Mr. Frescobaldi stays in Florence with our daughter.'

'Are you heartbroken, like I was when I heard what the witch Anne had done behind my back?'

'My heart is in my chest and ready to work for Your Majesty.'

'No, Thomas, you are in a state of pure agony. You cannot think, you mumble and slur your words. Your skin is ill-coloured, your walk bent. You grieve.'

'I am above grieving, Your Majesty. I must be, to do my duty for the realm.'

'No one is above grief, Thomas. Not even me.'

A panicked knock on the door echoed through the stillness of the privy chamber, occupied only by the King, his chief minister and a roaring fire. The chamberlain rushed in, a wet hat in his hands. 'Your Majesty, an urgent message from the Duke of Norfolk.'

Henry snatched the letter and ripped it apart in a moment as Crumwell leaned forward in his seat. 'Is the Duke well?' he asked.

Henry's eyes scanned the brief note, his face reddened to match his hair, even with its growing number of silver streaks. ''Tis the rebels,' Henry said, his voice rising in tone, his fearful panic returning. 'There is talk, through your man, Ralph Sadler, that the Percys in Northumberland are funding and angering the rebels into returning once more to rise and take the north. I gave those men a pardon!'

Crumwell watched Henry throw the letter on the floor and he swiped it up for the King. 'Where is this rebellion forming?'

'They want to take the port city of Hull and then stretch out through Lincolnshire from there,' Henry said while Crumwell read the same words, written in Norfolk's own hand. Norfolk had been in the north listening to whispers from the gentry, who still wanted to overthrow the Chief Minister.

'Find Sir Francis Bryan,' Crumwell said as he read the message, 'for he is a man much indebted for his poor decisions and spending,' Crumwell told the King. 'Also, John Hallam, he was one of those who rose in the first Pilgrimage of Grace. These traitors have taken your promise of peace and negotiation and thrown it back. They want York and Durham in open revolt against Your Majesty.'

'I want heads for this!' Henry cried as he limped from his chair and Crumwell followed suit. 'How dare they presume to rebel against my mercy?'

'I shall get the armies together at once, Your Majesty,' Crumwell said. His thoughts instead went to his family, for now, they were back at Austin

Friars for Christmas, but now there would be killings. The angry expression of the King's face said such.

'I shall have the head of every man, woman and child, as I warned them,' Henry said as he paced a little, one hand on his bejewelled chest. 'I warned them once, and now they shall suffer! I will have Suffolk put them all to the rope!'

The door banged again with a messenger, this time the chamberlain accompanied by one of Crumwell's men.

'Your Majesty, Your Lordship,' the messenger said. 'A message for Lord Crumwell, fresh from a ship docked in Dover.'

Crumwell grabbed the letter and sent the messengers on their way, distracted by the sudden panic, after hours of drinking warm wine by the fireplace, playing cards and dice with the King, his only friend. Crumwell could not recognise the seal on the letter and cared not; the damp letter had come a long way and was in Italian. Now, finally, perchance news had come to England, and yet war was about to strike. Only war could take Crumwell's mind from Nicòla and his pain over losing her, and yet now she and war came in the form of letters at the same time.

My Lord Crumwell,

The news comes fresh to us from Florence this eve of a most incredible tragedy. Inside the fortress of the Fortezza de Basso in the central city, where Alessandro de'Medici, Duke of Florence lives, is the most lamentable tale. They say they lured the Duke to a room for a sexual encounter with a woman named Laudomia, the widow of his cousin. But the Duke had been drinking wine poisoned by Laudomia's brother, Lorenzino de'Medici. Duke Alessandro died the most painful and horrid death while waiting for his whore. But to make this worse, Alessandro had not been drinking alone, for he had been in the company of his brother-in-law, Nicòla Frescobaldi, lately of your service, who believed you to be "The Prince" of Machiavelli's writings. They found both Medici and Frescobaldi dead in the fortress, a slow and bloody death came to each of them.

We quickly rolled the bodies in carpets and carried them to hidden tombs at St. Lorenzo. The Spanish king shall hold a small vigil for the deaths in Valladolid, Spain. The anti-Medici families have not risen in joy, so Lorenzino de'Medici could not raise an army to overthrow Florence and is now in hiding. I am sorry to tell you of this occasion without many details, but it was known that Frescobaldi was a close friend to you for many years.

They have not seen the Duchess of Florence since the deaths of her husband and her brother and shall be in hiding. Nor can anyone find the

385

bastard child who travelled with Frescobaldi, stolen from the fortress. Frescobaldi did not get a true Catholic burial and has been buried with Alessandro, as the threat of war in the area over the poisonings was a terrible threat to everyone's safety. I am sorry to tell you such poor news in haste, but for tonight, we know little but disaster.

The letter fell from Crumwell's fingers onto the carpet. Somewhere in the dark distance, he could hear the King's strong tone, as if calling from underwater, ordering Crumwell to start a civil war, while Crumwell thought of his daughter far away. The heat of the room soared as Crumwell felt himself falling, darkness encircling him. Nicòla Frescobaldi was dead.

To be continued...

PART III OF THE QUEENMAKER SERIES:
NO ARMOUR AGAINST FATE

The moderate man shall inherit the kingdom.
That man needs to be the Queenmaker.

London, January 1537 – Thomas Cromwell is in deep mourning. His new queen is on the throne at King Henry's command, but the personal cost is too high. Nicòla Frescobaldi is lying dead inside the Medici tomb in Florence, and Cromwell's only daughter Jane is missing. Now, the people of England have rebelled against their king, marching to London to start a civil war. The Pilgrimage of Grace has two demands: remove all the Reformation changes from religion and cut off Cromwell's head.

Cromwell needs his friends, allies and the king's favour more than ever, but he can do nothing when Queen Jane dies giving England its son and heir. Cromwell's son has married the Queen's sister, but the Seymours will disappear from favour if Cromwell does not eliminate all those able to take their place. There is only one solution; become Queenmaker yet again and find a foreign princess for Henry, one to seal religious change and create stability in the war of Catholic against Protestant.

Nicòla Frescobaldi may be dead, but Duchess Nicòletta of Florence is not, so Cromwell and his creature can rule politics again to control England and Ireland. But when war with the Holy Roman Empire threatens, all of Cromwell's powers, titles and schemes cannot save him from his oldest enemy in England, and a betrayal deep in the heart of the powerful Cromwellian faction.

There will be blood…

ALSO BY CAROLINE ANGUS

The Thomas Cromwell Queenmaker Series
Frailty of Human Affairs
Shaking the Throne
No Armour Against Fate

My Hearty Commendations:
The Letters and Remembrances of
Thomas Cromwell – *non-fiction*

The Secrets of Spain Series
Blood in the Valencian Soil
Vengeance in the Valencian Water
Death in the Valencian Dust
also available as a complete set

The Canna Medici Series
Night Wants to Forget
Violent Daylight
Luminous Colours of Dusk
Cries of Midnight

Intense Professional Countess

Available soon –

Hatred Gained by Good Works:
Thomas Cromwell in Florence

The Private Life of Cromwell – *non-fiction*

The Indulgent Nursery of King
Henry VIII – *non-fiction*

Printed in Poland
by Amazon Fulfillment
Poland Sp. z o.o., Wrocław
04 January 2022

6eba9e29-1041-4ef0-ad15-1ad41deb23e9R01